FARNSY

A NOVEL

WILLIAM ANTHONY

Farnsy
Copyright © 2022 William Anthony

ISBN: 978-1-63381-304-5

All rights reserved. No part of this book may be reproduced in any form or by any electronic or mechanical means, including information storage and retrieval systems, without permission in writing from the author, except by a reviewer, who may quote brief passages in review.

This is a work of fiction. Names, characters, places, and incidents either are the product of the author's imagination or are used fictitiously, and any resemblance to actual persons, living or dead, is coincidental.

Cover photo by Lorna Stern.
Photo used with permission of the Jacobs and Reny families.

Designed and produced by:
Maine Authors Publishing
12 High Street, Thomaston, Maine
www.maineauthorspublishing.com

Printed in the United States of America

For Carolyn

Prologue

In 1912, Alfred Wegener, a German scientist, hypothesized that all of the earth's continents were slowly floating around more than 200 million years ago, having once been jigsawed together in a huge *Urkontinent*, a primal landmass he called *Pangaea*. Like all new theories, it was ridiculed until, many years after Professor Wegener's death, modern geologists determined that the good man was right all along.

In other words, if you were out on Pemaquid Point in Maine 200 million years ago, you might've seen Morocco from your Adirondack chair. But *Pangaea* split up, and the pieces drifted apart like old friends. When the mile-thick sheet of ice blanketing Maine began to melt 25,000 years ago, the state's flooded coastline unzipped in a tattered confusion of peninsulas and speckled islands.

The first humans arrived in this region around 12,000 years ago and found land and waters teeming with life. Wabanaki speakers still refer to their land as the Dawnland, or *Ckuwaponahkik*, which means "place where the sun first looks our way." Maine is often referred to as "Down East" because in the old days ships out of Boston heading to Maine sailed downwind, due east, down the coast. Fly over this ragged ocean-scrubbed coastline in a puddle jumper out of Boston on your way up to Bar Harbor, and you'll see why a lifetime in Maine isn't long enough.

For all of Maine's 3,400 miles of coastline, there can't be more than a dozen sandy beaches, most of them buzzing with a succession of summer swarms: tourists, black flies, no-see-ums, and greenhead flies. In July and August, the ocean's so cold only a few of those beaches are swimmable.

The coast of Maine is a rock-bound, pine-forested, fog-soaked, tide-rounded place where fishermen bumblebee from lobster pot to lobster pot, sunshine pleasure boaters poke around coves, and shop owners, innkeepers, and roadside blueberry stands do brisk business while teeming hordes of visitors "from away" look for the perfect lobster roll and a balsam-scented refuge from city noise and stifling offices.

Maine may be "Vacationland," as the state's license plates boast, but a summer vacation in Maine requires appreciation for simple things: waiting for the morning sun to break through; enjoying a good mystery and a cup of chowder on a rainy day; scooping ice cream onto a slice of warm blueberry pie; finding the best chocolate donut; looking for the perfect stone or seashell at low tide; staying up late to watch the Perseid meteor shower streak overhead.

After the summer people leave and the autumn leaf peepers drift away as if with the ebb tide, winter settles in like a grumpy uncle at Thanksgiving dinner. Clipper winds pick up; the ground turns hard as the granite underneath; and snow commences falling in fat wet clumps, then turns to powder flakes and drifts up as high as anyone can remember, one storm after another. Now and then, an overnight ice storm glazes trees like so many candy canes and large branches locals call "widow-makers" snap and crash, unheard, mid-forest. Some fall on power lines, prompting men with angry chain saws to clear away branches and trees. Late afternoon, the roads slick up, and night winds rattle windows and doors up and down the Maine coast.

In late winter, storms sputter like empty threats, the ground warms up, the last icicles drip, and mud season commences. Back roads rut up from runoff; lakes start to turn over after ice-out; loons commence their lonely mating calls; and the whole cycle

Prologue

starts up again around Memorial Day when schools of silvery alewives swarm up the Damariscotta River, across the Great Salt Bay, then wiggle their way up the fish ladder at Damariscotta Mills to spawn in Damariscotta Lake's fresh water, while Morocco slips another centimeter or two farther away.

Truth is, the Damariscotta River isn't really a river. It's a tidal estuary, a pulsing, salty, moon-tugged artery of the sea, with wicked high tides, teeming with life: stripers, oysters, clams, scallops, heron, harbor seals, horseshoe crabs, cormorants, osprey, eagles, dolphins, lobsters, fishermen, pleasure boaters, kayakers, and a few resolute swimmers.

The village of Damariscotta, with about 2,000 year-round residents, is a two-stoplight town nestled off US Route 1, a two-lane highway built in the 1920s, the oldest and once the longest stretch of interstate highway in the country. It is about halfway between the northern tip of Damariscotta Lake and open ocean to the south. The original inhabitants, the Wawenock, called the area *Madamescontee*: "place with many alewives."

Damariscotta is where Police Officer William Phineas Farnsworth grew up. And Damariscotta Lake is where his father taught him how to J-stroke and paddle a canoe quietly enough to be able to net a sleeping sun turtle. It's where Farnsy and his younger sister Grace paddled out to a little island to pick blueberries for their mother's pies and their father's pancakes. And it's near where Farnsy's grandfather took him every spring to a secret spot to show him how to pick fiddleheads so the ferns would grow back the next year. It's where his father, Jack, once cast a fishing lure with such power that it wrapped around a branch too high up to get it down. And it's where his mother, Lilly, told him, "There are a lot of fish in the sea, Willie," which is what his parents called him then, when his first girlfriend in high school, Lucy, broke it off. Farnsy was too serious, she'd said.

FARNSY

After college, Farnsy knocked around odd jobs down in Boston like a boat with a broken rudder. Late March one year, on an impulse, Farnsy hopped on a bus back up to Damariscotta so he could get out on the lake with his father on opening day of fishing season. One morning, as Farnsy remembered it, while his father was frying up some bacon on the griddle, his mother mentioned something about the Maine Criminal Justice Academy over in Vassalboro. She'd heard the Chief was looking for a patrol officer. Looking back, Farnsy said he could almost feel the tide turning.

SUMMER

The Atlantic Horseshoe Crab (*Limulus Polyphemus*)

Tugged by the spring tide and a full moon, the horseshoe crab's barnacle-crusted carapace stirs the water's surface at the edge of the Great Salt Bay. Propelled by his spindly legs and desire, he scuttles over tide-smoothed rocks through a tangle of seaweed toward the faint scent of a female crab. When he reaches her, he clings to her with clawed grip, expels his seed over her briny eggs, then disengages and scuttles off, concluding a ritual at least 20 million years old.

The Migration

It was a quiet weekday morning in downtown Damariscotta early that June and was setting up to be a real scorcher. Police Officer William Phineas Farnsworth of the Damariscotta Police, known to most folks as Farnsy, was sitting in his new cruiser, tucked away on the side street next to the Lincoln Theater, thinking about this and that while he watched summer folks stroll up and down Main Street, peeking into shops, mesmerized by all the doodads for sale. Wooden lobster Christmas ornaments, made in China. Ladies' handbags with little red lobsters sewn on them, made in China. Paper napkins with lobsters, printed in China. T-shirts, sweatshirts, pants, socks, boxer shorts, didn't matter. Stick a lobster on it and summer people will buy it, Farnsy thought.

He wondered what folks over there in Shanghai thought about all this stuff they were making. Had they ever even seen a lobster? He imagined a pretty Chinese gal sweating away at her sewing machine with a big poster of Chairman Mao on the wall behind her looking out over a sea of workers' bobbing heads, which reminded Farnsy of the lobster buoys that were popping up everywhere, which reminded Farnsy of Earl the lobsterman, which reminded him of Earl's ex, Lucy, who, he'd heard, was back in town. He thought he'd seen her in the vegetable section of Hannaford supermarket around Memorial Day, but it was someone else, from away. Farnsy remembered that dream he had now and then, when he thought he'd spotted Lucy on Boston Common, where he'd pedaled gaggles of tourists around the little pond in a swan boat that summer after college. All he could do was watch Lucy disappear into the crowd. She'd never heard him call her name.

Farnsy's thoughts swirled another minute or two as he tried to remember the last time he'd seen Lucy, until a huge summer fella waddled past with a *Where the Hell is Damariscotta?* T-shirt stretched drum-tight across his belly, a proud tsunami of human flesh that briefly eclipsed Farnsy's view of Main Street. Just then, Professor Tuttle's old green Pontiac, the kind with a dark visor, like sunglasses, at the top of the windshield, rolled by headed north, barely missing a startled tourist on the crosswalk.

What caught Farnsy's attention was the yellow dog driving the car—sitting there, cool as a cucumber, looking out the window but mostly paying attention to the road, just like any experienced driver. As Farnsy learned later, the Professor's yellow dog had actually accumulated a fair amount of serious driving time, most of it on back roads.

Farnsy waved a little girl and her mom over the crosswalk from Renys toward Sherman's Maine Coast Book Shop. Then he lit up the lights, burped the siren once or twice, and, as soon as the crawling summer traffic parted for him, turned left onto Main Street and followed the Pontiac, which was now several vehicles in front of him and stopped for the light at the intersection in front of the Baptist church. Farnsy couldn't tell if the yellow dog was going to take the road out toward Pemaquid Point when the light changed or head straight up Business Route 1A toward Hannaford and Round Top Ice Cream. Maybe he's headed to the veterinarian farther down the road, Farnsy thought. An out-patient drop-in. He'd read somewhere that vets were recommending that dog owners start brushing their dogs' teeth. Farnsy shook his head in wonderment. What's next, he thought, as he and the dog waited for the light to change—doggie psychiatrists? Which he assumed someone was probably already doing out in California. A bucket of looney-tunes on that other coast, Farnsy thought, pretty much the opposite of Mainers.

Then the light changed, and the dog shifted into gear somehow and got rolling up the road to where Farnsy could pull in behind and hit the siren a couple of short taps. Didn't want to scare the dog. But by then, the dog had steered the car off onto the soft shoulder, and Farnsy pulled in behind him. Chuckling to himself, Farnsy wondered, what do I do? Ask for a dog license and proof of rabies shot? Tell him to "Sit, stay!"?

Farnsy considered the driver's window with all the caution he had been taught and even more curiosity. As he inched nearer the car, the yellow dog, whom he could hear panting in the heat with the driver's side window rolled down, commenced a low growl. A moment later, Farnsy saw Phoebe Tuttle, Professor Tuttle, *emerita*, to be precise, one of the morning coffee regulars at Waltz's Soda Fountain, sitting in the driver's seat with that big yellow dog on her lap. The dog smiled up at him, still panting, as if waiting for a picture to be snapped.

"Well, hello there, Professor!" Farnsy chirped, leaning down to peer in the window. "Looks like you got a new dog."

"Why, hello, Farnsy. Pemmy? She's a rescue. Didn't think I was speeding. So, do I have a taillight out? Now look here, I've got some errands to run, so if you don't mind...Officer," she added to ice up the cake. The Professor was off and running, at least her mouth was, like she was giving one of her college lectures. Like she told the early-riser coffee drinkers at Waltz's Soda Fountain, her students called her "Mad Dog" because she gabbed so much, she'd sometimes start to foam a little at the corner of her mouth, especially when she got up and running about the overlooked women of history. Farnsy flipped out his warning book and started writing. The Professor was a good friend, but rules are rules.

The yellow dog started a low growl.

FARNSY

"Remind me, what's the driver's name, Professor?"

"Her name's 'Pemmy,' short for 'Pemaquid.' But her full name is Pemaquid Rumphius Tuttle. Rumphius, after the lupine lady, Miss Rumphius. Pemaquid, like the Point, you know, Pemaquid Point, but she's not a pointer, she's an English Lab, and they're—"

"That's okay, Professor. If it's okay with you, I'll give Pemmy a little treat." Farnsy always carried a couple of dog treats in a vest pocket because you just never knew, so he held out his palm and fed a treat to Pemmy, who stopped growling and nipped the treat off his outstretched hand as fast as a frog snaps up a fly.

"Now maybe you and I can talk about why Pemmy's sitting in your lap there, looking like he's driving your car."

"She's a she," the Professor corrected.

Like most traffic stops, this one ended with a W&C—a warning and a chat—and Farnsy watched the good Professor pull out into the long line of summer traffic, that yellow dog now hanging her head out the window over on the passenger side.

Early snowbirds arrive in Maine about the middle of May, after mud season and before the bugs start buzzing. Around Memorial Day, some folks from away come up for a weekend getaway. But by mid-June, after the end of the school year, one-week renters and visitors from away start to choke up roads everywhere in Maine. And Damariscotta puffs up like stovetop popcorn.

The Chief, Elwood Grenier, Farnsy's boss, had just heard a lunchtime talk over at the Skidompha Library and told everyone at the meeting the next day that the speaker, a fella who was a member of the Optimists, had said it was going to be a long, hot summer for the economy. Things were just starting to percolate, was the way Chief said the man described it. Which meant even more renters coming and going every Saturday, all of them squeezing through that highway bottleneck in New Hampshire, headed

SUMMER — *The Migration*

Down East, more folks asking which way to East Vassalboro, and more nut cases than usual, on road and off.

After a bowl of haddock chowder outside Larson's Lunchbox, still chuckling about that yellow dog, Farnsy pulled into his favorite spot for radar control in the cool shadows under a copse of oak trees near the old Round Top Ice Cream stand, where a nice breeze was stirring up from Great Salt Bay.

Farnsy's squad car, a new Ford Interceptor, was classic black with a bold blue stripe, the Damariscotta town seal, and the word *POLICE* on both sides. It had a radio antenna, tied back for good aerodynamics, a light bar on the roof, a black-handled sweeper searchlight outside the driver's window, and a serious-looking heavy-duty brush bumper mounted over the grille in case he ran into a deer, because you never knew when one would jump into the middle of the road and stare into your headlights.

Inside, he had a radio scanner with a corded mike clipped to the dash so he could communicate with the Lincoln County boys if he needed backup, a cell phone on the center console so he could call anyone on the Damariscotta force, a laptop on a swivel with Internet, a small video camera mounted on the dash, and an assault rifle sheathed in a scabbard that looked just like the one Farnsy saw in that Alaska state trooper show.

Farnsy also had several blocks of tickets and warnings; a town map; a Class B UL-rated fire extinguisher; a box of breathalyzers; rubber gloves; a pair of rangefinder binoculars; a black 800-lumens waterproof LED flashlight; a nightstick; a tactical knife to either break a window, cut a seatbelt strap, or scale a fish; a 100-foot tape measure; a notebook; a pen and pencil; a couple of pieces of chalk; a can of Mace pepper spray; two pairs of Smith and Wesson Model 100 chain handcuffs; a first-aid kit with two 4mg doses of Narcan nasal spray for overdoses; two epinephrine auto-injectors for allergic reactions to bee stings; plus a bag of dog treats.

FARNSY

In the glove compartment and on the passenger-side door, Farnsy kept a couple of lollipops and a roll of Junior Police Officer stickers for kids; a pack of stale Marlboros with some matches; a pack of spearmint Nicorette gum; a pack of Big Red chewing gum; a pouch with dog treats; and at least a half-dozen rolls of Necco wafers, his favorite. The only firearm he carried on his person was a Glock that he'd used once on duty to put down a deer that had jumped in front of a pickup one fall.

In the trunk, Farnsy had a box of road flares; a jumper cable; a tactical first aid kit; a spike strip; two orange traffic cones; a pair of collapsible crutches; a teddy bear he'd gotten from the found property closet and thought might come in handy sometime; and, in case there was a standoff or an overnight emergency, a bug-out bag; two bottles of water; a variety of snacks, including four strips of the Chief's best jerky; a hand warmer; gloves; and an army blanket. And because this was Maine, Farnsy stored a box of bear bangers and a canister of bear spray, along with a pair of tracker snowshoes, a hand axe in a leather sheath, a variety of household tools, more rounds for his Glock and the rifle, a roll of silver duct tape and a roll of yellow tape that read "POLICE LINE DO NOT CROSS," Nature's Miracle Skunk Odor Remover, Skeeter Skidaddler bug spray, two rolls of two-ply paper towels, and a roll of quilted toilet paper the Chief got a good deal on. Of a personal nature, Farnsy kept an old bamboo fly rod and reel his grandfather had used, a wicker trout creel his father gave him when he graduated from the academy, green hip waders, a fishing vest, and a clear plastic flip case with six flies that his grandfather had tied. One of them was the Maple Syrup, his grandfather's favorite lure. Farnsy never had time to use the fishing gear, but he liked having it there.

Farnsy had all the bells and whistles in his cruiser. But what he really needed right then was a fly swatter—a SWAT team, Farnsy thought, as he watched a fly buzz along his windshield, bumping along, looking for any crazy way out. Farnsy tried to steer him with his cap toward the driver's side window, which he'd slid down halfway, but the fly was having none of it and landed on the opposite end of the dashboard as if to wipe off the sweat, take it all in, and make a new plan. Farnsy lowered the passenger window a notch farther, but the fly bounced back up and resumed head-butting the windshield with renewed vigor, ignoring the second opportunity that Farnsy had created for his escape.

Farnsy wondered if he wasn't just as stuck as that fly. Which got him back to thinking about Lucy again. Seemed like most anything reminded him of her. It didn't take much. Every now and then he'd catch himself doing a double take, especially after he heard she was back in town, thinking that was her he just saw, coming out of the bank, the way she walked or the way she had her hair, or that curve of her back just above her hips, and that last time out at the lake.

Farnsy checked his gear and made some notes about the yellow dog incident. Chief would love that story when Farnsy told him about it later that day. And that reminded him of the stick of homemade moose jerky Chief had given him that morning, so he pulled it out of the glove compartment, and just as he was unwrapping the wax paper around it, his radar started beeping. Farnsy watched an upscale SUV with Illinois license plates shoot past him, headed due north to somewhere fast, hell-bent for Lexington, like his father used to say. Five miles per hour over was a gimme, a warning maybe, but 10, or in this case, 15 over the limit was ticket time. So Farnsy lit up the lights and siren on his cruiser and slipped into the traffic, which had slowed down to let him in, and he tailed the wagon until it pulled over onto the shoulder of Business Route 1A, just across from the Damariscotta Veterinary Clinic.

Farnsy hated making a mess of someone's holiday in Vacationland, but laws were laws for a reason and he was there to enforce them. It was all about safety, Chief reminded the crew every day. Like the Chief said, every time you pull someone over, whether you give them a warning or a ticket, a dozen cars slow down soon's they see the blue lights flashing, glad it's not them pulled over. "Nothing wrong with slowing traffic down a dite," Chief said.

This stop started out cheery. How's the weather out in Chicago? You a Cubs fan? Then: You know why I stopped you, right? Farnsy gathered the driver's license and registration and walked back to check his laptop. Valid license, so it was a simple ticket. He wrote it up, then strolled back to the vehicle and handed the man the ticket. Motioning to the fishing poles on the roof rack, Farnsy said he hoped the fish were biting and wished him a nice day. But as Farnsy walked back to his cruiser, thinking that hadn't gone too badly, he heard the man's wife shout that they hadn't driven a thousand miles just to have some small-town cop ruin their vacation.

Chief always said it was important to stay calm, so Farnsy leaned back in his seat and took a deep breath. The air conditioner felt good. But he had a mind to walk back over there and tell them Damariscotta wasn't some hick town. It had all the same problems and emergencies as Chicago, or any other place in these United States, just fewer. If being a friendly place that was small enough for anyone living there to know what anyone else was doing made Damariscotta a hick town, that was fine by him. Chief was always telling the officers it's not the quantity of cases that counts; it's the quality of their relationships in town. If all it took was a warning to set a kid straight, that was more important than a ticket. But his police work wasn't any less dangerous than it was for any officer wearing a badge and carrying a firearm anywhere in the country. As far as Farnsy was concerned, he was holding up one end of that thin blue line of justice just like Joshua Chamberlain and his

SUMMER ~ *The Migration*

Maine boys held off rebels on Little Round Top at Gettysburg. Big city summer folks could think whatever they wanted. Nice to see them coming, as long as you weren't a lobster, and most of them were nice folks, happy to be in Maine, but it was also nice to see the last of them head home after Labor Day.

As the motorist from Chicago put on his directional signal and nosed his SUV into the northbound traffic, Farnsy looked up to see two cute little girls, not older than 10, smiling back at him from the rear window. Twins, he guessed. Expecting a little wave from them, Farnsy was getting ready to wave back when both of them, suddenly, like they'd done this before, gave Farnsy the finger. The bird.

Jeez, Louise, now that's real nice, Farnsy thought, watching their car melt into the northbound traffic. But he was too tired to even think of lighting up the cruiser, going after the whole lot of them again, and lecturing those girls and their parents about respecting police officers. Tough crowd, those Chicago folks. But not as bad as "Massholes" or New Yorkers. They were the worst. Took the cake, that's for sure, he smiled. And they'd eat it too. It was late in the day, early summer, and already he felt like he needed a vacation. But Labor Day was months away.

"That was a certified synchronized double flip-off they gave you," the Chief told Farnsy afterward. "Now that is a first. Twins, too." Chief shook his head and chuckled all the way down the hall to his office.

Next morning, Farnsy told the regulars sipping coffee at Waltz's Soda Fountain that the Chief had said the Maine economy was turning around. Doc Adams—Perry Adams, a widower, retired, Mainer born and bred, who'd been the town dentist for as long as anyone could remember until his hands started shaking—took a sip of the coffee Julie'd just topped off for him and said the only thing he'd seen turn around recently was Julie behind the counter when she did the refills. Doc once told Julie that he liked the way she wiggled. That got him a one-week ban from the counter.

Doc could still hold a pen, and, like he told anyone who asked, he was writing the real town history, the stuff that's in between the lines in the weekly paper, the *Lincoln County News*, which came out every Thursday. Doc said he just wanted to make sure folks a hundred years from now could see what daily life was really like back then, which was now. Eyewitness history. And the best place to record it, fresh, Doc told Farnsy, was right there at Waltz's Soda Fountain.

Doc picked up his pen and resumed scribbling away in his notebook at the counter. Julie gave Doc that look of hers and said, "If anything's turning around now, it's the weather. Won't need to reheat the coffee it's getting so hot."

Farnsy thought that was probably as accurate as any weather forecast. Yes, it was officially summer in Damariscotta. Finally. Winter in Maine was always way too long and wicked cold and was followed, in slow succession, by mud season, tick season, bug season, then tourist season, and sometimes it was hard to tell which was worse.

The Haircut

The Chief kicked off the last staff meeting in June by handing out what he said was an updated Maine Police Grooming Guide. "Big changes," Chief said. "Turns out Augusta thinks Maine police, the men, that is, are getting a little shaggy." He paused. "All of you, and I'm not talking about you, Dottie, okay? Well, let's just say the good folks in Augusta think we need to clean up our act, you know? You can let your hair down some in winter, when most of you are wearing hats anyway, but come summer we got guests, visitors, and headquarters says we need to make a good impression on these folks from away. Good for tourism and all."

Chief looked around the table. Old John, who worked the parking lots and supervised the summer intern, was bowling-ball bald. The only reason he went to the barbershop in the back lot near the harbor was to read last month's *Field & Stream* magazine and catch the latest gossip. Investigative work, John claimed. Dottie, the dispatcher, always had a nice perm, nary a hair out of place. Farnsy looked up from the handout and saw the Chief looking straight at him.

"So," Chief said, "I know what you're wondering. What's all this mean for us?"

Silence. Everyone glanced around the table for an answer.

"Well—" The Chief paused for effect, a new trick he'd learned at Toastmasters. "Okay, Farnsy, looks like this memo only applies to you here—"

More silence.

FARNSY

Farnsy felt the top of his head. His hair was a scootch over his ears if he tugged on it. The hair on the back of his neck might be over the collar, but if it was, it was just a tad. Fact was, Farnsy kind of liked his hair short. Wasn't that the way Lucy said she liked it?

"Well, Farnsy," the Chief continued. "It just so happens that someone gave me this coupon here for a free trim at that MECasa hair salon, you know, the swanky new place where they serve you espresso while you wait. So I figured I'd give it to you. Maybe they can help you look almost normal, you know?"

The team burst out laughing.

"Anyway, Dottie got you an appointment over there." Chief looked at his watch, "in about 15 minutes. And Winnie, she's the owner, says she's got a new stylist in training. Says she needs some heads to practice on. So you just got volunteered, Farnsworth. And relax," Chief said. "You're off duty, Officer. It's lunchtime. And the haircut's free."

Farnsy saw her standing there as soon as he opened the door, both of her hands on the back of the swivel chair, and realized the whole thing—the new state haircut guidelines, the coupon, the appointment, everything—was a set-up. He was on stage without a script and everyone else was in on it. Lucy Granger smiled that smile of hers, the one that started slow, then grew. Her hair looked different than the last time he'd seen her, a touch of blond now, and he had all he could do to keep from asking her if she wanted to come out to the cottage for a glass of wine, then crossed that idea out as fast as he thought of it. Never mix police work with pleasure, he'd learned at the academy. Now here she was, again. And it all came back to him, fast.

"I was going to call you, Farnsy, but the Chief called me first." She confessed. "Well, anyway, he said he needed some help with a little surprise. So, I figured, okay, it's a Monday. The shop's usually closed, but Winnie said I could give you a first-timer freebie touchup. For old time's sake, she said. And, you know, if you want, we could talk, you know? I mean, it was my idea. I wanted to talk. You know, after last fall and all. You know, when Earl, I mean, it was after the divorce, when Earl came out to your place and, well, I was there. You know what I mean."

Farnsy knew exactly what she meant, and he didn't know if he should give her a hug and kiss her right there or just take off. Like she had last fall, just when they seemed to be getting back together again. The door closed behind him. Farnsy sank into the chair as Lucy enveloped him with a snappy new striped cape and tugged it around his neck, snug, then pinned it. Trapped. No escape now.

Lucy'd been on his mind off and on all winter and spring and now here she was—and she'd never looked better. Those brown eyes of hers. And that smile. How he missed the sound of her voice and those conversations they had that just seemed endless. And when they did end, he liked how they usually ended. Lucy always surprised him. She was a mystery he'd probably never solve. But like Doc once said, "Some mysteries you don't want to solve. Because if you did, then they'd be over for good."

"Okay, Lucy. You got me now."

She sized him up, looking from the mirror to his face then back again, like she wasn't sure which Farnsy she preferred. "You know, I think Chief's right. Your hair's getting a little, let's say, rakish. Some girls might like it that way, Farnsy, but for a cop, it's kind of shaggy."

All Farnsy could think of was Samson and Delilah as he watched her in the mirror, combing up tufts of hair, her scissors clicking and her shorts rustling against his arm now and then. He couldn't think of a thing to say that was honest.

"Thanks for coming in, Farnsy. I know this is a surprise and all, but it's really good to see you again. This time, no Earl…"

FARNSY

Farnsy decided the best bet was to pretend this was a hostage situation and go with the flow, so he let her talk and listened. Wasn't that what women said they wanted in those magazine surveys? he wondered.

"Earl's just Earl. Can't help it if he smells like fish. Always spent more time out there on his boat with baitfish and lobster than he ever did with people. Or women. Or me." Farnsy looked up and their eyes met briefly. Why was it, every time they met, it felt like they were two ships passing in the night.

"I was young and old Earl was all talk. Promises me he's gonna sell his boat and get a camp out near Rangeley, take the Maine Guide exam, he says, and start taking "sports" out fishing. Sounded good. Then he says he could build cabins out there for people from away. 'Off-grid,' he says. So I told him he was off something all right, he was off his rocker. Next thing, he says he could maybe save enough for us to go down to Florida every winter. 'If those Canucks can do it, so can we!' Earl says."

Lucy paused. "So then I'd tell him, well, Earl, I took French in high school, maybe I shoulda married some guy from Quebec then."

She continued around to the back of his head, taking slow measure of each cut. "Anyway, if you're wondering why—"

Farnsy looked up and caught her eyes in the mirror again and followed them as much as he could while she snipped here and there. He assumed she was trying out some new technique.

"If you're wondering why, why I'm here, well, it's simple. I've done a lot of thinking since I saw you last fall out at Pemaquid, when we went out to your favorite spot there on the rocks and we just sat there."

She snipped some off the side. Farnsy could almost feel her breath. He remembered having oysters at Eider's, then driving out to Pemaquid to watch the moon rise over Monhegan. He'd wanted to kiss her back then, but the ink on her divorce papers hadn't even dried yet.

"You were just listening, like you are now, while I was trying to figure out things with Earl." She fluffed his hair, and their eyes met in the mirror. "That really helped me, Farnsy, you know what I mean? To figure some things out. What's right."

All Farnsy could remember was that magnetic feeling that he had then, same as now, that he just wanted to hug her, but he couldn't. Now here he was again, immobilized by contrary forces. Seemed like the timing was always off. Never just right. Would it ever be? And that winter, he'd come to think maybe their time had run out. Maybe it was all just about timing.

He wasn't even going to try to figure out what she was trying to say to him now. Doc told him once that men and women communicating is like an Irish movie where you know they're speaking English and you get the drift, but you can't understand a damn thing they're saying. Farnsy couldn't tell if Lucy was trying to jump-start things or tell him goodbye for good. He tried to listen to her, but his thoughts wandered. How'd the Chief set this up? Should he ask her out? Would he invite her to his cottage again? This time no Earl, that's for sure. Earl had already found a new squeeze. Was she warming up to tell him she's getting married? Wouldn't someone at Waltz's have told him? Broken the news gently?

"...so that's why I left Earl. Had to. And then one thing after another, and things go from 'Stand by your man' to 'Can't stand that man.' Three years was all it took, Farnsy. You opened my eyes. How's that look on top?"

Farnsy said, "Good, but why'd you call? Just now, I mean?"

"Because I wanted to tell you I need some more time. Just because I married too early doesn't mean it's too late to figure things out. Like my next step. You know, where I'm going with my life and all."

FARNSY

"Time, Lucy? That what you're saying you need?"

"Might say that."

She worked one side of his head, then stepped back and started on the other side, measuring his sideburns. Neither of them said a word. Farnsy thought she never looked prettier. He liked her hair that way; it was new, looked a little shorter, but not too short. He remembered she liked to tuck it behind one ear like that. Not much makeup. What's this? Here he is with a woman he once loved, maybe still loved, whatever love is, and he's going into full detective mode? He thought he could see a few lines near her eyes. From crying, maybe. Long eyelashes. Those were new. And one button unbuttoned on her white blouse. That western belt with the blue stone on the buckle that he'd undone a couple of times.

"...so anyway, Farnsy, that's why I decided to get in some practice cutting here this summer. Besides, Winnie always needs help when the summer people come back and, you know, she has the best Japanese shears." She held up the shears and clicked them once. "So I'm going up to Augusta this fall. Get my cosmetology certificate, you know? Follow my dream, like my mom says. Stay at a friend's place. Then figure some things out between us. I still got time, you know?"

Farnsy didn't know if there was anything still between them. Ever since high school, they'd been on again, off again Finnegan so often it was hard to remember where they were. As for time, Farnsy knew what she meant. He was coming up on 35 real fast. The halfway point to somewhere was how he'd started thinking about 35, and he wasn't sure how much more time he had. But a "friend"—what friend? Was she trying to tell him something? Let the cat out slowly?

"Luce, you're what, 33?"

"Almost, Farnsy. Next February. Aquarius, remember?"

How could he forget?

SUMMER ⁓ *The Haircut*

"So, you were saying you need time? Or is it distance? From what, you don't mind me asking? From me? Jeez, Luce, I haven't even seen you in months. Talk about time. I mean it's been almost a year since..."

She stopped to pick up the comb she'd dropped on the floor, then slid it into a glass filled with blue liquid to soak next to a few other combs and pulled a new comb from a pocket in her smock.

"Yes, distance from you, Farnsy. Space. Time to figure things out, you know. I know what you're thinking."

Probably not, Farnsy thought.

"Like you know, I get you in here, just the two of us, just to tell you I'm leaving again. Crazy, right?"

Farnsy smiled. "No argument there."

She lathered up his neck with warm shaving cream, then unfolded a straight razor and gently shaved the back of his neck and the area near his ears. Judith and Holofernes, Farnsy thought. Right out of the Old Testament.

"Farnsy, sometimes you have to take 10 steps back just so you can see clearly, you know? I mean, you put your nose on a tree and you can't see the forest around you."

She brushed his hair with both hands, then squeezed a dollop of something into one palm, rubbed her hands together, fluffed the stuff into his hair, then held up a mirror and showed him her work.

"You look good, Farnsy. Always did."

"Jeez, Lucy, you too. I mean, real good."

She set the mirror down, tugged the cape off his chest, then stood there and held her arms open. "Okay, Officer, give me a kiss? You're not on duty."

Farnsy was surprised, uncertain, but he did. They did. He could feel her softness and all the old aches coming back. He remembered the last time they were together out there at Pemaquid Point, her giggling, telling him they were like pieces from a puzzle that just fit together. He also remembered how empty his cottage felt last fall when she left.

She pulled back to look him in the eyes and said, "You're a good man, Farnsy, a real good man. I can see it in your eyes. But not now. I can't. At least not right now. I gotta let you go. You better go. You know, catch and release."

"Okay, Luce." He brushed a few hairs from his tunic. Some of them looked gray. "Thanks. For the trim. And everything. You take care, you know?"

"I will, Farnsy. You know, it's not like it's 'goodbye' forever. More like 'see you later.' Around town, you know. Not like you're going anywhere. Wait, I didn't mean it that way! Shoot, I'm so sorry. I just gotta figure some things out."

Farnsy waited. Good cop technique. Let them talk.

"I need space, Farnsy. I feel like life is closing in on me sometimes. Trapped. Like one of Earl's lobsters. Can you believe I've never even been to Boston?"

Farnsy didn't think she'd missed all that much.

"No offense, Lucy, but there's more space up here in Maine than in all of Boston. You're probably right, though, taking time..."

"I love you, Farnsy, always will. Take care of yourself out there. You're a good cop. But be careful."

He was going to give her one last hug and maybe say something like "Love you, too," or "Don't worry about me," but she was already on her way to the back room, so he turned around and walked out into the summer sunshine. A new man, maybe, but more confused than an hour earlier. When it came to Lucy, it seemed he always thought of the right thing to say the next day.

Waltz's

Waltz Soda Fountain, Waltz's to locals, is on Main Street in Damariscotta in the old red brick Professional Building, which has been owned for many years by the Jacobs and Reny families. Some years ago, when Waltz Pharmacy went out of business, Renys Underground next door (so called because Renys had operated in the building's basement for many years) expanded into the space where the pharmacy had been, and the Jacobs and Reny families agreed to keep the old Waltz Soda Fountain up front in its original location.

All eight of its round red stools are still lined up along the beige linoleum countertop, which stretches from the cash register and the display of fresh homemade donuts under a glass dome at one end over to the big storefront window at the other end facing Main Street. Red wooden booths hug the wall opposite the counter. Everything is where it should be: the newspaper stand near the entrance and the Boston bus schedule tacked on the bulletin board with a few hopeful business cards. The old neon Waltz's Rexall sign still hangs outside. On a corner a block away, the other Renys store sells clothing. It's the flagship store of the Renys chain. Renys' motto is: "If Renys doesn't have it, you don't need it."

Even if young folks don't seem to have the time anymore to take a stool at the counter and have a morning coffee and a homemade donut, or a grilled cheese for lunch, or an ice cream cone or lime rickey or root beer float on a hot afternoon, there are always a few loyal regulars, who go to Waltz's to catch up on the local, fresh gossip, chuckle at old stories, and share their amazement about the crazy things folks do. Now and then, a summer visitor will drop in for a sundae with their grandkids to show them what life was like when time moved slower.

Some people from away flock to the new café that opened up across the street, where there's Wi-Fi and they can sit alone at small tables and eat a croissant or a scone or have a chai latte or a cappuccino or a bowl of lentil soup with a dill sprig while they connect with the world on their phones. But over at Waltz's, the news is local and fresh.

Farnsy preferred Waltz's. Waltz's was where he felt at home because he knew most everyone who showed up at the counter, and he knew their stories and they knew his. It's where Farnsy went most every morning he was working to get a hot black coffee and a fresh homemade donut. And it's where he'd go if he needed to find out what was going on in town, the latest scoop, sometimes even before it happened.

A sign on one wall at Waltz's proclaimed to anyone from away who sat down at the counter that the locals gathered there were "Counter Intelligence," and by the time they'd finished their coffee and overheard the chatter, most of them had to agree.

Behind the counter, facing Waltz's customers, was a wall of handwritten signs describing an array of floats, sodas, ice creams, melted cheese sandwiches, and the soup of the day. Julie brews fresh coffee all day, while four flavors of Round Top ice cream wait in their tubs under old freezer lids for Julie to scoop ice cream for floats, shakes, and sugar cones with a practiced flick of her wrist. The only changes over the years were the prices, the faces behind the counter, and the locals who'd staked their claim on a favorite stool.

Most every morning, sitting there at the old Waltz's counter, sipping coffee and nibbling fresh donuts, was over a hundred years of human experience, starting with Julie behind the counter, who had heard it all twice. Other than Farnsy and Doc Adams, there was the Professor, Phoebe Louise Tuttle, who was from away but transitioned from seasonal to full-time resident after she retired. More than a decade later, she was still considered from away. Once a history professor, she fed Doc all the town news she heard. But she was careful to leave an empty stool between herself and Doc, who told her he needed room for his notebook.

Tourists sat on the stool next to Doc at the risk of a stern gaze. Nice folks. Dollar tippers. Other regulars stopped by whenever they could in season, like the Captain, who came in on his old wooden boat when the tide was right. Skinny as a rail, Captain always got a lime rickey. Didn't matter if it was still morning. Said it reminded him of when he was a kid. He went south come winter. And Bob, who lived in Edgecomb, and came in a couple of times a week. He'd wait quietly there with his coffee mug in front of him, until he heard the conversation slack, and he'd jump right in and tell about the times he used to walk all the way into town some Saturday nights just to dance with a girl at Lincoln Academy. Even if you weren't a regular, if you dropped by a couple of times, Julie'd remember how you liked your coffee, and if you kept your mouth shut and your ears open, you'd hear some good stories. One fella from away said sitting there at Waltz's was like a Berlitz course in Mainer.

The bells on the back of the door to Waltz's Soda Fountain jingled that morning as Farnsy pulled it open and took a seat midway between the Professor, who was over near the glass donut display, and Doc, who always sat at the end of the counter nearest the storefront window so he could observe history as it happened and still have room for his writing arm.

Julie, who'd been working the fountain counter as long as anyone could remember, slid Farnsy a white mug filled to the brim with coffee, black, the way he liked it. The sugar dispenser sat there

FARNSY

in front of him, tempting him to break his new diet. Lined up next to the sugar were salt and pepper shakers, a napkin holder, and a small glass with sugar substitutes in thin yellow and pink packets.

"Something on your mind there, Farnsy? You look serious today." Julie had a knack for picking up folks' "vibrations," as she called them.

Farnsy took a sip. The coffee was piping-hot perfect. He looked Julie square in the eyes and said, "Trying to figure something out. Just doesn't make any sense."

"You want to be a little more specific, Farns?" Julie said, wiping the counter off. "A lot of things these days don't make much sense."

"Let me take a wild guess," the Professor said, "if you don't mind me butting in."

"Why not?" Farnsy said.

"Is it maybe," the Professor paused, "something to do with Necco wafers? Out at the lake?" She wiggled her spoon in the air as if stirring up trouble.

Fact was, something had just reminded Farnsy of Lucy and he was still trying to figure out if she was just trying to let him down gently and was really breaking up. Not that there was anything to break up.

"Necco what? What are you talking about, Professor?" Farnsy asked. He was reluctant to leave his reveries about Lucy.

Doc, who was sitting on the other side of Farnsy, tapped the Portland paper, which was in front of him, turned to Farnsy, and said, "Son, most of what you read in the paper's as stale as yesterday's sandwich by the time you read it. Same with the radio." He paused. "You want real news, you sit right where you are."

"You mind telling me what you heard, Professor?" Farnsy asked.

The Professor took a breath. She reminded Farnsy of a professor he'd had at Colby who knew how to hook his students' attention. Being a cop, Farnsy loved a good mystery.

"Well," the Professor began, "this friend of mine has a brother up in Jefferson, and his neighbor's wife, Gail, does a little housekeeping on the side. You know, opens up some summer rentals there on the north end of the lake. Works for an agency that hires a new team of cottage cleaners every summer. But she does my place, too, on the side."

"What's this about Necco wafers, though, Professor?" Farnsy asked.

"Anyway, so she's out at my place the other day, when she stops in her tracks, middle of vacuuming, and I mean, with Pemmy, you met her, well, that dog sheds like crazy, so Gail's got to empty that vacuum pretty often. Have to laugh, you know. Gail told me once she thought she could make a good pillow with all the fur she'd vacuumed up."

"The wafers, Professor? You were saying..."

"So anyway, all of a sudden, she stops vacuuming and tells me she remembers thinking something was a little off when she opened up a couple of the cottages on the lake, earlier this season, you know, airing them out before Memorial Day. Front doors to both cottages were closed, she says, but she remembered they were both unlocked. Now, you and I both know, Farnsy, most locals leave everything unlocked. Half of them don't even know where the key is. But seasonals, renters from away, well, they lock everything up. Like they're still back in the city. You see, these were rental cottages Gail was getting ready. She says she'd locked them up tight as a barrel after closing up last fall. She didn't think much of it. Not until she was vacuuming in my place and started thinking about the second thing that was a little off and that was the rolls of Necco wafers. That's when she remembers those cottages she was cleaning that day, the same ones with the doors unlocked, well, both of them had rolls of Neccos sitting right out there. One was on a kitchen counter, unopened. Not on a shelf, where it would've been if she'd seen it when she was cleaning up last fall. She thinks the other one was on the kitchen table, not in the pantry. Opened. Said she ate a couple wafers, couldn't resist. You following me, Farnsy?"

Farnsy, tight-lipped and listening, nodded, then turned to his right. "You getting all this down, Doc?"

Doc nodded.

"Well, that's not all." The Professor leaned toward Farnsy like they do in spy movies. "This is where the real mystery starts. Because she says it wasn't until then, right there in my living room, as she starts to pull up the rug near my fireplace. She stares off and says to me, 'Now that's strange…' Then she says to me she just remembered the owner of one of those cottages is what she called a 'born-again' granola vegetarian. Everything organic. Lets her husband fry up some bacon now and then to keep him happy. Candy? Maybe, but Necco wafers? Not the type, knowing her, probably sour balls, Gail says. I mean, personally, Farnsy, I don't know anyone doesn't like Neccos."

"Any chance it was some renters just left them behind?"

"Nope. I asked her and all she said is they'd cleaned that place up real nice last fall, then her husband went over and blew out the water pipes so they wouldn't freeze up, poured some antifreeze down the toilet, shut off the electricity, and locked up for the season. Lock, stock, and barrel, closed up tight. No off-season renters. Then, like some ghost planted it there, this roll of Necco wafers pops up this spring, if you please. Out of nowhere."

"She mention anything missing from the cottage? Anyone report this to the cleaning agency?"

"Didn't ask, and you don't mind me saying it, but isn't this something you boys in blue should look into? I mean, if they'd been missing anything, you know they'd have mentioned it."

"She say anything about seeing footprints?"

"Farnsy, these are hard-working gals with a job to do, who do it, then pack up and drive over to the next place, cleaning up cobwebs and dust bunnies and getting those places aired out and all. They don't have time to go snooping around. I mean, she did think it was off and checked around, but she says she just cleaned up and got on to the next job. Of course, she thought it was kind of funny, the wife being a carrot lover and all. Figured maybe it was someone's idea of a joke, don't you know. But she didn't start to think about the unlocked doors at both places where she'd seen some Necco wafers until she was talking to me."

"Last question, Professor. She say if they were all-chocolate or mixed flavors?" Farnsy asked.

"Huh? Okay, sure, got it, cops like details. She didn't say, but I'm guessing mixed flavors. All three of those Necco rolls," the Professor said.

"Wait a minute. I thought you just said there were only two rolls of Necco wafers. One in the veggie's place, and the other in a second cottage nearby?"

"Well, now, this is where it gets interesting," the Professor said, lowering her voice so that only Farnsy and Doc and Julie could hear her. "You see, Gail says it wasn't a week or so later she was talking with her sister-in-law who has a camp over on the other side of the lake, just across from those two other places with the Neccos. And she tells Gail she found a roll of Necco candy in her place too, when they opened up, only this time the roll was open, just a couple of Neccos left. She figured her husband left it out there on the kitchen counter. His idea of a joke, maybe."

"She ask her husband if they were his?"

"Farnsy, like I said, this was a month ago maybe more. So if you were thinking you might dust some fingerprints off one of those candies, you can forget it. Long gone and in the trash. Sorry."

"So that makes three camps. That we know of. With Necco wafers."

"Hmm," Doc muttered. "Two's interesting. Three's a story. So maybe I'm sticking my neck out here now, Farnsy, but three rolls of Neccos, well, that's a—What would you call it, Farnsy? A coincidence, maybe?"

Farnsy stared into his coffee. "Maybe, Doc. But in my business, we call that a pattern. Now here's the question, Professor Tuttle: You sure nothing was missing from those camps? Those gals up at the lake say anything about anything missing? They file a report? I mean, I don't remember Chief mentioning any reports."

"All I can tell you is what I heard, Farnsy. When I asked Gail, she said nothing was missing. Just those rolls of Necco wafers sitting out there, almost as if someone was trying to have one over on all those folks. Except, well, now there was one more thing she happened to mention that I thought was kind of interesting. And that's why I'm telling you about it now."

"What was that?"

"Well, she calls me yesterday, Gail does, after work, and says she was talking about the whole thing with a friend who has a place next to hers over on Pemaquid Pond. She says her neighbor told her they opened up their cottage right after fishing season started. Gail says her friend calls it a cottage, but it's really more of a fishing camp, even though they closed up their privy years ago. Anyway, so her friend tells her that her neighbor says her hubby always takes his Lund over to his favorite spot on the lake on opening day, but when he was looking for his fishing gear this year, he asked her if she'd tried to reorganize his stuff. He says it looked like someone'd been messing with his fishing tackle. Couldn't find the old tackle box, the one with his grandfather's favorite lures. He thought something was off, but he couldn't tell what. Besides, she says he was so anxious to get out to the cove and get his hook wet before anyone else got out there, he didn't have time to figure out where that tackle box was, or what was missing, if anything. He just went over to the hardware and got a couple new lures. So when I mentioned something about the rolls of Necco wafers popping up, she says, oh my gosh, she found a roll of them, too, right after they opened up. Thought maybe the grandkids'd left them out last fall. All she could remember was her husband shouting about someone hiding his tackle box. So she gave him the Neccos. Distract him, you know. Sweeten him up some."

"I guess there was no police report? And no insurance claim filed, right?"

"How would I know, Farnsy? But it's kind of strange, all these coincidences, don't you think?"

"You can say that again, Professor. Have to agree. Keep your eyes and ears open. Let me know if you hear anything else, okay? And thanks."

Farnsy dunked one end of his cruller into his coffee. That made four rolls of Neccos. So far. Weird.

"Doc, you getting all this down, now?" Julie quipped.

Doc smiled and kept writing.

"Say, Julie," Farnsy blurted out, holding up what was left of his cruller, "you know, I just thought of something. You never did tell me who makes them, these donuts. All you've ever said was 'homemade.'"

"Homemade, for sure. Can't you tell from looking at them? You want store-bought perfection, you can get that anywhere. But you want a donut that tastes like a donut, you want homemade and that's here. I thought you were a good cop, Farnsy. Chief tells everyone you've got a detective's eye for details and all that."

"Not a detective, not yet, maybe sergeant someday. But like Chief says, a good cop always asks questions. So spill it, Julie, who's your supplier? Who's your source?" Farnsy paused so it didn't sound like a cross-examination and dipped the other end of his cruller in the coffee. "If you don't mind me asking."

"Course I mind, Officer. Some things stay secret or they lose their, their, what do they call it?"

"Luster?" Farnsy offered.

"Luster. Their luster. They lose their luster. You know, like after you're married a few years. So, let's just say those are real donuts, man-made, no machines."

"Julie, you know as well as I do there aren't many secrets in this town."

"Farnsy, seriously? Oh, my, you got no idea. Every town's got secrets. Even if everyone knows them. So let's leave it there, okay?"

"A good cop can be discreet. Your baker's name's safe with me. I mean, did I ever tell you who burned down old man Shaw's outhouse that time?"

"You kidding, Farnsy? Everyone in town knew who lit up that privy. Doc probably has it all right there in his little diary." Julie nodded over toward Doc.

Doc tapped his notebook. "It's a journal, Julie. But it's all right here, Farnsy. If you want, I could check last year's journal, but it's back home. I remember the story."

"That's okay, Doc. Anyway, Julie, who bakes your donuts?"

"Not on your life! That recipe was handed down. And let me tell you, the first dozen sold fast."

"Okay, you said 'man-made,' not 'handmade,' so I'm guessing it's a man, then." Farnsy looked up at the ceiling. "Got to be older than 40. Probably older than that. Retired. A retired baker maybe, with some free time on his hands, and he started thinking about his family and the old country. Maybe he's in that genealogy class over at the library, tracing his roots. All I have to do is ask that new librarian over there, and she'll spill the beans. So tell me who he is..."

"Not even close. Look, Farnsy, they wouldn't taste any better if you knew who made 'em. You know that. Might even taste a little off, you know, once you put a face with the hands that rolled the donut dough." She paused good and long, then added, "Besides, what's life without a few mysteries, Farnsy? I thought men liked mysterious women."

"Mysterious, sure, but not secretive. But if I've learned anything, Julie, secrets leak out. As soon as I figure out who your baker is, it'll cost you a donut to keep it secret. You on?"

"The game's afoot, Sherlock. If you figure it out, I'll give you a free coffee and one of those chocolate donuts. Every day, for a week, free." She started wiping down the counter around Farnsy.

"Deal, Julie." Farnsy said, reaching out his hand for a shake to seal the deal. "Wait a minute now. We talking about a five-day workweek or a full week, Saturday to Saturday?"

"A week's a week, Farnsy. Now, don't you have work to do?"

Julie started another pot of coffee. She wrapped up a raisin muffin in a paper napkin, then slipped it into the microwave, beeped 60 seconds on medium, and told Doc he'd have his breakfast in a minute.

Farnsy turned back to the Professor. "Last question, I promise. You happen to know the name of the cleaning agency those gals work for?"

"Farnsy, sure. Midcoast Dusters. But you're not gonna get any more out of them."

Farnsy'd heard of the agency. Mostly summer rental cleanups. Twenty-thirty jobs a weekend, he remembered someone telling him, sometimes more, rental turnarounds, all summer long, late May into September, Saturday to Saturday bookings. Heard it was hard to find cleaners who'd work a whole season. The younger gals got tired of cleaning summer people's toilets and picking up after them, four or five cottages a day.

FARNSY

Farnsy drank the last of his coffee, which had gone cold but still had the flavor. "Thanks, Professor. You too, Julie," he winked, and headed out. By the time he got back to his cruiser and buckled up, he was convinced that there was something about those Necco wafers, and he was going to find out what. Just didn't pass Farnsy's smell test.

The Lake

One Saturday, late June, Farnsy was driving his pickup back out to his cottage on Damariscotta Lake after getting in some early morning target practice out at the range. Like the Chief always said, "A firearm's involved every time an officer's on duty, so even if you never have to use it, you'd better know how." Farnsy was a good shot with his Glock—three headshots out of 50 rounds in the silhouette every time he requalified at the range. But those were paper targets. Farnsy hoped he'd never have to use his sidearm. Or the rifle.

It was one of those crisp, blue-sky summer mornings in Maine that Farnsy's mom used to call a three-season day, when you'd wear a sweater in the morning, put on shorts around midday, and when the sun dropped behind the trees, you'd be back in long pants and a sweater. Farnsy loved driving the narrow road that snaked along the lakeshore over the rock-bound farmland, now and then catching a glimpse of the lake through the trees on the way to his cottage.

The overlook at the top of Bunker Hill offered a picture-postcard vista of Damariscotta Lake and, if you knew what you were looking for, off to the east, the bay where the lake opened up, and you could just about pick out the speck of a rock that Farnsy's family had dubbed Blueberry Island.

When Farnsy was a kid, his father would stand there at the lookout, sweep his arm from one end of the lake vista to the other, and tell Farnsy and his little sister Grace, "There you are, Willie, Gracie, that's our lake!" Farnsy would cup his hands around his eyes and imagine he was a north-woods game warden piloting a floatplane, coming in for a water landing.

Farnsy pulled over at the lookout. He spotted a silver boat out on the lake, off in the distance over toward Muscongus Bay, and could make out a man standing up, casting. Farnsy could've told him that's not where the fish are biting this time of day, but then maybe all the guy wanted was an excuse to get out on the lake and hear the loons, have a little adventure of his own and let the wife sleep in. Just because you were out fishing didn't necessarily mean you wanted to catch a fish.

About a half-mile past Bunker Hill, Farnsy turned onto his old fire road, which was still rutted up from all the spring runoff. Farnsy nosed his pickup down the short slope that was once the old lakeshore, past a thicket of aspens and some underbrush that hid an old water pump. Farnsy and his father used to wade through a chest-high tangle of pricker bushes and burrs buzzing with mosquitos and bees, just to fill a couple of plastic jugs with fresh well water.

His father always left an old plastic gallon jug out there, filled with water, so the next time he could pour water down the spout and prime the pump. After a half-dozen rackety clanking pumps on the curved pump handle, just when it seemed like the well might've gone dry, the old pump would cough up rusty water and soggy leaves, like a cat's hairball, and after a couple more pumps, up came a stream of cold clear well water, and they'd each hold an empty gallon milk jug under that bountiful flow from deep in the earth until the jugs filled up. Then they'd screw the caps back on the jugs and trudge back to the cottage like returning warriors. When he was little, Farnsy had all he could do to carry one sloshing jug back to the cottage. And his mother would say, "Oh, Jack, Willie, look at the two of you! Burrs stuck all over you."

The well they'd drilled later near the cottage had good water, but his father still went out to the old farm pump in the middle of the field once or twice every season, just for the taste of that cold artesian water. Eventually, trees and a tangle of bushes grew up all around the pump. Farnsy guessed it was still there. The last time he could remember going out to it was a few years before his mother died, when the pump sucked air and he and his father had to replace the worn valve with a piece of leather cut from an old glove. With a tight seal, the pump could draw more water. That same summer they painted the pump bright red, "So's Gracie's kids can find it in the thicket when they get older," his father said.

Last Thanksgiving, a year after Lilly passed, Jack was about to slice the store-bought pumpkin pie when he broke into a sobbing mess. Thanksgiving just wasn't the same without her, he said, weeping. No turkey with the fixings and her giblet gravy, the way he liked it. Just a couple of burnt frozen turkey pot pies and a can of store-bought cranberry sauce. The smells were wrong, he said. They all hugged and said they loved each other more than anything and would stick together. But then Gracie flew back to California, where her kids were with her ex. And Farnsy went back to work.

A month or so later, Jack drove off in a beat-up RV he'd found in *Uncle Henry's Swap or Sell It Guide*. He wrote them both letters and told Farnsy the camp was his now. He knew Farnsy would take good care of it and hoped Grace and her kids would still come out every summer. Jack said he was real sorry, but he just couldn't live there alone. Had to get away and hoped Farnsy and Grace would understand. He wished Farnsy would find a gal as sweet as his mother. Farnsy read Jack's letter over and over, trying to figure things out, but it was like trying to untangle balled-up fishing lines.

After a while, his father started sending them postcards from all over the country. The mermaids at Weeki Wachee Springs. Devil's Tower. The Grand Canyon. The one from Las Vegas said only "weekend misspent." It seemed to Farnsy like his father was just chasing the sun, getting something long pent up out of his system.

Grace had married young and, two babies later, she'd divorced young, but she promised Farnsy she'd still come out to Maine with her kids, Maggie and Lulu, every summer. But every summer she seemed just a little different to Farnsy. Not bad. Small stuff. How she talked. What she wore. Later, what she wouldn't eat. After a few years, when her kids were older, it didn't seem like Gracie was really a Mainer anymore. He told her she was still his little sister, always would be. And he was still her big brother and always would be, she'd said.

On the phone, Gracie told Farnsy she was worried their father would end up in a cabin out west, like the Unabomber. Farnsy pictured him fishing for marlin in the Gulf Stream, like Papa Hemingway, a cigar in his mouth. But the postcards never stopped, and they hoped maybe he'd find the road back to Maine.

Farnsy pulled into the drive at the last cottage at the end of the road, shingles weathered gray from the sun and hard winters, on a slight rise overlooking the cove, just past two other smaller cottages, which were vacation rentals now, because their original families and the kids Farnsy and Grace had played with had all grown up and grown apart. The three cottages were close enough that their occupants could wave and be neighborly, but not so close you could hear the Red Sox if they were on the radio next door. The Farnsworth place, as neighbors called it, was the oldest, the first one built on the cove, and was originally just a simple summer place like a thousand others, a weekend fishing camp his grandfather had built just after the war, with an outhouse and no electricity. A dowser had found a spring out in the field back of the cottage, so that was where they drilled the well. Power lines came in from the lake road in the late '50s after two other places went up nearby, so Farnsy's folks tore down the privy and had old man Sprague install an indoor toilet and a septic tank—a late wedding gift to each other.

In the early years along the lake, come summer, it was all kids running around, local and from away, made no difference, teasing and playing, squealing with tickled joy as if life were just one long summer. And then those kids' kids. And when those families grew up and spread out, or when there was a divorce, there were renters, sometimes new ones every Saturday, coming and going. One-week renters tried to squeeze everything into six days—a day at the lake, and a day at the beach, and maybe a day in Freeport if it rained. Two-week renters had time to get a canoe from Ralph over at Pemaquid Canoe and poke around the coves or paddle out to what his family called Blueberry Island with a plastic pail. One-weekers didn't even have time to learn the J-stroke, in spite of Farnsy's dad's best efforts to help the poor folks paddle straight. Like old Ralph once told Farnsy's father, those young couples from away who thought canoeing was romantic didn't understand that for some beginners canoeing was an argument waiting to happen.

Farnsy's parents never rented their place out. His father said that was like sharing your underwear, so they never did.

After Farnsy moved in, he added a heater and some insulation, and settled in, surrounded by the clutter of old memories. He never locked the cottage because he figured there wasn't much to steal if someone was bent on it.

On this day, when he opened the front door, he decided the place needed some fresh air, so he opened a couple of windows, and a sweet lake breeze soon wafted through the cottage, which was really still more camp than cottage. Even though it didn't have a privy like a camp, it felt cozy as a camp, and Farnsy liked that. A cottage was what the high rollers up at Bar Harbor used to call their mansions on the sea. Some had half a dozen flush toilets, and

FARNSY

whenever anyone brought up the topic, Farnsy's father used to say to Farnsy's mom, "Jeez, Lilly, who needs that many toilets? You only got one butt...!"

Farnsy sensed Lucy's presence there even though it'd been almost a year since they'd driven down the cottage road last fall the day after her divorce from Earl was in the *Lincoln County News*. "Just to talk," she'd said. Then she'd stayed for dessert, then one more glass of wine, and a few more stories, then a long silence, and when the last log in the fireplace rolled off the andirons into the glowing embers with a thunk, one thing led to another, and Lucy spent the night. "Just for old time's sake," she said. After all, she'd said, "I'm a free woman now."

"Not really, but nearly," Farnsy'd said as he led her to the back bedroom, where it all had started long before she met Earl.

That next morning, Farnsy'd heard a car clatter down the road, kicking up the gravel, and crunch to a stop just outside, then someone pounding on the screen door so hard it might break off its hinges.

Farnsy had looked up from breakfast and wasn't exactly tickled to see old Earl standing there, banging on the screen door. If the door wasn't unhinged, Earl was.

Farnsy had hoped Lucy had enough sense to stay in the back bedroom or at least put some clothes on. He wondered how in blazes he'd landed in the middle of this mess. It was like having your own little summer theater right there in front of you.

"Can I do for you, Earl? What's all the commotion?"

"You know damned well, Farnsworth. Open up. We need to talk. Now." Earl had squinted into the screen, his face pressed against it so close Farnsy could see little squares etched across his forehead.

"Door's open, Earl. Always is."

The screen door had squeaked open and then flapped shut two or three times. Farnsy's father had said that was all the burglar alarm system they needed. Could hear that thing slam across the lake. Wake up the dead in Fairhaven, he'd say.

Earl had stood there, just inside, his muck boots still on from the dock.

"Coffee, Earl?"

Earl'd commenced pacing back and forth across the braided rug Farnsy's grandmother had made out of his mother's skirts and jumpers when she outgrew them.

"Settle down, now, Earl. S'matter? Something eatin' at you?"

'You know damned well what's eatin' at me, Farnsy."

Earl had his arms wrapped up, so it looked like he was his own straitjacket trying to keep his hands from doing something awful.

Wound up tighter than a winched rag was how Farnsy'd thought Earl looked at that moment. Which was when Farnsy recalled a trick he'd learned in Boston at that workshop on hostage negotiations Chief sent him to. So he tried that empathy technique they'd practiced, where the negotiator validates the emotions the hostage-taker seems to be exhibiting. Farnsy had tried to soften up his voice the way you did when you talked with a kid.

"You seem pretty upset now, Earl."

That technique was supposed to calm folks down a little and looked good on the overhead: just figure out what someone was thinking, then tell them you know how they feel. Not Earl. He'd taken the bait like a striper and ran with it.

"Don't you try an' tell me how I feel, Farnsworth! How in hell you know what anyone feels, you all high and mighty there with your police stuff, struttin' around Damariscotta like a bull moose in rut. Ink's still wet on those divorce papers, and now you're out here cavorting—well, don't think I don't know what's going on here."

"What? What's going on here, Earl?"

"Jesus Christmas. That's her car out there."

"She's your ex, Earl. Ex. Water under the bridge."

"Farnsy," Earl said, "she always fancied you. Never said it. Didn't need to. I thought she was mine. Thought I had her in my trap, but you know, sometimes a lobster finds a way out."

Right about then, as best as Farnsy could remember, Lucy had strolled into the kitchen just as calmly as you please, barefoot, past the two of them, wearing what Farnsy recognized as his favorite flannel pajama top and not much else, poured herself a cup of coffee, stirred in a couple teaspoons of sugar, then turned around to face the two of them.

"First of all," Lucy had said, "I'm not a lobster and love isn't a trap. Second, Earl, you just gotta move on. Let me go. That goes for both of you." She stood her ground, waiting for one of the men to say something. It got so quiet, Farnsy felt like he was watching a daytime soap opera with the sound turned off.

"As for you, Farnsy, it was real good seeing you last night. Thanks. I'm just sorry, you know, the timing's always off."

Lucy wasn't a door slammer. She'd just taken her coffee into the back bedroom, then emerged a few minutes later with her things, stopping to put her coffee mug in the kitchen sink. She'd strolled past the two men, then got into her car and drove up the road.

"Well, Earl," Farnsy had said, sighing and waving an arm around his empty cottage parlor, "guess she's not in my trap, either."

Farnsy and Earl had talked a good while longer that morning last year, looking out at the lake, not at each other, because that made it easier to talk, two men who were still in love with the same woman, just in different ways.

After Earl had finished drinking his Moxie—he was on the wagon again, he'd told Farnsy—he'd sighed and slapped his hands on both knees, pushed himself to his feet, stretched, then said, "Guess I'll be going, too."

Farnsy'd stood up too, and said, "Okay then, Earl."

SUMMER — *The Lake*

When Earl'd reached out his hand, Farnsy thought he might be trying something funny, but Earl was just reaching out for Farnsy's hand, so they shook as Earl said, "Thanks for the Moxie," and "I guess that's that."

"What do you mean, Earl?"

"What I mean is, well, I guess that's it for me and Lucy. Won't bother you again."

"Earl..." Farnsy had said.

Earl had nodded. "I guess not. But you and I both know she'll come back. Always does. But not to me next time."

"We'll see, Earl." Farnsy had watched Earl get into his pickup, and that was that.

That was all last fall, but to Farnsy it felt like yesterday. The next time he'd seen Lucy was when she gave him a trim a couple weeks ago and told him she needed time to think things over, figure herself out.

Farnsy's fridge was almost as empty as the cottage felt now, just a few bottles of PBR, a half stick of butter, some moldy bread, and three slices of mortadella that were hard around the edges. Farnsy had picked up some stuff in town: a half-dozen eggs, some bacon, Velveeta cheese slices, individually wrapped, a bag of Fritos, a half gallon of milk (whole milk, not that 1 percent white water stuff), and a box of Wheaties with a picture of a baseball player he'd never heard of on the front. A couple of jet skis buzzed around the lake like angry bees, then it got quiet.

After tidying up and squaring things away, Farnsy scraped the mold off the bread, trimmed around the old mortadella slices with the kitchen shears, assembled his mortadella and cheese sandwich on a paper plate, tucked the bag of Fritos under one arm, grabbed a can of PBR from the fridge, went out on the deck overlooking the lake, and sat down on an Adirondack chair. His pickup may have been right there behind the cottage, but work seemed a million miles away. For Farnsy, work started to fade away as soon as he turned onto the fire road, and by the time he parked, he was as good as unplugged.

Farnsy glanced at the beer can in his hand and wondered when everyone started calling it "PBR." His father had just called it what it was, "Pabst Blue Ribbon" or simply "Pabst." All that mattered to his dad was that it was cold and cheap. He wondered what his father would make of all the micro-breweries popping up all over Maine, with their special farmhouse brews and their pale ales with catchy names. Dry hopped or barrel aged. There was even a beer made with clam juice and an ale made with blueberries.

Farnsy was about to take a last swig of his PBR when he stopped short. Had he just seen some Necco wafers on the shelf over the stove? He went back into the kitchen. There they were. The roll'd been opened. Then closed up again. But how long had it been there? Farnsy stared out the window and thought long and hard. He'd have noticed it for sure. Somehow, he must've missed it. Lucy sure didn't bring it with her last fall, and he hadn't had any visitors since then. He tried to remember if he'd seen anything unusual in the cottage or outside. He would have noticed footprints or tire tracks outside that winter or in mud season, which ran late that spring, and if there had been any, he'd certainly have seen them. After he flipped through all the possibilities, he concluded someone must've been in the cottage. Maybe when he went ice fishing up on Moosehead, and he just didn't spot the candy when he came back? Maybe they were left over from Halloween? But he just couldn't remember buying any Neccos that winter. Maybe he got a roll and just forgot? Then he remembered the Professor telling him about the Necco rolls some folks'd found a little up the lake from Farnsy's place—and a roll or two over on Pemaquid Pond.

Farnsy let the PBR sit. The mortadella couldn't get any staler. But he couldn't let the thing go. He scoured the whole cottage with fresh eyes, shifting into what he thought of as his detective mind, looking for anything out of place. The hardest thing was always to see what wasn't there.

So Farnsy surveyed each bedroom, thinking maybe he'd see something missing. Something that wasn't there that should be. Nothing. Same in the closets. Everything was where it was supposed to be. The only thing off was a half roll of Necco wafers sitting right there in the kitchen on the shelf over the stove next to the salt and pepper shakers and the napkin holder. He tried to remember if he'd sensed anything was off when he'd come home a few months ago after the weekend ice fishing up at Moosehead.

The trouble with memory, Farnsy'd learned as a cop, was that it wasn't very reliable. Ask any two eyewitnesses what they'd just seen, and you'd think they were in different time zones or that one of them was lying.

Like the Chief said, once you're aware of something, it's hard to get unaware of it. So that roll of Necco wafers was on Farnsy's mind all that Saturday, even as he mowed the lawn and took a few casts off the dock late in the day. What would he tell the Chief: he'd found a roll of candy he couldn't remember buying?

It wasn't until he was sitting at the kitchen table, wondering what he'd have for supper, staring at that half roll of Neccos, turning it around in his hands, tempted to sample the evidence, when he remembered he hadn't checked the tool shed out back. That was where he and his father had spent hours working on projects—making bird feeders, fixing broken stuff, side by side, sometimes talking. Most times not.

FARNSY

Farnsy unlatched the shed door, and as soon as he swung it open he could see the outline on the wall where a small picture frame had hung, the only spot that time hadn't faded. His father's old fishing lure was gone. That little box frame with the lure inside was lock, stock, and barrel, gone, and only a small white patch left where the lure had hung.

That smooth white Jitterbug with the red head, perfect little glass eyes, and a curved silver spoon for a mouth that made the lure jiggle on the surface of the lake when you reeled it in. The same lure that his father said hooked the biggest largemouth bass ever caught on that cove. The same lure that Farnsy's dad had tried to cast across the cove but had wrapped around a big oak limb two or three times.

When Farnsy was growing up, he used to think it was amazing that his father could get a lure up that high, but when he started doing serious fishing, he realized that dangling Jitterbug wasn't heroic. It was a bungled mess of a cast. And there it hung, as if to taunt Farnsy's father, until years later he'd climbed up and cut it down. That was when Farnsy's mom, Lilly, had it framed, with a shiny brass plate: *Jack Farnsworth, age 25, caught a live oak with this Jitterbug in 1980.* She presented it to Farnsy's father on April Fool's Day, opening day of fishing season in Maine, the same year Farnsy was born. Like Farnsy's dad told him, it was a reminder not to get all full of yourself. At least not if you're a Mainer.

By the end of the weekend, Farnsy had contacted the owners of the two other cottages on his side of the cove. One of them said they'd found the wrapper from a roll of Necco wafers, which they'd thought was a little odd, but had tossed it out. They hadn't noticed anything missing when they opened up their camps that season, so they figured one of last summer's renters might have left it. The neighbor on the other side said his cleaning lady opened up their cottage every summer but hadn't mentioned anything

SUMMER ~ *The Lake*

about finding Necco wafers. They said they'd ask her next time she cleaned the place and let Farnsy know.

Back at work that Monday, the Chief said he'd never heard any mention of cottage break-ins. Besides, he reminded Farnsy, Damariscotta Lake wasn't exactly in their jurisdiction. Pemaquid Pond was, and Biscay Pond, but not Damariscotta Lake. So Farnsy let it go. Maybe it was just one of what his father called life's little mysteries, but he made a note to himself that he'd keep an eye out for that little framed Jitterbug. There was just something off about the whole thing. And now his father's favorite lure was gone.

Like the Chief always said, TV mysteries get solved in an hour. Real ones simmer like soup on a back burner. Just a matter of patience, he said. Like a good fisherman, you just have to wait for the bobber to start wiggling. Maybe the Chief was right, but Farnsy still felt like something was off. Back burner didn't mean twiddle your thumbs. After all, it wasn't just a few rolls of candy. More like five. He'd forgotten to mention what the Professor had told him about the Neccos that cleaning crew had found over on Pemaquid Lake. And then there was his father's missing lure. It had hung on the wall over that workbench in the shed for years and now it was gone. And what, if anything, did that roll of Necco wafers have to do with his father's lure? Nothing made any sense.

Farnsy found himself staring out at the lake, just thinking. It was something his mother used to tease him about, that off-somewhere else stare of his. Farnsy usually told her he had a lot on his mind and sometimes that was true and other times it was the opposite. He remembered the time he and his father had rowed across the cove to that rented cottage with the wind chimes that woke up his father, whether it was his afternoon nap, at night, or early morning. Didn't matter. His father'd said the damned things were driving him batty. So he told Farnsy one night when there

FARNSY

wasn't a moon, they'd row over there after the cottage lights across the lake were out and cut the blasted thing down, stuff it in a pillow sack to keep it from clanging, and row back home, careful not to splash the oars.

The plan worked with military precision until they were halfway back, middle of the cove, and a spotlight lit them up. It was the renter, and he was shouting that he saw them and was going to call the cops. Farnsy's father shouted something about how that wind chime was an environmental danger to the loons, disrupting their nests, and he was going to report the man to the game warden.

The next morning, Farnsy's mom had made him and his father row back over there to return the wind chimes and apologize. Farnsy thought that might've been when he started thinking about how laws protect people from each other and keep things running smoothly. Turns out the renter hadn't called the cops. Said he liked a nap as much as the next man, so he agreed to take the chimes down if Farnsy's dad would tell him where the fish were biting. They shook on it and waved to each other every summer after that until the renter stopped coming.

The Cleaning Crew

The Fourth of July was approaching fast, but Farnsy had time near the end of his shift to make a few calls. No one at either of the real estate companies doing summer rentals in the area had heard about any break-ins. At least not yet, and if they had, they weren't talking. Bad for business, Farnsy figured. He didn't mention the rolls of Neccos those cottage owners had found when they opened up that season because he didn't want word to spread any faster than it already had. Plus, it wasn't a good idea to reveal a key piece of evidence, especially if it was something that linked all the break-ins they'd heard about so far. If word got out too soon, it might spook the burglar or burglars, if that's what they were. Both summer rental agents swore they'd let Farnsy know if they heard anything.

He may not have had a breakthrough yet, if this even was a case, but at least Farnsy'd thrown out a good net. If they were break-ins. But there was no doubt about it; something odd was going on. After all, who breaks into a place just to leave some Necco wafers? And then, there was his father's missing lure. Nothing else in his place seemed to be missing, besides, who would take old stuff like that? The only value of that lure was sentimental, and people don't steal stuff for sentiments. Especially not other people's sentiments.

No one breaks into a cottage and just leaves candy. Not in at least half a dozen summer cottages. Doesn't make any sense. Like his father used to say, you got five senses, everyone does, even the summer people. But not all of them have common sense. Besides, every one of those cottages was a small family camp. Nothing much of value inside. No silver cutlery, no jewelry, and no fancy paintings. Maybe it was just someone with a sweet tooth who likes classic candy. Or maybe whoever got into those cottages just lifted small stuff that no one would notice was missing. Maybe they took some little doodad, like a souvenir to remember their break-in. But why break in at all?

Farnsy leaned back in his chair and closed his eyes. What had he missed? Who could it be? Why? Who'd break into a bunch of old camps? It wasn't like these were McMansions on the sea. Just cottages. Three-season places mostly. There had to be some link. So what was it? If rental folks hadn't heard about any thefts from their rental properties, that didn't mean there weren't more. Maybe the owners would eventually spot something missing when they returned after the renters left. Or maybe never, if their place was a chock-a-block full of a lifetime of stuff like most old cottages.

Farnsy tried to picture what might be of value to someone that you might not miss right away. An old watch forgotten in the back of a drawer? A monogrammed silver cigarette lighter? Fancy golf clubs? Any boats of value would be either out of the water and stored under a cottage or towed back to Massachusetts or wherever. He couldn't think of anything that might be in each of those cottages that would make it worthwhile for someone to break in and steal stuff. So maybe it's too early in the season yet. After all, some of those places had just opened up. Could it be that more things were actually missing—their absence just waiting to be discovered?

Farnsy knew from previous burglaries and talking with a couple of insurance agents in town that it usually isn't until folks need something and start looking for it that they find it is missing. And that could be months or even a year later. And then they'd just assume they'd misplaced it. Something told Farnsy that when the

SUMMER — *The Cleaning Crew*

owners of other camps started dropping by to check their properties in between renters, someone would be looking for something, figure it was just somewhere in the cottage, lost to memory, and never report it. Like Chief said, you can't eat just one cookie. You always go back for more, until someone catches you with your hand in the cookie jar. Plus, amateur burglars, which Farnsy thought this had to be, make a mess of things. Pros, Farnsy had learned, knew just what they were looking for and left everything else just as it was. Quick in and out. Leave no trace. Maybe they left the Necco rolls behind when they got spooked? But spooked every time? Didn't make sense. Maybe they get a kick out of confusing folks, Farnsy guessed, trying to think like a burglar who loved candy. Maybe the Necco rolls were just a joke? But Farnsy could hear the Chief: "We're on River Time," he'd say. "Slow and easy, same way you smoke jerky..."

That may be, Farnsy thought, but he couldn't quite let it go. By then, he'd driven all the way back to his cottage, lost in his thoughts, and couldn't remember how he got there.

Farnsy always tried to put himself in the role of the victim, and that was tough sometimes. On the other hand, for some reason he could never figure out, because it seemed like a strange thing for a policeman to do, Farnsy felt comfortable trying to get into the criminal mind. It wasn't just that he'd found half a roll of Necco wafers in his own place on the lake. That bothered him, but it just made him feel some sort of kindred link to the other victims of the "Necco Caper," as the Chief was calling the case. Farnsy's mind was spinning like a fishing reel feeding out line to a hooked bass.

What was it about those Necco wafers? "The Original Candy Wafer," it says on the paper wrapper. Made since 1847. Named after the New England Confectionary Company near Boston that once produced them. Maybe the Necco man was a proud Bostonian? But then Farnsy couldn't imagine anyone who liked

Neccos breaking into summer cottages. The wafers are like communion wafers. The same size as a U.S. quarter dollar and a little thicker. Eight flavors of subtle sweetness: clove, orange, wintergreen, cinnamon, lemon, lime, licorice, and chocolate. Thin, round, and perfect. Around 40 in one roll. Farnsy used to squabble with his sister, Grace, over who got the chocolate wafers. And though he tried every time to let each wafer melt in his mouth, he couldn't resist crunching them in his teeth. One after the other. Whether he was reading Superman comics as a kid, or watching traffic from the roadside in uniform, Farnsy couldn't remember ever leaving a half-eaten roll of Necco wafers.

Mid-reverie, sitting on his sofa with a can of PBR on the table next to him, Farnsy spotted a dust bunny under the easy chair across from him, which reminded him he'd meant to call that other cleaning service that had been working the midcoast for a few years. See if they'd heard anything about rolls of Neccos.

Farnsy found the company's card under a magnet on the fridge and called Daphne, the owner, over at Midcoast Dusters, who said business was picking up and she was sorry but she couldn't spare the time just then. She was checking in girls from the afternoon shift who'd just come back from opening up a big place down near Southport. But Daphne said it sounded serious, which Farnsy confirmed, so she agreed to meet him for lunch at Larson's Lunchbox the next day, when she had a little break.

The line at Larson's was long, even though tourist season hadn't really gotten into full gear, but it was worth it for the haddock chowder. By the time Daphne backed into the last parking spot, Farnsy had already picked up two bowls of chowder and found a picnic table with some shade. He recognized her from the Yellowfront, where she'd worked the meat counter before starting her cleaning business, and waved her over.

SUMMER ~ *The Cleaning Crew*

"Thanks for agreeing to meet me, Daphne. I know you're busy. Hope you like chowder."

"Thanks, Officer," she said, looking around at the tables and the crowd of folks from away.

"Farnsy, please," he said. "We've known each other how long?"

"Okay, Farnsy, thanks, but let me pay for my soup." She handed him a 10 and he gave her a five back.

"So what was it you wanted to know? Something about Necco wafers?"

She opened up the packet of oyster crackers, sprinkled them on top of the chowder, then added a shake of black pepper. Farnsy offered her a pat of butter, which he always liked to see melting in his chowder, but she shook him off.

"Thanks, but I've gotta cut back on butter."

"You, too, huh?" Farnsy chuckled.

They started on the chowder while it was still hot. The lumps of fish in the white broth were tender and fresh. Diced Maine potatoes and a sliver or two of onion. Homemade. From scratch. Like the donuts at Waltz's. Farnsy tried to remember what else he liked that was homemade—the meatloaf at Moody's up in Waldoboro, the eggplant parm at the A-1 Diner in Gardiner, and the chicken pot pie at Becky's Diner in Portland—when Daphne asked how she could help him.

"Well," Farnsy started, "a while ago, over at Waltz's counter, I heard about a cleaning gal who said one of her friends was cleaning a place, opening it up for the season. They had some early renters, you know, and she finds some Necco wafers. Right out in the middle of the kitchen table. Said she remembers she'd cleaned the place real good last fall, a special 'deep clean' she said, which cost more, and never saw a roll of Neccos. But there it was when she opened up nine months later, this spring. Empty. Which is weird, you know?"

Daphne stopped eating. "You're kidding, right?"

Farnsy shook his head.

"Well, now, this is really weird. One of my girls told me a week or so ago about a roll of Neccos she found, like you said, just sitting out there. Only it was on their fancy granite countertop, all alone. She said it really spooked her. And this gal's a pro, real clean freak," Daphne said. "I mean, she's the one who tells the young gals just starting out how to clean, how to wash windows so they sparkle, and how to make a place smell fresh."

Farnsy looked up now and then from his notes to nod. A good interrogator lets the talker talk.

"Anyway, this is where it gets really weird. She was telling me about that roll of Necco wafers when, just then, another gal comes in to drop off her cleaning gear and she hears us talking and says, hey, she found one, too. Jeez. I mean, who does this?"

Farnsy put down his pen to take another spoonful of the chowder. The pepper he'd sprinkled on it from that little paper packet gave it a nice kick. He didn't miss the butter.

"Those the only Neccos your team found?"

"So far. Might be more. We haven't finished setting up all the cottages. Have to wait for the tradesmen to turn on the power at some places and get the water running again before we can clean, you know."

"Call me if you hear any more reports, will you?"

"Sure will."

"I mean, anything, not just Necco wafers or wrappers. Call me if there's anything missing, okay? Anything odd or unusual."

"Well, you know, one thing comes to mind, Farnsy. Just thought of it."

"What's that, Daphne?"

"Must be some kind of candy gourmet, if you ask me."

Farnsy made another note, then looked up. "You happen to remember the location of these cottages?"

"Course I do! Both of them were on Biscay Pond. Damariscotta side. Good tippers, too."

"Any chance your gals kept one of those rolls? You know, I'm thinking maybe we could dust them and get some prints. Something we can go on to link these rolls. Maybe there's a batch number or expiration date on them, something like that."

"Sorry, Officer, like I said, our gals clean up wicked good. Those rolls and wrappers just went straight into the trash and are long gone. But I wouldn't blame 'em if they'd eaten the candy, you know?"

"They say anything else? Like maybe they saw something else? Like, you know, a cigarette in an ashtray?"

"Yes—no. Well, there was a big clam shell on the kitchen counter she thought someone might've used for an ashtray, but it was clean. Like someone washed it. Which makes it all the stranger, you know? I mean who does that? But the other roll was unopened."

"Daphne, that's exactly what I'm trying to find out. Thanks for your help today."

"You're welcome, Officer, Farnsy, no problem. Any time. Say, you don't mind me asking, how's Lucy? I hear she's back in town."

"You heard right, Daphne. Just the summer, though."

There were times when Damariscotta felt even smaller than it was. He stacked up their empty soup bowls and napkins and tossed them in the bin.

Lucy's back, all right, he thought, but she might as well be miles away. And here he was, puzzling his way through a fog, with just some candy rolls and a missing fishing lure to go on.

Fireworks

The Fourth broke hot. Not a breeze stirring. Farnsy had the morning off, then parade duty in town, which was mostly riding a bike alongside the marchers, keeping folks on the sidewalks. He poured a cup of coffee, black, into his favorite mug, the one his grandfather had liked. With the mug in one hand and a couple of local maps in the other, Farnsy went out to the picnic table by the side of the lake. He had a hunch and thought if he took a look at the maps of the lakes, he might find some pattern to the Necco sightings.

Farnsy spread out the maps and put a big red N everywhere there'd been a sighting of a roll of Neccos and added a T where that fella reported some missing tackle and another T next to his own cottage. Were there any other things missing that had just gone unnoticed? Was the prowler, if this was a prowler, just snooping around and hanging out, or were these breaking-and-entering burglaries? It reminded Farnsy of that hermit in the woods out near some lake in central Maine who'd been living off nearby camps for years. Same thing—folks thought stuff was missing but couldn't figure out what. Maybe this was a hermit, but then, a hermit couldn't hit cottages on three different lakes and go unnoticed.

After an hour or so, Farnsy rolled up the maps. Time to get into town. The day was promising to be a scorcher, but Farnsy knew there'd be a breeze when they started the fireworks that evening. And the good news was, Chief had things covered after the parade finished up, which meant Farnsy had the rest of the day off and

SUMMER — *Fireworks*

could go into town to see the fireworks. Anything to get his mind off the Necco mystery.

The parade was splendid. Balloons and flags fluttered everywhere, and a string of marching bands wended its way over the bridge and through town, led by the Chief in his cruiser, burping the siren every now and then, smiling and waving. A few peaceful protesters stood on the bridge, holding signs. Something about lobsters having feelings, too.

Farnsy pedaled down Main Street, taking it easy. The sidewalks on both sides were chock-a-block full, especially around the hot dog stand and the burger grill. Seemed like most everyone was smiling, except for a boy whose ice cream cone had just fallen onto the sidewalk outside Wicked Scoops. Farnsy hopped off his bike and shepherded the boy and his surprised parents back into the ice cream shop, apologizing to the folks standing in line, telling them he had a little ice cream emergency. He asked the college kid scooping ice cream if she had any "ice cream insurance" that might cover a dropped cone. She hesitated a moment, then got what Farnsy meant and asked the boy what flavor. Last thing Farnsy saw before he hopped back up on his bike was that little boy with a chocolate mustache licking around the new cone, two scoops high, trying to keep up with the drips.

Of course, some of the locals, seeing Farnsy on a bike for the first time, and him in shorts and out of his cruiser, well, they had to get their two-cents' worth in:

"Nice legs, Farnsy!"

"'Hey, Farns, slow down, you know there's a speed limit."

"Chief gonna upgrade you to a motorcycle next year, Farnsy?"

Farnsy laughed. Had to admit it was kind of odd to be out there in the open like that, looking like some overgrown teenager in a Boy Scout uniform, but the Chief had a point. It got him in closer touch with folks. And if he had to stop in traffic on the bike, there was no need to roll down a window—he just pulled up alongside a car and chatted folks up if they had their window down. Gave some folks directions. Answered some of their usual questions.

"Which way to East Vassalboro?"

"Can't get there from here," Farnsy said, playing right along with the joke.

A driver with Tennessee plates, who was stopped in the traffic behind the parade, rolled his window down, waved Farnsy over, and asked him to say something "in Mainer," like it was another language. Farnsy thought a moment, then said, working up his best imitation of a Maine accent, "Well, sir, I could, but then you wouldn't understand one iota. See those folks in that caahh behind you they-ah? Well, they're from Auguster, our state capital, which isn't wicked faah from he-ah, but they can't understand a word of what I'm saying if I talk in my Damariscotta dialect. Ayuh, fact is, some husbands and wives here can't understand each other at all, don't cha know."

The man from down South, whose wife was sitting in the passenger seat, chuckled. "Got that same problem all y'all got, back home in Knoxville, Officer." It was that happy sort of day. Farnsy radioed in now and then, and it was the same everywhere in town all day long, no big problems, only little ones, nothing the team couldn't handle.

After his first round through town, Farnsy got a hot dog from Sully's stand over in Newcastle. The next round, he stopped for a fish taco from Mike over at the new red Mexican food truck across the street, figuring he could work the calories off with a few more rounds through town. Then he'd get half a Reuben at Fernald's or a grinder at Metcalf's.

The kayak rental place was hopping. Schooner Landing was jammed. And a long line of folks jabbered away, waiting to board the *Teciani*, for a cruise around the river to see the oyster farms. The whole town was buzzing. Then, late afternoon, around the time his bicycle shift was over, the town quieted down as if in anticipation of the fireworks.

Farnsy drove back out to his cottage for a few hours to catch the second game of the Red Sox double-header on the radio and take a nap. For supper, he opened a can of Maine sardines, drained out the oil, and squeezed a slice of lemon over the headless fish lined up tight in the can.

As he harpooned the last sardine with his fork, Farnsy smiled. What was it his mother had said? Something about there being a lot of fish in the sea? He remembered when he and Lucy were high school sweethearts, long before she met Earl, and they sat on a blanket on the Newcastle side to watch the fireworks across the harbor. He remembered watching those fireworks go off, cuddled so close he could feel her breathing, then the big climax when she grabbed his arm real tight. But then it wasn't long before she called it off, said they were getting too serious, and went out and had a fling with a summer fellow. Farnsy left for college, then she started a cosmetology course a year later. They got together a couple of times one summer for picnics on Pemaquid Beach and moonrise at the lighthouse. She was a nanny one season for a family out on Vinalhaven, so he didn't see her much that year. Then he fell in love with a girl at Colby, but she broke it off just before they graduated and married their classmate from Portland. It was all a tangle. And he knew Lucy wasn't the only one fussing with the on-off switch. After she finished her course, he'd started at the police academy. Maybe he saw her a couple of times around town. Like Lucy told him out at the lake after her divorce, she just gave up on him and figured it wasn't meant to be, so she'd married Earl.

Well, Farnsy thought, maybe Doc was right, even though he'd been a dentist, not a marriage counselor. Maybe the best way to start over, now that Lucy was off again, was to get out of the cottage, out of uniform.

"The universe works in strange ways," Doc told Farnsy. And Farnsy was starting to think maybe Doc was right. So around seven that evening, Farnsy slapped on a couple dollops of Skedaddle mosquito spray, which smelled almost as good as his Old Spice, put on his Red Sox cap, grabbed a sweatshirt and a folding chair, and drove into town, a civilian.

Most days now after work, all Farnsy wanted was a nice quiet evening. But tonight Farnsy was looking forward to the fireworks, because he'd read in the *Lincoln County News* that the selectmen, in a close vote, had approved a big increase in the fireworks budget at the annual town meeting that spring. According to Julie, whose sister worked in the town hall, the show was going to feature a whopper of a finale that year.

Farnsy pulled his pickup into a spot on the hillside near the Lincoln Home and waded into the gathering crowd on the small, sloped field overlooking Damariscotta Harbor.

The music from Schooner Landing wafted across the harbor, and he could smell popcorn and grilling hot dogs and spent sparklers and the smoke from firecrackers that popped here and there. Dusk was falling, and if you looked downriver, you could see fireworks popping up over the trees now and then across the river. Like summer heat lightning, they lit up the thin clouds that were drifting high above.

Farnsy unfolded his beach chair and sat down near a nice older couple from the Lincoln Home and, as he chatted them up, he spotted the *Teciani* gliding back into the harbor. Trailing behind, a string of small boats motored in, their red and white running lights glowing in the dimming evening light, then moored up and waited for the fireworks. It was like watching a movie theater fill up with people, all of them chatting and gabbing before the feature.

SUMMER — *Fireworks*

Clusters of families settled into the empty spots sprinkled on the hillside all around him. Little kids ran around waving glow sticks as if they were cowboy lassos, and older kids lit sparklers that sent off sparks like a spray of lightning bugs. The older couple next to him tugged a blanket over their laps and held hands like it could be their last fireworks together. Farnsy wondered if, years back, they'd ever been on-again, off-again like he was with Lucy, then he glanced around, knowing she was back in town, and wondered if she were there with someone else.

A kid close by set off a string of lady finger firecrackers that crackled and popped, startling a baby in a stroller, who started crying. Farnsy watched a woman nearby get up and walk over to talk to the kid. No yelling, but it looked like he gave her his matchbook. Nice, he thought; it takes a neighborhood. But knowing that he knew the difference between the sound of a firecracker and the report of a gun firing made him feel older.

A few dogs ran around off-leash, yapping and stopping to sniff each other. The people from away were in full mosquito defense: slapping on repellant, spraying each other, and tugging long-sleeved sweatshirts over their heads. Folks wearing hoodies pulled them tight around their faces to keep all but the most resolute mosquitos away.

Locals stood around, chatting up neighbors. Mainers wore festive short sleeves, even shorts, as though they hadn't a care in the world about bugs or bites. Just waved them off. Most of the little ones were in pajamas so they could go straight to bed after the fireworks.

As the sky darkened, Farnsy made out two guys across the harbor holding up safety flares, getting ready to light the rockets and start the show. There was a smattering of applause and a couple of woo-hoos as folks on both sides of the harbor watched them stroll over to the float where the fireworks were set up.

FARNSY

Then the two guys started setting off the fireworks, working their way through the assembled canisters like choreographed dancers. Volleys of rockets arced up overhead, burst in ever-expanding colors, mirrored in the water, sputtered out, and drifted safely down into the river.

They settled into a steady pace, and the crowd was entranced by the rhythm of the pounding explosions of the larger fireworks, colors bursting within bursts into crackling shapes like electric flowers that melted into waterfalls of silver glitter. One after another and then another, clusters of rockets shot into the night sky, burst once, then once more.

After a short pause, Farnsy heard the pops of a few small rockets followed by a fountain of spewing colors and a trailing pop-pop-POP-BOOM! as if to say, "Here we go!" Surely this was the buildup to the grand finale. The men on the float, enveloped in clouds of spent rocket smoke, commenced launching a thunderous cataclysm, an end-of-the-world fireworks fury like the last artillery battle of a world war. Then, as silence settled in around the harbor, the two men threw their flares, in twin arcs, up and into the river.

The crowds huddled around the harbor, stunned by this silence, watched as the night breeze carried off the lingering smoke to reveal the two guys on the float, taking bows. The harbor erupted with waves of enthusiastic applause. Cheers and gleeful whistles, fueled by sheer delight and appreciation, echoed around the harbor. People on boats tooted air horns. Locals who'd watched from their cars, refugees from relentless mosquito swarms, honked and flickered their headlights in appreciation.

Folks started to pick up their things, fold up lawn chairs, roll up blankets, pack up picnic baskets and coolers, count their kids to see if everyone was there, and trudge back to their parked cars, the smell of the fireworks lingering in the cool night air.

SUMMER — *Fireworks*

Farnsy slid into his pickup and sat there a moment to watch folks struggle up the hill, kids in tow, their neon necklaces still glowing, then pack up and drive off to their homes. Just as he was thinking how good it felt to have some time off, his phone buzzed. It was the Chief.

"Farnsworth, you at home?" Chief asked.

"In town. Just watched the fireworks. You see 'em?"

"Sure, from the cruiser in town. Some of us got to work. Good show, though. You there with Lucy?"

"Just me, Chief. Watched the fireworks from over at the Lincoln Home."

"You know it's too early to retire, Farnsy, right?"

"What's up, Chief? Why you calling me this time of night?"

"Farnsy, this Necco thing—I can't shake it. Got an interesting phone call this afternoon. So, look, I think you may be on to something."

"Same here, Chief. I got out a couple of maps this morning. Thought maybe I could find a pattern or something. But what's this about a phone call?"

"Let's meet tomorrow morning, okay? I'll fill you in. But bring those maps."

"Okay, Chief. You want me to bring a donut? Waltz's? They're homemade."

Chief paused the pause every dieter takes, then sighed. "Sure, why not? Plain cruller'd be my first choice. Or maybe jelly. Yes, jelly. But bring your maps."

Maps

Chief poured himself a coffee and tugged a jelly donut out of the bag of donuts Farnsy had brought in. "So I get this call in the station yesterday, out of the blue. This woman says she's up on Damariscotta Lake, not far from your place, I think. She tells me she heard about the Necco break-ins from her cleaning lady. Sounded reliable. Anyway, Dottie got her number. So the woman says she thought she ought to call us. Says they have a neighborhood watch back in Boston. See something, say something. So she says she remembers chatting up a jet skier—this was last summer, you know? Little too friendly, she says, but she didn't make much of it at the time. Not until she heard about the Necco rolls. Seems she was sitting out on her dock last summer getting some sun. Remember, this is out on your lake, there, Damariscotta. So anyway, she says this gal skis ups and starts asking all kinds of questions. Claims she's thinking of renting next summer, which would be this summer. Tells her she's looking for a quiet place. She said it seemed funny to her afterward—her being on a jet ski and all and wanting a quiet place. Now here's where I think it gets interesting. She says the gal asked her if she knew any old fishermen on the lake, and did she know where they lived? I mean, who asks a question like that?"

"She give you a description of the woman, Chief?"

"No, just said she thought something was a little off, you know. But you want to follow up, we've got her number."

"Okay. That makes one tackle box someone might've messed with, right? Plus my father's Jitterbug that's missing."

SUMMER ~ *Maps*

"Right. One tackle box, okay—and don't forget, Farnsy, that first guy's box with the old lure might just be lost somewhere. Misplaced. Under a bed for all we know. But then there's that Jitterbug of yours. Have to admit, it's a little curious." Chief was chewing a stick of leftover venison jerky he'd made for the Fourth. "Spicy Fireworks," he'd named it.

"Show me what you got, Farnsworth," Chief said.

Like a general tracking Allied troop movements, Farnsy rolled out his map of Damariscotta Lake next to the maps of Biscay Pond and Pemaquid Pond already spread out on the Formica table in the staff room, taking care to leave room for the bag of donuts from Waltz's. Chief's venison jerky held down the corners of each map.

The Chief studied the maps and listened intently as Farnsy briefed him. He told the Chief he'd spoken with folks in the only two summer rental agencies in town to see if they'd heard anything about rolls of Neccos or gotten any complaints about things missing. Between the two agencies, he figured he'd covered most of the rentals. It was a scattershot approach, a wide net, and Farnsy thought for sure he'd stumble on some connection, even some hint of a possible link between the Necco wafers and fishing tackle, but he couldn't find one, at least not yet.

"Has to be some link, Chief," Farnsy said, shaking his head. "Gotta be."

Farnsy explained that he'd learned that most of the listed cottages were seasonal rentals because the owners tended to be older folks who visited less frequently than they had when their families were younger. They might come out for a week around the big summer holidays, but otherwise they rented their places out by the week. If they were lucky, a renter might take a place for a month. But one- or two-week rentals were pretty standard. Which meant sporadic witnesses on the lake. Which meant no witnesses.

And none of the rental agents could say for sure which cottages on the lakes were occupied year-round and not rented out. Now and then, one of them might pop up on a broker's multiple listing service, but they'd usually sell fast, an agent told him. Then the new owners would rent the place out to cover taxes.

"Plus," Farnsy added, "it means some of those cottages might be empty for as long as a week or two, early June or after Labor Day, when rentals thin out."

That meant only a handful of possible local witnesses who lived at the lake all seasons and might've seen any suspicious behavior. Otherwise, there were only renters from away on the lake and they were just too busy vacationing to pay attention. To Farnsy, most renters from away were either arriving or leaving. In between, summer folks just buzzed around, ticking things off their summer bucket lists, like they were on a scavenger hunt. It would take some digging to find anyone who might've seen something a little off and develop new leads. Maybe find a pattern or a connection. Farnsy was starting to feel like he was lost in the weeds. Too many loose ends leading nowhere.

He stared at the maps. He took a sip of his coffee. Lukewarm, getting cold. Like these leads. A cicada buzzed outside the open window. It was only mid-morning, but it was already hot. Not a breath of a breeze. Like everything had stopped moving. Then Farnsy pushed his chair back, stood up, and stared at the maps from above, bird's eye view, hoping he'd see something he'd missed. Judging by the Ns, it looked like the Necco man might have hit some places on the Damariscotta side of Biscay Pond first, then Pemaquid Pond second, and then moved up to Damariscotta Lake, because those reports were the freshest. Biscay and Pemaquid were linked by a small passage. Might get a jet ski through there, a canoe, or a kayak, but not a boat, not even a small outboard.

SUMMER — *Maps*

For now, there was no way Farnsy could pin down the exact date someone had left a roll of Neccos in those cottages, but it was getting clear there was a plan linking these bits and pieces and, if he was right, that meant they were up against pros. Amateurs, he'd learned, have short attention spans. Smash and grab. But the pros? You'd hardly know anyone'd been there, which gave them time. And time cools off any trail of clues. And then memory fades. Most folks had so much stuff, even if they knew their place'd been hit, they couldn't tell you if anything was missing.

As the Chief pointed out, they couldn't even say the Necco burglar was a burglar, "Except for maybe your dad's missing Jitterbug, Farnsy, which might not even be connected. And, fact is, your dad's lure might've gotten clipped last year or the year before. When's the last time you went into the shed, anyway?" He waited but got no response. "Thought so. So this is a prowler, at best."

"Well, wait just a second, that's not completely true," Farnsy said. "Don't you remember? One of the cottage owners over on Pemaquid Pond, I think he was from New Jersey, called the station last year after he opened up his place to report that he couldn't find his fishing gear. Didn't he say something about a missing tackle box?"

"That's right," Chief said. "Guy said he'd looked everywhere for it. I remember now. Said he always took one last cast when he closed up for the season in late September, and he clearly remembered putting the tackle box back on a shelf where he kept all his fishing gear. Whoever took the box didn't touch the old fly rods or reels, even though they were a lot more valuable than the tackle box, the guy said. Way more. Made no sense, which was why the owner said he waited a couple days to call it in. His wife had no idea where it was. Said she wouldn't touch his fishing gear.

"Well," Chief said, "like I was saying, one missing tackle box, you might get curious. But two? Well, I think you've got yourself a mystery."

Farnsy shook his head and looked over at the Chief. "Well, sir, with all due respect, we've been staring at these maps for almost an hour now, trying to get in the mind of the perps, assuming there's more than one, which I'm inclined to believe, and I'm coming up with a whole lot of nothing. Tell you the truth, I don't even think we can assume it's a Necco man. Could just as well be a Necco woman."

"Could be, but I mean, seriously, Farnsy, can you name one woman who's nuts about old fishing lures and loves Neccos?"

Farnsy smiled. He was thinking maybe Lucy.

"Okay, forget it, Farnsworth. Have to admit, you've got the mind of a detective, always looking at all the angles. You remember to mark your place on the map?"

Farnsy pointed to the spot where his cottage sat. "Right here." Then he added a new T for the second tackle box on his map. Then a J for the jet ski report. The Ns were sprinkled along the west side of Biscay Pond and Pemaquid Pond, a few at the southern end of Damariscotta Lake, not far up from the eagles' nest at the very south end. And, of course, the three Ns that were across the lake from Farnsy's cottage. And only the one J for where someone had seen a jet ski on Damariscotta. Farnsy wondered if jet skis were even allowed on Biscay Pond or Pemaquid Pond. Have to look into that. It looked to Farnsy like this case, and it was starting to look like a real case, was going to be a slow burner. The west sides of the two ponds, Pemaquid and Biscay, were part of Damariscotta, so they were relevant to the case. Damariscotta Lake wasn't on his beat, but it was his home. And it was his father's lure. The case was personal.

Dottie waived Farnsy over to the dispatch desk and said in a half-whisper, "Got that new game warden on hold, Region B, says he needs to talk with you, Farnsy. Right away. Something about loons." Her grin gave Farnsy hope it wasn't something serious.

SUMMER ~ *Maps*

"Yup, what's up out there in the woods? Bob is it? This is Officer Farnsworth."

"Bob, Bob Petit here, that you, Farnsy? I think we crossed paths a few years ago, back there up in Stockton Springs. You know, when we collared those Unitarian nudists at a wedding out on Sandy Point?"

"Jeez, Bob, how could I forget? Still my biggest bust. So to speak. Must've been a couple dozen of them, all decked out in their birthday suits. But what brings you to call this fine summer day? Something about loons, I hear?"

Farnsy winked at Dottie. "We talking about those folks down in Washington, are we? Or maybe some summer folks."

"Farnsy, this is serious. You know that loon nest up at the north end of Damariscotta Lake?"

"I do."

"Well, I was trolling, not far from there, you know, undercover, had the wife with me as decoy, two lines in the water, no hooks, like we were hoping for a bite. I'd just ticketed some nitwit who drove up from Baltimore, you know, fishing off a wharf on the cove across from that kids' camp. I pull up to where he's standing, and I ask him if they're biting, and he says he hopes so. That's when I flip up my cap, show him my ID, and ask to see his license. Should've seen the look on his face when he sees the fine. Anyway, like I told your gal there, I'm calling about the loons' nest."

Farnsy waited.

"So, we're out there, about mid-morning, I'd say, this was the day before the Fourth, so right after I write that ticket, the wife and I head out of the cove, south, when this nut case of a jet skier comes racing up the lake, does a couple of figure-8s, rooster tails around us, then between us and the loon nest in the cove, spraying us real good. Thing is, those loons' eggs were about to hatch. So the male and female take off. You know, it takes them a good while to get off the water. And they flew so low, right over us, I could've heard them breathing if it weren't for that knucklehead on the jet ski."

"You arrest him? Isn't there a No Wake sign floating out there near that nest?" Farnsy asked.

"I'm getting to that. Anyway, wouldn't you know? As luck would have it, for me, the guy's jet ski sputters out a couple hundred yards down the lake, you know, right around the narrows there. So we pull in our lines and hop over there, and I flash my badge and wipe that shit-eating grin right off his face. I tell him about the nesting loons nearby and the No Wake sign then I get his ID."

"Masshole?"

"Nope, 'Live Free or Pie.' Claims he never saw the sign. I tell the guy there's good reason for that, him going so fast and all."

"Okay, Warden, but what's this got to do with me? Why'd you call us?"

"Sorry. Anyway, it wasn't five minutes later someone at a camp across the lake waves me over. And this's where it gets good. Where you guys come in. Because the fella renting the camp tells me how some guy'd been jet-skiing all weekend, driving him and his family nuts. Says he's sitting out there on a folding chair at the end of their dock smoking a cigar when the jet skier pulls up near his dock, only the jet skier isn't a he, she's a she, and she starts asking him all kinds of questions. At first he said it was all chatty and pleasant."

"But?"

"But then, after he told the jet skier he'd been renting there for at least 10 years, the jet ski woman starts asking questions. Does the renter know anything about summer rentals on the lake and how much they cost and where the good fishing spots are and which houses are new and which ones are the oldest? Also, does he know any old fishermen? The renter told her he had no idea, never really got to know folks on the lake that much. So then the gal guns her jet ski, thanks him, and flies off down the lake. He couldn't tell where, but he remembered thinking if she was renting, well, it was way past the narrows. So, anyway, wasn't long after that I remembered hearing something about your little Necco roll mystery and thought, well, maybe there's some connection, you know?"

"Bob, this is interesting. Any chance you could drop by here later today or maybe tomorrow? Maybe fill in a few more details? Appreciate it if you could."

"Sure thing. Happy to help, Farns. Gotta tell you, though, I think there's something odd about her. For starters, like the guy said, she didn't look like she did much fishing. Said she looked more like a gal who got her fish by the pound over at Hannaford."

Farnsy wanted the Chief on hand when Bob dropped by the next day, and by the time they'd studied the maps and the markings, drained their coffee mugs, and the warden had tried to eat one of the Chief's new jerky sticks, they'd agreed that this gal sounded like the same person who was jet-skiing over on Pemaquid Pond and asking the same sort of questions. Odd, but not illegal. And they agreed to keep their eyes peeled, their ears to the ground, and, like the Chief said, their asses in the saddle. Farnsy thought the Chief must've heard someone say that in a Western because he knew the Chief would never climb up on a horse unless it was with his grandkids and the horses were going up and down and around in a circle.

Farnsy could sense the circle tightening now: first the Necco rolls, then the missing tackle boxes, then this jet skier. Had to be some connection. And if he had to guess, maybe more than one person was involved. Maybe they cased the places on a jet ski, checking out which places to hit, something to do with fishing and therefore maybe the tackle boxes, then probably hit all those places off-season when there's not a soul around.

FARNSY

"Makes sense," Chief said. "You know, I think you're on to something, Farnsworth. Hardly anyone out there on the lakes in winter, so less chance of witnesses. Maybe a couple of ice fishermen, but they'd be watching their lines. Most all those cottages are empty. Only problem is footprints in snow. Or driving in, when most of those gravel lake roads are rutted and iced up even if someone plowed."

Farnsy bit a good chunk off one of the Chief's jerky sticks.

"You need any help with this, Farnsy?" Chief asked him.

"Thanks, Chief, I think I'm good. For now. I'll get in touch with that informant who called you about the jet skier last summer. Meanwhile, I've got to talk with some of my neighbors, the ones who fish, because I don't know what you're thinking, Chief, but it sounds to me like they've hit all the places they're gonna hit on Biscay and Pemaquid and maybe moved on to case out Damariscotta Lake last winter. Anyway, that's what I'd do if I were in their boots. Which means they'll hit a few more camps on my lake this winter."

Farnsy wondered if the perpetrators were out there trying to think like cops, the same way he and the Chief were trying to think like the perps and anticipate their next move. These guys were smooth. Pros.

"Real police work," the Chief confided to Farnsy as they were staring at the maps and the places marked, "real police work isn't just cops in uniform, showing the blue, Farnsy. Public safety depends on a little vitamin C, you know—connections, all those little connections we have in the community."

"We're good, Chief. But we still haven't figured out why they might be after tackle boxes."

"You got any ideas?"

"Actually, that's a yes, Chief. I've done some thinking and we can eliminate the tackle boxes themselves. Most are just plastic. The old ones are metal, but those are pretty rusty, especially if they've been used. So no value there. I think it's got to be something inside the tackle boxes. And that means we can rule out spools of fishing line. And fish knives, even the old ones. And the lead weights and bobbers and bare hooks and spinners. And that leaves only one thing: the lures inside the tackle boxes. Someone's after lures. Which means my father's lure is part of the whole caper. And based on the reports we've got, especially the questions that jet skier asked about where the old fishermen lived, well, I'd guess it's the old lures that have some kind of value, because that's got to be what they're after."

Farnsy thought for a moment about his father's old Jitterbug. Wouldn't be the first time someone from away took home old stuff from Maine and thought it was a treasure.

"Okay, Sherlock, so where you gonna go to find out the dollar value of rusty old gummed-up fishing lures?"

"Got just the place in mind, Chief."

"Wait, you don't mean checking in with that cute new librarian over in Skidompha, what's her name? Eva, something?"

"Nope, Charlotte. Real cute. But real married, sir."

A couple of days later, Charlotte called the station. Dottie took the call, smiled, and said she'd transfer the call to Officer Farnsworth, who was having lunch alone in the canteen. Farnsy put down his slice of pizza from the Hilltop Stop. It was already lukewarm, so he told himself he'd just take the call then zap the pizza in the microwave afterward. Charlotte said she'd found five books about antique fishing lures. The library had one of them. The others she'd gotten through interlibrary loan. They were waiting for him there in the main office behind the checkout counter in the Skidompha Library. Farnsy told her he'd be over there soon as he could.

FARNSY

Charlotte spread-eagled the book she thought would be most helpful for Farnsy on the desktop. "I opened this one up just to show you something crazy. See that one there?" She pointed to an old black-and-white photo of a dull gray metal lure in the shape of a minnow. It had a simple single hook coming out underneath its tailfin. Farnsy guessed maybe if a fish were blind that lure might look tasty. But not as tasty as he thought modern lures might appear, with all their colors, speckles, and streamers. Then he read the caption.

"Ca. 1850 The Minnow, Auction value $12,000."

"Holy…"

"Okay, Farnsy, but don't get your hopes up. Book says there are maybe only half a dozen of them left. But check out the other lures, early 20th century. You recognize any of them?"

"Might. I'll check these books out if you don't mind. This is really great, Lucy."

"Charlotte."

"Sorry."

"Guess I know who's on your mind, Farnsy. Anyway, bring 'em back in two weeks, okay? Wouldn't want to see your face on our Wanted List over in the Post Office, would we?"

"But here's the kicker, Chief," Farnsy said back in the station. "Want to guess how much the best antique fishing lure is worth? It's called 'The Minnow.' Looks like a fish with one hook coming out its rear, just a hunk of melted metal with a couple of bug eyes and a big fin. The fish'd have to be blind to think it was a real minnow. Anyway, take a guess."

"What? Fifty dollars? A hundred? On a crazy day maybe a couple hundred. Good condition more. Okay, you tell me Farnsy, just how much would a collector pay for one of those things?"

"Chief, we're talking thousands. 10. Maybe more, maybe a lot more. Book says there's only a handful left."

SUMMER — Maps

"Christmas, Farnsy. You serious?"

"That'd be a yes, Chief. Affirmative. Dead serious." Farnsy crossed his heart, Boy Scout style. "So look, we're talking big money. Mint condition? Original box? More."

"Well, Farns, gotta hand it to you, guess you've found the link. Now we're looking at a crime that pays. This is more than just a couple rolls of candy. Some smarts behind all this, Farnsy, no amateurs. And you know what that means, right?"

"Yes, Chief, plans like these need people, and where there's people, one or more is all it takes, so there's gonna be a screwup somewhere. And pretty soon, one of 'em's bound to make a mistake."

"You got any ideas where to dig around now, Farns?"

Farnsy poured himself a coffee from the urn. Stone cold. He walked it over to the microwave and punched in a minute on high.

"Yeah, as a matter of fact, I do, Chief. Thing is, we know what they're after, and why, and even when—it's got to be off-season—and my guess, from the reports about unusual jet ski activities on the lakes late last fall, I'm guessing these guys are scouting out cottages in season, then getting down to business off-season. No witnesses. But Chief, it sure sounds to me like these guys are pros, scouting out the locations, looking for good fishing spots, figuring that the best old lures might be in those cottages. Least if I were after old lures, that's what I'd do."

Chief nodded. "This is good police work, Farnsy. Keep your eyes peeled and your ear to the ground. It takes them time to find these lures and steal them. And it takes them more time to sell them. And that gives us time, too. Time is on our side. Which makes me think: where would they sell these things? Maybe we work backward? Gotta think like they do. Like they say, 'follow the money.'"

"Chief, could be online. eBay, Craigslist, auctions, antique shops, and antique fairs. Flea markets in the summer, maybe, but there are hundreds of places to buy and sell these things."

"You try looking at *Uncle Henry's Swap or Sell It Guide*?"

"Not yet, but I'll check it out. Good idea. But if these guys are big time, they're not swapping old lures worth a couple dollars. They're after big bucks. Folding money. You ask me, that eliminates online sales. Too public, too open. Traceable. Same thing for auction houses. And antique fairs are for browsers and a few dealers. Last I heard, these little summer shows aren't drawing folks like they used to. But antique dealers, well, they're all over the place, one on every street corner, and they're always on the lookout for stuff on sale. But that's not the big money. The big lures, the oldest ones, the ones collectors want and decide they have to have, well, my guess is they take them down to Boston or New York. Or Philadelphia. Same cities where the sports that Maine Guides take out fishing have always come from. That's where the money is. The collectors. That's where the big bucks stop."

Henry

The Chief opened his office door and waved down the hallway to Farnsy, who was headed out to his vehicle. One hand cupped over his phone, the Chief said it was a missing person. Farnsy thought something was up because the Chief had a little grin.

"This one's for you, Bud," he quipped.

Chief liked to joke. Said police work was serious enough. A little humor now and then was good for morale. Most of his jokes were room-clearing groaners. The play on "This Bud's for you!" was his new favorite.

Farnsy stepped into the Chief's office and sat down in front of his large oak desk. Hanging on the wall behind the Chief, for every visitor to see, were a career's worth of marksmanship plaques, buttons, police patches, badges, framed citations, civic awards, and the Chief's certificate from the academy in Vassalboro. Along the wall near the door hung a row of baseball caps from police forces around the world. Above the file cabinet on the wall behind Farnsy was a huge street map of Damariscotta. On the front panel of Chief's desk was the big, round, wooden seal of the Damariscotta Police Force. On top of his desk, next to a leaning stack of reports and memos, was a Rolodex too stuffed to turn and a mug of black coffee that looked forgotten. Flipped open as though the Chief had been studying it was a dog-eared book, whose title Farnsy could read upside down from where he was sitting: *The Idiot's Guide to Making Jerky*!

FARNSY

Chief hit the speakerphone button and leaned back to let Farnsy take the call.

"Officer Farnsworth. How can I help you?"

"Farnsy, that you?"

"Doc! Now who else would take a call from you? What's this I hear about a missing person?"

"Missing person? Who told you that? Farnsy, it's Henry."

"Who's Henry, Doc?"

"You know him, Farnsy. Jumped onto your lap that time you came over for cribbage last winter."

"Jeez, I'd forgotten his name. Guess it's been a while since I've been out to your place. Big fella—Maine coon cat, right? Say, you know we're on speakerphone. Glad the Chief can hear this. He just loves cats."

The Chief rolled his eyes and mimicked strangling a cat.

"Best damned cat ever, Farnsy. Sorry Chief, forgive my French. I swear, if Henry could talk, he could play cribbage. Just not like him to take off like this. Overnight, maybe, but he's been gone a week now."

Chief shook his head and dunked one end of his cruller into the mug of cold coffee. "Neighbors of ours had a cat take off once," Chief chimed in. "Kid next door other side of us set off a string of firecrackers and that darned cat scrambled up the nearest tree and wouldn't come down for love or money. They tried everything. Catnip, treats, even a can of tuna. She was glued to that branch. The cat, I mean."

"What'd you do?" Doc asked.

"Well, it got late in the day, and wouldn't you know, that cat was still up there, so then the wife, Edna was her name, I think, she calls the fire department. So they send out a truck and ladder and this fireman goes up and gets her down."

"That's great, but..."

SUMMER ~ *Henry*

"Well, it was. Until they burped the siren on the way out, as if to say goodbye, and don't you know, that cat was back up in that tree like she'd never left it."

"So what'd they do, Chief?"

"The wife—I heard this from her husband, you see—well, she calls the fire department again and tells them the cat's back up that tree. She listens a while, then her husband hears her say, 'No,' so then she hangs up the phone and starts bawling her head off."

"Why's that?"

"Well, she says the fireman asked her if she's ever seen a cat skeleton up in a tree. So she goes, 'No,' and he says, 'That's right, any cat up a tree will find a way to climb down when it gets darned good and hungry.'"

"Did it?" Doc asked.

"Yup. Right after it got dark, that cat came right back, scratching on their kitchen door."

Chief dunked his cruller again, then bit off the mushy part, as if he were punctuating the end of that story.

"Well," Doc says, "Henry's been gone a week now."

"You go outside and holler for him?" Farnsy asked.

"Did that two days runnin' and still no sign."

"Well, if you got a picture of him, Doc, we could put up some Police Wanted posters around town," Farnsy offered. "You got a good one?" he asked Doc, and the Chief started waving his arms "NO!"

"Somewhere, back in my desk drawer, I think."

"Okay," Farnsy said, "you bring me that photo and we'll have the good folks up at that office supply place make us a poster and we'll put it all around town. From Round Top to Louis Doe's and every place in between. Won't be long before someone comes up with a lead."

"Thanks, Farnsy. Let's hope so. Don't know what I'd do without that cat. Hate to think a hawk might've gotten him."

A week later, someone from the Lincoln County Animal Shelter spotted one of those wanted posters with Henry's picture on it and recognized "Sasquatch," which was the name they'd given a big cat that had been hanging around a house about a mile away from Doc's, as it turned out. Folks there brought him in because they were tired of feeding him and they knew the shelter was no-kill. A volunteer at the shelter noticed a resemblance to the picture in the poster and called Doc's number. After his shift was over that afternoon, Farnsy drove over to Edgecomb with Doc to fetch Henry.

It took the two high school girls on duty half an hour to find him. They said "Sasquatch" liked to curl up in a nice, quiet, sunny corner somewhere and take a nap.

Doc said, "Yup, that's my Henry all right."

Farnsy remembered Doc talking about that cat following him around his house just like a dog, the big old Maine coon tomcat that he was. Doc said he named him Henry David Thoreau. Henry for short. And "Thoreau" like "thorough," Doc said, "the way they pronounce it down in Concord."

Finally, one of the volunteers emerged from the back of the shelter holding up the biggest cat Farnsy'd ever laid eyes on, her hands under the cat's armpits, his long body and legs hanging down, his paws almost dragging on the linoleum, he was that big.

"Jeez," Farnsy blurted out, "big fella, isn't he? I'd forgotten."

"Well, it's been a while since you came over for cribbage," Doc said.

One of the girls said, "He sure is heavy. A real Maine coon, sir, for sure. But he's a sweetie-pie. Nicest cat we've ever had. Listen to him—he's purring!"

Farnsy could hear Henry from all the way across the room. Then the cat got loose, padded right over to Farnsy, and started sidling up to his leg, like the cat had picked him out of a police lineup.

"Well, I'll be."

Halfway back to Doc's place, Henry was stretched across Farnsy's lap and fast asleep.

Next day at Waltz's, Doc told Farnsy it was obvious to him that Henry had taken to him. Doc said something about how he'd been doing a whole lot of thinking while Henry was gone, and said he was getting on in years and probably ought to be finding Henry a good home. "Besides," he added, "I thought you could use a little companionship, Farnsy, now that Lucy's out of the picture again, at least for now."

"And you know," Doc continued, "you could always bring Henry over to visit when you come over for a cribbage lesson."

So that was how Farnsy came by that cat.

That first week with Henry, Farnsy thought about taking him along in his cruiser, and figured the cat could stretch out the whole length of the rear window. Police dogs, why not police cats? Then he thought the better of it. For starters, where'd he put a litter box? But Henry made himself right at home in Farnsy's place real fast. Found the coziest places to nap and the best windows for bird watching.

Farnsy wondered what they'd think at Waltz's if he told them Henry was keeping him company most nights, a regular little furry bed buddy, curled up near him. Farnsy hoped Henry'd have the good sense to sleep on the couch if Lucy ever did come back for a visit.

Henry was more reliable than an electric alarm. Come morning, at the crack of dawn, just as the sun started to peek between the trees across the lake, which was later and later now, Henry started his routine. A symphony of sounds: all the coins Farnsy had emptied out of his pockets and put on top of his dresser, one by one, hitting the wooden floor. If that didn't work, Henry would rattle the little brass handles on the dresser drawers, clack-clack, clack-clack. And if that didn't work, Henry would jump down and run right across Farnsy's sleeping face, front paws, back paws, two thumps on Farnsy's nose. Like Doc said, that cat was half human.

It was hard to get angry with a cat, Farnsy learned. And that was just one of the lessons Henry taught Farnsy that summer. His favorite was what Farnsy called Henry's "cat stare," the "you kidding me?" look, which Farnsy used whenever someone said something stupid. One guy trying to talk his way out of a traffic violation said Farnsy's stare reminded him of Clint Eastwood. But the truth was, that stare was all Henry's. Farnsy never let on where he'd learned that trick. But it worked like a charm, every time.

Nedda

During his Monday morning head-to-head with the Chief a week later, the Chief told Farnsy there'd been an incident out on the *Teciani*. The tour boat's owner, Chuck, said one of the passengers had had a little too much wine with their oysters, and somewhere around Glidden Ledge, the fella slipped overboard trying to photograph a seal. Chief said Chuck asked him if he knew anyone interested in earning a little overtime, just to keep an eye on folks while he was at the helm, the big Labor Day weekend coming up and all. Chief said he knew Farnsy could use a little extra income, so if he wanted it, Farnsy had his permission to work security off-duty, as long as he wasn't in uniform.

That was how Farnsy found himself sitting at the stern of the *Teciani* late one Friday afternoon watching a boat full of passengers out on the river. As they boarded the vessel, Farnsy chatted up everyone and winked at any locals, as if to say, let's keep this between you and me—none of this Officer Farnsworth stuff. Farnsy always enjoyed hearing summer folks' stories, where they were from and where they were headed, and he found most everyone onboard to be pretty nice. Just happy to be out on the water. But if one of them leaned over the side a little too far or tried to stand up on the gunnel for a selfie, he was ready. Most of them were enjoying Chuck's humorous stories about the early years of shipbuilding on the river, the old brickyards, the seals and the oyster farms and the eagles' nest on Merry Island.

FARNSY

Being on a boat out on the water—didn't matter what kind of a boat or water—Farnsy figured it had some kind of sweetening effect on most people. His theory was that every one of them had an ancestor who'd crossed some water at some time to get somewhere new, and these folks probably still had that yearning to go somewhere else, just around the next bend in the river, to see if things might be just a dite better. Not everyone had to go off chasing white whales. Sometimes all it took to get the ya-yas out of your system was an hour in a kayak poking around the coves, or a tour on the *Teciani*, singing Carole King songs along with that pretty Maine gal Katie and her guitar.

If you had a place on the river, you'd hear the gentle throb of *Teciani*'s engine before you'd see it between the pines, sliding downstream or chugging upstream into the current. You'd wave to folks onboard, and they'd wave back, and the *Teciani* would become just another welcome afternoon sight.

Farnsy often daydreamed on duty, and this gig on the *Teciani* was no different. It was something every good police officer had to contend with—the inevitable boredom of waiting for something to happen and sometimes even wanting something to happen, nothing bad, just something, anything. So, even if it looked like Farnsy was about to doze off and his mind was a million miles away, he was, in reality, a coiled spring, ready for action.

On this particular Friday afternoon, late that August, his second tour on board the *Teciani*, Farnsy was drifting off, watching pleasure boats come and go, lost in his thoughts. Maybe it was the burble of the boat's wake and the gentle throbbing of the boat's engine, or maybe it was the fresh air and sunshine. Or maybe it was listening to Ursula showing folks how to shuck an oyster or Chuck on the loudspeaker telling tourists about the oyster farms spread out along the river, the best in North America, he boasted over the loudspeaker. Farnsy smiled when someone

SUMMER ～ *Nedda*

from away asked Chuck about all the colorful "bobbers" floating here and there in the river. Chuck was explaining that those were lobster buoys, each one with a trap at the end of the line, and that every fisherman had a different color, when, out of the corner of an eye, Farnsy spotted the unmistakable shape of a Friendship sloop. It was slipping by as quiet as a leaf on the water, sailing in with the rising tide, her dark hull slicing through the river chop, her white sails stretched tight, popping as they caught the late afternoon breeze.

In Farnsy's mind there was nothing prettier than seeing a wooden boat under sail like that, white foam under the bow, leaving a burbling ripple behind, the sails puffed up and tugging in the wind. You could take that boat anywhere, he thought. Down east, up the coast, to Camden, Bar Harbor, or across Fundy Bay to Nova Scotia. Or south, to the Vineyard or Key West and beyond.

And now here was that boat, as elegant as any boat that ever was, slipping by the *Teciani* so close that he could hear her skipper's dulcet voice when she returned the captain's wave with a cheery hello. Sunglasses, black shorts, white visor, her hair dancing in the fair breeze, one hand on the arched wood tiller, she glanced up at her mainsail, which looked pretty trim to Farnsy, but her sails quickly caught some air and Farnsy watched as the *Aphrodite* out of Castine beat upriver. Then, after she was well past Dodge Point, he watched her tack around the green can where the oyster farm spreads out and head down the narrow channel toward Goose Ledge and a mooring in Damariscotta Harbor.

In an instant, Farnsy felt trapped—couldn't wait to get off and find her, find out who she was, this woman who was sailing such a sweet boat, solo, up a tidal river, lobster buoys scattered everywhere, just waiting to tangle up rudders, and enough rocks, narrows, ledges, and currents and eddies to confuse even the best boaters. Who was this woman? She looked familiar, like someone from a past life. She looked like a protean beauty from a world of water, and he felt landlocked.

"Nice boat, eh?" Farnsy heard someone say behind him.

"Sweet lines," Farnsy said, looking back to see Chuck.

"The boat or her captain?"

"You know her?"

"Oh, yeah, the *Aphrodite's* a corker—a Friendship sloop, gaff-rigged, old working boat, classic, wood, Maine made, her tender too, not an ounce of plastic on her."

"I could see that. You know her skipper?"

"Read some about her. Serious sailor. Blue water, you know, offshore stuff, that sort of thing. America's Cup."

"America's Cup?"

"Ayuh, all woman-crew. Maybe 10 years ago. Contenders. Her name's Nedda. That's right, Farnsy, Nedda Barnes. Wonder what she's doing up here? Wait, isn't there a regatta or something up there on Eggemoggin Reach, end of summer, around Labor Day? Bet that's where she's headed."

"Maybe," Farnsy said, wondering what a woman like Nedda Barnes was doing sailing solo anywhere.

The *Teciani* chugged upriver with the rising tide toward Damariscotta, past several more oyster farms, hundreds of dark bins bobbing in the boat's wake, millions of tiny oysters trapped inside, cormorants perched on top, their wings spread out to dry. Then, when the *Teciani* nosed around Goose Ledge and eased into Damariscotta's harbor, Farnsy spotted the *Aphrodite* moored up over at Paul Bryant's place, the Riverside Boat Company, her sails trimmed neatly and no sign of life. The tender was missing. She was in town, somewhere, Nedda Barnes was.

Process of elimination, Farnsy thought as he stepped onto the dock after the last passenger was off, process of elimination. Detective work. A woman like that probably didn't need anything at Renys. Wasn't likely she was looking for a *Where the Hell is Damariscotta?* T-shirt. So that eliminated a few other places. Not Jeff's gallery. Closed anyway. Not Wicked Scoop, the Gifford's ice cream place. And the banks were closed by now.

Farnsy was trying to think like she might think, same way he always tried to get into the criminal mind, so he figured she probably wasn't going for a grinder at Fernald's. They were closed now, anyway. Probably wasn't picking up fish to grill at the Fisherman's Catch. Now she might be a reader, but Sherman's Book Shop was closing soon, this time of day. Probably wasn't going to the laundromat, though he'd check it out if he didn't find her before. So that only left one possibility, Farnsy deduced.

Since it was late afternoon, she was likely headed for a cold drink and dinner in town. And that meant either the Schooner Landing right there on the town dock or the River Grill or King Eider's Pub on Main Street. There were a few other options, like that Thai spot or the new bistro, but Farnsy was thinking Nedda Barnes was probably more of an Eider's gal and pictured her sitting at the oyster bar there upstairs with a martini—or an Oxbow summer ale—and a plate of oysters, enjoying the lively bar chatter in Eider's. That was it. King Eider's.

Halfway up the ramp from the dock, Farnsy turned to wave to Chuck, who wished him luck. A blues band started warming up the small crowd gathered on the patio outside Schooner Landing, their beer glasses glowing in the late afternoon sun. Anyone who had a worry left would've lost it there fast.

Just as Farnsy was about to head over toward Eider's, he spotted Nedda Barnes sitting at one of the tables on the patio bathed in golden late afternoon sunlight, in the middle of all that weekend laughter and a cloud of smells of onion rings, burgers, beer, and the great salt sea, whose waters lapped at the dock, reading the menu, all alone.

FARNSY

Farnsy knew he'd regret it the rest of his life if he didn't do something or say something. No way he could go back to his place on the lake and have a can of cold Pabst and a hot dog all by himself with Henry.

"Seat taken?" he asked her.

She cupped her ear, "What?"

"You alone? I mean, is this seat taken?"

"Yes," she said, but seeing the look on his face, she added, "I mean, yes, I'm alone, and no, that seat isn't taken."

He sat down across from her and realized she was probably the most beautiful woman he had ever seen, and there she was and here he was and he was just a small-town cop without any idea what to say next. Hadn't even given it a thought. When he was a kid calling up girls for a date, he'd write out his side of the conversation in a spiral notebook. Now here he was, an actor on a real stage, waiting for a prompter to whisper him his lines.

"Menu?" she asked, handing him the weekend menu, encased in plastic and greasy to the touch.

"Me? No, thanks, I know it by heart."

After they went through the whole "you're from here, where're you from, didn't I see you on the *Teciani*, yes you did" conversation, Farnsy asked her if she'd like to go someplace quiet. When he saw the look on her face like maybe he might be an ax murderer, he said, "Sorry, I don't mean my place. I mean Eider's, King Eider's Pub, just over there." He pointed across the street. "You know the place?"

"Never been here before. But sure, I'm game. As long as I can take Pearly here." And she pointed to a yellow lab, curled up at her feet. This woman was full of surprises.

"Not sure they'll let her in, but they've got a couple of tables outside."

"I'm Nedda Barnes," she said, offering her hand. If he hadn't known she was a sailor, he might have figured she was a rock climber, she had that kind of a grip. The self-assured grip of a woman who could handle herself. No wedding ring.

"Farnsworth. Actually, it's Officer Farnsworth," he said, showing her his wallet ID.

"Officer William Phineas Farnsworth, Damariscotta Police," she read. "Libra, I see."

"Is that good?"

"We'll see," she said. "I'm Aries."

Farnsy never could remember which signs went with which signs.

They crossed the street after cars stopped, with Pearly now on a leash. Farnsy felt protective, and didn't know why.

"Aries?" He asked.

"Yes, William Phineas Farnsworth."

"Folks here just call me Farnsy."

"I like Finney," she said.

"Nice boat you got there, the *Aphrodite*."

"My father's. And before him, my grandfather's. Long story. Finney, let's get something to drink and you tell me all about Damariscotta. And a dozen oysters. For starters."

Inside Eider's, at the register, Jock took quick measure of Farnsy and Nedda, looked down to check his reservation calendar, out of habit and, for Farnsy, pure formality. Then, with a conspiratorial wink and a smile, he showed them the corner booth, which Jock knew was Farnsy's favorite. As a final flourish of good-will, Jock set a bowl of water down next to Pearly, who'd curled up under the table. He could tell it was an evening for an exception to the no-dogs rule. When Nina, the new waitress, handed Farnsy his menu, she gave him a wink and Farnsy knew the news would be all over town before he even got the check, probably even before his seafood stew arrived. And that meant Lucy would hear. But he reminded himself that Lucy had told him she wanted her space and more time. And that was weeks ago, over a month, and not a peep from her since she'd given him a trim.

As Doc had once advised Farnsy, conversation's the best foreplay. They talked right through the oysters, dinner, two black coffees, and some of those M&M's that Jock's waitstaff always left with the check to sweeten up the bill-paying and maybe encourage a good tip. They emerged into the cool summer night. Farnsy asked Nedda if she'd like an ice cream across the street at Wicked Scoop before the college girls closed up. They finished their cones on a bench overlooking the harbor. The tide was headed out. Time and tide, Farnsy thought.

"Where do you live, Finney?" Nedda broke the silence.

"Got a camp—well, a cottage, really—on the lake."

"Which lake would that be?"

"Damariscotta," Farnsy said, not sure where this was going.

"Want to show me?"

"Now? You mean tonight?"

"Why not, Finney? You've seen my boat. Gets pretty ripe after a few days out. Besides, it's a full moon. Got anything for Pearly to eat?"

Farnsy thought a moment. "Cat food, the dry stuff. I don't think Henry would mind."

"Henry?"

"Maine coon cat. Real big, real smart, like a dog, only he purrs."

"I like him already."

They found Farnsy's pickup in the back lot and drove in silence out to the lake, the night air growing ever cooler as they got closer to the lake. Then Farnsy headed down his winding gravel fire road through the woods, which quickly enveloped them in darkness. When he and his sister Grace were kids, Farnsy's father would stop halfway down to the cottage and turn

SUMMER — *Nedda*

out the headlights. And Gracie, a dripping ice cream cone still in her clutch, would scream. "Dark as a pocket!" Farnsy's mother would always say.

It seemed to Farnsy that time was speeding up, because they were already there at his spot on the lake. Farnsy turned the engine off and they sat there briefly in silence, lights off, when Nedda jumped out and ran down to the lake, her dog Pearly arf-arfing alongside her. Farnsy caught up with her on the wharf, and they watched Pearly leap into the dark lake and chase bubbles in the water. Pearly got out and shook herself off. They sat on the end of the dock, surrounded by water, and listened to the loons. They talked, avoiding the obvious, until they were all talked out, shivering in the cold night air, and then just gave in, exhausted, and watched the moon rise over the trees on the opposite shore and begin to light up the lake.

"Necco wafers!? Wait, a whole carton of them? How many rolls you have here? Finney, are you serious?" Nedda tightened the belt of Farnsy's bathrobe a little and picked up a roll of Necco wafers, holding it up in the Saturday morning light that was sparkling off the lake and flooding Farnsy's cottage with dappled sun shadows. It was as though the whole place was under water the way the sunlight sparkled and danced and shimmered.

"It's research, Nedda. Long story. I mean, okay, look, well, I confess: I really like 'em. Reminds me of when I was a kid. And I always keep some in my cruiser. But I can explain. I mean, if you want to try them go right ahead, they're related to a case I'm working on, but it's not like you'd be eating police evidence."

"Maybe after breakfast," she laughed. "But first, you know what I want to do??"

"You tell me, Ms. Barnes."

"Let's go for a swim."

FARNSY

Henry the cat, who was stretched out on the windowsill above the kitchen sink, lying against the screen in the early morning sun, perked up, then watched with detached interest as the screen door slapped shut and Nedda Barnes walked outside, barefoot, Farnsy's plaid bathrobe all loose around her, and tossed a stick off the dock. Pearly chased after it with a great cannonball splash, and Nedda Barnes let the bathrobe slip off her, forming a pool of soft cloth around her pink ankles. Farnsy watched from the screen door as Nedda ran down the dock, dove into the rippled surface of the lake with a shriek of sheer joy, then bobbed up, swept her hair back, and waved back to Farnsy.

"Come on in, Finney!" She slid onto her back and backstroked out to his float some distance away, her altogether slipping through the same water he'd swum in all his life, as if to bless it now in some different way.

Farnsy slid out of his shorts, prompting Nedda to whistle, and he did his best dive off the dock into the dark lake water. He swam out to her, and when they were behind the float, laughing and hanging on, out of breath, he kissed her and she kissed him back in a way that seemed different from the way they had kissed the night before.

Post-swim, Nedda found some oranges in the fridge, sliced them in half, and squeezed their juice into two tumblers. Farnsy started the bacon frying on one griddle while Nedda scrambled some eggs on another. She stirred in a dollop of chive cream cheese she'd found in the back of his fridge. After they ate, Farnsy told Nedda her coffee was perfect and needed no sugar. It was a corker of a day on the lake.

They took Pearly out in the old rowboat and paddled over to the cove, which was brimming with lily pads, whose flowers were opening and filling the still morning air with sweet fragrance. Farnsy told Nedda his grandmother would row out there with him when he was a kid and he'd tug on some lily pads until they popped loose, and they would paddle back to the cottage and put them in a big bowl on the deck. They'd watch the pond lilies open and close, until a week would pass and they would go out to pick more. He told her about netting sun turtles there with his nieces. And when he told her about swimming out to Blueberry Island, he wondered: If he kept telling her stories, might a whole lifetime pass? They talked about driving back into town, but Nedda found enough supplies for a spaghetti dinner right there, and Farnsy came up with two bottles of red wine.

That evening, Farnsy lit an old kerosene lamp and they took it out on the dock and sat there, feet dangling in the water, like two kids, nibbling on a couple of Neccos, until the bugs got them and they had to skedaddle back indoors. Before they did, Nedda insisted on one more skinny dip, which was perfect because the moon was up again, this time even brighter, and it bathed the lake and the land in its soft white glow.

Back inside, Nedda found a joint in her jacket and lit it with a kitchen match. She inhaled as though she were inhaling the whole day they'd had together, taking it all in. Farnsy shook his head when she offered him a puff, but said it didn't bother him if she did, so she did. Farnsy made busy starting a fire in the fireplace, and Nedda flicked the end of the joint into the fire and said, "Come on, Finney, let's snuggle, okay?"

Farnsy tried to memorize the feel of her body, her slender weight atop him, astride him. The touch of her fingers. Her buttery smoothness in the cool night air. The feel of her hips, the curves he could hold and bring closer to him as they rocked, gently, then faster.

They made love once, then again before falling asleep. Farnsy guessed it was sometime just before dawn's early light when Henry stirred, then Pearly, and Nedda whispered in Farnsy's ear and asked if he was up for just one more, but he said he was spent. He regretted it soon and then for a long time afterward. Never disappoint a woman, his father once told him. Farnsy was too young to understand what his father had meant back then, but now he thought he knew.

"This your girl, Finney?" Nedda asked. Her back was turned, but Farnsy knew it was the photo of Lucy that he'd had framed and had forgotten was still on top of his bureau.

"Was," he said.

"Was?"

"Was."

"Then why keep her photo? She the one who got away?"

"I think so. Maybe. Not sure. Just put it in the top drawer there."

"She's pretty," Nedda said, still holding the photo. "What's her name?"

"Lucy."

"Nice name. She must be nice."

That Sunday morning the wind was too light for sailing, so Nedda started the engine and they motored with the ebb tide down the Damariscotta River, the *Aphrodite*'s diesel chugging like a heartbeat. Pearly curled up and slept in the sun in the cockpit. They could feel the day warming up and could see folks in their cottages on the other side just starting to stir, coming down to river's edge, coffee mugs in hand. One of them waved. The *Aphrodite* motored quietly past boats tied up along the channel, as if the current were pulling her toward the sea, toward some kind of a decision, faster than Farnsy was ready to make it.

Just past Merry Island, just past the osprey nest atop a green day marker, the river widened and either side of the channel was sprinkled with tide-tugged lobster buoys as far as the eye could see. The morning breeze picked up, so Nedda cut the engine and told Farnsy which line to haul. It seemed as though the *Aphrodite* started to breathe again, and Farnsy could feel that it was all coming to an end, faster than he wanted. She was heading Down East, up the coast, to Eggemoggin Reach, just like Chuck said, and Farnsy wasn't. Couldn't.

When Farnsy woke up Monday morning, he felt like he had lived a whole lifetime with Nedda Barnes that weekend. It was a dream more real than any he'd ever had. Her fragrance, her essence, still lingered in the quiet cottage air. He could still remember the sound of her voice and her giggle and wondered why he'd gotten off her boat in East Boothbay and watched her sail out to open ocean. He sensed it all slipping away like a dream dissolving. He lay there in bed as Henry the cat started knocking stuff off the top of his dresser, Farnsy trying to hang on to the memory of her and fix it all in his mind so that he'd never forget her there in his cottage, her fragrance, the feel of her skin and that silk, and her voice whispering in his ear in the deep of night when they clutched again. Try as he might, he couldn't any more memorize those things than he could remember the sound of her voice, which bubbled with life and then, in the darkness, became a whisper.

"Magical," Nedda had told him when she gave him that last long hug on the pier in East Boothbay, "Finney, it was magical." They both seemed to know it was just a slack-tide moment where time and tide seemed to stop, briefly, then commence flowing again.

Pemaquid

The whole coast of Maine was socked in when Farnsy drove out to Pemaquid to think, and the fog got thicker the closer he got to the point. Drizzle turned to rain, and the rain was hard and wind-driven. Any folks with boats still in the water kept them moored up. Only fishermen who needed to check traps ventured out. Waves were running three to five feet, and the Coast Guard issued a Small Craft Advisory. Farnsy slowed down as he got close to the parking lot out at Pemaquid Point, where he drove a couple of times a year just to get away and think. It's where he'd taken Lucy late last fall, after her divorce from Earl was signed, to hold her hand and listen as she sobbed and told him she needed time to think.

The fog hung thick around the pines, and the pines seemed to shrink the closer he got to the coast and the lighthouse. By the time he pulled into the parking lot, the lighthouse, which was only a few hundred feet away, was barely visible through the fog. Though the rain had stopped, the air felt thick with water.

Farnsy tugged on a rain slicker and his Red Sox cap and found the path over to the rocks just beyond the lighthouse. That was his spot for sitting and watching the ocean churn and boil over onto the huge rough-edged granite rocks, which weren't the least bit rounded in spite of all the millions of years of being battered by waves, and were still beautifully dangerous even on a sunny summer day. He remembered it was near high tide when he'd left town, so it was definitely high tide out at the point. The waves seemed to have tentacles that groped up into the crannies of the rock ledges

SUMMER — *Pemaquid*

as if they were looking for someone or something, anything to pull back into the surf. A few gulls rode the waves, out where they started to break, floating as if levitating, up and down as each wave, dark green, almost black, rolled beneath them, then rose up in a white froth and broke on the rocks, which were black and gray in that weather. Farnsy sat down and watched.

He felt like he was approaching some kind of crossroad. He'd known Lucy as long as he could remember. From back in high school, when he wished she were in more of his classes and then, when she was, he couldn't pay attention to anything the teacher said. That time he took her to see *Titanic* in the Lincoln Theater and they watched until Farnsy snaked his hand around her and they kissed. Wasn't much later Lucy dumped him and Farnsy went off to Colby and they lost touch, in different worlds, except now and then they'd bump into each other at Thanksgiving or Christmas and, by chance, some summers. They'd laugh, because it was almost always in the Hannaford veggie department, as if they had timed it. Just two old friends, catching up.

He'd knocked around in Boston for a year and she'd gone up to Bar Harbor to wait tables. She'd saved up to go out West, but started cosmetology school, then she met Earl. For the life of him, Farnsy never could understand her attraction to Earl. Lucy lifted up everything around her, like a rising tide. She laughed easily. And she was smart. Sassy smart. But then she and Earl ran into hard times because Earl was an unlucky fisherman. When Lucy and Earl had split up one spring a few years earlier, Farnsy had bumped into her in the veggie department again. The only thing he could recall from that time was that he'd just wanted to take her in his arms. But he'd pulled back because the last thing he needed then was complications, so he advised Lucy to give it another try with Earl. She did, but it sputtered again, and by fall last year their divorce was final.

FARNSY

After the weekend with Nedda Barnes, Farnsy had no idea where anything stood. That weekend left him feeling lonelier than he'd felt in a long time. There was still a flicker of something deep for Lucy. For the life of him, he couldn't figure out what it was. And he couldn't seem to shake her. The best he came up with was that she was a real Maine gal. Tough, but soft in all the right places. Trouble was, no one wrote a book with the answers for the questions on Farnsy's mind. And now, when summer was over, Lucy was headed off again, over to Augusta, to learn how to color hair.

Farnsy had other things on his mind, like his birthday, his 35th, coming up in September. He wondered if he'd be stuck in Damariscotta the rest of his life, like a piece of driftwood hung up on some rocks, and never know what police work in a real city was like. He'd once thought about going to law school, but now that felt like someone else's dream.

When he joined the force, Farnsy believed he could make a difference. And maybe he was. But sometimes he asked himself if handing out warnings and tickets to speeders, getting tourists headed in the right direction, and responding to parking lot fender benders really made life in town any better.

Labor Day marked the end of the season. And it seemed to Farnsy like just about everyone else was leaving town, headed somewhere else, back South or out West. And here he was.

Pumpkinfest would be crazy, people from all over, but after that it was just the locals and a few leaf peepers. Even the lobsters headed out to colder waters, and it wouldn't be long before the hummingbirds would disappear, one day to the next, headed south. Pleasure craft on the river had melted away, parking was easier, and the traffic around Red's Eats in Wiscasset was getting lighter. The season was almost over, and Farnsy wondered if he'd just plain missed his time. The big 35 was coming up and that was half of 70. Halfway to retirement. By this age, his parents had been married more than 10 years and had two kids in a small cottage with a big mortgage. Now, all Farnsy had was the cottage. And Henry. Henry. Farnsy had to laugh. Henry. Great guy. Almost like the brother he'd never had. Or son. Of course, he had his friends at Waltz's, too. But something was missing.

The rock Farnsy sat on had grown cold, so he stood up, stretched, and headed back toward town. Fall was coming, ready or not. Time to start his shift and take a slow spin around town in the cruiser. It was the same old parking lot tour: fender benders and lockouts. Or old folks who forgot where they'd parked. Now and then a lost kid. After dark, he might stop to check a parked car that hadn't moved in a while. A knock on the window was all it took, and the kids inside would jump up and drive off before Farnsy could finish the ticket he was pretending to write up. They'd have another Farnsy story to tell their friends, and maybe Farnsy'd spared the girl a lifetime of misery married to that numbskull. Every once in a while, he'd run an out-of-state plate and find a bail jumper or someone with a few priors and a skipped court date. Being a cop, a policeman on the Maine coast, Farnsy saw a lot of things most folks would never see. But what he couldn't see was where he was headed.

FALL

The Ruby-Throated Hummingbird (*Archilochus colubris*)

The ruby-throated hummingbird, the only hummingbird common to Maine, returns each May after traversing mythic distances. It weighs as much as a penny and dazzles bird watchers with its dizzying acrobatics. The only bird able to fly backward, a hummingbird can hover like a honeybee to draw nectar from a flower, then dart, a silver blur of red and green, from tree to tree, a master of three dimensions. In mid-September, Maine nights chill, the nectar slows, leaves begin to turn, and the ruby-throated hummingbird commences its long migration south, toward Florida and across the Gulf of Mexico to Central America. Hummingbirds are not monogamous.

The Speeder

"Willie, what about you? Still a cop?"

Farnsy opened his eyes. The room was still dark, but he knew the sun would be rising soon. That voice seemed to have come from close by. His father? Couldn't be. He was in an RV out West somewhere. Just a postcard now and then. But that voice, his father's? He used to call Farnsy "Willie" when he was a kid. This is crazy, Farnsy thought. Of course I'm a cop. Who wants to know, anyway? Farnsy closed his eyes and tried to get back to the dream, maybe get a good look at the man with the voice, but gave up and emerged from sleep as if he were wading up the lake bed onto shore. He was certain he knew that voice from somewhere. He didn't feel threatened, just wanted to know who it was and what it meant. It was a simple question: Once a cop, always a cop?

Farnsy wanted to know the answer, too, because he had been mulling over the same question for some time now. In a few weeks he'd be 35. Halfway to 70. The tipping point: where the roller coaster pauses, briefly, at the top, before it wavers, teeters, tilts, then starts the long race down the slippery slope to the bottom of the hill. As much as he loved his work and this little town he patrolled, he wondered if this was it. Or was there something more waiting for him, just around the corner? Farnsy had read somewhere that women have a nesting instinct, a biological clock ticking away. Lucy had talked about hers once, but now Farnsy wondered if maybe men had one, too. Just different time zones probably.

FARNSY

Farnsy propped himself up on his elbows and looked around. Then he spotted Henry, stretched out atop his bureau. They locked eyes. Henry yawned a meow.

"Don't even think about it, Fuzzypants," Farnsy said, but Henry started tapping Farnsy's spare pocket change off the top of the dresser, and Farnsy heard the coins clatter, one after another, onto the wooden floor, then roll around and scatter. Farnsy sprang out of bed and Henry jumped off the bureau, landed with a thump, and scurried off toward the kitchen, tail upright, mission accomplished, celebrating another good morning victory, and waited, perched on the kitchen counter, for Farnsy to come fix his breakfast.

As Henry ate his special seafood medley, the sun rose a notch up over the treetops on the other side of the lake, bathing the cottage in a warm yellow light. Sunday was starting up without Farnsy, who wanted only to go back to that dream. But the more he struggled to remember it, the less he remembered. The room. The darkness. The familiar voice. All that faded away and Farnsy was left with a lingering question he couldn't answer now, awake.

Farnsy adjusted his rearview mirror and checked to make sure his radar device was on. Then he waited. It was a quiet September Sunday morning. When he assigned Farnsy the fall Sunday morning church speed check, Chief said even though most churchgoers probably weren't all that anxious to hear a sermon, it might be a good idea to set up a speed trap out that way. "Speed stops are a lot like fishing," Chief had said. "You throw out a lure—in this case, a quiet open road on a Sunday morning right about where folks start to hit the gas, especially the back pew late risers—and you just might nail a scofflaw or two and slow traffic down a while. Sort of like catch and release, only with motor vehicles."

"And you have to keep 'em guessing," he'd advised. "Always vary your tactics." Didn't matter to the Chief if they were Baptists,

Episcopalians, Congregationalists, Catholics, or Quakers. In the Chief's mind, every one of those churchgoers was a potential driving sinner.

Farnsy took another peek in the rearview and wondered what Lucy might be up to now. It'd been some time since she'd given him a trim that summer and she'd told him she wanted space, time to herself, to think about her future. She'd told him she was starting a program in hairstyling, maybe it was hair coloring, over in Augusta that fall, but someone at Waltz's had said they'd heard from the friend of a neighbor that Lucy was visiting her mom's auntie over near China. Farnsy remembered Lucy's auntie and that old camp of hers. He'd gone out there one summer years ago when he and Lucy were dating, and he'd spent a hot September day crawling around her garden with trimming shears and leather gloves, pruning her raspberry patch. Sometimes the news got delayed before it reached Waltz's, so Farnsy figured Lucy could be anywhere by now, but she was on his mind, and he couldn't shake her for the life of him.

To pass time on radar patrol, Farnsy sometimes played license-plate bingo, like he and Grace used to do when their father decided the family should go out for a Sunday drive and have a picnic lunch instead of sitting in church. They'd compete to be the first to spot all the New England license plates they saw. It was their mother's way of teaching them a little geography. Memorizing all the New England state capitols. Starting, of course, with Augusta.

Farnsy bingo-ed in 20 minutes. Most all of the cars were migrating south. To New York, Massachusetts, Connecticut, Rhode Island, New Jersey, Pennsylvania, even Maryland, Virginia, or Florida. And Texas, that was an odd one. A rental, Farnsy guessed. Every car packed up tight as an engorged tick, roof racks loaded. Families with kids headed back to school and work. Kayaks tied down on top or bicycles strapped on back with stretched bungee cords, the bike tires spinning slowly in the tailwind as their owners retreated. Retirees, most of them, this time of year, Farnsy speculated, snowbirds headed south. Or empty nesters who came up for one last long weekend of summer. Or folks with cottages who'd had their big leftover dinner the night before, then locked up that morning, dropped a trash bag off at the town dump, and left.

Another month or so and leaf peepers would start to arrive. Older folks, blue hairs, in leaf peeper buses with big picture windows, or couples in RVs, stopping along the roads, slowing down traffic, ooh-ing and aah-ing at all the pretty leaves and grateful, probably, for the last few golden days of fall before the leaves dropped. In the fall of their own lives, leaf peepers followed the trail of speckled colors up the Maine coast as overnight frosts turned leaves bright orange and red and yellow.

Farnsy thought the leaf peepers he chatted up seemed happier than the summer folks, especially the tired one-week renters, stuck in backed-up traffic with a car jammed full of stuff and whining kids. Maybe, he thought, some of the older leaf peepers were happy just because this might be their last road trip together and they wanted to squeeze the most out of it. Like apples in a cider press. Seeing all these folks headed somewhere made Farnsy feel like a clam, stuck there, buried in the sand while the tide goes out.

Farnsy watched a fly land on the granola bar in his right hand. Chief, who always looked out for his team, had told them it might be good if they all dropped a little weight and handed out Granola bars at the end of a recent team-building meeting.

"Like eatin' wood chips, you ask me," John, the parking officer, had muttered to Farnsy as they walked out of the meeting. Chief used to joke that John couldn't see his belt buckle unless he took it off, but John had joined Weight Watchers online. "Now never you mind how many calories they have, Chief said, watching John squint as he tried to read the ingredients on the packet. Chief was always onto something new. That summer it'd been beef jerky, then moose jerky, and, most recently, venison, trying out new spices. The original protein diet, Chief claimed.

Now the Chief was big on roughage, too. Probably some magazine he'd been reading. Next thing would probably be a vegetarian diet. Or yoga. Yes, Farnsy thought, as the first cars started to head home after church let out. Chief'd said something about how he'd read in that *Oprah* magazine in the barbershop that yoga was good for the core muscles. That was when John had told the Chief he didn't have a core anymore. "Just six-pack flabs," he'd said.

The fly landed on the granola bar again, and Farnsy shook it off. Last fly of the season, Farnsy thought. Sort of like the tourists and all the summer people from away. Except flies don't migrate. One short season is all they get.

Summers always made Farnsy happy. All those memories of school days when summer finally arrived—and back then it seemed like summer would just last and last—a long string of sunny days stretched out before him like a string of lobster buoys one after the other and the other. Then, a little after Labor Day, like right now, when fall eased in, Damariscotta settled back into its quiet routine again, everyone busy doing things they couldn't get to in the summer because it was summer, and they all figured there was still plenty of time. Out at Farnsy's cottage, that red maple would drop its leaves overnight, like a woman letting her dress slip off and puddle around her feet. This fall, Farnsy noticed the leaves falling off one by one, a few at a time, like paint flaking off. As if to slow down time. The leaves on the big oak, where Farnsy's father had wrapped that Jitterbug fishing lure around a branch, were always slow dropping.

As Farnsy tugged a granola bar out of its wrapper, his radar alerted and he watched a black car zip by, hell bent for Lexington.

FARNSY

Farnsy'd just glanced in the rearview, had seen nothing, and now his radar was beeping like crazy and that car just whipped past and headed out of town, wicked fast, at least 20 over, he estimated. This was a ticket, for sure, no excuses and a warning. He made a mental note: black Lexus. Older model. Mass plates.

Farnsy dropped the granola bar on the floor, knowing he could find it later, radioed Dottie in dispatch, telling her, "10-83, Dot. A hot one, headed south on Bristol Road." He lit up the light bar, burped the siren a couple of times, and took off in pursuit. By the time he caught up with the Lexus, it was hitting 70, 75, in a 45 mph zone, clearly marked. It kept driving, but slowed, and passed what Farnsy thought were a couple of good spots to pull over, until the driver finally found one worthy of his Lexus.

Farnsy pulled up behind the car as it came to a stop, and he left his lights strobing like a loud noise on this quiet Sunday morning. Locals passing by would know Damariscotta's finest was on the job, putting their tax money to good use. Plus, they could take secret pleasure knowing it was a Lexus—and, better yet, from Massachusetts.

Farnsy called in to let Dottie know he was about a mile past the hospital on Bristol Road, then read the license plate to her. If anything happened, backup could find him fast. And they'd know what car to look for. He took a minute or so to catch his breath and settle down before he made his way up to the car. Thirty over the town's limit was no joke. It was a menace and a danger. And Farnsy was worried that he might just reach right inside the car and yank the man out like a forceps delivery in the maternity ward, then spank him. Not that he'd ever actually do that, but Farnsy thought he'd like to try it once.

He stepped out of the climatized cruiser into the warm September air, tugged his uniform straight, put on his cap, and felt the gear around his waist with both hands to make sure it was

FALL — *The Speeder*

all there. He tapped his sidearm for reassurance. His engine was still clicking, cooling down from the chase. It hadn't taken but a minute, start to finish, but it seemed longer, and Farnsy was just getting his breath back to normal by the time he reached the trunk of the car, watching the driver for any sudden movement. You just never knew what might happen. Appeared to be no passenger up front, and the back seat was empty. He stopped by the rear window of the Lexus and heard the driver's window glide open with a purr.

He'd seen the driver briefly from his cruiser and noted that it was probably a male, though he couldn't tell. Farnsy was about to tell the driver why he'd stopped him, when the driver reached toward the glove compartment—every cop's worry, something they trained for and discussed all the time. What if he turned around with a weapon and started firing? Farnsy had his right hand over his Glock, ready, and tugged his cap down tighter with the other hand. Times like these, show force, Chief said. Show the uniform. Half the time most folks, after they see the uniform, spilled out their stories, their lame excuses, apologies, explanations, and sometimes, tears, too. Sometimes just the tears. Farnsy took several steps backward, out of the line of fire if there was a gun, his right hand on his Glock.

"Hands on the wheel. Please. Do this now!" he commanded. Hearing nothing and expecting the worst, Farnsy continued to inch backward, to the safety of his cruiser door, which he'd left open.

"You really have no idea who I am, do you? Officer. Do you? Officer?" Farnsy heard the man blurt out.

Farnsy heard himself say, "No, sir, I don't. But I am going to find out. So, now, sir, please take out your license and registration. Slowly." He added, "Hold them in your left hand out the window so that I can see them. Keep your right hand on the steering wheel."

"Must be a slow day in Maine. What did you stop me for? Mind telling me?"

The man sounded like he was a champagne cork about to pop.

"Sir, show me your license and registration. Now!"

"Do you know who I am?" the man bellowed. "Do you have ANY idea who I am?"

Farnsy could see the man's hands gripping the top of the steering wheel, his fingers flicking like they were playing notes on a piano.

"You don't have any idea, do you, who I am, do you, do you?" the man said out of the corner of his mouth.

Just then the man lurched as if to reach for something on the seat next to him and, just as fast, Farnsy had his Glock out.

"NOW!"

The man froze, his left hand still on the steering wheel and the other just inches from what looked like a cell phone, propped up in the center of his dashboard. Farnsy heard its insistent pinging. Then silence.

"Sir, leave your left hand on the wheel and with your right hand, find your license and registration in the glove compartment and hand them to me, slowly. It's a beautiful Sunday in Maine, and like you said, it's a slow day." The documents emerged from the window.

"Thank you, sir," Farnsy said, then strolled back to his cruiser to run the name and numbers and let the man cool down. He flipped open his laptop and entered everything in the computer—his license, the car's make and model and registration. Negative. The man's record was clean. Then Google told him the man was the owner of an antique shop in Boston. Another click and Farnsy saw a photo of Mr. Lexus with a full head of hair, in his younger, skinnier days, smiling, arms akimbo, in front of a shop, whose specialties, its sign said, were "Olde New England collectibles," whatever that was. The extra "e" probably meant $100 more per item. At least. Whatever floats your boat and to each his own, Farnsy thought. One man's junk, another man's treasure. Never a

FALL — *The Speeder*

dull moment. Another story for Waltz's, this stop was shaping up to be. He remembered Doc telling him that Germans say every Mercedes comes with built-in right of way. Maybe Lexus drivers think they got free passes, too?

By the time Farnsy returned to the man, he seemed to have cooled off a bit. But when he saw the ticket Farnsy'd handed him and the amount of the fine, he stared at it long and hard then said, "You're kidding, right? This a joke? That's outrageous!"

"You don't mind me asking," Farnsy said, "you want to tell me why you were driving so fast? I mean, there's not much going on around here on a Sunday that requires that kind of speed to get to, if you get my drift?"

"A meeting. I was supposed to meet a man in Round Pond about a collection of fishing tackle." He pointed to a little tied fly hooked in the band around his fedora, sitting on the seat next to him.

"You a fisherman?" Farnsy inquired.

"Not for fish," the man said, "You could say I fish for antiques. Old stuff," he added, as if Farnsy might not know what an antique was.

"Come here often?"

The man looked up at Farnsy. "Like I said, I'm headed to Round Pond."

"Well, Round Pond'll still be there. Hasn't moved much since last week."

"Very funny. So tell me, Officer Friendly, now that we've gotten acquainted, I don't suppose you know a nice place to get a bite to eat, do you?"

"Well, there's King Ro's over in Round Pond. Muscongus Bay lobster pound's still open, so you could get yourself a nice lobster and some steamers. They're right on the harbor. Just before the turn-off to Round Pond, there's Deb's Bristol Diner. Great soup."

FARNSY

Farnsy checked his watch. "But they close at noon Sunday's. Now Reilly's, down in New Harbor, will make you a wicked good grinder."

The man in the Lexus had the look of a beached whale all tired out from struggling and just waiting for high tide.

"Say, you don't mind me asking, since you say you're an antiques expert, what do you think I could I get for my father's old Jitterbug?" Farnsy watched the man's face for a reaction.

"Condition's everything, Officer. You have the original box?" No reaction. Poker face. He's either a rank amateur or he's a pro. Hard to tell.

"Nope. No box. Used. Caught a lot of fish with it he did, though. Back in the days."

The man smiled at Farnsy. "Well, Officer, then I'd say just keep it. As a memento. Most you'd get at a flea market'd be a buck. Tops. On a good day." The man's grin wouldn't stop, and Farnsy watched him drive off, gravel crunching under the wheels of his big black Lexus.

When Chief pulled up behind Farnsy's cruiser to take the next speed check shift, it was around noon and the church crowd had thinned out. It was a Sunday traffic slack tide. Mostly late risers now, headed into town for the paper, something they forgot to get at the hardware, or brunch with the wife at Chrissy's.

Farnsy pulled over next to Larson's Lunchbox and found a nice spot at a picnic table in the sun. Normally Larson's lot is full. But they're closed Sundays. He poured himself a cup of black coffee from his thermos, pulled out the baloney and cheese sandwich he'd made that morning, and sat there alone at a picnic table, trying to figure out what it was about the man in the Lexus that he just couldn't put his finger on. Seemed like there was a connection to something.

FALL — *The Speeder*

Back at the station, Farnsy made a note about that stop in his daily report. Something about the man didn't make sense. But then a lot of things in life didn't make much sense, not until you turned a corner or plunked in the last puzzle piece, and then it all made sense, clear as day.

Chat with a Cat

"Well, Henry," Farnsy said to the cat, who was sitting across from Farnsy on top of the kitchen table meditating. In his off-hours, Farnsy couldn't stop thinking about his father's Jitterbug, which had hung for years, framed, proudly, over the workbench in the shed, with an inscription on a little brass plate his mother had special ordered. Now, whenever Farnsy went back to the shed to see if he'd missed a clue, the empty spot on the wall seemed to stare back at him, as if taunting him to find the lure. And the person who took it. Why do people do things like that? Farnsy looked over at the cat.

"Well, Henry, sure wish I knew what you were thinking. Maybe you've got some idea who might've taken that 'bug. Sniff out the Neccos, you know."

"You're probably just wondering when I'll play that birdie-on-a-string game with you again. Been a while, I know. You're a good boy, Henry. Best cat I ever had, hands down." Henry flicked his tail. "Okay, you're right. You're the only cat I ever had. But I'm a lucky man. So was Doc." Henry flicked his tail. "I bet you miss Doc. That's right, meow. I know he misses you. Maybe I'll take you with me next time I go over there for some cribbage. He probably still has some treats for you."

Farnsy sighed. Here he was, talking with a cat. Dog owners talk to their dogs. Why not cat owners? Farnsy recalled something he'd heard, maybe it was his psychology professor, maybe it was someone at the academy in Vassalboro, or maybe it was the Chief.

One of the above, he thought. But it went something like this: good conversationalists listen more than they talk. They just take in what they hear. Some folks never stop talking. Like that time when he was a kid and picked up a party line and heard what sounded like three ladies jabbering about something. Farnsy interrupted to ask, "How do I know when I can use the phone?" There was a pause, and one of the women said, "When we've stopped talkin." So Henry just sat there and listened. All ears. The best sounding board a man in a quandary could ask for. A furry conversationalist.

"So, okay, Fuzzypants, here we are, almost officially fall, and all I know is that someone who really likes Necco wafers broke into maybe half a dozen lakeside cottages last winter, including this one. Someone with a real sweet tooth. An old-time classic candy gourmet. And it's not as though it was exactly a break-in. I mean, some of those places all they had to do was open the door and walk right in, because they never were locked up, even at the end of the season. Most every one of the owners told us they didn't figure they needed keys because there wasn't much of anything really valuable in there. Like the Jitterbug on the wall here. It didn't have money value, just value to us. Memories attached. Like one of your toys, Henry, the ones that get lost under the bed. Out of sight, out of mind. Until you remember it and start looking for it."

Farnsy took a sip of his coffee, which had chilled in the morning air, and remembered his toast. He smeared a streak of butter across it and watched it try to melt, then sprinkled some cinnamon on top. He felt a sudden urge to smoke a cigarette. Old habits. Like they say, we go back to them when things get bumpy.

"So, okay, Henry, hear me out. We've got no evidence. By now every last one of those Necco wafers has probably been eaten and the wrappers tossed in the trash. So that means no fingerprints and no code on the wrappers we could track. Not even sure you can get a fingerprint off a Necco wafer. So we've gotta find out who bought them. I know what you're thinking Henry, good luck with that. And then we've got a couple of missing tackle boxes. Maybe more we just don't know about. And my father's Jitterbug. There's got to be some connection. Some of those old fishing lures are pretty valuable. To the folks who collect and sell them. To the fishermen who bought them, they're just a way to hook a fish. Value's in the eye of the beholder."

Farnsy sipped his coffee.

"All we know is that this seems to be a coordinated operation. Looks like the perpetrator or perpetrators probably started at Biscay Pond. Perfected their techniques, then moved up to Pemaquid Pond. I checked Lake Pemaquid Campground and there's no connection to any campers there. First of all, jet skis aren't allowed. But that doesn't mean someone didn't sneak one out on the water one day and got away with it."

Farnsy put his coffee mug in the microwave and tapped 30 seconds on high.

"You ask me, Henry, it looks like maybe they started scouting for good targets up on Damariscotta Lake last summer. Then last winter they hit a few places. And mine. Probably poked around here when I was up ice fishing on Moosehead last year. You got any ideas, Henry? Not talking? Cat got your tongue? Okay, bad joke, sorry."

"But seriously, that's it. Necco candies, tackle boxes, some lures that might be worth something. And, if they find one, there's one lure that's the mother lode of lures and might be worth big money." Farnsy paused to sip his coffee, then continued his chat with Henry. Maybe just talking it out would help him get a new angle on things.

"I've checked with cleaning crews and summer rental agents, and, when I get a chance, I'll chat up some jet ski rental and repair places, see if they've seen anything unusual going on. As for that gal who was asking questions this summer about where the old fishermen lived, she could be a person of interest. But no one can ID her. All we know is she told that renter who was sitting out on the dock that she lived in town. But the renter's been coming to the lake since she was a kid and knew something was off when the jet skier pronounced the town "Da-MARA-scotta."

Farnsy heard the microwave beep and pulled his coffee mug out. Now it was too hot. Henry flicked his tail again.

"Maybe you're right, Henry, best just to listen. And wait. That's how you catch a mouse, right? You just sit and listen and watch and wait. Then pounce. But I'm a cop, and I think I need to talk with a few more folks. See if the rental folks have seen anything new. Heck, I should probably check out Necco wafer sales at Yellowfront and Hannaford. And now we got winter comin' up pretty soon. Snow means footprints. Only trouble is, the wind whips up and tracks disappear. I know what you're thinking, Henry, maybe I need to set a little mousetrap of my own. Good idea, Henry. Thanks. You're a good boy. Okay, now it's time for your backrub and some play time. Where'd we leave that birdie toy?"

The CLYNK Kid

Dottie took the call from the day manager up at Hannaford and paged the Chief, who was back in the station kitchen demonstrating how to make moose jerky to Farnsy and John.

"It's all in the spices," he was saying when Dottie's voice chirped over the intercom.

"Got a sit-u-a-tion up at Hannaford," Dottie announced in the sing-song-y stage voice she'd practiced when she was in a play the summer before over at the Heartwood Theater.

Chief stopped talking. A piece of moose jerky in one hand, he pressed the speaker button and groaned. "Not another fender bender in the parking lot, Dottie?"

"No, Chief, manager's a new fella, from away, just started up there. Says he's caught a thief red-handed. Citizen's arrest. Got him tied up good and they're holding him in the men's room near the front door. Over."

"Roger, we're on it. Thanks. Over and out."

"Now, like I was saying," the Chief said, "it's all in the spices. But I'll save that secret for next week's meeting. Farnsy, you take the Hannaford call, and while you're there, pick up some teriyaki sauce for my jerky. But wait. Here, it's almost lunchtime. Take a stick from my last batch with you." The Chief wrapped up a wrinkled strip of dried meat in a napkin and tucked it into Farnsy's top pocket.

The station wasn't but a couple of minutes from the store, so Farnsy took his time. He was already thinking that if this citizen's arrest turned into something serious, he'd have to take the culprit to the Two Bridges lockup over in Wiscasset, because there was no holding cell in Damariscotta. The Chief had been pushing for one, but the selectmen were keen on getting in some benches along the harbor because they said there were more tourists and tax-paying locals who liked to sit down and look at the harbor than there were drunks and skunks.

Farnsy caught a whiff of the Chief's newest jerky recipe wafting up out of his front pocket as he parked his cruiser and walked over to the Hannaford entrance. Halfway there, he heard a dog yipping from a parked car, its head stuck out the driver's side window. Farnsy thought he recognized that bark, and, sure enough, it was the Professor's car and that was her yellow lab, Pemmy. Probably helped the Professor park the car, sniff out empty spaces. Here was a chance to solve two problems at once, so Farnsy unwrapped the Chief's venison jerky and held it out. The dog inhaled it two chomps.

Inside, Farnsy headed straight for the men's room door, where he found the new manager waiting, arms crossed.

"Thanks for getting here so fast, Officer."

"You can call me Farnsy."

"My name's James, Jim. Jim Noonan. I'm the new manager. Nice to meet you. Heard a lot about you, Officer, Farnsy."

They shook hands. Farnsy's dad always said you can tell a lot about a man by the way he shakes hands. Then he'd give Farnsy a little demonstration of the various handshakes, asking Farnsy to tell him what kind of shake each was. The new manager's handshake was hesitant, nervous. He was new. Give him a month or two and he'll be all right, Farnsy thought.

"So where's our prisoner?"

"In here. Follow me."

FARNSY

Sitting on the hopper in the only stall, its jail-gray door open, the prisoner was wrapped up with gray duct tape like a moth in a cocoon. He was a kid around 14, 15 tops, Farnsy figured. Skinny as a wet cat. Short hair, brown, a buzz cut. Probably his mom or dad cut it for him because Farnsy could see a few white spots where someone'd dinged him with the clippers pretty good. Trying to save money in tight times. Old Converse high tops, classic black. But way too big for his feet. His brother's hand-me-downs maybe. T-shirt with some kind of rock 'n roll death skull on the front. The kid looked up at Farnsy with a hang-dog look, like a deer with a leg caught in a snap trap. His face said guilty all over it. He didn't have to say a word.

"What's your name, son?" Farnsy asked.

"Frederick Hallbert. Friends call me 'Freddie.' Guys at school call me 'Burt.' Or 'Halibut.'" The kid paused. "Or 'Big Foot,' sometimes, 'cause of my shoes."

"Caught him red-handed," the manager said, as if he'd nabbed Dillinger outside the Biograph Theater, "in the act! And we've got it all on security footage. I can get it if you want."

"Tell me what happened. And what did he take?"

The manager started from the beginning. For a couple of weeks, the store staff had been watching the kid lurk around the CLYNK recyclable area near the main entrance. Every Hannaford was linked up to the CLYNK recycling system, which was where folks could pick up a roll of green plastic bags and a free strip of stickers printed with their own personal barcode. Back home, they'd drop their returnable plastic or glass bottles into the green bag, and when it got full, they'd twist a little wire doodad around the neck of the bag to hold it closed, then stick on one of those personalized bar code tags. Next time they went shopping, they'd go into that little alcove near the store entrance, use the hand scanner to enter their barcode for that bag, pull open the little hatch door to the CLYNK storeroom, drop their bag onto the ramp, and

FALL ~ The CLYNK Kid

watch it slide down and join all the other bags stacked up in there, waiting for someone from the store to come in through the staff door, open up the bags, count the returnables, 5 cents for cans or small bottles, 15 cents for liquor bottles, and credit each CLYNK card holder's account. Then all the customer has to do is check the account now and then and either use the accumulated recycling refunds to defray the cost of groceries at the checkout or cash out with a paper coupon at the Customer Care counter.

It seems that the suspect, as the manager called him, had raised suspicion, not just because he seemed to be hanging around—"lurking about," as the manager described it—but because of the frequency of his withdrawals and the dollar amount, which their records showed tallied at least a few hundred dollars already this summer, though they were still cross-checking that amount.

"So it could be higher. Way higher," he added ominously. "This kid's been running his own tag-over scam all summer. Like the CLYNK recycling bottle deposit system was his personal bank account. Gotta give him credit for ingenuity, I guess."

"What do you suggest I do?" Farnsy asked, looking at the manager, who stood, arms akimbo, outside the stall, guarding the prisoner.

"Well, we've got a sign out front that says loud and clear that we punish shoplifters to the fullest extent of the law, so I say we throw the book at him. There's a lesson to be learned here, and none too soon."

Farnsy thought a moment, uncertain whether this was exactly a case of shoplifting. He turned back to the manager and said, "Now, of course, we need evidence of a crime, you know. Law doesn't think much of hearsay. Like the Chief always says, 'Hearsay's just poor man's gossip.' So I'm thinking we'll need to fingerprint the bags in question, which will take a day, assuming we can even pull some prints off those plastic bags. Then we'll need to send those

FARNSY

prints over to the lab in Augusta and that'll take a week at least." Farnsy let that all settle in with the new manager. "And, as you know," he added, "fall's pretty busy and all."

Farnsy paused, then asked, "Mind if I talk with the, uh, the prisoner, Jim? Alone?"

"Sure, Officer, I'll wait outside." The manager side-stepped around Farnsy and the prisoner.

Farnsy chatted Freddie up a bit, but it wasn't long before the boy's voice started to quiver and it looked like he was about to cry. He told Farnsy, yes, he'd tagged over other people's CLYNK bags. Then he shrugged. Said he figured most of the bags of bottles were left by summer people who could probably afford the missing spare change. On that, Farnsy thought the boy had a point. Freddie said he was really sorry and wouldn't do it again. Said it wasn't what he was taught, but his mom couldn't pay the electric bill and end of most months they had to go up to the food pantry, and even then, his family had to skip meals. Freddie had tried to come up with a way to make money to help out. Said every time his mom went to Hannaford for stuff on sale, he went with her. Sometimes they had their own CLYNK bag, but that was how he got the idea to get his own CLYNK stickers and retag bags left by other people. Whenever he went shopping with his mom, he'd retag four or five bags. And once, after the Fourth of July, he'd tagged over at least six. All that money added up fast, and it sure made his mom happy. But he told Farnsy she had no idea what was going on. It was all his idea. Freddie said he'd told her he'd been mowing lawns and doing odd jobs in their neighborhood. But there wasn't much money in that. Right then, Freddie started to cry. Said he wasn't sure what his mom would do if they locked him up. And maybe they'd lock his mom up, too.

Farnsy took it all in. He told the boy to wait there. But he had to smile because it wasn't like the boy was going anywhere, all taped up, sitting there on the john.

"Look, sir, Jim," Farnsy said to the manager, "it's your call. I can't tell you what to do with your company policy. It's in Hannaford's hands, after all, and you're the boss."

"But?"

"But if you asked me, and I know you didn't, but if you did, I'd tell you I think there's a better way to teach young Freddie here a lesson."

"And that would be?"

Farnsy paused, "Let him go."

"Let him go? I don't get it."

"Right. Just let him go. Not scot-free, mind you, but I think Freddie's a good kid, just made some wrong decisions. Did some wrong things for the right reasons. Wasn't like he was using the money to buy beer or a new video game or something. Just trying to help his ma. And if you look at it another way, his mom used all those ill-gotten gains to buy groceries right here in your store. And the kid's got a point. I'm not saying it's right, what he did, but it's not like those summer people will miss a few bucks."

"Jeez, I don't know, Officer."

"We can pull his stickers off those bags you caught him with today and get the change to the right people. But look, how would it be if I tell him we'll let him go? That is, if he agrees to work right here in your store? We can even tell him it's your idea. Yes, I kind of like that. What do you think?" Farnsy thought a moment. "You could even wait until the CLYNK folks give you an estimate for the damage here. That won't take more than a couple days, you know. Then the boy could work off that amount. Minimum wage, of course."

The manager mulled it over, looked over at his assistant, who looked familiar to Farnsy and seemed to be taking all of this in. "Okay, but he does his time as a bagger up front, where we can keep an eye on him."

FARNSY

They went back into the men's room and the boy, who had stopped crying but was red-eyed and still had that hang-dog look, agreed to the plan. Freddie would start off as a bagger up front, where they could keep an eye on him, all fall, 10 hours a week, especially weekends, when the store was busiest. Then, if he passed that test and they needed help going into the holidays and he wanted to stay on, they'd start paying him hourly and he'd work Sundays, because he played basketball on Saturdays.

As they began peeling the duct tape off Freddie's wrists and ankles, the boy tried to thank Farnsy, but Farnsy waved it off and said, "Don't thank me, Freddie, thank Mr. Noonan here, he's the manager, and he's the one came up with the idea. It'd been up to me, I'd have asked the judge for a one-year minimum in the Wiscasset lockup, or some hard time up there in Thomaston, you know, maybe reduced time for good behavior."

Farnsy winked at the manager, who shook his hand and said, "I think a couple of us have learned a little lesson here, today, Officer. Sorry—Farnsy."

"Hey, almost forgot, Jim. Chief needs some teriyaki sauce."

"It's in the international aisle. Want me to show you?"

"Thanks, I'll find it. Good luck with your new job."

"Thanks, Officer. For everything."

"All in a day's work," Farnsy said, smiling at the kid. Like the Chief always said, a good cop is one part cop, one part priest, one part psychologist, one part judge, and one part something else, but he never could remember what that thing was. Whatever it was, it added up to way more than 100 percent.

Word about Farnsy's community service idea spread fast on the gossip grapevine, and by the next morning it had reached Waltz's Soda Fountain. Chief was concerned it might start a new trend, but when he told the town manager about it, he liked it too, so the Chief liked it even more. And according to the folks who worked with that new Hannaford manager from away, he continued to learn some important lessons from the Mainers he supervised. By Thanksgiving, young Freddie was bumped up to part-time bagger on Sundays and holidays.

The Pet Lobster

When the director of the Skidompha Public Library invited Farnsy to come in and read *Police Officers on Patrol* to the little ones during preschool story time a year ago, his performance had been a big hit. After the *Lincoln County News* ran a photo of Farnsy in uniform with the kids, word spread, so this fall, the principal over at Great Salt Bay asked Farnsy if he'd come over on their September Career Day to talk with the first-graders about his life as a police officer. In uniform, too, she asked.

In his new Look Back–Look Ahead team-building meeting just before Labor Day, the Chief had told the team that they were trying this sort of personal outreach down in Portland, getting out into the community more, and the early reports were that it seemed to be working.

"Gotta nip things in the bud," Chief said. "You plant your tomatoes in a row, and they'll grow up straight as a bean."

Farnsy thought the only tomatoes he'd ever seen in a garden grew up kind of helter-skelter, and he knew string beans never grew straight. But when Miss Creeden, the new first-grade teacher over at Great Salt Bay, called the station to confirm his visit, he thought she sounded nice. Besides, Farnsy thought it sounded like a lot more fun reading a story and handing out police stickers to first-grade kids than Chief's other option, trying to convince high school kids to say "NO!" to pretty much everything most of them either wanted to do or had already tried.

FALL — *The Pet Lobster*

When Career Day rolled around middle of September, summer was already a distant memory to students and teachers, and both needed a little R & R before Pumpkinfest and the long slog to Thanksgiving. That was how Farnsy had found himself that morning thinking about Miss Creeden as he'd tried to tuck himself into his uniform, hoping the buttons on his tunic would stay put at least until he'd finished the Pledge of Allegiance. Henry looked skeptical.

One of the girls led the class in the Pledge of Allegiance, and after the students had taken their seats and cleared their desktops, all the paper rustling, chair scraping, and whispers ceased. All eyes were on Miss Creeden, who Farnsy thought looked like a bottle of softness poured into a dress. She waited patiently in front of the class for the kids to settle down, her arms folded, with a serene smile. Then she introduced Farnsy, who was surprised how much she had found out about him, including the story he'd told the year before in the library about his pet lobster. How she'd heard about that, he never did find out. Like Doc told him, some women are mysterious; most men, not so much.

After she'd warmed up her students, Miss Creeden welcomed Farnsy to come up to the front of the classroom, and he did so to considerable applause, which the kids had probably practiced. Not that they needed much. Farnsy knew from his sister Gracie's children that kids that age just like to make a lot of noise. Miss Creeden took a seat on a small chair in the back of the classroom near the coatroom. Farnsy looked out over the sea of bright, smiling faces and thought he recognized a couple of them. One boy for sure had Tib Tibbett's nose. Farnsy could smell freshly sharpened pencils. One of Miss Creeden's bulletin boards had happy letters in different colors spelling out her theme that year, Readers Are Leaders! The other bulletin board was quilted with her kids' art projects. Silhouettes of lobsters, all shapes and sizes and colors.

One had three claws, but most were fairly accurate, speckled dark green, with long antennae. A few of these kids obviously had a lobsterman in the family. And every kid in Maine knows that the red lobster on the Maine auto license is a cooked lobster.

Start at the beginning, Farnsy thought, so he told the kids about the police academy and the tests that officers have to pass before they can put on the uniform and the firearms proficiency training every officer had to undergo twice a year after the academy. He told them he was a patrol officer but hoped someday to become a sergeant. Then he told the kids how he'd bumped into the Chief at Pumpkinfest a few years earlier and Chief had asked him if he'd be interested in joining the force.

Farnsy was about to show and tell the kids about all the gear and stuff he was wearing around his waist when one kid in the back raised his hand and said, "Farns...Officer Farnsworth, that's all interesting and stuff, you know, but we want to hear the story about your pet lobster!" The class erupted. The kids clapped and cheered and whooped, and the bigger boys in the back stomped. The first question grownups asked Farnsy was if he'd ever used his gun, which only meant they wanted to know if he'd ever shot anyone like in the movies. But all these kids wanted to hear about was his pet lobster.

Farnsy glanced at Miss Creeden for a little help. It was pretty clear her students had zero interest in how police apprehended criminals and kept Damariscotta safe.

"All right, class, and thank you, Miles, very much for your suggestion." She thought a moment, then said, pointing to the art on the bulletin board, "Well, we are studying creatures living in the Damariscotta River this month, and the lobster is one of them, so why not? I mean, if Officer Farnsworth is willing?"

The kids hurrahed—"YAAY!"—and then commenced chanting, "LOB-STER! LOB-STER!" at which point Farnsy grinned at

Miss Creeden. As she'd told him over the phone, these kids were still pretty good at turning off their TV minds and listening to a good story.

Farnsy gave in to the rising tide of public opinion and forgot momentarily all about Miss Creeden sitting there in the back of the room, lest his other thoughts get in the way, and he started telling the story about when he was around their age a long time ago and he was down on the Damariscotta River, only it wasn't a river. Folks just called it a river.

"Actually," he said, "it's what they call an estuary, which is an arm of the sea, with seals, and fish, and oysters and barnacles and lobsters, too, right alongside all the other animals, sort of like a big seafood stew." He thought maybe he'd ask Miss Creeden to share a seafood pie over at Eider's sometime.

"So I had a hook in the water," he continued, "mighta been a worm on the end, I forget, but anyway, I sat there for some time, probably an hour, just thinking, probably about my homework…"

The kids groaned.

"…when all'va sudden like, there's this wicked hard tug on my line."

Farnsy gestured and mimed a big bend in his fishing rod. Then he remembered that all the fishing gear he'd really had back then was a weighted hand line and a little wooden contraption his uncle'd made that he had to crank, like something at the end of a kite string, but the story sounded better with a nice silver reel and a bendy rod, so he left it that way in their minds. "Anyway," he proceeded, "I finally got that fish up close to shore, reeled it in… only I saw that it weren't a fish—"

"Wasn't a fish," Miss Creeden piped up from the back of the room, ever the teacher, and Farnsy knew it wouldn't work—a seafood pot pie date with Miss Creeden would probably come with a grammar lesson—so he soldiered on with his story. "Only it wasn't a fish, 'twas a gigantic lobster. Must've been a good 35 to 40 pounds."

The kids oohed.

"Maybe more. Well, you can imagine my surprise. That lobster was about as long as I was tall. Maybe you kids've seen that big old 50-pound lobster hanging on the wall over at the Pemaquid Fishermen's Museum? So anyway, this lobster just walks right up onto shore, like a dog coming out of the water, big crusher claw about the size of a catcher's mitt, and he stops and he looks up at me, his two antennae twitching away, and says, 'Your name Farnsy?' Just like that, clear as a bell, like we were old pals, you know?"

A kid in the back of the classroom muttered, "No way!"

"Well, I don't know what you'd do, but I backed up a bit, and just before I was about to take off running, the lobster says, 'My name's Lou.' Well, it took some time that morning before I got near enough to Lou so I could remove that fish hook. But he stood there just like a tired old dog got caught up with a porcupine and let me do it. Didn't say a word. When I got done, we commenced talking and talk we did, most of the rest of the morning. I shared my lunch with him. Learned a lot about what it was like, life on the bottom of the ocean, watching big schools of alewives head upriver come high tide every spring, or seeing some of his lobster buddies crawl into a few lobster traps to nibble on some bait, and then getting hauled up into some old boat never to be seen again, or talking with the oysters, who took a while to come out of their shells, but like Lou said, they had a fine sense of humor. The clams weren't as happy as folks said they were."

He could see Miss Creeden giggling, one hand over her mouth. Maybe that seafood pie at Eider's could work, after all.

"Anyway, like I said, Lou was a pretty nice fella, so we agreed to meet every Saturday about that same time. High tide was best, Lou said. I just had to call out 'Lou-Lou, come in Lou!' and after a while he'd come crawling out of the water, like he promised, his big old antennae ranging around, on the lookout for big people or dogs or eagles, things that might swoop in and grab him. Old Lou seemed to live in a world of fears, and these little talks we had were a quiet time when he felt safe, so I guess you could say we made friends. Truth is, he was one of my best friends. So it wasn't long before I asked him if he wanted to go to school with me."

"You mean, walk? Like a dog? On a leash?" Lou asked me.

"I say, okay, it's only a mile, but I can take you in my knapsack."

"Just wrap me up in a towel—get it good and wet first with some seawater."

"So I took Lou to school on the big yellow bus, probably the same one all you kids ride in, and he sat way in the back of the classroom with me. I don't think anyone heard him, but he was whispering me the answers to all those math problems, he was that smart. So when my teacher asked if anyone knew what animals lived in the river, well, Lou fed me a critter list so long that my teacher said I knew so much about the river that I must live in it. And that's when Lou shouted, 'Hell, yes!' Which surprised me, but later he told me he learned that word from the first fella who trapped him, and Lou had to talk his way out of that trap. But that's another story."

About then, Miss Creeden pointed to her watch. Farnsy sighed. "Well, kids, I took Lou to school with me a couple more times. And it wasn't much later that I took him back to the river and sort of lost touch with him. He sure taught me a whole lot, and I think he may have had something to do with the lousy lobster haul in that part of the river these past few years, telling all the lobsters there what I'd told him about what folks above water do after his friends wander into those traps, and the place where most of them end up. Meaning in a kettle of boiling seawater. You see, I had to tell him what happens after they leave the river. Took Lou a good while to believe me."

FARNSY

Farnsy could see he was starting to lose some of his audience, so he sped things up and jumped right to the last chapter. "Last time I saw Lou, he told me, 'Look, Farnsy, I've gotta go out a bit deeper downriver and offshore this winter, and I may stay out there a few years, but after the summer people've gone back to wherever, you'll know when, just holler out my name and give me some time, and I'll come back and we'll catch up.' Now the very last thing he told me…"—and hearing this, Miss Creeden flashed that smile of hers—"…was that I should read a lot of books and study hard…"

Hearing Farnsy's obvious propaganda again, the kids groaned in united chorus.

Farnsy wrapped up the story, telling the kids that was the last time anyone had ever heard Lou's voice. "I just hope he didn't end up in a lobster tank somewhere," Farnsy said. "But then, I think Lou could probably talk his way out of anything. He was wicked smart that lobster was."

And every last one of those school kids, first thing that afternoon, soon's they got home, told anyone who'd listen about Farnsy's pet lobster, Lou. One girl's father, a lobsterman, said he wanted whatever Farnsy was smoking. A couple of the boys and girls snuck down to the riverbank and tried their best to call Lou, until it got dark and they had to go home for supper.

The Surprise

Jock called Farnsy from the reservation desk at King Eider's Pub just after five. Farnsy heard the usual bar chatter in the background, indistinguishable spirited voices and the clank and clatter of glasses and plates. The front door slamming. People coming and going. Farnsy could almost smell the beer and juicy burgers and pictured Jock looking down at the old reservation book—circles for the round tables in the center and squares for the booths around two walls—colored red or green for the two regular servers.

Farnsy knew that book because he'd peeked in it when he met Lucy there last fall to celebrate her divorce from Earl. It was a blur of names, in pencil and pen, some crossed out. Some reservations were accompanied by margin notes: "A REGULAR, NICE," or "LOUSY TIPPER." Someone had penciled "LOVEBUGS!" on the square for his favorite corner booth. After dinner, Lucy had suggested they drive back to his cottage...for dessert, she'd told him.

Jock told Farnsy there was a line of folks trying to get in to hear that night's singer and the line went out the door and around the corner, past their big sign on the side. Farnsy knew that sign well. "Home of New Englands Finest Crabcakes," it boasted. Jock had once done a citizen's arrest of the head of the English Department at the Lincoln Academy when he'd caught her just as she was trying to add a possessive apostrophe with a big red marker. Farnsy'd had to stop by and square things away. Jock said he told her if she wanted to get that sign repainted, she could. Her expense. Up to now, he told her, he'd never had any complaints. Which meant none of her former students had ever spotted the missing apostrophe, he added, and he was sure they'd all seen that sign more than once.

"Line's that long?" Farnsy asked. "Jeez, Jock, what do you want me to do about this? Sounds pretty good to me, business hopping, shoulder season and all, you know. And if those folks are behaving themselves, I don't think there's much I can do."

"Farnsy, you need to get your butt over here. That's all I'm sayin'." Farnsy heard the door at Eider's slam again. "Gotta go, Farns. I'm gonna hang up now." The line went dead. Farnsy wondered if any of the young kids nowadays wondered why older folks said they were hanging up the phone. Now you just folded it shut. Or tapped a button. He still remembered actually hanging a phone back up on the wall. Back when kitchen telephone cords were always long, curly, and tangled up.

Farnsy thought about it a moment. It wasn't unusual on Thursday nights for folks to start the weekend a day or two early after the summer people left. But Jock sounded real serious, so he figured he'd better get over there, at least check up on things. A friend's a friend. Besides, it was Farnsy's birthday, the big one he'd been dreading and trying to forget, even after Doc reassured him the week before, telling Farnsy he was twice that age and still had gas in his tank. But no one seemed to have remembered this was the day. No funny "Old as Dirt!" birthday cards at work. No cake, no pie. Not even a free birthday donut at Waltz's that morning. Doc was scribbling away as usual, and everyone else had their noses buried in the *Lincoln County News*. And nothing in his mailbox in town.

All Farnsy could think about now was, here he was, the same age as his father, Jack, when he'd been married for years and had two kids. And what did Farnsy have? Henry? A cat? And Lucy,

FALL — *The Surprise*

his now-and-then girlfriend, who wasn't really a girlfriend, not anymore, so maybe she was just a friend. He couldn't define it and, besides, she was over in Augusta, living in a friend's place.

And what if something happened to him out at the lake, who would know? Would anyone care? Chief'd have half a dozen qualified applicants for the opening in a week, easy. Okay, his sister Grace might care. And her kids. Her kids for sure. And probably Henry. His father was somewhere out west, Farnsy knew. One postcard said he thought he might go visit Gracie. But she'd never heard anything about a visit. Still trying to shake off his dark clouds was what their father had written.

So if that's what comes of love, all that sadness after years of marriage, even if most of them were happy years, then maybe marriage wasn't for him. Thirty-five is half of 70. And what had he accomplished? Here he was, still on patrol, still daydreaming about making a mark, doing something noteworthy before he was 40. Stuck in the same town where he grew up. From where he was just then, at 35, it certainly didn't look like a wide-open sunny field of boundless opportunities, all ripe for the plucking. Nope, here he was, sitting in his musty cruiser in a uniform that was starting to tighten around his middle, donut powder dusting his chest, all alone on his 35th birthday, as the sands of time started to speed up like they were slipping down through an old sieve. He was on the outbound tide, headed downriver toward an island of loneliness.

Farnsy pulled out of his favorite speed trap next to the bank some 500 or so feet away, his lights flashing, no siren, happy to be doing something, anything, to get out of his funk, but when he pulled in front of the pub, he was confused: no line. What gives? he thought.

When he opened the door to Eider's, he was met by the warm, mouthwatering smells of steaming seafood and cold beer. And darkness. No music. What the hay? He squinted in the dim light and spotted Jock standing behind the bar with Nina, the summer mixologist, who'd come up from Boston to help Jock around the Fourth and stayed on to wait tables. There were a few rumors flying around town late summer speculating why Nina was still there, but she'd proved herself and become part of the scene, as if she'd always been there, or should've been. She was still from away, but in her case, it didn't seem like so far away. And Nina was the one, when Farnsy and Nedda Barnes had come in and slid into the corner booth in August, who gave Farnsy a wink as if to say, "Nice catch!" She and Nedda had even exchanged a few "female pleasantries," which Doc told Farnsy was a linguistic code that women shared and which only a few men had ever cracked. Like the Enigma project in the war, Doc explained.

"What's this?" Farnsy spat out, confused by the darkness and the quiet rustle just out of sight inside the darkened pub. Power out? he wondered.

"HAPPY BIRTHDAY, FARNSY!! SUR-PRISE!!" a chorus of voices shouted as the lights popped on, bright as the light out at Pemaquid, and the packed room was suddenly lit up with faces from all around town. Farnsy glanced around the room. Looked like everyone was there.

Jock handed Farnsy a frosty can of his favorite brew, PBR, and everyone raised a glass as Jock crowed, "A toast to Farnsy, everyone!" Farnsy looked over at the Chief, who was in the second row, next to Doc, and pointed to his uniform as if to ask, "Okay if I drink in uniform?" The Chief pointed to his own uniform, as if to say, "Exception to every rule." And the Chief tipped his drink Farnsy's way, then said, "Thirty-five? Like the skier said, it's all downhill from here."

Someone shouted, "Old fart!" then "Geezer!"

Doc stepped forward and said he'd heard enough about the aged and started to tell the story about Farnsy's first day on the job,

FALL — *The Surprise*

when someone cut him off and said, "Heard it a thousand times, Doc!" To which Doc said, "Some folks just need reminding, is all."

Farnsy waded into the gathered crowd, chatting with this person and that. Folks he'd given a ticket or a warning, didn't matter. Freddie Hallbert, aka the CLYNK kid, was there, too, smiling, with his mom, and sipping a soda, of course. Even Jim Noonan, the Hannaford manager who'd wanted to have Freddie arrested, was there. They were telling Farnsy stories, chatting and laughing. And the room was heating up. It was the closest thing Farnsy'd ever had to a family reunion. Except his little sister Grace and her kids were out in California. His father, Jack, was somewhere. And Lucy was in Augusta.

Jock and Nina waded around the crowd with plates of scallops wrapped in bacon, fresh oysters, and little squares of tuna sushi. One after the other, the kitchen doors swung open and something new would emerge and by the time they got to the other side of the room, the platters were cleaned. There was a second round and by the time folks were starting on a third, the lights dimmed, there was a pause in the conversation and the kitchen doors burst open and Jock and Nina came out with a huge cake shaped like a police cruiser, black, with red-colored icing on the roof for the light bar, and silver icing on the side that looked like a genuine Damariscotta police vehicle. The lettering on top said, "HAPPY BIRTHDAY FARNSY!" and there were 35 candles, with one extra for good measure, blazing away as the crowd sang, "Happy Birthday, dear Farnsy, Happy Birthday to you!" Jock and Nina placed the cake on the bar so that Farnsy could blow out the dripping candles. Before Nina cut the cake, someone from the *Lincoln County News* took a photo of Farnsy standing next to it, trying to smile but still feeling caught off guard by how fast he'd hit 35.

Jock made great theater of presenting Farnsy with a special mug he'd commissioned from Edgecomb Pottery for the occasion.

FARNSY

Farnsy's name was on one side and a special glazed ceramic police badge on the other. After Farnsy thanked Jock, Jock reached up with a boat hook and added the new mug to the hundred or so others hanging from hooks along the ceiling beams, each one for a regular customer, most of them still alive.

Farnsy was about to get all sorry for himself, thinking they were right, he was halfway to 70 and what did he have to show for it, when Bruce, the postmaster, handed him an envelope. "Came in late this afternoon, Farnsy, special delivery. Thought you might want to see it."

"Thanks, Bruce," Farnsy said, almost whispering, "appreciate it." Lucy's handwriting was unmistakable. The return address wasn't Augusta. It was Lucy's mother's place in Bristol. As happy chatter filled Eider's, Katie Duggan plugged in her guitar and struck up a joyful cover of the Beatles' song "You Say It's Your Birthday!" and the crowd sang along. The party had started.

Out in the cruiser, after the party, Farnsy leaned back with a smile on his face. Sitting on the passenger seat next to him was a small pile of knickknacks and doodads—gifts that he'd unwrapped: a whole box of 24 classic Necco wafer rolls, a booklet of Dunkin' Donuts coupons, and an old handbook on antique fishing lures.

Farnsy stared at the envelope from Lucy a good long time before he opened it up. She said she wished she could've been there, but with his birthday coming right around the first anniversary of her divorce, well, it was too much. You don't just stop loving someone you once loved just because you don't love them anymore, she wrote. Which made no damn sense to Farnsy. Especially because she signed it, "And I still love you, Officer Farnsworth."

Looked like fresh car tracks going down the road toward the cottage, so Farnsy drove slower than usual, not knowing what

FALL — *The Surprise*

might be waiting for him at the bottom of the hill. Thought ran through his mind it might be the Necco guy. Catch him red-handed. But then he turned the last corner and saw Lucy's car sitting there next to the cottage. And Henry sitting in a window, looking back at Farnsy. The outside light was on.

Stepping inside, Farnsy heard her voice come from the back of the cottage and he followed it all the way down the dark hall.

"That you, Officer?"

"You the famous Necco burglar I'm after? I may have to put you under arrest."

"Handcuff me, Officer. I could be dangerous."

"Danger's my game."

He nudged the bedroom door open, half expecting her to jump out from somewhere. But there she was. In her birthday suit.

"Sorry. I couldn't make it to Eider's, Farnsy. By the time I decided, I was late leaving work in Augusta, and you know the traffic on the Augusta road. So I thought I'd bring you this, Special Delivery." She swept one hand across a thick eiderdown comforter that draped across his bed and hung down the sides like melted vanilla ice cream. "Thought you could use something else to keep you warm this winter, Farns."

The Lure

Farnsy sat on the red vinyl swivel seat nearest the donut display at Waltz's Soda Fountain that Monday morning, flipping through last Thursday's copy of *Uncle Henry's Weekly Swap it or Sell It Guide*, thinking he might spot some old lures for sale, maybe get an idea of what they're worth in trade and, if he were lucky enough, maybe pick up the trail of the perpetrator behind the break-ins. He was reading with one eye and listening with the other, like the Chief had said once, and happened to pick up a rumor just as it was about to get launched.

Doc was sitting two seats away and must've thought no one could hear him, but Doc's hearing wasn't what it once was, if it ever was, so his voice was clear as thunder all along the soda fountain as he read from one of his old journals.

"It appears," he tried to whisper to Julie, "that a woman doing some end-of-season cottage cleaning out on Damariscotta Lake told her neighbor, who told a good friend of one of my former patients, who told me she heard there was some funny business going on out there in one of the cottages. Way she tells it, she saw someone driving up the lake road, fast, just as she was driving in. Fancy black car, she said. Out of state plates. Fella driving didn't wave. Then, right when she pulls in behind the house, the one she's going to clean, she spots someone slipping out the back of the cottage next door, strolling down to the little wharf, and getting onto a jet ski, just as calm as you please. Skinny fella. Long hair. 'Coulda been a woman,' she said, 'not sure. And might've had a knapsack or maybe it was a canvas

FALL — *The Lure*

bag.' She watched the jet ski disappear up the lake, headed north. Didn't think much about it until she thought more about it. She would've let it all go if she'd thought it was just a little afternoon delight. Those things happened now and then out in those cottages. But when she found that roll of Neccos in the kitchen where she was starting to clean up, well, she thought for sure something fishy was going on out there."

Doc read this from the notebook where he kept the town's history, day by day. He stopped reading when the Professor appeared suddenly behind him and took a seat between Doc and Farnsy. Julie set a black coffee in front of the Professor, full to the brim and wicked hot, the way she liked it. Then, before he could say good morning, Farnsy spotted a couple lines in *Uncle Henry's*.

"WANTED! Old fishing lures. All styles. Any condition. No replicas."

Then, as if to prove Einstein's quantum theory of relativity and synchronicity, which is what the Professor called it later on after Farnsy left for work, the Professor slid a small, framed box down the countertop in Farnsy's direction. She smiled.

"Thought you might want this back."

It was the framed lure from the wall in the work shed behind Farnsy's cottage. Sitting inside, behind the glass, was his father's old vintage Jitterbug, rattling around loose but otherwise intact. Farnsy held the box with the lure in both hands and had a look at the little white shape with small black beady eyes and a curved metal scoop where the baitfish's mouth would be. Farnsy could picture it wiggling through a tangle of lilies in their cove, looking like a little fish in trouble: just what any lurking large-mouth bass or a pickerel would love to strike. Easy prey and a quick meal. The two clusters of three barbed hooks dangling off the lure were guaranteed to keep any fish that took the bait hooked good until it ran out of gas struggling to shake off the hooks. No two ways about it: it was the same original Fred Arbogast Jitterbug, made in Ohio, that had belonged to Farnsy's old man. Same frame. And his mother's funny inscription. The same dings and slightly rusted hooks, so Farnsy had no doubts this was the same lure his father had once, years ago, tried to cast out past the lily pads, only to end up wrapping it around a branch way up in an old oak at their edge of the cove, along with a tangle of leader and a few yards of new fishing line. There it dangled, taunting his father, until one day Farnsy's old man got so tired of the jokes he borrowed a neighbor's ladder, snagged the lure somehow with an old rake, and yanked it down.

Farnsy knew his old man well enough to know how much it must've gnawed at him to see that pricey lure and all that good line tangled around that branch up there. He guessed his father must've launched a volley of swears as soon as it landed up there, and he imagined his old man's shouts echoing all around the cove. Anyway, years later, after Jack had cut the lure down, his mother took it into town, got it framed, and had a little brass plate inscribed that read: "Jack Farnsworth, age 25, caught a live oak with this Jitterbug in 1980." She gave it to him on opening day of fishing season, about six months before Farnsy was born. And it hung there for years on the wall above his father's workbench in the shed out at the lake. Until the Necco burglar nicked it.

Farnsy stared at it in disbelief. "Where the devil'd you find this, Professor?"

"Well," the Professor explained to everyone still sitting at Waltz's Soda Fountain that morning, "you told us you were missing a fishing lure, Farnsy. I remember you saying it was in a little box, something about an old 'Jigglebug' I thought you said, only now I know it's a 'Jitterbug.'"

She took a sip of coffee.

"If you're curious as to how I came by it, well, I was just poking around over at the Montsweag Flea Market last Saturday, like I do pretty much every Saturday, but there was nothing much to look at, it being past prime tourist season, so I thought I'd stop at that place up north on Route 1, you know, the one that just says "Stuff" outside. I was headed up to Moody's for lunch, anyway. So that's where I found it, sitting out there on a table in the back room, the one with all the old tonic bottles."

"You ask the fella how he came by it?" Farnsy asked.

"Sure. 'New acquisition' was all he said," she sniffed, "'acquisition,' yeah, like it was from one of those hoity-toity Boston galleries or something. So I gave him one of the two-spots I keep for tipping and he snatched it faster than a frog grabs a fly."

"When was this, Professor?"

"Just this last weekend."

"You happen to ask the man to describe the fellow who sold it to him?"

"I did. Said he was pushing 60."

"That's it?"

"No, had a three-day beard."

"That all?"

"Yes, except he said the man wasn't much of a hard bargainer."

"Not much to go on, Professor," Farnsy said.

"Like I was saying, I paid two dollars for it, Farnsworth. Crisp $2 bill."

"Oh, sure, right," Farnsy said as he came out of his reverie and fished two singles out of his wallet. "And let me get your coffee, Professor, adding another dollar. That make us square?"

"It does if you include that last chocolate donut," Professor said, pointing with her spoon down to the glass dome next to the register at the end of the counter.

Julie fetched the donut with a napkin and put it in front of the Professor. "On the house, Professor. In honor of this special occasion. Besides, it's been there a day or two."

FARNSY

"Perfect. Just the way I like a donut," the Professor said, "crusty! Like Doc." She broke the donut in half and dipped one end into her coffee.

"Thanks, Professor. Might just make you a deputy detective."

"Town can't afford me, Farnsy."

After his shift, Farnsy checked in back at the station and wrote up some notes, including the news of the stolen property the Professor had found and the circumstances. Then he drove his pickup out to the Stuff place before it closed to see what he could sniff out, but, like the Professor said, the big man wasn't very helpful. Not because he wasn't willing, but his memory, the way he put it to Farnsy, tapping his head, wasn't getting backed up so much anymore.

Most of the stuff he just picked up at local yard sales or estate sales, he explained. "Sort of recycling for profit," he said. "Wasn't like the good old days," he said, when he'd drive up to Millinocket or over to Jackman or the Rangeley lakes, looking for specials and rarities, the price of gas being what it was and besides, he was just slowing down. Almost sounded like he was making Farnsy an offer to buy the place.

But as soon as Farnsy showed him the lure in the box, the old man stopped short. "Now that one I remember," he said. "Just came in. Then some old gal dickers me down and drives off with it. Hard bargainer she was. Wasn't on the shelf long, that's for sure. So, how'd you come by it? You know her?"

"Yes. Good friend. Knows I like old lures. But you want to tell me how you got it?"

"Sure, last week or week before. Might've been after Labor Day. You know, things had started quieting down. Fella stops by here with a shoebox full of fishing lures, old ones, missing hooks and all dinged up. I can see all's they need's a little paint and I can get a buck for each one of them, maybe a dozen of them in that box, so I offer him five bucks."

Farnsy let him talk. No sense trying to dam up a flowing river.

"'Jesus, mister,' he says, 'they're worth at least five dollars each, every last one of them.'"

"'Maybe when they were new they were,' I says. So he goes back to his car and says, 'Look here, I'll toss in this one someone framed if you give me a 20 for the whole lot.' Well, I give it a good look-see and think maybe that frame is worth five by itself. So I say, '18,' and he says something nasty about dickering with a Mainer, and hands it over and I give him a 10-spot and four two-dollar bills I won in cribbage."

"You describe this man?"

"55 maybe 60. Bald as a baby's butt."

Farnsy knew that most eyewitness accounts were as trustworthy as a carnival huckster, so he took it all with a grain of salt, but he was starting to get a picture. He asked the man what kind of car the fella was driving, and did he happen to see the license plate?

"Oh, that's easy, he was a Masshole. Car was fancy, black, a Lexus I think, but had some rust. But I mean, what car hasn't got a little rust, you know? Even if winters aren't what they used to be."

Farnsy figured that description would fit most cars in New England. But he had a pretty good hunch that the Lexus man was the same person he'd ticketed in September.

Farnsy drove back to his cottage and hung his father's Jitterbug on the kitchen wall where he could keep an eye on it. Maybe the puzzle pieces were starting to fit into place, but the mystery remained: Who stole these fishing lures? Who was the Necco burglar? And what was the connection? If there was one.

Back Burner

For a while, the Necco wafer mystery went dormant, no new leads. Farnsy and the Chief hadn't discussed the case since they'd tried to find a pattern in the maps Farnsy had marked up, but Farnsy was still working it over in his head like a good stew on a back burner. He'd stopped chasing down more clues. He had plenty of clues, but what he didn't have was the connection—and he knew there had to be one, some red thread that would connect all those rolls of Neccos, the jet skier, who seemed to be casing old cottages first one lake then another, from Biscay to Pemaquid to Damariscotta, asking oddball questions, the missing fishing-tackle boxes, his father's lure.

He tried time and again to visualize the connection. Get into the mind of whoever was behind this. He still couldn't figure out how the jet skier managed to get in those cottages undetected after the cleaning crews had finished up last fall. No reports of any jet skis on those lakes after Labor Day. So if they didn't break into those cottages late fall, when things were quiet, then when? He'd heard no reports of cars or tire tracks on any of the fire roads down to the empty cottages last fall or spring. He certainly hadn't seen any on his road. And there were no jet skis on any lakes until Memorial Day at the earliest, and then the cottages would be opening up and getting ready for renters. So whatever happened had to have happened between early October and late April. That was over half a year. The Lincoln County Sheriff's Office had no reports of any unusual activity last winter. If Necco man was active in winter, it was either by car, which Farnsy'd pretty much ruled out, or hiking in on foot, which made no sense. Too slow. Too cold. Maybe he was on skis, cross-country skis? Snowshoes? Same thing: too slow and too cold. He had a long-shot, hail Mary hunch, but he decided to talk to the game warden, who'd called him late summer.

"Bob, it's me, Farnsy. Thanks for picking up. I know you're busy now, it being hunting season and all."

"No prob, Farns. What's up?"

"Well, you remember that incident with the jet skier speeding out on Damariscotta Lake?"

"How could I forget? You want to see that report?"

"Thanks, but no. Here's my question: you work the lake, Damariscotta I mean, in winter, right?"

"That'd be affirmative."

"Well, you ever see any hikers out on the lake there? Or any cross-country skiers?"

"No hikers. Snowshoers maybe. Why?"

"I'm trying to figure out when these break-ins happened. You ever have any run-ins with snowmobilers?"

"Now and then. Hey, wait a second, I ticketed a couple of ice fishermen over the limit last year. They had snowmobiles. Why?"

"Anything else?"

"Well, come to think of it, I had to ticket one fellow for an OUI. Three times over the limit. I'm surprised he could even find his way out to that ice fishing shack of his. Had to strap him onto the back of my sled and tow his machine off the ice. Nice guy, apologized after we got him sobered up. Guess that's why some folks call it 'ice drinking.'"

"That it? You see or hear anything else out there last winter?"

"Well, now, come to think of it, I remember the fella I ticketed said he'd seen some snowmobiler racing up the lake, all the way to the narrows, before he disappeared into that cove east of that kids' summer camp. You know the one, right?"

"Sure do. Not far from my place. When was this? You remember?"

"Well, ice fishing season doesn't start until New Year's Day, and if memory serves, the ice on Damariscotta doesn't freeze up good until late January. You know, you need a good eight inches of ice before it's safe for jet skis. Course, not everyone checks first. Way it usually works is one guy sets up a fishing shack then everyone else figures the ice is good and there's gotta be some fish biting over there. You see one shack go up in the morning and pretty soon you got half a dozen. Every one of them drilling holes and setting up their shack and a little folding chair, putting a shiner on a hook and sitting there, can of beer in one hand, or a thermos of Allen's Brandy, just waiting for the red flag to pop up, hoping it's a nice brown trout. God, they taste good cooked up, squirt of lemon on top. What was your question? Oh, I'd guess if someone was casing those cottages in the summer, and the break-ins happened in the winter, then it had to be sometime between late January and late February, maybe early March. But late March is generally ice-out at Damariscotta. So that's your window of opportunity, there, Farnsy."

Farnsy thanked the warden and asked him to stay in touch, keep his eyes out for anything suspicious, and let him know. For Farnsy, this had become like four-dimensional chess: he had his network of law enforcement, the state boys, the county office, his town team; then he had his local network. Farnsy was starting to think of detective work as a sort of garden drip-hose, so he left little hints and favors here and there all around town to let the word get out. If the perpetrator or perpetrators were local, then maybe they'd get the message and stop the burglaries. He'd nab them eventually, but the main point was to stop crimes before they happened. And if the perps were from away, then Farnsy had his network of eyes and ears alerted. Like a Venus flytrap waiting to snap shut.

"Real police work," the Chief confided to Farnsy when they were staring at the maps again back in the station, "real police work isn't just cops in uniform, Farnsy. Public safety depends on all these little connections we have in the community. That's why we get out there and fly the colors."

Chief continued, "I mean like prairie dogs. All of them eyes out for danger and barking when it's bad, you know?"

"Chief, I been thinking."

"Good Farnsy, that's a good thing."

"You remember that game warden I spoke with last summer? About the jet skiers?"

"Sorry, no. Wait, yeah, said he ticketed a guy without a fishing license, something like that."

"Same guy."

"And?"

"I called him earlier today. Thought maybe he might've remembered seeing something out on the lake last winter, since that's pretty much the only time these break-ins could've happened without someone spotting him. Or them."

"You thinking what I'm thinking?"

"What? Some new moose jerky recipe?"

"Seriously. I'm thinking you need to stop beating around the bush."

"Okay, here's where I am now: snowmobiles."

"Snowmobiles?"

"That's gotta be it. They case cottages on jet skis in summer, check rentals, identify older cottages and anyone who does any serious fishing, you know, where the tackle boxes might be, where there's a Lund tied up. We know old lures are their target. Some of them, the rare ones, even some beaters, bring big bucks."

The Chief sat down across from Farnsy and listened. "And?"

"So, I think we need to be looking for someone on a snowmobile on Damariscotta Lake during ice fishing season when the ice is thick enough, when there are other ice fishermen out on the lake. That gives them a cover story."

"Last year was warm, so the lake iced up late, but it was thick enough to fish by late January, and those ice houses had to come off the ice by mid-March, latest, before ice-out. So we've got a window of maybe six weeks. Mid-January through February, maybe a scootch into March."

"Okay, Farnsy, we got time. That gives us this fall to poke around before things ice over. Maybe we'll get some more clues. But come New Year's, we better have a plan. You better have a plan. This is your case, Farnsworth. You broke it, you close it. We good?"

"We're good, Chief."

Pumpkinfest

Pumpkinfest excitement was growing in Damariscotta all week. This annual festival celebrates the giant sumo-sized first cousins of the smaller orange gourds that ripen on farms and fields all over Maine. Farmstand pumpkins for pies and Halloween carving you can carry under an arm or with two hands. The gargantuan pumpkins (*Cucurbita maxima*) that are the celebrated stars of the Pumpkinfest tip the scales at over 1,000 pounds and require a wooden pallet and a forklift.

The week started with the pumpkin weigh-in outside town. Then, on Thursday morning, trucks lumbered into town, transporting the winning pumpkins, spectacular gourds of all shapes, each one having been tended with care and watered all summer at nearby farms and gardens. These behemoths were reverently set down in front of every shop on Main Street and a few other shops and businesses around town. But the proud gourds on Main Street were the royalty, the obese nobility of Lincoln County's pumpkin patches.

And early the next day, Friday, artists of all ages appeared with paints and glitter and stick-on doodads and started to carve and decorate those super-sized vegetables. At day's end, the pumpkin in front of Fernald's Country Store had the most folks surrounding it, scrambling to get a picture on their phones to send somewhere. It looked like a Georgia moonshine still that was making Moxie. Sherman's had a giant gourd out front that appeared to be reading a book about the Pumpkin Patch Kids.

King Eider's had one carved to look like an oyster. Chief said it looked like that oyster'd been sitting out too long. The pumpkin outside the Fisherman's Catch Seafood Market was carved and painted to look like a fishing boat with a lobster named "Lou" trying to escape from a trap. The pumpkin outside Renys looked like a whoopie pie, "low-cal" painted on the label. Every storefront pumpkin had a small crowd of gawkers, ooh-ing and aah-ing and taking photos that went straight to Facebook or Instagram.

Everywhere you looked there was a pumpkin or something with a pumpkin. Kids raced soapbox derby-style wheeled pumpkins down a ramp or hunted for pumpkins like Easter eggs. Some folks sat down for the pumpkin pie eating contest and others ran in the five-mile Pumpkinfest footrace. Shops all over town sold pumpkin pancakes, pumpkin cupcakes, pumpkin paintings, pumpkin caps, and pumpkin T-shirts. Waltz's Soda Fountain served pumpkin-flavored coffee, which folks from away tried because they assumed it was a local tradition. Regulars weren't having any of it. Doc heard about the new menu item and muttered, "You might's well put a clam in it and call it New York style chowder." Like some locals, Doc and the Professor stayed out of town during Pumpkinfest.

They were the only sourpusses, though. Everyone else, shopkeepers, folks from all around and far away, babies in strollers, babies strapped to their moms or dads, little kids, teens, parents, tourists, leaf peepers, old-timers still able to get out and about, folks with walkers, folks in wheelchairs, folks with canes, and couples holding hands snaked through the crowded sidewalks, and the rest cruised through town in their cars and pickups as slowly as the sidewalk strollers walked to gape at the gigantic pumpkins outside every shop in town for all three of the blocks, or four, if you counted the Baptist Church up the hill, which had a different pumpkin Bible scene every year.

FALL — *Pumpkinfest*

The Yellowfront grocery couldn't keep enough Table Talk pumpkin pies, big or small, on the shelves. You'd have thought everyone in town was practicing for the pie-eating contest.

That Saturday afternoon was the Pumpkin Parade, which started up the hill around Lincoln Academy and proceeded at a walking pace downhill through Newcastle and across the Twin Villages bridge into Damariscotta, led by the Chief in his polished-up cruiser, the lights flashing and the Chief burping the siren every now and then or when a kid waved. Sidewalks were so crowded you had to wend your way through a brambled thicket of humanity and a cloud of smoke from grilled hamburgers and bratwurst just to get somewhere. The place was abuzz, and music was everywhere.

Dogs with little lobster hats, tattooed bikers, teenies, and BoSox fans in full regalia crowded past volunteers directing traffic and pedestrians munching on hot dogs, pizza, and kettle corn. Folks with apartments in town leaned out their windows and took it all in.

Folks who weren't seeing their first parade knew there were good places to sit or stand over near the library. And shortly after the Chief drove through town, music from the first band drum-rattled down Main Street, bagpipes squawking like an approaching Scottish army. Smiles and grateful applause broke out all along the route as the musicians passed.

The only incident that might've been worthy of note in the *Lincoln County News* came when Dottie radioed Farnsy about some college protesters outside the Fisherman's Catch, so he picked up his pace and headed over there, curious as to what these college kids were doing with their clipboards gathered on the sidewalk outside the fish store. Farnsy watched them from Fernald's across the street.

Jeez, he thought, how'd those girls pour themselves into those jeans? Something else, he thought. But nice. When one of the girls spotted him, Farnsy pretended to adjust his belt a little and strolled across the street. A girl with a blond bob bounced up to him, clipboard in hand.

"Hi, Officer, um, Farnsworth," she said, reading the name on his badge. "I'm Alice from Colby College, and here's my permit."

"Well, hello there, Alice from Colby. Nice to meet you. Don't mind my asking, what's this all about? I got a call—"

"Well, Officer, we're here trying to help the lobsters."

"Didn't know they needed any help, really."

Alice handed Farnsy her clipboard so he could read the petition. Her photo ID was clipped at the top. He recognized a few of the signatures. Professor must've signed it by mistake, because Farnsy knew she always went to the lobster bake over at the Lincoln Home. Maybe she forgot her reading glasses because there, at the bottom of the petition, Farnsy read:

"SAY 'NO' to BOILED LOBSTERS!

"SAY 'YES' to MERCIFUL LOBSTER CONSUMPTION!

"LOBSTERS HAVE FEELINGS, TOO!"

Alice watched closely as he read down the page, then jumped right in when he finished, a summer's worth of experience petitioning on behalf of lobsters under her belt. "I know what you're thinking, Officer Farnsworth. I know it sounds crazy, because that's what my folks told me." Thinking she'd trapped her audience, she started hauling up the pot. "My whole family's Mainers, some of them out west near Rangeley, a few down near Mexico and Rumford, a couple up the coast in Stockton Springs, some cousins up in the county, Fort Kent—Mainers, all of us, lobster lovers—but then, I took this bio class at Colby and the professor explained the nervous system of the lobster and how it feels pain, too, just like us. Lobsters have feelings, you know, for sure. So anyway, a few of us got together in the dorm that night and that's when we started this campaign to end the lobsters' pain."

"You don't say."

"Now look, we're not trying to close down the lobster industry. We're realists."

All evidence to the contrary, Farnsy thought to himself.

"You ever heard a lobster scratch and scramble soon's you put him in the pot? They've actually recorded little shrieks the lobsters make. All we want to do is to get restaurants to kill lobsters humanely before they dump 'em right into boiling water. Just use a kitchen knife to put them out of their misery before they're tortured."

Alice showed him a picture of someone she said was a "really famous chef" in Portland putting a big knife into the skull of a nice big two- or three-pounder. Farnsy didn't see any fear in that old lobster's face. Looked pretty resolute to him. Sort of like he was ready to go meet his maker. Probably tired of crawling around the ocean bottom in the dark, eating dead fish.

"Alice, I appreciate what you're sayin', but I don't think they suffer much. I mean, it's not as though they have a lot going on in that teensy little brain of theirs. You ever take a good look? You ask me, a lobster's brain is about the same size as the brains in some of those folks down in Washington." Farnsy tried for a laugh.

The girl reached over and deftly snatched the clipboard out of Farnsy's hands. She smiled, then said in a sweet voice that he'd just started to like hearing, "Well, if the tables were turned and a giant lobster opened your brain up after you'd been boiled, he might think yours was pretty small too. You know what they say, don't you? Small brain, small..."

With that, Alice spun around and crossed the street to meet up with another college kid, who was dressed up like a Maine lobster and standing there with a big sign in his crusher claw. The big lobster was red, which meant he'd been cooked. Except he looked pretty happy to see Alice coming.

"Just a couple of college kids collecting signatures. One of 'em in a Halloween costume," Farnsy told Dottie when he called in with an update. "A giant lobster invading town!"

Farnsy slipped away from the curb and joined the tide of humanity strolling down Main Street, stopping in clusters to gawk at the carved pumpkins.

On Sunday, in a field near the old Round Top Ice Cream stand, pumpkins the size of a man's head were catapulted by a huge Roman-style trebuchet, built just for this occasion, and launched in huge arcs, farther than you'd think any pumpkin could possibly fly, through the cider-cold air over a stubbled cornfield to explode in orange chunks on the opposite hill. But the highlight on Sunday was when a construction crane hoisted a pumpkin the size of a two-seater outhouse up higher than any pumpkin had ever been, and then, after the crowd shouted a slow countdown, dropped the pumpkin onto a beat-up car someone had donated.

One year, just before the last pumpkin drop, some guys pushed out an old junked-up police car. Locals, standing four rows deep, knew this was the finale. They started chanting, "Drop it! Drop it!" without any cue from the guy on the megaphone. When that last pumpkin finally reached the highest point under the tip of the crane, it dangled there just a bit longer while the dramatic tension built up. When the hook popped open, the pumpkin, suddenly freed, seemed to hesitate. Then it started dropping and the crowd's roar crescendoed as it hurtled toward the waiting police car. When all 1,000 pounds of the vegetable exploded on its roof, crushing the cruiser, thousands of pumpkin chunks and stringy seeds splattered the front rows of onlookers with an orange spray. The crowd cheered riotously. For some of them, it was sweet revenge for every ticket they'd ever been handed.

FALL — *Pumpkinfest*

Farnsy's favorite event was the grand finale—the Pumpkin Regatta that took place at noon on Monday, when, at high tide, the announcer leaned into a microphone and started the first race. "Ready! Set! Get wet!" And the first small fleet of colossal hollowed-out gourds wobbled around Damariscotta's harbor, piloted by lunatic captains dressed as princesses or gnomes or bearded Vikings. With kayak paddles or tiny engines, they raced those huge, tippy pumpkins out and around a buoy, cheered on by thousands of spectators who wished them well but secretly hoped that one or two of them might take on water and disgorge the pilot, safely of course, before sinking unceremoniously.

As the pumpkins left the dock, in race after race, folks along the harbor squeezed shoulder to shoulder for a glimpse of the little fleet, plowing through the water as only a pumpkin big enough to hold a human being can, barely making headway toward the buoy, then around it. Each race was a new spectacle and was cheered on by thousands of spectators around the harbor and on boats anchored nearby. If one of the giant pumpkins started to wobble, then tilted and took on water, one of the fellows from the fire department who was in a wet suit would swim over as the paddler scrambled out to safety and the gourd sank, and there was more applause.

At the end of that happy pumpkin week, a few hours after the pumpkin Regatta, Farnsy had cleanup duty, walking the afternoon beat, up and down town, a big figure-8 loop that would take him just about an hour if he allowed time to stop to chat with everyone he knew or to answer a tourist's questions. Farnsy loved his little town, which he didn't think of as all that little. Farnsy's rounds got quicker as the afternoon went on and the town emptied out. Seemed like folks were headed home for a nap followed by supper with their favorite pumpkin-pie honey bunny.

FARNSY

That was when he spotted someone in the middle of the Twin Villages bridge, leaning over the guardrail. As Farnsy approached, slowly, he clicked on his lapel mike, whispered his location to Dottie on dispatch, and took care not to make too much noise, which, because he was loaded up, wasn't easy with all the gear strapped around his waist: his Glock, an ammo clip, a taser, a pair of handcuffs, some pepper spray, a nightstick, pen and notepad, and because it was the evening beat, a compact high-beam flashlight. In his vest pockets, he had an open roll of Necco wafers, some dog treats, and a piece of the Chief's jerky that he'd once taken a bite of. It all made Farnsy feel like he'd put on a summer gut, even though he was in good shape for a man who spent so much time sitting and waiting. But everything around his waist was, as he thought of it, his little office.

Now here he was, doing the toe-to-heel stealth walking technique they taught at the academy, but which everyone in Farnsy's class knew was the same technique any Maine Guide used to get close to whatever game they were after. Worked good on deer, and Farnsy'd used it on a moose, once, out of season, when he was just trying to see if it worked. It did. Could've spanked that moose, he got so close.

By the time Farnsy got close enough to the person on the bridge, he could see it was a man, not that old, looked familiar, thin build, six feet at least, khakis, sneakers, US flag on the back of his jacket, staring downriver. He looked about to put one foot up on the guardrail on the little bridge. The bridge is no more than 50 feet long, two lanes wide, and it runs over the falls between Great Salt Bay to the north and the start of the tidal Damariscotta River on the south, a drop of about 10, 12 feet at the most. It didn't seem all that long ago Farnsy'd jumped off that bridge with his high school buddies, mid-summers at high tide and the water always cold and swirling. Now, anyone jumping off the bridge into the

FALL — *Pumpkinfest*

river would have a short fall into the long autumn darkness and unforgiving cold.

"Say, buddy," Farnsy said, coming up on the fellow's left side so that he'd have his right arm ready if he needed to take action fast and grab him. ABT, they taught the future police officers at the academy. "Always Be Thinking!" the recruits chanted back.

Hearing no response, he repeated, "Say, buddy, you okay there?"

The man startled, but was already on the other side of the waist-high rail. He turned to Farnsy.

"Don't you come any closer, Farnsworth!" the man snapped.

Farnsy stopped up short. "Eddie, that you?" Eddie Levitt. He'd know that voice anywhere.

"Ayuh. I'm still me. Who else'd be here, this time of night?"

"Well, I don't know, coulda been anybody, I guess. Been a while, hasn't it?"

"Can say that," Eddie answered, then added, "lot's happened since I left."

"I hear you did some time. In the service, I mean. Navy, right?"

"You heard right, Farnsy, you heard right. Cruiser. Middle East. Other places."

It all came back. Eddie Levitt, Fast Eddie, Edgecomb Eddie, star runner from Edgecomb on the varsity cross-country team at Lincoln Academy his senior year, a class or two behind Farnsy. Talk of the town. Academic scholarship to UMaine Orono, and the next thing Farnsy had heard, Ed was serving in the Navy on a vessel that was built down in Bath Iron Works a couple miles south.

That was the last Farnsy'd heard of Eddie, until this evening at the end of a week of Pumpkinfest, the last big hurrah before the Early Bird Sale in November and Thanksgiving. Just Farnsy and Ed on the bridge to Newcastle. Or, to Damariscotta, depending on which way you were headed. Farnsy kept his eyes trained on Ed, who didn't look all that steady and was starting to take off his jacket.

FARNSY

"Not sure that's a good idea, Ed, taking off that coat. It's gonna get pretty cold tonight. Radio says a cold snap's coming in, down to around freezing."

"Don't much care what they say, Farnsy. Besides, those guys can't tell you what the weather was yesterday. Forget about predicting it!"

Farnsy let Ed's remarks ride. "You mind telling me what's on your mind now, Ed?"

"Long story," Ed said over his shoulder.

"I got all night, Ed, all the time in the world," Farnsy said in the most calming voice he could muster. "All night." Which wasn't really true. If he stayed another hour, Chief would be up at the station, waiting to hear Farnsy's report, and if he didn't show up, they'd put out some calls and the squawk-box on Farnsy's shoulder would light up. So Farnsy reached up and turned down the volume on the little square speaker on his left shoulder.

Farnsy waited for Ed to talk but watched him for any sudden movement, too. He'd never had a jumper before, and was trying to think of anything he could say or do to get Ed over on the sidewalk. He could try to pull Ed over backward, but Ed being ex-Navy and all, there was a good chance Ed might take Farnsy with him into the burbling water a dozen feet below them. So he sidled up closer to Ed.

"You need money, Ed? That it?"

Ed shook his head and stared at the river like he was getting ready.

"You need a job, Ed? I heard Yellowfront could use some help. Maybe the hardware has an opening? Lot of possibilities in town this year, they say. Things are looking up, my friend."

"Not for me, they're not." Ed looked down at the river.

"A woman, Ed? Is it a woman?"

Ed looked up. So it was a woman. Good guess.

FALL ～ *Pumpkinfest*

"Ed, okay, it's a woman. You want to talk about it? Jeez, I got some stories too."

"You got a cigarette, Farnsy?"

"Two, Ed, my last ones. Been trying to quit since I started up after Lucy went off again this fall." Farnsy slipped in that part about Lucy, thinking it might give Ed a chuckle. "Here, you take one and I'll smoke the other."

Ed took the cigarette and looked it over like he was facing a firing squad and it might be his last one ever.

"Not going to explode on you, Ed, don't worry."

Ed looked like he might smile but didn't. Still, it gave Farnsy some hope. Now all he had to do was keep Ed talking.

Farnsy struck a match, and it went out. Another, same thing.

"Look, Ed, tell you what—you let go of the railing there and cup your hands together over this way, so I can get this next match lit long enough to light up, okay?"

Ed nodded.

"Now watch yourself, Ed, don't want you fallin' in, it's a long drop. Likely as not you'd smash up on those rocks, then get rolled all around like you were in a tumble dryer over at the laundromat. Wicked cold that water. If the rocks don't get you, the cold will." Farnsy kept talking as he lit the match and Ed leaned over to get his cigarette going, then Farnsy lit his cigarette and flicked the dead match into the burbling water below. The lights near the parking lot at the Schooner came on. The two men leaned against opposite sides of the railing, Pumpkinfest a distant memory, and took deep drags on their cigarettes in unison, as if they were infantrymen in a Bastogne foxhole.

Farnsy started to say something but stopped. What do you tell a man who's trying to end it all in the dark? He was off script, on his own. Running on fumes and intuition.

Then Ed broke the silence.

FARNSY

"I went over to her place this week." He pulled on the cigarette, then spoke as he exhaled. "Was gonna tell her that was my last deployment. I'd be hanging it up, you know. Home duty. More time together, like she wanted. So then she says to me, she says she sent me a Dear John letter. Says she tried to tell me and all, but it came back, return mail undelivered." Ed looked at Farnsy. "'Spect me to believe that? Says she met some guy while she's waiting tables over at River Grill. Works at that sauerkraut factory up in Waldoboro, Morse's. Wears a nice white shirt, she says. Says she wanted someone who was going to be around for her. Not off saving the world." His voice trailed off, and he flicked his cigarette into the water. Farnsy finished his, too, and it landed in the water a second later.

"Women," was all Farnsy could say.

"You can say that again."

"Women," Farnsy said, still trying to get Ed to chuckle. And when Ed cracked a smile, Farnsy added, "Can't live with 'em and can't live without 'em."

"Got that right," Ed said in a whisper.

"Tits," Farnsy said, surprising even himself.

"Tits is right," Ed said. Then both of them laughed one of those shivery nervous laughs.

The two of them stared out into the dark harbor, where the last few working boats of the season were moored up, as if sleeping, noses headed into the night breeze coming from up north. That wind seemed to have a mind of its own, gusting up, the two of them there, out of cigarettes and out of words, standing on either side of the rail. Farnsy looked at his watch. Said he had to get going, Chief'd start to worry. Then he says to Ed, "Say, you want to go up to Moody's with me, get some homemade pie?"

"You serious?"

FALL — *Pumpkinfest*

"Dead serious," Farnsy blurted out, then regretted his word choice. "You remember that homemade blueberry pie they got there, don't you? They'll warm it up for you, then put a scoop of that Round Top ice cream on it, vanilla. Now I'm a Gifford's ice cream man, but still, there's nothing like Moody's homemade blueberry pie, or apple. Lucy likes their rhubarb and strawberry, but I like my pie straight up. Don't know about you, Ed—"

"Well, Farnsy," Ed said, cutting Farnsy off, "you'll be paying, 'cause my wallet's in the drink." Ed pointed to the river. "Tossed it in a couple hours ago, before you got here. Along with my car keys, her letter, and everything."

"Why sure, Ed, you just climb over the railing here now and we'll go see if my cruiser's still there."

"You worried someone might steal a police car?"

"Nope, I'm just worried it might've turned into one of those two-ton pumpkins I been lookin' at all week. Come to think of it, maybe I'll get a piece of their pumpkin pie, little slice of Vermont cheddar on the side."

"Thanks, Farnsy, real kind of you." Ed thought about it a while then asked, "How can I repay you? All I got's my old place on the lake."

"Pie first, Eddie, then we'll talk. You just stay on this side of the railing from now on, okay? I got some ideas for you." Truth was, Farnsy didn't, but he knew he'd think of something.

Undercover

Ever since he started thinking there might be a connection between the Necco wafers and the missing fishing tackle, Farnsy had tried to put himself in the mind of the perpetrator. Maybe if he tried sampling some Neccos something might come to him. Maybe sprinkle some crushed Neccos on top of a scoop of Gifford's or Round Top ice cream. He wondered if the Necco man chewed the wafers like he did, or let them dissolve slowly like Lucy did.

Farnsy was standing in the express line at Hannaford, in uniform, it being the end of his shift, two customers in front of him, with six rolls of Necco wafers in his cart, when he spotted Freddie Hallbert, the CLYNK kid, bagging groceries at the end of his register. The kid was bagging like a pro, heavy stuff first, vegetables and eggs on top, Necco wafers off to the side, and smiling at the folks checking out, wishing them a nice day.

Whenever he had time standing in line, Farnsy liked to check the magazines in the rack next to the register. *Cosmopolitan* always had a top 10 list of things he'd never done and hadn't ever thought of. The *Oprah* magazine lifted spirits and was nearly sold out. *Down East* had a new list of top 10 Maine lobster rolls. *Yankee* magazine had a list of top 10 New England day hikes. And *People* magazine was all Hollywood split-ups and divorces: people whose 15 minutes of fame was apparently expiring.

Farnsy watched the next shopping cart move up to the conveyor belt. It was heaped high with cottage staples: beer, wine, chips, dips, soda, and everything that Farnsy used to eat without feeling guilty. Way over the 15-item limit, but other than an eye roll directed to Farnsy, as if to say, "I guess they stopped teaching math," the cashier said nothing. Farnsy guessed the woman had a couple of sons waiting for her back home, judging by the snacks and Cheez Whiz cans. It was going to be a few minutes, so Farnsy pulled the latest *Uncle Henry's Weekly Swap or Sell It Guide* off the shelf, thinking whoever was lifting the fishing tackle might try to sell it that way. Leave no stone unturned and then check under the same stones again. Maybe you missed something. You never knew.

Next thing he knew, he heard Freddie call his name. Farnsy looked up as he put the Necco wafer rolls on the moving belt. The cashier gave him a raised-eyebrow look, as if to say, "Really?" Farnsy smiled. "Research," he said. "Long story."

After he paid up and took the bag from Freddie, Farnsy motioned him discretely to one side. He didn't want folks to think the kid had done anything wrong. And he certainly didn't want to embarrass him.

"They tell me you're doing a great job, Freddie."

"Yeah, I guess," the kid said. "Got a nickel raise."

"Hey, that's great. Your mom must be real proud. Every bit helps."

"You don't mind me asking, Officer," the kid said, "what's with the Necco wafers?"

Farnsy looked down at the box.

"Just my winter supply, Freddie. Every time I think about smoking a cigarette, I pop open a roll and have a few. You oughta try 'em. Necco wafers, I mean, not cigarettes. But look," Farnsy glanced around quickly and slipped the CLYNK kid his business card, "Freddie, I can use all the help I can get."

"You mean eating all those candies?"

"No, I'm serious. You see anyone, especially if you never saw them in here before, you see anyone buying a whole bunch of Necco rolls, you call me. Don't wait. Call me, okay?"

"This have anything to do with those break-ins I heard about?"

"Might," Farnsy said, "but I'd have to deputize you first and for that you gotta have a degree and take the police course over in Vassalboro." Farnsy winked. Smart kid, Farnsy thought. Might make a good cop one day himself.

"Don't worry, Officer. if I see anything, I'll call." The kid sounded excited.

The Auction House

About the middle of October, Farnsy drove over to Ames's Hardware in Wiscasset to get a big bag of cat food for older cats and a new cat toy. Henry'd started to put on some weight and needed a little exercise—or at least some quality one-on-one play time. Farnsy had to smile, because most of what he thought applied to Henry just happened to apply to himself, too. Like father, like son. Halfway there, he saw a sign at Atlantic Auctions announcing a big pre-Thanksgiving auction. They were looking for gold, silver, old art, and bric-a-brac. On a hunch, Farnsy pulled into the parking lot. One old pickup was backed up near the entrance, all jammed full of stuff.

As he stepped inside, Farnsy heard a voice from somewhere chirp, "Morning, what can we do for you?"

As far as Farnsy could tell, there wasn't any "we," just one woman there back in the office. He watched the voice lean from her chair to peek around the corner to see Farnsy. "Oh, my gosh, Farnsy, that you?"

"As far as I know, it's me, Maureen. That you?"

"Guilty as charged, Officer. But tell me, what brings about this visit? You need something nice for your place? Lucy trying to civilize you again?"

Farnsy winced at the mention of Lucy. Be easier to find out how many people didn't know about Lucy. Probably the only folks who didn't know were the leaf peepers coming through town.

"No, sorry, Maureen, Lucy's out of the picture at the moment."

FARNSY

"She's a good girl, Farnsy. I know it's none of my business, but you know what I mean. Like they say, 'love isn't catch and release.' Well, anyway, Farnsy, what can I do for you? Must be important if you're stopping by in uniform."

Farnsy had almost forgotten why he pulled over, thinking about Lucy now and the last time he'd seen her at his birthday party. After the party, to be precise. She was a regular box of mixed signals, and he was a Boy Scout still trying to learn women's semaphores.

"Fishing lures," Farnsy blurted out, now that he remembered why he'd pulled over. "Wondered if you know anything about them." Farnsy knew some fishing lures were worth real money, but maybe Maureen could help him find an expert who knew the big collectors. Someone who might help him find an angle he'd missed.

"No, I sure don't. If I want fish, I drive over to the Fisherman's Catch. Fresh off the boat. Nice red gills. Won't catch me putting a worm on a hook or pulling breakfast out of some poor fish's mouth. But today's your lucky day, I guess, because the fella who knows fishing lures is Mr. Marsh, standing right behind you there."

Farnsy spun around. It wasn't like him to be caught off guard that way, and he made a quick promise to himself to pay better attention, be alert, like Henry, when his whiskers picked up vibrations like some crazy antennae.

"Owen Marsh, this is Officer Farnsworth, with the Damariscotta Police."

"I know you, Officer, seen you around. How're things with Lucy these days?"

Farnsy looked over to Maureen, then back to Owen Marsh.

"Jeez. As far as I know, Lucy's okay. Off in that hairstyling school over in Augusta, last I knew. You guys probably know more than me. So, Owen. What do you know about fishing lures?"

"A little." Owen smiled.

"A lot," Maureen interjected. "A lot a lot."

"Okay, Owen, just one question: Why do you think anyone would want to poke around in some old tackle boxes?"

"How old?"

"I'm guessing these boxes had some lures going back a ways, maybe to the '20s or '30s, possibly older. You see, there've been some reports around the lakes up our way of missing tackle boxes. Maybe around a half dozen so far, and it wouldn't surprise me if there'd be a few more reports trickling in over the next few months. Some of these camps are rentals, and the original owners' kids have them now. None of them goes out fishing anymore. Too much trouble."

"What's your question, again, you don't mind me asking?"

"You know if old fishing lures have any value? I figure they must, or these guys wouldn't steal them."

"Some do, some don't. Depends. The old beaters, maybe just a few bucks."

"Based on what, age?" Farnsy remembered in the academy they taught the candidates to ask questions you already knew the answers to. Establish the contact's expertise. Then dig deeper.

"Value depends on the age of the lure, the style, the maker, the condition. You know: Hooks rusted? Packing original? Paint faded? One eye missing?"

"You any idea what they'd bring?"

Maureen chimed in, "Now that depends on where they're selling—at a roadside flea market, online, at auction, or some upscale antique shop. We've had some nice things here go for pocket change, next to nothing. But sometimes, you know, if the right people show up at an auction, like some of those heavy hitters from Boston, and a couple of them want the same thing, well, then that price just goes up and up until the last bid. Like they say, beauty's in the eye of the beholder. Why, I've seen some rusted dinged up stuff go for..."

"Okay, can I give you an example? Let's say my father's old Jitterbug lure, his favorite, the one he got from his father when he was a kid. That makes it maybe a 1930 or '40 Jitterbug. I've got it framed up in my cottage. A little worse for the wear, but that's a long story. What might something like that go for?"

"Like I said, depends. If it's like new, and I suspect it isn't, then it might go for up to $100. If it's got a little rust, maybe a little dinged up, maybe around half that. Really bad shape, I'd say a couple of bucks, five dollars, maybe, give or take. Depends. But you never know. Some collectors like things used a little and dinged up."

"Okay, so if this guy, or these guys, because we think maybe there's more than one, if they got, say, even 10 or 12 tackle boxes, and say there were only 20 lures in every box, well, that's still a lot, maybe around 200 lures. Even if most of them were five-dollar lures, that's a thousand-dollar profit. Minimum."

"But now let's say maybe a couple of the lures, say two or three of them are in mint condition, still in the original package? That might be another 200 dollars, maybe more."

"Okay, so it'd be more than a grand. And remember, that's on a good day—the perfect auctioneer and hungry buyers. All you'd need is two bidders. But look, it just doesn't make any sense, you know? All that trouble, casing the cottages, then breaking into all those places? The risk of detection and arrest. I don't get it."

"Well, maybe so. Might just be some kids with a good plan who found a way to sell their ill-gotten goods the modern way. Online. But..."

"But what?"

"But sometimes crime does pay. I mean, now, if they ever found a Haskell Minnow, that'd be a game-changer, Officer. Whole new level you got there."

"What do you mean?" Farnsy asked, trying to sound as if he didn't already know what the Minnow was.

"The Minnow is the original. From around 1850, I think. Saw one at a sportsman's show down in Boston. Ugly old piece of cast copper, you ask me, supposed to look like a minnow. With a hook coming out the tail end."

"How much?"

"Depends. On who's bidding. I read once, in *Field and Stream* I think, where a Minnow went for something around 10 grand. Maybe more, I forget. And they said it was in fair condition. Which just proves what they say, you know: a fishing lure doesn't have to catch fish. Just a fisherman who wants to buy it."

"That's what I'm learning. Now we got to catch the guys going after these lures. But keep your eyes open and your ears to the ground and let me know if you see or hear anything, anyone interested in selling or buying old lures, will ya?" Maureen and Owen nodded, looking like they'd just been deputized.

"One more thing, Farnsy," Owen said, catching Farnsy at the door.

"What's that?"

"Fakes. You gotta watch out for fakes, knockoffs, you know. Get an original Minnow and all you gotta do is make a cast of it, pour in some molten copper, then leave it outside over the winter. Get a little patina on it, and you could sell weathered Minnow replicas to unsuspecting collectors at antique fairs anywhere. Top dollar."

Farnsy looked at Owen square as if to say, *You kidding?*

"Not kidding, Farns. Big money in it. Big. Half the antiques I've seen at some of these summer fairs and flea markets are knockoffs made in China, and I don't mean China, Maine."

Cribbage

Farnsy rubbed his eyes. The ice-cold morning air on his feet told him he must've left the bedroom window open too wide. His toes were his personal thermometer, so if they got cold, it was wicked cold out. Which meant he needed to get himself ready, then jump out of bed, slip into his slippers, grab his bathrobe off the hook on the back of the bedroom door, make a dash for the fireplace, stir up any coals still glowing under the ashes, ball up a couple of pages from an old *Lincoln County News*, toss them onto the coals, blow on them to get the paper going, stack a few sticks of kindling in a little teepee on top of the paper, wait for them to catch, then set two or three small pieces of pine, if he had some, on top of the eager little fire.

After he made sure the first two pieces were laid square across his grandfather's brass andirons, Farnsy would stack split logs, two across, side to side, then two on top, front to back. Just a slight gap between the logs so the flames would lick up and the fire would take the logs even faster. Split oak, especially branches, burned long and hot and made the best coals.

Then Farnsy'd stand back, wait until the flames from the kindling licked the edges of the logs on top and those edges took light. Then he'd remember his bathrobe was open and his options were either to go back to bed and wait for the fire to warm the place up, which could take a while, or just heat up some water for coffee, turn on the radio, and make his favorite breakfast of the season. After the first fall chill, on those mornings, Farnsy would put three or four strips of bacon on the griddle, and after the bacon got crispy, he'd crack a couple of eggs and fry them. Over easy, not runny.

As he lay there that Saturday morning, his thoughts racing this way and that, waiting for a sign to get out of his warm bed again and get the day started, Farnsy felt Henry cuddling up next to him, purring, warm under the blanket's weight. Prompted by the smell of the crackling fire and the pine needles he'd tossed in to get it started, Farnsy's thoughts wandered back to other autumns when he was a kid, and he and his sister Gracie used to run and jump into a huge pile of leaves they'd raked up—until his father told him it was time to light the fire and the acrid gray smoke from those burning leaves corkscrewed up and up until it looked like it was part of the whole gray sky or maybe the source of all the clouds in it.

And there was that last fall in college when he was tangled up on a blanket beside that brown-eyed girl at Colby up on Mayflower Hill. "De-flower Hill," some guys called it. He remembered walking hand-in-hand with her up the hill late that afternoon, him with a blanket over his shoulder, shaking in the crisp fall air that smelled of winter coming, nervous and everything so new, not knowing what was next or what to do, but hoping he'd figure it out or that maybe she'd know. He remembered how their conversation slowed down and seemed to get more serious the closer they got to the crest of the hill, and then stopped when they turned to look back at the campus lights and the road that ran down into Waterville, students driving their cars to Big John's in town.

Shrouded in silence, as though they'd done this a thousand times before, they scraped the dead leaves aside, unfurled his blanket, and cuddled up. Farnsy's arm grapevined around her, never wanting to let go of the moment, and they kissed in the fading afternoon light and their awkward hands found places

FARNSY

still untouched. After they melted together and then slowly came undone and had rebuttoned and zipped up, they lay there afterward, shivering in the early night frost, each waiting for the other to make the first move to leave. Samantha.

Farnsy hadn't thought about her all that often since then, but whenever he did, he remembered what his mother told him when he told her his girlfriend wasn't coming home with him that Thanksgiving, they'd stopped going out. She'd dropped him, he confessed. His mother told him there were many fish in the sea, which was true, of course, but, until then, Farnsy had thought she was the one. Then everything was over, and she'd disappeared, lost to him in a school of fish. A few years later, when he'd read in the alumni magazine that she'd married that other guy, his mother said it again. He knew she meant well, but Farnsy couldn't help wondering if that brown-eyed girl was the one that got away. Once you loved someone, if it didn't last and if it was good when it was still real, then you don't hate them when it breaks up later. You still love them, just in a different way. And you always wonder what might've been.

Farnsy tried to shake off some of those memories whenever they popped up, though they'd softened over the years. Then he'd replay some of those scenes and think of things he might've said or done differently. Always the same questions, never any answers.

Henry leaped atop Farnsy's bureau, meowed, and commenced tapping Farnsy's spare change off the top, indicating his frustration at not getting his breakfast. The coins plunked on the wood floor, and he heard a few rolling under the bed. He imagined Necco Wafers.

"Comin', Henry," Farnsy said. "You're my furry alarm clock. No batteries needed."

Henry finished the coins and started tapping Farnsy's cell phone toward the precipice.

"Okay, Henry, okay, you win!" Farnsy laughed. "One order of warmed-up chicken liver medley for you, coming right up."

And then to himself and no one in particular, Farnsy muttered, "No use looking back, Farnsy. Everything works out for the best." That was another thing his mother used to say whenever he and Lucy broke up. He hoped she was right. But the last time he talked with Lucy it sure sounded like she was headed in another direction. Maybe it was time for him to explore his own space, too, whatever that meant.

The next morning, Farnsy reached into his mailbox, pulled out a letter, and saw Samantha's name and a Portland address. When he told Doc about the letter over at Waltz's, Farnsy confessed that he'd been thinking about her recently and thought maybe it was the smell of fall in the air, the leaves turning like they did that autumn back in college that reminded him of her. Doc, listening intently, stared into his coffee mug as though he were reading tea leaves. He took a deep breath and reminded Farnsy that he was a man of science and facts, but no, it wasn't a coincidence that Farnsy had been thinking of her and then her letter appeared, after so many years.

"Universe's a funny place," Doc said in a quiet voice. "Sometimes it's funny strange. Other times it's just plain strange, good strange, the way things work out." He paused. "Yup, like it can read your mind." Doc took a sip of his coffee, shook his head. "Scary sometimes. All quantum stuff."

Sam's letter, which he read over and over, thinking he might've missed a word or some new meaning, opened a box of memories for Farnsy, seeing the curves of her longhand and her signature, "Samantha." He could almost smell her hair again, that perfume she used. He even remembered the name, "Shalimar." Back then, for him, that was the scent of womanhood and it was all new.

FARNSY

She wrote that she'd read in the alumni news how he'd become a policeman, saying it didn't surprise her because she'd always known he was a good man and she'd never forgotten him and all the good times they'd had back then. She apologized, without directly apologizing, for dropping him like she had that fall, his senior year, when she was only a junior, for that skinny guy from Portland, who Farnsy knew now had a big office down there, something in law or real estate, or both. There'd been some talk about him running for office in Maine, and Farnsy had glimpsed her in a newspaper photo around that time, her next to him, both of them on skis, smiling, and him, handsome.

Now here she was, no kids, no mention of her husband, and would Farnsy be open to meeting for coffee in Portland sometime? She just wanted to reconnect, she wrote. Farnsy read the letter over and over, trying to figure out just what she had in mind and, more importantly, why now? After, what was it, 14 or 15 years? And "reconnect"—what did she mean by that?

Tempted though he was to call her, he had no idea what he'd say and didn't trust himself not to say something stupid like he had back then. So Farnsy wrote her a note saying he'd come down to Portland and meet her for morning coffee at Becky's Diner around 9 on the Saturday morning before Halloween.

"Farnsy, you okay there?" Julie whispered as she wiped off the countertop at Waltz's Soda Fountain and picked up the coffee mug Doc had left behind.

Farnsy looked up, as if Julie'd thrown a tumbler of water on his head.

"Ayuh, I'm talking to you. You okay, Farns'? You look like you just seen a ghost or somethin'. You got me worried, seeing you just sittin' there, twirling your spoon, round and round. Never seen you put so much sugar in your coffee. Now't I think of it, I can't remember the last time I saw you put sugar in your coffee."

FALL — *Cribbage*

Farnsy took some time climbing up out of his thoughts. He heard Julie talking but he was so wrapped up in his own tangles it was like listening in on a party line trying to figure out who was talking and about what.

"Hear you, Julie," Farnsy said as he stopped spinning the spoon. "Loud and clear as the Pemaquid gong buoy." Farnsy tried to smile, but all he could think about was how he felt back in college when the Portland gal told him it was over, that she'd met someone.

Julie took Farnsy's mug and dumped it in the sink. Then she pulled a clean mug off the shelf, set it down in front of Farnsy, and poured in fresh hot coffee, all in one fell swoop. Sometimes it seemed to Farnsy that Julie had more than two arms, like one of those Hindu goddesses. The high school kids who worked the counter some afternoons were cute. But they couldn't juggle coffee and a conversation like Julie. Or spot a middle-aged man in a pickle like Julie.

"Want to tell me what's on your mind there, Farnsy, or do I have to take drastic measures?"

Farnsy smiled a real smile this time, which encouraged Julie to press a tad harder.

"Let me guess: that cat Henry run off on you again?"

Farnsy's smile was still there, but he shook his head.

"Something up with Lucy?"

Farnsy shook his head.

"You still trying to figure out who the mystery donut maker is?"

Farnsy stared at his coffee and shook his head.

"Okay, and I'm just wondering out loud now: any chance you're thinking about taking that job at Bowdoin? You, know, the one where you'd be babysitting college kids?" she added "Or that opening on the force down in Portland? And didn't I hear someone say something about you might be going to law school?"

FARNSY

Farnsy looked up with a start. The job at Bowdoin was old news, but how'd she know about that Portland job? And law school? He couldn't remember the last time he'd had time to even think about those things.

"Aren't there any secrets around here?"

Julie thought a moment. "Nope. Not really."

"How'd you even hear about Portland?"

"Well, now, Officer Farnsworth, you have your sources and so do I. And that's all I'm telling you."

"Fair enough," Farnsy said, his smile coming back, a thin ray of hope for Julie. "The answer's no to both questions. I mean, what would I do without my morning mug here at Waltz's?"

"So, what is it then, Farnsy? There's something on your mind. I can tell. No one else here now 'cept you and me, that cup of coffee, and this fresh chocolate donut," which she produced on a plate like a magician and slid in front of him.

"You trying to bribe me now, Julie? Have to arrest you, you know."

"No, just the truth and the whole truth now, Farnsy." Then she took a wild stab: "It isn't a woman, now, is it? You need some coaching from the other team?"

She waited, then added, "You know you'll never figure women out. You've got a lot more in common with your cat Henry there than you do with almost any woman." She chuckled. "'Cept he's neutered,"

Farnsy sipped his coffee. It was hot but not too hot, and it was good, as near perfect as a cup of coffee could be. The letter was still folded up on the countertop. He looked over at Julie, nodded toward the letter, and said, "Got a letter from a girl I knew at Colby."

"You mean that one you were in love with, only you didn't know it really because you were too young to know, and then when you realized after you both graduated that it was love, so you wrote to her, only she was already engaged?"

FALL — Cribbage

"Jeez, Julie, what the... How'd you...?"

"Farnsy," she sighed, "you told us all about her. Last year, same time, I think. Something about the fall air, I guess, stirs up old memories."

Farnsy's phone buzzed. He picked it up and mouthed the word "Chief" to Julie.

"Yes, Chief, right, be there in three. Over."

"Gotta go, Julie," Farnsy said. "Sorry." He wrapped up the donut in a napkin and slid one of his crisp $2 bills on the countertop. "To be continued," he said, "and by the way, thanks."

Farnsy spent that whole day playing Whac-a-Mole with his memories of that brown-eyed girl, trying to focus on his police work. By day's end, he'd had enough, so when he saw that it was a little after 5, which was about when Doc usually poured himself a shot of Jameson's, Farnsy drove over to Doc's place to see if a game of cribbage might shake those memories.

Doc offered Farnsy a shot of whiskey, but Farnsy waved it off.

"Moxie, Doc, you got any? Wouldn't want to cloud my judgment, Doc. Not when I'm up against Lincoln County's cribbage shark."

Doc shuffled the cards and Farnsy lost the cut, so he dealt first, and the game was under way. Except the letter kept popping up in Farnsy's mind, and as soon as it did, he'd hesitate just a little too long with his pegging or walk right into one of Doc's tired old cribbage tricks and lose more points.

"Farnsy, something's off." It was the second time that day someone had told Farnsy that. "Anything you want to talk about? The Necco case, maybe? Last I heard it was stalled."

Farnsy paused a moment, hesitant to brief Doc on the Necco maps and the possible snowmobile connection. So he told Doc about the letter and what'd happened back in college and how she'd dropped him back then and how it felt like the bottom had fallen out from under him and now she wants to "reconnect," she says.

Doc let Farnsy talk. He'd heard the story a few times. He pushed his chair back from the table and said, "Look, first of all, a game's a game, Farnsworth, so you owe me two crisp two dollar bills. You got skunked fair and square and I need some coffee money."

Farnsy pulled out two crisp sequential $2 bills, the way Doc liked them, and handed them over. Doc took a deep breath and looked away, like he was going through some of his own memories.

"Well, for starters, I subscribe to the theory that time is like an arrow. It sails along in one direction. Time doesn't curve around, Farnsworth. There's no going back, not in dreams and not in real life. If all this is real. I mean, I think it is, but you never know. How's that ditty go? 'Merrily, merrily, merrily, life is but a dream.'" Doc drew a deep breath. "I mean, who would want to curve around in time and relive all the crap we go through growing up, I mean all of it?"

"I might want to go back and behave a little differently with that gal from Portland," Farnsy blurted out. "You know, maybe things'd be different now."

"Sure, maybe someday we'll be able to go back and kick ourselves in our collective behinds, too. But let's say you could, let's say that's possible, wouldn't you forget what you were there for, standing behind your old self, you know, forget your purpose just like you forget most of your dreams? They're two different worlds, Farnsy, the same way one end of the Damariscotta River never meets the other end. Quantum physics, you know. Something like that. Light can bend, not time. But probably there's no man or woman alive who wouldn't want to go back and do things a little different. Or undo some things. Be a little kinder."

"Or tell someone you love them," Farnsy added.

"You mean that gal who left you back then? The one who just walked away?"

"More like ran away, Doc. But yeah, that's the one."

"Timing, son, timing. It's all timing. When things line up right, you just feel it in your bones, sort of like that dowser you told me about, the one who drilled that well out at your folks' place. That's hard to tell when you're young. Too many signals beeping and sirens going off. Older you get, the better you get at this intuition stuff. But way I see it, if you start getting all jangled up and can't stop thinking about someone, you'd better do something."

Doc took a long pause.

"Or you'll regret it as long as you live. And you want my honest opinion? It's a hell of a way to live. Like one of those new GPS things they got there, telling you to turn around, go back, recalculate the route. Doesn't work that way. And it's probably a good thing you can't, otherwise everyone would be turning around, going every which way, undoing things. Chaos, Farnsy. No, you ask me, I think the arrow of time works just fine way it is. We get over most of those regrets anyway. Or we just forget them, like they were dreams."

"Well, Doc, this time, for once, you're starting to make sense. I think you may be right."

"Now that's a first, Farnsy. You heard what I said, and you listened. I'm gonna mark my calendar, make an entry in the town history."

"But you see, Doc, sometimes you can go back."

"What do you mean?"

"That gal I was telling you about?"

"Ayuh?"

"She wrote to me last week."

"And?"

"And I wrote back."

"You don't say."

"I swear, Doc, I could hear her voice in that letter. It was like we were back there in her dorm room."

"Farnsy, you been listening to anything I've said?"

"Taking notes, Doc. It's all up here," Farnsy said, tapping his forehead. "And she asked me to come down to Portland. To talk."

"So you're going down there to see her, then, right?"

Farnsy nodded.

"Like a moth to the flame, Farnsy. Icarus to the sun. You watch yourself, son, you hear?"

"I hear, Doc. I hear."

"You may be listening, but I'm not sure you heard a damned thing I said."

Portland

"I'll have a small V-8, slice of lemon, Tabasco if you have it, two eggs, over easy, not runny, a piece of toast, white, oh, couple strips of bacon and a stack of blueberry pancakes, real maple syrup, I'll pay extra, and a refill of my black coffee when you come back." Farnsy paused, looked up from the menu, and added, "Please."

"Canadian or American?."

"Bacon? American."

"How you want them?"

"Crispy."

The waitress glanced up over her glasses. "Like, burnt?"

"Nearly. Oh, and a side of your corned beef hash."

Her eyes still glued to her order pad and her pen poised to scribble, the waitress nodded to Samantha, who had said a minute earlier that she needed more time.

"Cappuccino. Do you have cappuccino?" Samantha asked.

Farnsy could see the waitress's nostrils flare as she inhaled deeply, then sighed. "No," she said, but in a way that sounded more like, "Really? What kind of place you think this is?"

To which Samantha responded calmly, "Okay. Then I'll have coffee, with cream."

The waitress pointed with her pen to the cream in a small metal pitcher sitting there with the salt and pepper and napkins smack dab in front of Samantha, who added, "And a piece of toast. Whole-grain organic farm bread."

The waitress's eyes closed, her pen wiggling, waiting for an order. Samantha said, "Okay, scratch that. Whole wheat, if you..."

The waitress made a quick note, flipped her pad, stuck the pen back behind her right ear, glanced back at Farnsy, as if to say, "Good luck with her," chirped, "Be right back with that coffee, sir," and disappeared into the clank and clatter of the kitchen behind the swinging door. Farnsy and Samantha sat at a square white Formica table in a booth at Becky's Diner, next to a window with a glimpse of Portland Harbor on a busy Saturday morning, surrounded by people coming and going, catching up and making small talk, and the smells of pan-fries, bacon, fresh coffee, and warmed up sticky buns, their cinnamon fragrance permeating the air.

"Hash?" Sam smiled. "You haven't changed one bit, Farnsy."

He looked at her, trying to take her all in. She still had that short-cropped haircut. And those eyes, those brown eyes you could almost dive into—and he once had. That voice. That same dulcet voice with the giggle that he hadn't heard in years. He felt like he'd changed. But there was a chance, he thought, that she was right, maybe he really hadn't changed. If that was good or bad, he didn't know. The way she said it made him feel like maybe he ought to have changed. At least a little.

"You either," Farnsy said, "You either. So how are you doing, Sam, you and...uh..."

"Jed?"

"That his name? I'd forgotten. Jed, right." Farnsy remembered her husband's name now, because it reminded him of Jeb Bush and the Bushes' summer place in Kennebunkport. Money.

The waitress set plates in front of them with little ceremony. "Get you two lovebirds anything else?"

Farnsy said, "No. No, thanks. Not now."

He remembered the feel of her that fall night when he'd slid his hand under her sweater and then the lace...and Farnsy struggled to get his mind back to where he was sitting now, putting butter on his pancakes so it could melt the way he liked it, before they got cold.

"So," he started, "how are you doing?" not looking up from the fake maple syrup he was pouring over the pancakes. The waitress had forgotten to bring the real stuff, but the pancakes were still hot, and the waitress seemed busy, so he poured the slow sugary goo over the pancakes, lifting up each one like he was peeking under a blanket.

She looked out the window where a ship was pulling away from the dock. "Oh, I'm okay. All right. I guess."

"Just all right? Any kids?"

"No kids. Jed wants them. Says it would look good if he were going to run for office."

"You?"

Farnsy watched the ship. It created the illusion that the whole of Becky's Diner was pulling away, leaving the ship behind.

"He said it like he was thinking about getting a dog at the shelter."

"Sam, what about you? Did you want kids?"

She looked at Farnsy and paused. "Not yet. Not with Jed. We're running out of time…"

Farnsy stopped working on his eggs and put his fork down.

"Look, God, Sam, it's really good to see you. But your letter…" He tugged the missive she'd sent him out of his jacket, which was folded up next to him, and slipped it onto the table between them.

"You said you'd…"

"Yes. I mean, no, I never stopped loving you," she whispered, emphasizing "never."

"That's the truth, Farnsy," she added.

Take a sip of coffee, he thought, let her talk, just listen, like Doc said. How did Doc know women so well?

FARNSY

"I meant every word I wrote, Farnsy. That's the truth. Jed's a good guy and he's been good to me. And he's done well. We've done well. That's what people think. But Farnsy, you only have one first love and that was you, and you only live once. That's what I've been thinking about. For a long time. Real long time," she said.

They sipped their coffees in silence. Farnsy wished the waitress would come by to top off their mugs, break the silence.

"I guess I never completely forgot you, either, Sam. Not that I didn't try to, you know. You dropping me like that. Well, truth is, you knocked me for a loop. A couple of loops."

"Always said you were kind of loopy." She tried to laugh.

"Seriously, Sam. It hurt. Bad. I went into a tailspin. Into the woods. For a good while."

"I'm so sorry, Farnsy. That I hurt you. That I left. Broke it off. Stupid, you know?"

"Sam, don't be so hard on yourself. We were just kids back then. I mean, can't you guys work things out? Maybe this is just one of those dry spells you read about? You know, I just don't believe all that stuff about finding your soul mate. Like that song? You know, the Beatles, what is it? 'Love don't come easy now,' or something like that."

"Farnsy," she whispered, "he hasn't touched me in almost a year. Once, maybe. Farnsy, I really don't know what to do." She started to cry, then caught herself. "Farnsy, I keep thinking about all those good times we had. You always made me laugh. I never stopped loving you. That's the truth. After all these years."

All the old memories started to trickle back. And now here they were in Becky's Diner, holding hands like one of them had fallen overboard. When Farnsy became aware of her hand in his, he reached for the letter and slipped it back into his pocket and held his mug in both hands.

FALL — *Portland*

They talked, caught up, and filled in most of the years. They even had a few laughs and he told Sam about Lucy, on-again, off-again Lucy, to which Sam said, "You haven't changed, Farnsy." And they talked until their coffee went stone cold and the refills, too, and Farnsy could smell Becky's chicken pot pies coming out of the kitchen because all the breakfast people had been replaced by the lunch people. Sam said she wanted to show him her favorite paintings up the hill at the Portland Art Museum, maybe spend the day with him. And by that, Farnsy could tell she meant the weekend. But he told her he had to finish up an investigation report. It was a promise he'd made to the Chief, he told her. But the look on her face as they walked out to their cars told him it was obvious to her it was a lie.

She said, "Thanks for seeing me, for coming all the way down to see me, Farnsy. Lucy's a really lucky woman. Maybe she'll come back, Farnsy. Like I did," she said. Farnsy told Sam he'd call her now and then, stay in touch, maybe do this again sometime. But he thought they probably both knew they wouldn't. They kissed outside Becky's, and he watched her back out and drive off up the hill.

Farnsy wound his way through Portland, looking for the sign to 295 North. The rain was picking up, his windshield wipers were doing overtime, and he could still smell her perfume. He was lifting his collar to see if he could smell it again when he spotted the sign for 295 and headed over to the highway, which would take him to Route 1, up the coast, and back to Damariscotta.

After all these years, there she was again. Out of left field. Not exactly free and available, but available. He never did like Jed and besides, as Samantha had said, what's Jed got to do with this? This was between her and Farnsy. Unsettled business, old business. Old flames. Still there under the ashes, tiny embers still glowing, waiting for someone to sweet-talk them, whisper them into life again, and rekindle old flames.

She was in Portland. Married. Sort of. A city gal now, and he was just, what? A small-town guy, walking the beat in a two-stoplight town? Local color for tourists? Maybe he should apply for that college post. He'd be only 20 minutes from her. Like old times, but like new. No Jed. No kids. Just Henry. What about Lucy? And that weekend with Nedda? What was that all about?

Farnsy paused at the crosswalk in Wiscasset to let an older couple make their way over to the line of bundled-up tourists waiting in the cold for their last lobster roll of the season at Red's Eats. He'd long ago stopped getting angry at the slow traffic snaking past Red's. Farnsy had stood in line once with all the folks from away just to see what the fuss was all about. He listened to them talk about Maine and where they were headed with their kids. Hearing all that made him proud to be a Mainer, a Mainer who'd stayed.

As he drove over the Wiscasset bridge, he rolled his window down. It was low tide and he inhaled the sea air, that briny smell of fish and seaweed with a hint of the pines, and could almost feel that perfume of hers fade away. Sam made him feel lonely, in a way Lucy never did.

Early Bird

Six a.m. sharp the first Saturday of November marked the start of the annual Early Bird Sale in Damariscotta, and the whole town was abuzz with folks scurrying from store to store. The rules were that you got a 30 percent discount starting at 6 a.m., 25 percent at 7, 20 percent at 8, 15 percent at nine, and 10 percent at 10. Deeper discounts given for anyone wearing PJs. The locals knew this, but folks from away who happened to be passing through town were startled seeing folks running around in their Superwoman onesies and red flannel bathrobes, bedroom slippers slapping the sidewalks, a couple of women still in hair rollers, towing their menfolk along, giggling, bustling from store to store with bags of wool socks, winter boots, flannel shirts, knit hats, paperbacks, knickknacks, doodads, scarfs, and sundries.

The Early Bird Sale was like Halloween for grownups. Renys gave out free cups of coffee and a choice of crullers or chocolate donuts. The Barn Door Cafe next to Sherman's Book Shop offered free hot chocolate with little marshmallows. Around 8 a.m., the Lincoln Academy jazz band set up next to the Lincoln Theater, and pretty soon you could hear Scott Joplin's "Maple Leaf Rag" echoing around Main Street. But by the time all the late risers and lazy bones dragged themselves out of bed and into town around 11, the discounts were optional, the donuts had run out, and the free coffee was stone cold.

If you wanted to bring a town together, this was someone's brilliant idea. Of course, the Chief made sure that his team in blue was showing its colors, but for safety's sake and because some of the officers wouldn't be caught dead wearing pajamas in public, the Chief required that they wear their uniforms. Chief said it was okay with him if they wore a night cap, like the one the father wore in "'Twas the Night Before Christmas," if they had one.

Farnsy had been on duty since five that morning making the rounds, on foot, stopping by Waltz's every now and then for another coffee and donut or to chat someone up. That was the best way to take the temperature of the town, Chief always said. Just talk. A simple "How you doin'?" conversation, was the way he described it. "They don't know you, they won't trust you. And if they don't trust you, or they stop trusting you, nothing you can do will get it back."

Farnsy wasn't above making a purchase or two of his own. He stopped in briefly at Renys to pick out a new flannel shirt. He figured one new shirt a year and a new pair of Wrangler jeans was all he needed. As he stood in line waiting to pay, a pretty young thing in line ahead of him, wearing jeans that looked like she'd painted them on, swiveled around to look at the flannel shirt Farnsy was holding and told him she just loved that new lumberjack look.

Around noon that day, as Farnsy was about to go off duty, he was zapping a bowl of chowder in the station's microwave when he heard Dottie at dispatch shout down the hall, loud and clear, "Farnsy!" He stopped the spinning chowder bowl and heard Dottie bellow, "Farnsy, the Professor!" just as he popped his head around the corner to ask, "She okay?"

"She's called twice this morning, non-emergency, she says, and I told her you were on duty, that I'd call you first thing when you were off. Now she's called again. I think you need to call her, Farnsy, sounds like it could be important."

Farnsy asked, "What's up, she say?"

"Said she found evidence of mice in her kitchen. 'A swarm of them,' was the way she put it."

Farnsy chuckled. He knew you see one mouse, you know there are more.

Dottie gave Farnsy the Professor's number and he pretended to listen carefully and write it down, but he had it on speed dial. He called the good Professor as soon as he finished the last of his cup of chowder, which was just the right balance of clams to potatoes and had bits of bacon he'd sprinkled on top.

The Professor said she had a corker of an idea. "Elegant," was the way she put it. She had mice and Farnsy had a cat. Pemmy wasn't a mouser, but she got along with cats.

"So, let me guess, you want my Henry to come over to your place, do you, and hunt mice?"

"That's right. You know, like a farmer lends out his stud bull."

"You serious?"

"Would I waste your time with trivialities, Officer Farnsworth? Long and short is, I've got a serious mouse problem. As you well know, being a Mainer, mice like warm places, so when the temperature drops, they head indoors, and now they're in my place. What's more, I read somewhere that mice have ticks and some ticks carry all sorts of diseases, not just Lyme, so what I have, you see, is a public health hazard right there in my kitchen. Seems to me the least you can do is to lend me your Henry for a week or so and let him hunt mice. I'll feed him, that's not a problem."

"I understand, Professor, and I'm willing to help you. Henry probably would like a change of scenery, but there's no way I can part with him for a whole week. He's all the company I got now."

"Good. Then let's try three days and four nights. Cats are nocturnal, so four nights seems fair to me. How soon can you bring him over?"

FARNSY

"Later today? How about you make corned beef and cabbage for dinner and call it even?"

"Six p.m.," the Professor said, "sharp." Then she hung up.

"Nice lumberjack shirt you got there, Farnsy," the Professor said as she opened up her front door. Farnsy had just arrived with Henry, sulking in his travel crate, a bag of dry food, and the cat's plastic litter box.

Professor poured Farnsy a beer and he sat down to a proper New England boiled dinner while Henry trotted off to explore the Professor's cottage.

"Henry a good mouser?" she asked.

"Not sure. But I haven't seen any mice since I got him from Doc."

Farnsy cut off another piece of corned beef.

"Doc have him neutered?"

"Why?"

"They say neutered cats don't catch mice."

"News to me, Professor. Never heard that one." Sometimes Farnsy wondered who "they" were, saying all those things.

All the talk at Waltz's that week was about the weather and how the *Farmer's Almanac* said it was going to be a long hard winter. Julie said she heard somewhere that if squirrels' tails are bushy, that means it's gonna be a cold one. Doc looked up from his history notes, glanced out the storefront window, and said, "Well, you need proof, it's starting to snow, little flakes, and that means the first layer is dropping already. And it's only a week or so to Thanksgiving."

If you want to get a Mainer talking, ask how to get from here to there. Or mention the weather. The whole coast is a collection of micro-climates, so TV weather folks have a hard enough time telling you what kind of weather you just had yesterday, much less predict what's coming overnight or the next day. Now here it was, the first plowable snow of the winter, and it was starting to build up. Kids would be excited and some folks would think it looked pretty, but Farnsy and the team in blue knew that early snow meant trouble because drivers were out of practice driving in the stuff, and by the time the sun went down, that pretty white snow would ice up. Add to that it was a Friday night and Farnsy knew the Chief would call a special weather meeting before he heard Dottie's voice on his collar radio telling him Chief was calling a meeting.

"Take a donut with you, Farnsy," Julie said as she handed him a takeout coffee she'd poured as soon as she heard Dottie's voice. "Matter of fact, take a whole box of them. They're day old, just the way Chief likes them, and the boss says we're closing early. The weather," she added, not needing to explain this to Farnsy.

Farnsy disliked confirming any clichés about police work, but in this case, a donut was a donut, and what the homemade donuts at Waltz's might lack in the uniformity of store-bought plastic-wrapped donuts, they more than made up in flavor. It was like seeing a photo of something, a shadow of a tree on the wall, then seeing the real thing. As he watched Julie put the rest of the donuts in a takeout box, Farnsy remembered he still needed to figure out who made those donuts.

As if on cue, Julie asked, "Still trying to figure out who makes them, Farnsy? Give up?"

Her question startled him, but Farnsy wouldn't admit that he'd forgotten about her little bet that he couldn't figure out who made the donuts.

"Oh, I'm on the case, Julie." He winked. "Just a matter of time, you know."

As soon as Farnsy pushed open the front door to the station, he bumped into the Chief, who appeared on the way to somewhere.

FARNSY

"Oh, Farnsy, say," Chief said, not expecting to see Farnsy that early, "good, glad you're here. Why don't you take the call that just came in? From the other Renys, you know, the 'clothing Renys,'" which is what Chief called the flagship Renys that sold clothing just down the street from Renys Underground. "A shoplifter. Red-handed."

Farnsy handed the Chief the box of donuts and headed back out to his cruiser, coffee in hand. Good thing he'd thought to put a jelly donut in one pocket. He ate it in three bites, and by the time he'd licked the sugar off his fingers, he'd pulled in front of Renys. He took a quick sip of the coffee, but it was still too hot.

Inside, Farnsy spotted Louise Willette, one of the sales clerks, standing next to a youngish woman, maybe early 30s, a stroller with what appeared to be twins, babies, and two more children, one of them holding her hand and the other clutching one of her mom's legs.

"Farnsy, thanks for coming over so fast. This lady here tried to swipe two pairs of kids' boots. Just now. Stuffed one pair in there behind her twins in the stroller and hid the other pair underneath." She took a breath. "Caught it all on the CCTV, if you want to see it, but I got a witness, new gal over there who just started. She was coming out of the toilet in the back and caught the whole transaction," she added, then crossed her arms as if to say to Farnsy, now what are you going to do about it?

"Thanks, Louise, good work."

Farnsy turned to the young woman with the stroller, "What's your name, Miss? I'm Officer Farnsworth."

"I'm Emma. Emma Spencer. And I can explain, Officer."

"These the boots in question here?" Farnsy asked, pointing to the boots Louise had up on the counter as evidence.

Emma nodded. "My kids keep growing," she said, "faster than I can keep up. And my husband's off somewhere." Then she broke down, sobbing. She said she knew it wasn't any excuse. "I wasn't raised that way." Her sobs came from somewhere deep down. Farnsy wondered if she was okay, if maybe there was something else. He couldn't see any bruises, but winter scarves cover up a lot. He asked her if things were okay at home. She nodded yes. No hesitation.

Farnsy and Louise looked at each other. Louise looked away, at the register, then the boots again, and finally back to Farnsy. Same thing Henry did when that cat wanted Farnsy to feed him: first that stare, then a glance over to the bag of cat food, then back to staring at Farnsy. Like the Chief said, most language isn't spoken. Louise looked back at the boots, sitting there all brand new.

Farnsy asked Louise, "How much for the boots?" She'd already printed out a receipt as evidence, so she handed it to Farnsy, who pulled a debit card out of his wallet and handed it to Louise. "This should cover it."

Louise looked startled but nodded.

Then Farnsy pulled out five fresh ATM twenties and slipped the bills into Emma's hand. "Get yourself something warm too, Emma. Winter's comin' in."

Emma hesitated, then looked at Farnsy as if to say, You for real? She tried to give him a hug, but he waved it off.

"Wouldn't want folks to start talking now, Emma. I've already given them enough to talk about. But you're a real good mom," he said, loud enough for the folks standing in line to hear. "You were doing your best to keep your kids warm. You just made a little U-turn here now. And say, if you need winter jackets and mittens for the kids, they've got a good supply over at the Baptist Church. Everything's free there."

Emma gathered her kids up, wiped one kid's nose, then took the big bag with the boots from Louise, who had no idea what to make of all this, and Farnsy held the door for Emma and watched her push the stroller out of Renys and up the sidewalk.

FARNSY

"Now," he said, turning to Louise, "I want to thank you for your assistance, Louise. But let's keep this one between you and me and the fencepost, you know? No sense mentioning any of this to anyone, if you get my drift."

"That was a nice thing you did there, Farnsy."

"That may be, Louise. We all make mistakes now and then, some of us more than others, and sometimes you make just one wrong turn and have to find a way out of the puckerbrush. Happens to all of us one time or another. But thanks."

A crackle on his walkie-talkie, and Farnsy heard Dottie's voice. "Farnsy, call from over at Yellowfront. I think you'll want to take it. ASAP," she added.

This weather, the snow coming down harder now and it getting dark early, it had to be a parking lot fender-bender, Farnsy thought. But as soon as he pulled in front of the store, he was met outside by the CLYNK kid, who was working the afterschool shift at Hannaford and sometimes Yellowfront. He heard the kid was doing all right for himself.

"Farnsy," he sputtered, looking back inside the store, "he's here!"

"Who?"

"That Necco guy you said I should keep an eye out for. You remember? Last summer? You said anyone looks a bit odd or off and's buying up a lot of Neccos, I should let you know. Well, he's here. Only, I mean, like, you know, it's a she. See her over there at the end of the express line? The one with that stack of Necco rolls?"

Farnsy peeked in the window and found the woman's face at the end of the line. Looked like someone had missed counting after 15 items and was holding things up.

"Nice job, Freddie, thanks. But I think I know that lady, so I'll take it from here, okay? But keep your eyes peeled!"

"Hi there, Farnsy!" Lucy's mother waved.

"Good to see you, Corrie. You buying up all the Necco wafers in town?"

"Sure looks like it, doesn't it? But you know, you're to blame, Officer. Lucy tells me you love them. Well, anyway, I thought I'd get ready for Thanksgiving, you know?"

Farnsy didn't know.

"Lucy hasn't invited you yet? Oh, my gosh! Shoot! Well, cat's out of the bag now, I guess. So what do you think? Come over for some turkey, watch the game on TV with Lucy's uncle? Lucy makes great cranberry sauce, you know. And my stuffing, well, it's an old family recipe." She hesitated. "But look, if you've got other plans, I understand."

"Sure, Corrie, that'd be nice. Lucy know about this?"

"Her idea, Farnsy. All hers. She thinks the world of you, you know."

"Thanks, same here."

"By the way, that shirt looks great on you there. Real lumber man look."

Back in his cruiser, Farnsy tugged the plastic lid off his cup of coffee. Stone cold.

A Keeper

Henry hopped off the bed as soon as Farnsy stopped giving him his early morning back massage. Farnsy took a deep breath, jumped out of bed into the cold air, slipped into his slippers, and scuttled over to the bathroom, where Henry was already scratching away in his litter box. Great minds think alike. Farnsy smiled. That cat was part brother, part son, and the other part something else he couldn't quite put a name on. Fur-pal, maybe.

It was Thanksgiving Day, so Farnsy opened a can of turkey with giblet gravy cat food and scooped some into a bowl next to Henry's dry food and water dish. He couldn't imagine what shape he'd be in if Henry hadn't dropped into his life, as though the universe knew he needed someone to cuddle with. He was also thankful for this sweet little cottage, for his job, and even for the Chief and his crazy recipes. As content as Farnsy felt at that moment, with a long weekend off and time to get a few things done around the cottage, he still had the sense that there was something missing.

Farnsy filled the coffeepot with fresh water and spooned some Eight O'Clock coffee into the basket. While the coffee percolated, he put a couple of strips of bacon into the skillet. The meat began to hiss, and when his toast popped up, he swiped a pat of butter across it, then a dollop of blueberry jam. He cracked an egg next to the bacon, and pretty soon he was eating his favorite breakfast, listening to the morning news update and midcoast weather, while Henry looked down from his perch on top of the fridge, one of his long paws hanging over, like a rock climber chilling out in a hammock halfway up Yosemite's Half Dome, the picture of contentment. Heat rises. Smart cat. And a fine mouser, the Professor had told Farnsy when he dropped by to pick up Henry after his gig.

Farnsy wasn't sure he looked forward to seeing Lucy again for dinner because he couldn't remember if they were on again or off. Or maybe things might be good, but then maybe she'd tell him she still needed more space, more time. For that matter, maybe the whole thing was all her mother Corrie's idea. He should've called Lucy to see if she was on board with him coming over. Corrie had said so, but maybe he should just call the whole thing off. Make up some excuse. Tell Corrie there was a break in the Necco case, maybe. After all, he had a frozen turkey pot pie in the back of his freezer and a can of cranberry sauce. And a box of stuffing. Or he could go up to Moody's for the turkey special with all the fixings. And a piece of apple pie. No, make that pumpkin pie. With whipped cream.

Farnsy folded up the *Lincoln County News*, unable to concentrate. Most of the news wasn't all that new to Farnsy anyway. And the letters to the editor were the usual mixture of complaints and compliments. Republicans, Democrats, and others somewhere in between or from out in left field. Farnsy thought most folks wanted pretty much the same things. Just had different ways to get there.

Thanksgiving had always been Farnsy's favorite holiday because it never had all the glitter of the next holiday, and it was all about family, food, and football. But this year he felt more alone. First, it was a reminder that his mother had been dead now two years. And his father had left after Thanksgiving about a year ago and was somewhere out west. And this year, Grace told Farnsy she was dating someone nice and was going to stay out in California so her kids could get to know his kids.

"Besides," she said, "it's pretty expensive flying out with two kids, and anyway, I'll see you next summer. You know how much the kids love turtle hunting with you. By the way, how's it going with Lucy, Farnsy?"

Farnsy had hoped she wouldn't ask him about Lucy because he couldn't think of anything to say that made any sense or any way to describe their off-and-on slow dance. He didn't want to get Grace's hopes up and tell her that Corrie had invited him over, so he said, "You know, Gracie, same old, same old."

"Oh, Farnsy," Grace sighed, "you guys."

"I know, Grace, I know. But look, I gotta go."

"Okay, Farnsy, but promise me you'll go out, maybe up to Moody's. You like their stuffing and gravy you said. You really need to be around people. So no more turkey pot pies home alone, okay?"

"Okay. Promise. I'll make a reservation over at Moody's."

"Very funny, William Phineas Farnsworth. Love you."

"You, too, kid."

To shake off this carousel of distractions and try to refocus, Farnsy decided to get some fresh air, so he tugged on his heavy fall coat, grabbed a mug of coffee, and stepped outside. He inhaled the scent of sweet lake water and fallen leaves. Someone, probably over in one of the cottages across the lake, had a woodstove going. He couldn't tell which cottage. But it felt strangely reassuring to know that he wasn't completely alone.

There was a sprinkling of frost on the ground waiting to melt if the sun ever broke through the overcast sky, and the frost crunched underfoot as Farnsy walked down to the lake shore. Something about water. He had to live near it. He'd hauled his old wooden dock out of the water weeks earlier. The last echoes of the loons' wails were weeks gone and the waters of his cove and the lake nearby were still. The only sound was a light wind from the north rustling in the treetops. The *Almanac* had predicted gusty winds for late November and the first snow in early December. Farnsy found a good skipping stone and skimmed it into the cove. It bounced twice, then went under, and the water's surface swallowed the ripples. In another couple of months the lake'd be iced in.

Farnsy scanned the opposite shoreline to see which of the cottages had a wood fire going. He had to smile, thinking about the place across the way that had those noisy wind chimes. He could see the cottage where the cleaning crew had found the first roll of Neccos. One by one, he mulled over the details of the Necco case: the open doors, the rolls of Neccos, some of them open, the tackle boxes and old lures, jet skis, and wondering why it had taken him so long to piece things together and figure out that after the perps cased the lakes on jet skis, they must have done their work on snowmobiles. The easiest way to get from cottage to cottage, undetected, was in winter, when the lake froze up and no one was around. He wasn't sure, but that was the only piece of the puzzle that seemed to fit. As bad as winters were in coastal Maine, that still left only a few weeks, late January to early March, when the conditions were right for that sort of activity. Like the Chief said, there was no doubt about it, he was up against some real pros. It was just a matter of time, and all Farnsy wanted was simple justice. He sensed the thieves were probably doing the same thing he was: trying to find the cottages most likely to have a box of old lures. Just a question of time, he hoped, before they crossed paths. But he knew there was a chance they might not show up that winter. Maybe they got wind of things, heard folks were talking about those Necco rolls. Might've started scouting cottages on other lakes where no one was on the lookout for them.

FARNSY

Farnsy puttered around outside the cottage. Tarped his firewood. Tarped his canoe. Then he tarped the Adirondack chairs. The picnic table benches he put underneath the table, then he tarped it all. The two Tiki lights came indoors. He spotted a few places under the eaves where he'd need to touch up with paint come spring, but they'd be good for one more winter. He'd removed the screens on the front and back doors and replaced them with the glass windows that he kept in the storage shed behind the cottage. The trees were almost bare of leaves and the ones that had fallen he'd mulched up with the lawnmower the weekend before. The huge oak where Farnsy's father's lure had once hung was a magnificent skeleton. Waves started to whitecap out in the middle of the lake as the winds picked up. It looked like rain but could just as easily be snow.

Farnsy heated up some soup and put a slice of bologna on a slice of white bread, squirted on some yellow mustard, folded it in half, and sat in the living room looking out at the lake, having a small lunch, anticipating the turkey feast coming later that day. Henry was curled up behind Farnsy on the back of the sofa, and Farnsy could feel Henry's tail flick now and then, as if in response to some inaudible sound.

When the alarm went off, Farnsy propped himself up, groggy. He briefly forgot where he was and what day it was, but it came back to him fast, and there was no wiggling out of this now. Too late for excuses. So much of his life as a policeman was unpredictable that when confronted by the inevitability of spending Thanksgiving dinner with Lucy and her mom, he suddenly felt trapped.

He plugged in his electric shaver, showered, slapped on some Old Spice, pulled on a nice pair of corduroys, slipped into his new shirt from Renys, tugged a sweater over his head, found his coat and, because it was still hunting season, his orange ball cap by the door, and started driving around the lake over to Corrie's place. He couldn't remember when he was last there, but he remembered the way.

On the way up his drive, before he reached the main road, Farnsy stopped short as a flock of wild turkeys darted across the fire road. The turkeys in the woods around Farnsy's place were lean and hungry. Wouldn't make much of a meal, that's for sure. Enough for a sandwich, maybe. Not like the engorged butter-infused turkeys you could get at Hannaford. These turkeys scurried about like released prisoners who knew they'd narrowly missed the chopping block. Farnsy watched them melt into the underbrush and tangle of branches and disappear.

He was halfway over to Corrie's when he realized he'd forgotten to bring something, so he stopped at Yellowfront to pick up a nice bouquet and wondered what he was getting himself into. What would Lucy say, seeing him suddenly there on her mom's doorstep?

"Farnsy! Well, come on in," Lucy said. She seemed happy to see him, but he wasn't sure. Corrie was standing right there behind her, smiling.

"Beautiful flowers, Farnsy," Corrie grinned. "Come, give them to me, they need water. You two..."

Farnsy stepped in and was enveloped by the aromas of Thanksgiving. Turkey in the oven. Simmering gravy. And a pie, either pumpkin or apple, Farnsy couldn't tell. But it all felt warm and wonderful and made him forget anything unimportant. It was as if his mother were still alive and his father still there.

"Oh, and Farnsy," Corrie pointed to an old fellow napping on a sofa in the living room. "That's my older brother, Stubb, over there, Lucy's uncle. He's 'Stubb' because he was a sawed-off little shaver when we were kids. Just closed his camp up north. Headed back down to Florida. But don't get him talking about fishing. He'll never stop."

Stubb shook off the nap as he got up to shake Farnsy's hand. "Farnsy, eh? You the fella Lucy's been yakkin' about?"

Farnsy looked over at Lucy. "Guess so, guilty as charged."

Lucy shrugged a smile and gestured toward the family room, where a football game flickered on mute, and they sat down as if on a first date. They caught up and filled each other in on the two months since Lucy'd surprised Farnsy on his 35th birthday. By spring, she said, she'd be a master colorist, and with her stylist experience, that meant she could set up shop pretty much anywhere.

Farnsy told her about his work on the Necco case and how he'd followed a couple of leads but hadn't turned up anything just yet. He said he had a plan but wouldn't be able to set that trap until sometime in winter.

"Farnsy, you ever find time for anything else? Other than police work, I mean?"

Farnsy shook his head. "Not really."

"You ever think about law school, remember?"

"Luce, that was years ago. Besides," Farnsy said in his best Clint Eastwood voice, "I'm the law in these here parts."

Lucy poked him in the ribs. "Yeah, sure. Bet you tell all the girls that."

Corrie summoned them to the table with a chirpy voice. "So good to have you with us, Farnsy. It is. And I know how hard Thanksgiving must be for you, what with…"

"Mum, please."

"Okay, Lucy. You want to say grace? No? Okay, maybe you do, Farnsy?"

"Not sure I should, but here goes. As my father used to say, 'Praise the Lord—and pass the potatoes!'"

It felt to Farnsy like he was embraced that whole long day by love and laughter, and the conversation never stopped. It was the easiest thing in the world. No mystery, like Doc once said. One story after the other. How they'd met at the swimming hole in Bristol Mills. The time Lucy and Farnsy snuck a kiss in the balcony of the Lincoln Theater and spilled popcorn on a guy sitting in the last row, right underneath them. She told Farnsy about the time she turned a blonde into a redhead by mistake. Then she asked Farnsy to tell her mother the one about the Unitarian nudists. The wine tasted good, so Farnsy agreed to one last little sip. Then Corrie jumped up, "The PIE!" she exclaimed.

And out she came with her apple pie, perfect crust, browned, smelling of cinnamon. And behind her came Lucy with a pint of Gifford's vanilla ice cream, four plates, and an ice cream scoop. "Hope everyone kept their forks. Hey, Stubb, I forgot, are you a Round Top man or a Gifford's man?"

The question was not unlike asking folks if they voted Republican or Democrat. Lucy's uncle said, like he did every year when Lucy asked him that question. "Round Top cone on a summer day, but Gifford's vanilla with pie." Lucy beamed. Good answer. She caught Farnsy's eye. She knew he was a Gifford's man. And he knew she loved Round Top. The pies and ice cream disappeared quickly as all conversation ceased and everyone murmured their contentment.

"That Gram's recipe, Lucy?" her uncle asked. She nodded. "Thought so. A man could get used to that pie." Stubb loosened his belt a notch and gave Farnsy a look.

As Lucy collected the plates and cleared the table, Stubb leaned over to Farnsy and whispered in a conspiratorial voice, "Now, Farnsy, what's this I hear about Neccos and fishing tackle? I know a few things about both, you might say."

Farnsy followed Stubb back into the family room, where two new college teams were on the screen. They sat down and Farnsy filled him in on the basics of the case, how it all started with some Necco wafers, then how they linked up the missing tackle boxes with the Necco break-ins and were hoping to pick up the trail again this winter when they thought the Necco burglar would hit a few more places on the lake.

Stubb tilted the Lazy Boy back a notch. Said it helped his digestion.

"What is it you figure they're after, son?"

"Chief and I figure it's lures, Uncle Stubb, old ones. Antiques." Farnsy glanced at Stubb, who'd closed his eyes, thinking maybe the old man had fallen asleep, and added, "Some of them might even be older than you."

"You know about the Minnow, do you? Ever heard of it? The Haskell Minnow. Be about 150 years old now." Farnsy knew when he was being tested.

"Read about it," Farnsy answered.

"Well, saw one once. Had it right here in my hand like this." He held out his right hand as if hefting a small weight. "Bigger than most lures these days. Heavy, too. And ugly, if you ask me. But it'd sure put a smile on your face if you had one now."

"Big money, I heard."

"Could say that. Real big money. 'Course price depends on condition."

"What happened to the one you saw?"

"Oh, I was just a kid. About your age, I figure. This sport I was fixing lunch for one year tells me he'd just picked up a Minnow at some antique auction. So he pulls it out of his tackle box and lets me hold it. Now, I'd heard of the Minnow but never even seen a picture of one, so here I am, trout frying up in the pan, with that old lure in my hand. Funny how the mind works. I coulda pitched it into the drink right then and there. But I didn't want to burn the fish on the grill, so I handed it back to him. And this sport, he says to me, 'Some folks'll pay a hefty price for an old lure like that, son.' Then he tells me he's taking it back to Philadelphia to auction it off.'"

Farnsy saw Lucy peek around the corner and roll her eyes at him. To Farnsy it looked like she was happy to see him getting along so well with Stubb. Maybe she was worried that her uncle was boring him. But Farnsy gave her a quick smile and gestured that he was okay.

"Ever find out how much he made, selling that lure?"

"A lot. King's ransom, someone told me the next summer. But you see, my point was, Farnsy, that some of those old lures have more value than most of their owners know. Passed down, one generation to the next, and in 50 or 75 years, all someone sees is an old lure no one's used and no one's ever going to use again."

Farnsy was tempted to ask Stubb if he knew the value of an old Jitterbug but held back because he really didn't want to know. It had gotten quiet out in the kitchen, just some whispers, and Farnsy could see that Stubb was reaching for the lever to tip his Lazy Boy back again and take a nap. So he asked Stubb, "Ever done any ice fishing?"

"Not my pleasure, but now I had a good friend, Eldon was his name, ayuh, Eldon Levitt, lived out on your lake and used to raise hell come winter. Built himself a wooden ice boat that he'd crank up good. Sailed one end of the lake to the other one time in something like 20 minutes. Must've been good ice back then, I guess."

Farnsy did the math. That was about 30 miles per hour.

"But now, you asked me about ice fishing and, well, that guy was crazier about ice fishing than I was. He spent many a weekend out on the ice, even after he got married, mostly drinking Allen's Coffee Brandy and smoking cigars. Oh, now and then he caught something. Told me one time that he'd promised the missus he'd bring her some fish. Well, seems old Eldon had a bad day, so he wound up buying a fish at Hannaford, you see, and tried to pretend he'd caught it at the lake. So his old lady says she'd believe it, if he could prove haddock ran in Damariscotta Lake. Now, where was I?"

Farnsy was about to ask himself the same question when Stubb picked up his thread.

"Now, I think Eldon's passed. They took real good care of him down in Togus, but his son lives around here and I think he still does a little ice fishing. Probably still uses his old man's ice shed. You might know him. Eddie Levitt. He's a Navy vet, like his old man."

"Sure, Stubb, I know Eddie. Ran into him at Pumpkinfest. Hadn't seen him in a good long while. Real nice fella. We had a coffee and pie over at Moody's this fall. Did some catching up, we did."

They talked until Lucy came in and gave Farnsy her look.

"You worry me, Farnsy, all business, 24/7, 365. Once a cop, always a cop. Let's go, Officer. Mom says you should take me over to the Bunker Hill lookout near your place so we can neck."

The football game was at halftime, the TV muted, and someone dressed up in something sparkly was singing something. Lucy had a small shoulder bag over her shoulder and a smile, all ready to go. She kissed her mother goodbye and told her uncle she'd see him off before he left the next day. Farnsy got a big kiss and a hug from Corrie, who whispered to him, "Remember what I said, William Farnsworth. She's a good girl. A keeper. Don't you let her get away." Then she gave Farnsy a gentle tap on the shoulder that was almost a nudge to get going.

WINTER

The Painted Turtle (*Chrysemys picta*)

The lake loses its summer heat long before the fall sun dims and the night air shivers. The water in the lily cove grows heavy as a blanket, then ices up, and the painted turtle claws backward into a layer of dead leaves underneath a sunken log that had once been a tree leaning over the piney shore. Time slows as winter falls and her shell becomes her dark refuge. Now and then, she floats up to open water at the cove's edge to inhale, briefly, the frosted air, then scratches back into the murky lake bottom thick with leaves and spiny twigs from too many seasons past to remember. During her muddy sleep, she dreams of basking with other turtles on a sun-drenched log. A skater scratches overhead. Now and then the throb of an angler's ice auger. Ice-out is months distant.

The Big Snow

A week after Thanksgiving, the first big snow dropped on the midcoast. There had been a few earlier flurries and an overnight dusting, but they'd melted fast because the ground wasn't frozen up yet. The first week of December, all winter broke loose with a wallop. Snow fell out of the night sky like an old farmhouse ceiling finally giving way, as though it had been building up above the slate gray skies for some time, then busted through and dumped a thick layer of white that announced winter had arrived overnight.

Farnsy woke up to look out his bedroom window and saw what he guessed was at least a foot of the white stuff covering everything like a new skin. Not much wind in the treetops, he noted, which meant no drifting, not yet. But the Portland radio said the wind would pick up later in the day. That meant snowbanks and drifting. And drifts meant accidents and accidents meant long days. The lake had started to ice up, but the ice was still soft, and he could see it undulate. The empty cottages across the way looked hunkered down. They stared back at Farnsy.

"Well, Henry," he said to the cat, who was standing on his hind legs next to Farnsy, looking out the window, "guess winter's here."

Farnsy turned on the radio to get the latest midcoast forecast and heard a breathless reporter call it a "storm system." Farnsy wondered when they started calling a snowstorm a "system."

"Jeez, it's only snow. We're all Mainers," Farnsy said out loud, as he fished his good gloves out of the bottom drawer and found his favorite winter boots in the back of the closet. "You too, buddy," he muttered to Henry, who was watching a couple of mothballs roll across the floor and under the bed.

Mainers up and down the coast were tugging on old mittens that smelled of camphor. And Farnsy knew that somewhere in town a few generators were probably jumping to life because an iced-up widow-maker had taken down some power lines. Folks were bringing in more firewood to take the edge off the cold. Water pipes somewhere were freezing up and bursting. And an old-timer would slip trying to shovel the first layer of snow and break a hip. Farnsy sensed it happening all at once, everyone scurrying around like the ants in an anthill he had kicked as a boy.

There are times to daydream and there are times to get up and at it, his pop used to say. His mother always let him sleep in because she knew Farnsy stayed up late most nights, reading *Hardy Boys* mysteries under the covers with his Boy Scout flashlight. But his dad made an early riser out of Farnsy. And Farnsy came to love the early morning quiet just like his dad.

Farnsy gave Henry more dry food and fresh water, started the coffee, showered, and shaved. Then, after he'd buttoned up his still-wrinkled uniform, he snowshoed up the hill to his pickup, glad he'd had the foresight the night before to park in the clearing up near the main road in case it snowed. Twigs were scattered here and there and Farnsy stopped to drag a few branches off the road, thinking they'd make good kindling. He'd pick them up on the way back. He spotted a line of turkey tracks and, farther up, the tracks of a solitary deer, small, a doe, he thought. Snow had a way of dampening all sounds.

Farnsy knew that Tib Tibbetts, who lived a ways farther down the Bunker Hill Road, wasn't going to plow out Farnsy's fire road with that new yellow rig of his until later that day or maybe early the next, because Tib had some big jobs in town that paid the bills, he'd explained to Farnsy. Farnsy's road in was mostly gravel, and

WINTER — *The Big Snow*

Tib knew how to set his plow just right so as not to gum up the road any more than it already was, being still rutted up from the spring run-off.

This was just another winter workday for Farnsy—his shift starting in the dark and ending in the dark, which meant the whole work day seemed dark. Overall, Farnsy felt pretty good. He'd had a good Thanksgiving with Lucy a week or so earlier, but he wasn't exactly any clearer on where things stood with her. And he wondered if he'd ever crack the Necco case.

He got his pickup started and let it warm up while he scraped ice off the windows and brushed snow off the hood, the roof, and the bed cover. He figured there had to be over a foot of the white stuff, and it was still snowing hard. Small flakes, not the puffy kind, and not the wet kind you get in late winter. Small flakes coming down so fast and hard that by the time he slid back into the driver's seat, the whole vehicle was good and dusted over again. Have to laugh, Farnsy thought. Maybe Eskimos have a word for endless snow. He could be there all day, brushing that stuff off, trying to keep up with it as it fell, but there was work to do and no backup for a cop on the coast. Chief needed all hands on deck.

Grasping the steering wheel, which was stiff and stubborn cold, even with his gloves on, he nosed the pickup onto the two-lane road that wound around the west side of the lake toward town. The first snow always brought out the worst in some drivers. Some of them outright forgot what it was like to drive in snow. And folks with four-by-fours and SUVs seemed to think the laws of physics somehow didn't apply to their vehicles. But Farnsy knew the laws of physics were impartial, apolitical, and fairly meted out—to geniuses and idiots alike.

Sure enough, by the time Farnsy got to the station, calls were coming in from all over, a steady stream. Spin-outs, fender benders, a rollover, and a snowbank that ate a car. Dispatch said AAA was backed up for hours, but Farnsy knew most Mainers either dug themselves out, tossed down some sand or cat litter, or knew someone with jumper cables or a pickup with a towing chain. Every Mainer had been at one end or the other of a jumper cable sometime.

The station was piping hot because everyone let Dottie control the thermostat after she'd announced that she was post-hormonal. Meanwhile, the Chief was already knee-deep in calls, sorting out the emergencies. One call came in from a lady in a year-round place out on Biscay Pond, who said her husband had just started to shovel them out when she watched him keel over and disappear in a puff of drifted snow. She called back a few minutes later to say sorry, her hubby had only lost his balance and then crawled back up their driveway. Folks often said the first snow was the prettiest, all that white snow covering everything like frosting on a cake. But for anyone who worked behind the scenes, for the front-line folks in blue—police, firefighters, EMRs—it wasn't postcard pretty for long.

Chief glanced up over his computer screen to see Farnsy come in the front door and watched him stomp clumps of snow off his boots. Didn't bat an eyelash at Farnsy's slept-in look.

"Good thing we put a couple 50-pound bags of sand in every cruiser's trunk last week. Chains too. And a box of those new hand warmers. You never know."

Chief looked back at the screen. "Farnsworth, you do a run through town, report back ASAP. Stay in touch. Plows should be out on the state roads, but we need Main Street clean and sanded. The hospital has to be open. And Hannaford and Yellowfront. And that co-op place there with all the lettuce. Folks need supplies, so don't forget the hardware stores. You know the routine, Farnsy, we need some eyes out there. Be safe."

On his way out, Farnsy grabbed a couple sticks of the Chief's new spicy Cajun Caribbean moose jerky, which the Chief had concocted because he figured the team needed something hot in winter. Halfway out the door, Farnsy heard Dottie take a call from the Professor's caretaker. She was missing from her home.

The Professor had been slipping that fall and had started forgetting things. Little stuff at first, then important things. Once, in Sherman's Book Shop, over near the Staff Picks, she'd started delivering a lecture on Francis Perkins and the New Deal to a kid from Lincoln Academy who was just trying to get a book for a class assignment.

About a week later, she had a little bumper dinger in the town parking lot, and the Chief agreed with Farnsy that he probably ought to go over to the Professor's place just across the bridge to sweet-talk her and get her car keys—just for a little while, he lied. It hurt like hell to see that crusty old gal start to tear up, losing her freedom and all. But public safety was important. Nip things in the bud, Chief said. Shortly after that, the Professor had some good days and some bad days, and they found a good forever home for Pemmy.

Farnsy guessed that storm must've triggered some old memories because Tib, who happened to be making a second plowing run down Main Street, spotted the Professor in her pajamas and bathrobe, making her way between the snowdrifts on the sidewalk, over the bridge into town, and called in to report seeing her out there. Farnsy was sure the Professor was headed to the library, which he knew was her second favorite place in town after Waltz's counter, so he told the Chief he'd get the Professor and bring her back home safe and sound.

And sure enough, there she was, at the front entrance, top of the Skidompha Library steps, a good half a mile or so from her home, knocking on the front door. Farnsy kept an old army blanket folded up on the back seat in winter, ready for just such a situation, so he brought that with him as he stepped out of the cruiser and made his way carefully up the snow-crusted steps to the library.

FARNSY

"Professor, fancy meetin' you here now, this fine winter day!" Farnsy said in a calm voice so as not to frighten her. "Wanderers" was what some senior care staff call residents who find a way off the premises, looking for something they forgot or a long-lost friend they were supposed to meet, as if they were wandering in a dream, which, in a way, they really were.

The Professor's slippers were all crusted up with clumps of snow and her gray hair was powdered with it. She looked like one of Waltz's sugar donuts, Farnsy thought. Truth was, she looked kind of cute, if it weren't for the oddity of the situation.

She turned around slowly. "Now, Farnsy, I'm late to class. Won't you help me open this door so I can get started? Wouldn't want students to miss a snow day now, would we?" She smiled.

"Well, okay, I'll do my best, dear, but let's get you warmed up first." Farnsy couldn't tell if she was shivering because of the cold or because she had the shakes—or a combination of the two. As he wrapped the blanket around her, he could feel the bones in her shoulders, and it took him aback.

But it was obvious she'd lost some weight, and he guessed it was serious. It had been only a couple months since the Professor had found Farnsy's missing fishing lure at that place out on Route 1. Farnsy had told her daughter all about the fishing lure her mother had found, and the daughter's eyes started welling up with tears. Her mom had always liked a good mystery, she said. Now here she was, Farnsy thought, skinny as a chicken bone.

There were times in life, Farnsy thought, when everything just seemed to slow down or speed up. You went along, everything all normal, predictable, and routine, then all of a sudden, it seemed, little kids were teenagers and old folks started failing. And before long they were smiling back at you from an obit picture in the *Lincoln County News*.

WINTER ~ *The Big Snow*

Farnsy guided the Professor down the library steps, salt granules and ice crunching underfoot. The snow had paused momentarily. The town plow rattled by another time and Tib behind the wheel gave Farnsy a quick two-finger wave and kept right on plowing. Wasn't the time for small talk and the usual Hi-how-are-ya's.

"Where are we going, Farnsy?" the Professor asked. "This isn't the way to class!"

"Now don't you worry, Professor, I'll get you there. You were just at the wrong door."

He helped the Professor slide into the front seat of the cruiser and buckled her up and then, back at her house, he helped her shuffle indoors, where her caretaker had a wheelchair and a wool blanket ready and waiting for her.

During the short drive over the bridge back to her home, the Professor had confused Farnsy for her husband, who'd passed away years ago. She'd told everyone at Waltz's that he'd been her handsome blue-eyed Professor when she was a coed and a decade younger than him. She leaned toward Farnsy and told him she'd like to cuddle up when they got back. "Nothing like cuddling up next to you in cold weather, dearie," she cooed.

Farnsy played right along and smiled. "That would be nice." Which reminded him how much he missed cuddling with Lucy. Wherever she was then, he wished she were back in town. Must be something wrong with him; he was thinking of her so often. Just couldn't shake her.

By the time Farnsy got back home that evening, he was too tired to think. But he played the string game with Henry, who'd been alone all day and seemed a little clingy, as if he thought Farnsy might have forgotten him. Then Farnsy flopped onto his bed, still in uniform, too tired to take it off, with all the old questions pinballing around his mind before he drifted off: Who stole the fishing lures? Once a cop, always a cop? What if he and Lucy married and what if they had kids—how could he afford that? And what about Nedda? Where was she? Off in the Caribbean, sailing around? And Christmas? Another holiday alone? Thanksgiving had been surprisingly cozy with Lucy and her mom and Uncle Stubb, but what would he do for Christmas? Should he get something for Lucy? Would she expect a gift? Jeez, he thought, must be the Chief's new moose jerky got me all jangled up now. And then New Year's? Alone, again? Even with Henry's company, it was hard to be alone on the holidays.

Farnsy sat in the chair next to the Professor's hospital bed. She'd come down with something right after her little winter escape attempt, and the hospital had notified her daughter out in Chicago, who said she'd try to get out there as soon as the weather cleared up and the flights and connections got unscrambled. He held her hand. It was light as a feather. The bones in her fingers reminded him of the skinny white bones he'd found once scattered on the forest floor when he was a kid. Her veins were blue against her pale white skin. He squeezed her hand gently, then let go. She was still breathing. But her breathing had slowed and there were times when he thought she'd slipped away quietly while he was thinking about work or wondering how her yellow dog, Pemmy, was doing, the one he'd arrested last summer for driving. He thought about Henry and how glad he was he had that cat.

He shifted her hand to his left hand so that he could scratch his nose, and his eyes found the chart on the wall next to her bed: "Professor Phoebe Louise Tuttle," "Duty Nurse: Connie LaVerdiere," and "DNR" below that. Then a note, scribbled in washable green longhand: "No local family. Daughter in Chicago." He knew the Professor wasn't one for formalities. She was simply a common-sense Mainer who didn't bet on an afterlife.

"Just plant me under an apple tree," she'd once told no one in particular at Waltz's, when the conversation turned to the cost of a good gravestone and high-priced funerals. "Not gonna put me in formaldehyde like some kind of biological specimen," she said, "nothing logical about it. And make it a crab apple," she added, squeezing out a smile.

A few days later, the call came. Farnsy heard the night nurse at the hospital tell him that the Professor was slipping. The nurse said he'd heard the Professor talking to her husband as though he were standing right there in her room. The nurse knew the Professor's husband had been dead for as long as the Professor had lived in town, and he said that was a sure sign that she wouldn't be here much longer, so if Farnsy wanted to say goodbye, now was the time. Farnsy shook off the sleep, splashed cold water on his face, and put his uniform back on, figuring that he might be there all night and would just go straight from the hospital over to the station for the start of his 6 a.m. to 4 p.m. shift. He kept an electric shaver in his locker at the station for just such emergencies, and a can of Right Guard deodorant for what his father called "a captain's shower," meaning a hefty spray to cover up a long night's accumulated sleep and sweat.

The nurse came in to check on the Professor to see if all the monitoring wires were connected and the oxygen tube in place, and he gave Farnsy a knowing smile and a nod, then left him with the Professor. The door closed with a whisper, and Farnsy heard muffled voices out in the hallway and the hum of the monitors next to the Professor's bed. The green lights on the machine blinked in time with her heartbeats. Farnsy wondered how things were going outdoors. This new storm was bigger than forecast and it looked like the whole coast was going to get walloped. He reached for the *Field and Stream* magazine over on the side table. Even though it looked like a cover he'd read at the barber's last summer, it gave him something to do with his free hand, flipping pages while he held the Professor's hand in his other. He didn't want to let go because he'd heard somewhere that folks in hospice could feel more and hear more, even though they looked like they were asleep. It was too late now to take the Professor over to Pemaquid Point for one last sunset after the parking lot closed. That was something she'd been asking Farnsy to do, and they'd agreed it was their favorite place to go to think. But something had always come up that fall.

The green light stopped blinking. The Professor's face seemed to relax. Her chest didn't seem to be moving, not even slowly. When he was a kid, Farnsy would always watch the chest of the cowboy who'd gotten shot in a Western film to see if the actor was faking it, and if he saw a faint motion, he knew everything was okay. The Professor's chest was still, so he lifted her hand nearest him and gently placed it on her chest, where people place the hands of the dead, and he tapped her hand one last time. It felt cold and the room felt emptier than it had moments earlier, so Farnsy said a little prayer, hoping that if the Professor could hear him, she'd know Pemmy was okay and that he was glad he'd known her and grateful she'd found his father's Jitterbug. When he tried to picture her sailing peacefully down the Damariscotta River out to the open sea, he remembered the Professor didn't like boats, so he changed it to the *Teciani* tourist boat, thinking maybe she might like that more, the wine and oysters and lively music. The duty nurses, who'd seen lights flash on the monitors down the hall, whisked into the room and started bustling about, a well-rehearsed ritual they conducted as if the Professor were napping, just resting her eyes, like his grandfather used to say. Farnsy thought she looked like she was checking her lecture notes, about to start lecturing again.

Farnsy slipped out of the room, then sat in his pickup and cried as if he'd lost his own mother. He might feel bulletproof in his regulation vest, but the vest didn't protect him from tears. Or from feeling love, however unexpected. He had an overwhelming urge to find the warmth of friends and a black coffee as soon as he was able.

He sat there a good while, staring out the windshield at nothing in particular. It was going to be a lot quieter at Waltz's Soda Fountain. Doc would miss her for sure. Everyone would. And that dog of hers, Pemmy, was probably yipping around that farm up in Jefferson with her new family. Plenty of room to sniff around and no chance they'd ever let that dog drive their car.

The Professor's daughter, Lizzie, finally arrived in Portland, drove up in a rental, and met Farnsy in town at the new Barn Door Café next to Sherman's because Waltz's didn't do decaf lattes and scones. They chatted about her mother's last hours, memories of happier times, then, after Farnsy finished his oatmeal raisin cookie, he let Lizzie know they'd reminded him that the ground was too frozen to dig a grave so her mother would have to wait until June to be properly buried. Lizzie stared at Farnsy. "You're kidding, right?"

"No, sorry. This is nothing to joke about. Ground froze up real early this year. Caught a lot of folks off guard. I'm really sorry, but your mom's going to have to wait until after spring thaw."

"So what do they do with her until then?"

"You really want to know?"

She didn't answer, but the look she gave Farnsy was answer enough.

"Deep freeze," he explained. "They put her in a big freezer over there in the mortuary."

"Like a piece of meat? Like frozen hamburger? Oh, jeez, Ma." Lizzie laughed. Then she started crying, years of stored up happy memories, Farnsy figured.

Nibbles

As the days grew darker earlier and earlier, Farnsy sensed that the trail on the Necco case had gone stone cold. There'd been no new breaks or leads and neither he nor the Chief nor, for that matter, anyone at Waltz's had any new angles. Whenever Farnsy had a moment to think, to review what he knew, or thought he knew, it was always the same: they'd established a link between the rolls of Necco wafers and the missing fishing tackle, and there was good reason to believe that this was the work of pros because the cottages hadn't been ransacked and trashed like amateurs would do. Apart from the Neccos, these cottages were intact. Except, of course, the fact that some old fishing tackle was missing. And some of it might be valuable, very valuable. Otherwise, there were no fingerprints, no matchbooks with telephone numbers inside, no lipstick on a cigarette butt, not even a boot print or a tire track. And then there was the man in the Lexus. A lot of dots but nothing to connect them.

He assumed the Necco wafers were some sort of trademark they'd left behind. Maybe someday Farnsy'd find out what the candies meant, if they ever nabbed the culprits, who were probably connected with the summer jet skier who was asking odd questions about fishing. It was purely circumstantial. Sounded like it was the same person, but it was all guesswork. Plausible, maybe even likely. His theory that they might hit more cottages this winter was pure conjecture, but the Chief agreed with Farnsy, that it was still the best they had to go on.

Meanwhile, the ice on the lake was spreading, and by the time ice fishing season opened the first of the year it would be thick enough for snowmobiles and ice sheds. And they assumed the break-ins would continue out on Damariscotta Lake this winter, unless the perpetrators had gotten wind of their investigation and decided to move on and hit cabins on any of the hundreds of other good fishing lakes in Maine. Some police work ends up just snowplowing petty crime into another county. Depending on your location, that was good or bad, but in Farnsy's case, he hoped they'd make another run at cottages on Damariscotta Lake this winter.

The Chief hadn't brought the whole Necco matter up for a few days. But something the Chief said to him had stuck with Farnsy. "You gotta think like a hunter, Farnsworth. Set your bait, then you wait. Can't catch fish with a bare hook, you know."

Farnsy decided he couldn't just wait quietly, sit tight, and hope the Necco burglar would slip up. He had to take action, get a step ahead, and he had an idea. It was a long shot, but it might work. Chief was right. Lobstermen bait traps. Hunters bait bears. Anglers bait fishhooks.

At the station that Monday morning, Farnsy explained his idea to the Chief—how they could bait the trap, maybe flesh out the perps and get a jump on them. Chief was as tired of spinning gears as Farnsy was. He smiled, "It's crazy, but it just might work. Like they say, Farnsworth, fish or cut bait. Let's do it. I'll call over there to let the editor know you're coming."

Traffic in town was a bit pokier than usual. The strings of twinkling Christmas lights were a pleasant distraction, and drivers slowed down to see if they were anything like last year's lights. But Farnsy was over the bridge and parked outside the office of *Lincoln County News* in Newcastle before he'd even had a chance to figure out how he'd explain his crazy idea.

WINTER — *Nibbles*

When Farnsy told the obituary editor that he wanted to submit a fake obit, she said she'd never done anything like that. Farnsy said neither had he. She said she had to check with the editor first.

The editor was new, but she'd met Farnsy earlier that fall when Farnsy filled in for the Chief at the annual joint meeting of local Lions and Rotarians. She came out from behind her desk, gave Farnsy a broad smile and a firm handshake, and motioned for him to take a seat. The Chief had clearly already called to pave the way. Farnsy was optimistic. Maybe the wheels of justice were starting to get some traction.

"Good to see you again, Officer. So, tell me, what's this I hear about an obit for someone who didn't die?"

"Yes, ma'am, I'd like the paper's help. We need to post an obit for someone who not only didn't die, but never existed."

Farnsy filled the editor in on the details, why it was important to get the bait in the paper before the holidays. Then he swore the editor to secrecy. The editor said she wasn't quite sure that intentionally publishing bogus information was ethical journalism, but she was happy to help law enforcement. "After all," she said, "our paper is committed to serving the Lincoln County community and supporting our police. Besides," she said, rubbing her hands together, "didn't Sherlock Holmes put an ad in a newspaper once?" The game was afoot, and it felt good to Farnsy to have taken at least one small step toward breaking the case.

The next Thursday, the *Lincoln County News* ran a black-and-white photograph of Farnsy's father that his mother had taken of him after he landed a near-record large-mouth bass on Damariscotta Lake on opening day, half a year before Farnsy was born. The fictional dead man had a different name and a backstory that Farnsy hoped would hook the interest of avid fishing lure collectors and, with any luck, the Necco-loving fishing lure thief.

> **Otis Oliver Gould**
> Antique Fishing Lure Expert and Collector
> August 10, 1929–November 24, 2015
>
> Otis Oliver "Oggie" Gould died peacefully on Thanksgiving Day, 2015, in the Togus Veteran's Medical Center after a long illness. Oggie Gould was born in Jefferson, Maine, on August 10, 1929, the son of Wilton Tanner Gould and Francie (Tibedeau) Gould. Oggie grew up in the '40s and told folks he'd fished every corner and cove of Damariscotta Lake. But his real love was telling his nieces and nephews about fly fishing in the old days out on First Roach Pond in Kokadjo, near Moosehead Lake. Oggie was a proud Mainer, a veteran, and a dedicated bachelor whose first love was fishing and his second collecting antique fishing lures. Oggie's proudest possession was the Minnow, a fishing lure over 150 years old that is the rarest and most valuable of all collectible American fishing lures. A memorial service followed by the auction of his antique lures will be held next spring after the ground has thawed.

The following Thursday, both *Uncle Henry's Weekly Swap or Sell It Guide* and the *Lincoln County News* carried Farnsy's other fictional bait:

> **ESTATE SALE!**
> *The Worthley Collection!*
> Pristine Antique Fishing Lures, Vintage Rods, Reels, and Accessories.
> Once belonged to a Master Maine Guide and must be seen!
> No trades. Serious offers only.

WINTER — *Nibbles*

Farnsy left different contact information for each announcement. On the first one he left a Post Office Box number he'd set up with Bruce, the postmaster in town. At the end of the second piece in *Uncle Henry's*, Farnsy left his cell phone number. He'd baited his traps, and now all he had to do was to wait for a nibble, knowing that it might take a week or more before he got any responses. If he got any.

The first bite was a voicemail from a sportsman in Philadelphia who asked if he could see photos of the lures online. Farnsy called the man, who said he was looking for a couple of old lures. To complete his collection, he claimed. Farnsy replied that the dearly departed had insisted that the entire collection be sold intact. Farnsy felt bad for the man because he sounded legit and seemed disappointed, but he resisted the impulse to reassure the man and tell him the real story.

Several more days passed before Farnsy checked his PO Box and spotted an envelope inside. It was from a town in Connecticut that Farnsy had heard of, a short commute from New York City. A high-rent town, if anything there was rented. The note inside was on a small slip of embossed letterhead that made clear the sender was a serious collector and dealer. Farnsy called the number and the person who picked up wasted little time on chit-chat, peppering Farnsy with detailed questions about "Oggie's" estate. Farnsy described the fictional lure collection in vivid detail. He knew if you offer someone two or three concrete "facts," small details, they're more likely to believe whatever you're telling them. Con men everywhere use this trick.

Then Farnsy paused for effect and asked the dealer if she'd ever seen the Minnow. There was a brief silence. The dealer said she'd heard of the lure but hadn't seen one up close. Only a picture. Farnsy's "bullshit-o-meter" told him she was lying. Still, she could be legitimate, maybe just a cagey dealer feigning ignorance, hoping to score big, buying old lures from an ill-informed Mainer.

FARNSY

"Well, if you'd like to see it, let me know and I'll give you my address. It's real old, so I'll have to ask for $500 firm on that one." The dealer said, no, thanks, she wasn't going to drive all the way up to Maine again in the middle of winter just to see a box of old fishing tackle. Farnsy couldn't be sure she wasn't legit, so he kept the letter with her number. And she did say "again," so she'd been in Maine recently. If he called her back to ask if she had been to Maine earlier that year, she'd get suspicious and wonder why someone selling estate property would want to know that. So he made a note and put it on the back burner. Seemed to Farnsy like the kettle of miscellaneous things he'd been collecting on that burner was close to brimming.

As soon as the Chief came in around noon the next day, he and Farnsy sat down to go over their options now that they'd gotten a couple of nibbles. Chief agreed with Farnsy that the second call was more interesting, but probably not worth exploring.

The Chief's phone rang. He checked the number, then picked it up and cupped his hand over the phone, "Sorry, Farns, gotta take it. It's the boss."

The Chief had confided with Farnsy that he and his wife were trying to achieve what the Chief's wife had called "life balance." When Farnsy told Lucy about that on Thanksgiving, Lucy said she'd read somewhere that no one on their deathbed ever wishes they'd spent more time in the office. "You know me, Farnsy, I always did like you more when you're out of uniform."

The Chief held up a finger to signal to Farnsy that he'd be off the phone in a minute, then he put the phone down and shrugged. "Guess now that hunting season's over, I'm gonna have to spend a little more time with the wife down at the Maine Mall."

Farnsy wasn't a hunter so he just smiled and they picked up where they'd left off, discussing their options. Short of staking out every cottage on the whole lake, Chief admitted, there wasn't much more they could do. "You've set the bait, Farnsworth, now you just gotta wait. Two nibbles isn't bad. Speaking of nibbles, here, try this new jerky recipe. Tell me if you think rabbit tastes like chicken."

Farnsy thought he could wash the taste out of his mouth with a lime rickey over at Waltz's. Maybe get one of Julie's grilled cheese sandwiches with a slice of tomato and a dill pickle from Morse's on the side. See if anyone at the counter'd heard anything new.

Doc came in and took his seat over by the window. He looked up over his reading glasses and nodded in Farnsy's direction. Julie poured Doc his coffee and slid the milk and sugar his way. A spoon followed.

Doc closed his journal and leaned over to Farnsy. Julie was leaning in, too, like a co-conspirator. "Was that you put out some bait in the *Lincoln County* and a blurb in *Uncle Henry's*? If it was you, then nice touch, by the way, and good thinking, because take it from me, obits are addictive. Reading someone else's life story, you know. And the real estate listings. Most folks are just nosy, I guess."

Doc went on, "Hope you don't mind me saying it, but I'd bet dollars to donuts this Necco man will fall for one of those notices and take your bait."

Farnsy took a good long look at Doc. Why hadn't he thought of the real estate listings?

Julie went back about her business as if she'd not heard a thing.

"Well, Doc, for a dentist, you've got an eagle eye. Should've figured you'd spot the bait. And I think you're spot on about real estate listings. I should have thought of that angle."

Doc sipped his coffee and let Julie wipe the counter around them.

"So, that a thank you, Farnsy?"

FARNSY

"Doc, that was as close as you're gonna get to one today. I got work to do." Farnsy pulled a $2 bill out of his wallet. "Julie, this is for Doc's coffee. And one of those stale crullers, the ones he likes."

Farnsy's ad for "a classic Maine fishing camp" ran in the real estate section of the next *Lincoln County News*.

> Once owned by Carl Parker, an avid angler, retired CEO of Parker Fish and Game, who amassed a large collection of antique fishing gear, including bamboo fly rods, woven reed trout creels, hand-tied trout flies, and a box of old casting lures, some still in their original packaging. The estate includes one of the last remaining Minnow lures, once owned by Cornelia 'Flyrod' Crosby. Provenance provided upon request.

The ad ran with a photo of several cottages on Farnsy's cove. The address provided was vague: "Cove on the west side of Damariscotta Lake, north of Bunker Hill and south of the narrows. Where big fish are always biting!" Farnsy figured his cottage would be as good a place as any to keep an eye on the other cottages. If anyone recognized the cove and came poking around, he'd surely see them or hear them.

A few days passed, and then the call came. The only inquiry. With the holidays coming, Farnsy was surprised, but the caller was insistent. He wanted to look at the cottage, and the lures, he added, before Christmas. Farnsy said the cottage was closed up, but just as soon as he could get out to open the place up, he'd call the man back with the address. "But bring your Benjamins," Farnsy said, trying to sweeten the pot and set the hook, assuming this was the Necco man himself, or an associate, "because a couple of these lures are genuine antiques. Excellent condition, if I do say so, which is surprising for their age." The man said he could come up that weekend, would that be okay? The man sounded eager. Maybe too eager. "You interested in the cottage? Or just the lures?"

"The cottage? Yeah, sure. But the fishing lures sound interesting."

Farnsy thought a moment. "Well, then, if you're really interested in the cottage, I'll give you the address and you can peek in the windows, see if it's in the ballpark, you know? Then I could drive out and meet you, show you the lures, too. I'll have to get them out of Oggie's old army trunk under the bed."

The man took down the address, thanked Farnsy and said he'd call Farnsy Saturday morning. Something about the whole conversation seemed off to Farnsy. Maybe it was totally legitimate and the man really was interested in the cottage, not just the lures, or maybe he was just a regular guy who had a thing for lures. But Farnsy had a hunch, and without any clues or leads to go on, his hunch was all he had. The caller had said he was in Boston. If that was right, he had at least a three-hour drive. It was Thursday. The man might drive up that night, but Farnsy had a hunch he would drive up Friday, check the place out, then call Farnsy on Saturday. Maybe. After work Thursday, Farnsy kept the lights low and had an eye and an ear out for any cars coming down the road. If he couldn't hear something, Henry would. Every now and then, Farnsy glanced over at Henry. Asleep, no ears swiveling. It was a quiet evening.

Next day, Farnsy decided that Friday night was the night. If he drove home and his pickup were parked outside and the lights were on inside with a fire in the fireplace, the caller might come down but would turn around fast. His best option would be to leave some extra food and water for Henry, let his own cottage go dark, and watch from one of the cottages on the opposite shore. He could use the cottage where he and his father had cut down the wind chimes. Great sightlines and there'd be no tire tracks on the road down to his cottage. The trap was baited and set.

After his shift, Farnsy drove down the other side of the lake and parked his pickup behind the cottage. He pulled his winter pants on over his long johns and layered up, police balaclava and thermal mittens. He had his binoculars, a flashlight, a blanket, a Thermos of black coffee, two slices of Hilltop pizza, pepperoni and green pepper, and two rolls of Necco wafers. Enough to get him through the night. He took a blue tarp off some deck furniture and settled into a heavy Adirondack chair with the blanket wrapped around himself and the tarp on top, like a little tent, and he was warm and safe from the wind that gusted up every now and then. He wondered what Henry was doing across the way. Probably curled up on the sofa. Maybe he was looking out the window. Around midnight, Farnsy saw a light flicker across the lake. The wind in the trees made the light seem to move. Maybe someone with a flashlight. He looked through his binoculars and the only light he could see was coming from his own cottage. No car visible. No sign of anyone moving in the shadows. It was his living room. The timer on his night light. Farnsy stayed another hour or so, until he wasn't just feeling cold, bone-cold, he was feeling pretty foolish. Sometimes a hunch is just a hunch. The hot shower back in his place felt great. Then he noticed the flashing light on the cottage phone. Missed phone call. Lucy. No voicemail. Maybe Lucy was right, all cop, no wife.

Mittens

"Farnsy, woman says her name is Emma Spencer's here to see you," Dottie said. "I told her to have a seat, that you'd be right out. Or you want me to tell her to come back another time?"

"That's fine Dottie, be right out." Farnsy thought the name sounded vaguely familiar but just couldn't place it. When he saw her through the window on the security door as he pushed it open, he remembered. It was over at Renys during the Early Bird Sale, when they'd caught her trying to walk out with a pair of boots and a few winter things for her kids. It'd been more than a month, but he remembered her and wondered what she was doing now in the police station.

"Mrs. Spencer, nice to see you."

"Officer Farnsworth, hi. Good to see you again." They shook hands, and Farnsy sat down a chair away. Easier to make eye contact. Essential to good police work. But just common sense. And in the case of Emma Spencer, he just felt like he could relax a bit, though he didn't know why.

"Sorry to bother you. I know you must be terribly busy."

"It's okay; you caught me at a good time. Just making a few phone calls, checking out some leads. A little paper shuffling, you know. And I needed a break."

She smiled.

"So, tell me, Mrs. Spencer..."

"Please, call me Emma." She paused, then reached into the bag next to her and pulled out a small box with a blue ribbon. "I just wanted to do something to, you know, thank you for your help back then. I was so..."

"Miss Spencer, Emma, please..."

"Gosh, it was so embarrassing. I just didn't know what..."

"Emma, I was just glad I could help you. Not often a person has a chance to do something and just happens to do the right thing. All in the line of duty, you know."

Emma looked as though she were about to cry again. Farnsy looked away.

She handed him a small package, wrapped up nicely.

"Officer, I really just wanted to drop it off and leave it for you. But then the lady said you were here and all."

Farnsy held the box in both hands. "Should I open it now?"

"Sure. If you like. I mean it's really nothing. Just a little..."

Farnsy untied the ribbon, opened the box, pulled out some dark green tissue and saw a pair of mittens inside. Black, with a silver stripe across the top of both hands.

"I tried to make them look like policeman's gear, so I just used the colors of your cruiser, you know?"

"Emma, gosh, these are amazing!" Farnsy tugged them on. "They're really beautiful, and they fit perfectly. Wow!"

Emma shrugged.

"You made these? Jeez, perfect fit."

"Can you use them?"

"Are you kidding? The winters around here? Thanks so much, Emma."

"The wool is from sheep on a farm up near my place. And it's a tight pattern, so they should be warm."

"Emma, these are really great. Seriously, thank you so much." Farnsy thought a moment.

"You think you could make more of these? I mean, for sure you could sell these in town. I know you got your hands full with your kids and all, Emma, but, look, this is beautiful work. Hand-made, Maine wool, Maine knit."

"Well, I do have a couple pairs for sale over at the Weatherbird on Main Street."

Emma Spencer was smiling when she left the station, and as soon as she was gone, Farnsy showed the mittens to Dottie. And she said, "You know, Farnsy, and it's none of my business, but you ask me, I think Lucy might like a pair, don't you think? Christmas is just around the corner, you know."

Farnsy had a hard time deciding which color, but finally picked out a pair of crimson mittens for Lucy that had a tangle of cording on top that reminded him of pigtails. Then he bought a second pair for Dottie. A nice lavender color he thought she'd like. Farnsy liked knowing who made them, and he knew that if Emma Spencer was as careful knitting these mittens as she was taking care of her kids, these mittens would hold up on even the coldest day in Maine. And he was glad to hear they were selling as fast as Emma could knit them.

Late December was unusually busy, with the weather and all the holiday hustle and bustle. A week or so before Christmas, Farnsy realized he'd forgotten to mail the mittens to Lucy. His only option was to drop them off at her mother's place over in Round Pond. He could just leave them there on the porch next to the front door, with a note. Like one of Santa's elves. He wasn't sure he wished Lucy'd be there. When she'd left Farnsy's place the day after Thanksgiving, he remembered her saying that she had to get back to Augusta, but they should stay in touch. What did she mean by that? Whatever it was that tied them together, Farnsy was starting to think it was more like a bungee cord.

He drove over to the Granger place after work that week, the package all wrapped up and ribboned with a short note from

FARNSY

"Santa Farnsy" wishing Lucy a warm and merry Christmas and something about her being a good girl that year.

He had barely stepped onto the porch when he heard Corrie.

"Farnsy! What do you think you're doing, sneaking up here like this?"

"Uh, Corrie, hello there. I was just…"

"And what's that you got there? Well, I have to say, this is a nice surprise. Brrrr. Cold out. You want to come in?"

"Just wanted to drop off a little something for Lucy, Corrie. You know, holidays and all. From an old friend." He handed her the package with the note.

"Well, this is real nice, Farnsy. I know Lucy'll be happy to hear from you again."

What did that mean? Was he supposed to call Lucy or something? All she'd told him was to stay in touch. That could mean anything. Might as well say, "Have a nice day." Maybe she'd told her mom something. After all, according to Lucy, she still told her mom everything.

"She here?"

"Sorry, Farnsy, she's not. Right after her course was over, she and a friend flew down to Florida for the holidays. She didn't tell you?"

"No, she didn't say much about that. Not to me, at least. Florida?"

"Yup, said she needed time to think. About things, you know?"

"A friend?"

"If you mean a man, yes. Real nice fella, her coloring coach is. But I don't think you've got much to worry about in that department, if you know what I mean. Friend of his got a place down in Miami Beach."

Farnsy wasn't sure he should be hearing all that information. After all, Lucy was a free woman, like she told him, out of Earl's lobster trap, and it was her life, free to live. Sort of a modified New Hampshire license plate motto.

"Okay, Corrie. Look, could you please tell Lucy for me..."

"Farnsy, I'm sorry. Not to get all serious on you now, this being Christmastime, you know, but I feel like if you want to tell Lucy anything, you should really tell her yourself. Besides, she doesn't listen to half the advice I give her. I mean if she had, and I probably shouldn't say it, but she wouldn'ta gone off and eloped with that old fisherman, if you know what I mean."

Earl was only five or six years older than Farnsy, but he'd looked old since he was in his 20s. Corrie stopped a moment, then she said in a low voice that was meant for serious talk, "Okay, Farnsy, let me get serious for a minute, if I can, then I'll let you go because I know there are a thousand places you'd rather be than standing out here in the friggin' cold listening to an old lady."

She looked down at the gift Farnsy had brought, then back up at Farnsy, looking at him face to face. "All I'll say, William Farnsworth, is that life is real short and, sooner or later, there comes a time when you have to decide. The old fork in the road. And then you have to live with your decision. The other thing is, well, there is no perfection. Nothing is perfect. And, like Lucy knows, there's no perfect man. And, fair's fair, so that means no perfect woman. Lord knows, Mr. Granger, God rest his soul, and I sure rode the rollercoaster now and then. Ask Lucy. Everyone does now and then. But you just gotta hold on to whatever handle you got. And then, might be years later, you look back and you realize that you actually got pretty darned close to perfection." She took a deep breath. "So there you have it. Whatever happens between you and Lucy, I hope you'll stop by now and then, you know. For old time's sake, at least."

Corrie gave Farnsy a good hug, wished him a "Merry Christmas," and Farnsy drove back to his place in silence.

Lucy was a Mainer. A real Maine gal. Down to earth. Could be sweet as a jelly donut or tough as nails, blunt and honest. She'd size someone up slowly. Didn't matter where they were from, she'd take her time. And when she eventually concluded that someone from away was full of himself, or herself, that was it. There were, of course, some cases where she didn't need to deliberate. If you asked why there weren't any tides on Damariscotta Lake, since it was so close to the ocean, that's all the evidence Lucy needed. You were a fool.

Like most Mainers, she didn't have much patience for talkers. Big talkers. Loud talkers. Windbags. And folks who walked around like they owned the place and would sell it out from under you if they could. People wearing anything with a lobster printed on it were fair game. Like she told Farnsy, "You don't see those folks from Vermont wearing little yellow cheese wedges all over their pants, do you?"

But if you want to know why Lucy was a Maine gal, apart from the fact that she was pretty sure she was conceived in Maine and probably at the Skowhegan Drive-In Movie Theater during a summer *Star Wars* marathon—and then born right there in Damariscotta at the hospital—you could tell she was a Mainer because Renys was her go-to place for nearly everything. And she hit every sale they had. First of all, she had at least three different pairs of flannel PJs. The red plaid one was Farnsy's favorite. She had moccasin-style slippers for around the house, which she wore until the soles were paper thin and the furry top part looked like a dead squirrel. Then she'd watch for another sale at Renys.

Her favorite event wasn't the Pumpkinfest, she'd told Farnsy. It was the Early Bird Sale in November, when she could wear her flannel PJs and get the biggest discount at Renys. That's another thing about a Maine gal: she wasn't at all embarrassed to be seen wearing her flannels around town. Not in the least. Lucy liked fishing now and then, and she liked the company of women, her gal pals, and she had a couple, but she preferred the company of men, she once told Farnsy, because to her they were like big puppies. Feed them, give them something to drink and a bone to chew on, and they were happy, she'd said. As Farnsy knew, she never waited for him to make the first move. If she wanted a kiss, she went for it. Her favorite thing to do in bed was to cuddle. She told Farnsy it was the best way to get warmed up those frosty winter mornings.

She'd put on a pretty dress and a little fragrance for a dinner date and style her curls in different ways. But if she were taking a hike or going out fishing, she'd daub on a little bug repellant like it was a priceless Parisian scent. And Lucy had a little extra of herself, here and there, in all the right places, as Farnsy liked to tell her whenever she talked about maybe starting a diet. Maine women didn't have that lean and hungry look like New York models. They looked good just the way they were. Maybe a little rounder and softer, but that made cuddling all the more fun. As Lucy said, every couple started out with the hot stuff, but if they stayed glued together, with duct tape or by some miracle, it was because they cuddled. Pretty hard to argue or bring up something from yesterday or talk money if you're spooning, flannel on flannel, early some winter morning. And that's it, really: Maine gals are with you in the warm sunny days, but come winter, they're real partners, uncomplaining in the cold, shoveling out right alongside you. When it came down to it, like all Maine gals, Lucy enjoyed being a woman.

Fisherman's Catch

One bitter cold morning, as if summoned, a few folks who knew the Professor gathered at Waltz's Soda Fountain to take the chill off and have a coffee. They knew the Professor was hard-boiled about formal religion so they avoided talking about the afterlife, which the Professor always called retirement, or any suggestion that she might be looking down on them gathered there. Around 10, when Farnsy came in for his mid-morning coffee, he found every counter seat taken and more folks huddled around, jabbering away. When they saw Farnsy come in, they stepped back to let him get to the counter. Julie had his mug sitting there already, brim-full.

"Pick a donut, Farnsy," she said with a solemn air, holding out a box of chocolate donuts, the Professor's favorite. Julie knew Farnsy was trying to slim down, but she held out the donuts as if to say, this is a special occasion and one donut won't hurt, so just take one, will ya? Farnsy still hadn't figured out who baked Julie's donuts, but he had a mind to try to pin down the ingredients. There was something elusive about them, like maybe an old family recipe. And from scratch, homemade, because they were all slightly different in shape. What the donuts at Waltz's Soda Fountain lacked in the predictability of store-bought perfection, they made up for with homemade flavor.

Farnsy picked up one of the chocolate donuts, Julie smiled, and Doc watched the donut box circle around the assembled crowd, which had grown from a group to a crowd by that time. When everyone had a donut, Doc said, "Okay, folks, let's have a moment of silence and remember the Professor." There was a brief moment of silence, then some rustling, and then someone said, "Well, that's about long enough, seeing as she never did keep quiet that long herself." There were a few chuckles as folks thought of something the Professor had said or done. The silence settled back around them. Someone sniffled, then blew their nose. A few customers wended their way through the assembled faithful, curious as to what was going on, then wandered off, in search of something they didn't know they needed.

Finally, to the great relief of everyone gathered, Doc broke the silence and said, "Okay, folks, hold up your donuts!" There was a moment of silence. "Here's to you, Professor!" Doc took a big bite out of his donut and, as if synchronized, everyone took a big bite out of their donuts, then dunked them in their coffees, as the Professor had loved doing. "And Merry Christmas, everyone!"

Farnsy mingled with folks gathered around the counter, catching up on the latest, the weather, and answering a few questions: How was Lucy doing? What happened to Pemmy? He reassured folks that Pemmy had found a real good home and dodged the questions about Lucy because he knew anything he said about her would make the rounds faster than Jock at Eider's could shuck an oyster.

Farnsy asked Julie to freshen up his coffee, then snuck another jelly donut off the platter and found his way over to Doc, who was standing by the entrance to Waltz's, staring out the window at nothing in particular. It wasn't like in the summer when you could sit there and watch summer people wandering around. Winter was quieter. Snow blanketed the sounds of village life and everyone moved slower, but even though they were all bundled up, the town was small enough you could recognize your friends by the way they walked.

FARNSY

"Nice ceremony, Doc," Farnsy said, as both men stared out the window.

"You got some sugar powder on you there...." Doc said, brushing the lapel of Farnsy's uniform. "But thanks, Farnsy. Only surprise is the Professor didn't come back and chew us all out. She wasn't much of one for formalities, you know."

"Doc, look, sorry to talk business, but I've been doing some thinking..."

"Thinking is always good..."

"I'm serious." Doc was listening. "Okay, look, Doc, I need to take a look at your diaries."

"They're history, Farnsy, history. Journals, not diaries. And they're not ready for public consumption, if you get my drift."

"Sorry, I mean your histories, your notebooks there, the ones from last winter, say December through February."

"Mind me asking why?"

"Well, you never know, but I have a hunch there might be some detail tucked away in there or between the lines, some clue that you picked up and that I might've missed that might give us a new lead on this case. Other than the nibbles I've gotten, it's been pretty quiet. I figure that notebook of yours, your history, might just have some little clue that I missed. Even a small clue could break this case open." Farnsy steeled his jaw. "Far as I'm concerned, this case isn't closed until I say it is." Then he added, "Something about it just isn't right, if you know what I mean."

Doc took the last bite of his donut, dabbed his mouth with a napkin, then balled it up and tucked it into his empty coffee mug on the counter.

"Happy to help, Farnsworth. You want to read them yourself? Not sure I'd know what to look for."

"Thanks, Doc. Why don't you take a look through your notes first, see if you see anything that jumps off the pages and let me know. Maybe I'll have time to take a closer look after the holidays when things calm down some. Folks over at the Lincoln Home asked me to play Santa this year. Plus, the Chief wants us on call next couple of weeks. Always something up, you know, it being winter and all. People get to feeling pretty cooped up indoors and start doing crazy stuff around the holidays. Could be a domestic with the bills piling up or someone just needs some easy cash to buy things. But it'd be a big help if you could see if you made a note about any snowmobiles on the lakes last winter. Or snowshoers. Or cross-country skiers. And if you find something, it'd help to know the day and the date. And location." In setting this wheel in motion, Farnsy already sensed the futility of this trail. Most of Doc's journal was local material. And technically, Damariscotta Lake was out of Farnsy's jurisdiction.

"I'll take a gander, Farnsy, but I don't recall anything, so don't get your hopes up. Besides, what would the Professor say?"

"I don't know, Doc," Farnsy said, "Probably tell us to stop sitting on our thumbs. Anyway, I gotta go pick up the Santa outfit over at the Lincoln Home. So let me know what you find in those notebooks, will you?"

"On the case, Officer!" Doc sighed.

"You're gonna need a couple more pillows, I think, Farnsy," Edna over at the Lincoln Home said when she saw Farnsy emerge from the men's room with the Santa outfit on.

"Didn't think I'd lost any weight, Edna. Guess I should feel pretty good about that."

"No, it's just that our last Santa was, well, let's just say Milo was a big fella. I think he probably stopped walking years before he passed, but he kept right on eatin'. That's probably what killed him. A good soul. Sure liked hard cheese and Whoopie Pies. He could 'Ho ho ho' with the best Santas, and he didn't scare the kids who came here to visit their grammies. Anyway, it doesn't surprise me one bit that you've got some extra room in there."

She tucked a second pillow under the red Santa jacket and Farnsy wrapped the big black Santa belt around his middle.

"Now, tug it good and tight there, Farnsy. Wouldn't want anyone to see a pillow slip out and think you were having a baby, you know. Give someone a heart attack. "She took a good long look at Farnsy, head to toe. "All you need now, Farnsy, is a Mrs. Claus! Maybe next year?"

Farnsy wondered what he was getting himself into. He didn't feel much like celebrating this year, with the Professor gone now and Lucy off to Florida. But the nurses at the home said they thought they'd seen the Santa spirit in him when he came to visit the Professor. Then one of them confessed that the Professor had recommended him, told them he'd make a good Santa. Farnsy hadn't believed in Santa since he was a boy and got a Christmas present he'd seen at Renys—and he knew Santa didn't shop at Renys. Seems Farnsy was already a bit of a detective back then, so when he sniffed around his parents' closet and found a stack of gifts all wrapped up and marked for him and his little sister "from Santa!," well, the case was closed and the mystery solved. But he let his sister figure it out on her own.

When the day arrived for Farnsy to play Santa for the old-timers, he didn't quite feel the part yet, so he practiced a few "Ho ho ho" belly laughs as he tugged on his costume and checked himself in the mirror. He'd put on his beard when he got there. It had begun to snow and the flakes thickened up and came down faster as he drove. Clumps of snow, fat and heavy, smacked the windshield and the wipers tried to keep up. With Christmas tunes on the radio, he was beginning to get in the right frame of mind to pretend he was a jolly old soul. As he drove into town Farnsy could see sparkly Christmas decorations flickering happily here and there.

At the corner where he should turn right, Farnsy remembered he wanted to pick up a piece of haddock over at the Fisherman's Catch for supper that night and they'd be closed by the time he finished playing Santa. So he turned left onto Main Street, drove over the bridge and found a parking spot right in front of the fish market.

Strange, he thought, seeing a car in the spot just ahead of him, idling, someone sitting behind the steering wheel, looking over her shoulder. At least Farnsy thought it looked like a woman. Hard to tell in that light.

The old sign in the window at the Fisherman's Catch read, "In Cod We Trust," left over from when the shop was called Gilliam's. The store looked empty, except for the owner, Percy, who was fussing around the lobster tanks. Farnsy watched a skinny man step inside and saw the owner look up. The skinny man shook off some snow. Main Street was empty except for a few cars parked up by Renys and the one he'd just parked behind. Most folks were either home or headed there and darkness was settling in fast like a rising tide.

He sat another minute or so, then hit the windshield wipers, as if they could clear his mind. He felt the warm air from the vent and listened to the station in Portland babble on and on about this Nor'easter and how much snow they'd predicted by Christmas, just a couple of days away.

He turned the radio off and watched Percy move around behind the counter, the skinny man looking at the lobster tanks, with his back to the owner. Farnsy knew it was close to closing time and he was reaching for the door handle when he saw the skinny man pull something out of his right pocket and slip a Santa mask over his face. Farnsy took a deep breath, turned the engine

FARNSY

off, felt for his firearm in one of his big Santa pockets, then swung open the door of his pickup and stepped into a gust of wicked cold air that was coming in off the river and smelled of low tide and seaweed. The snowflakes were smaller now, and he knew that meant it would keep snowing, just like the radio said, in time for a white Christmas. Farnsy smoothed out his Santa outfit and ran his hand over the straggly beard he'd just hooked over his ears. No idea how those ZZ Top fellas could wear those long whiskers. Then he strode around the cruiser away from the car parked in front of him, over to the store.

At the doorstep, he looked around, but the street was empty except for his cruiser and the one car parked in front of his. Covered in snow, so it'd been there a while. Inside, Farnsy could see Percy with his back to the man with the Santa mask, doing something at the cash register. Something about it looked a little off to Farnsy, and one thing he'd learned as a cop was to listen to his instincts.

The door jingled as Farnsy entered the shop and the air was thick and warm and smelled of fish and salt and the sea. Before he could say a word, the man in the Santa mask startled and Percy behind the counter turned around and said, "Well, look who's here! Look, honey, it's another Santa!" A little girl, couldn't have been more than seven or eight, popped out from behind the counter, all pink-faced and pigtails, and let out a happy squeal, then ran back to hide behind Percy. Farnsy ho-hoed two or three times, trying to figure out what to do. Shoot, he thought, just my luck. Where'd that girl come from? Didn't know Percy had a kid that young. Where's the time go?

The other Santa ho-hoed too. Only it sounded more like "Who the hell are you?"

Percy weighed the haddock and looked down to the little girl as he wrapped up the fish. "Santa made it just before closing time, didn't he!?" and the little girl squealed a piercing squeal of sheer delight, so Farnsy Santa ho-hoed again, then stopped and just stood there like he'd lost his script, and Percy said "I'll bet this Santa's come to find out if you've been naughty or nice! That right, Santa?"

Farnsy ho-hoed, as if to say yes. But he was keeping one eye on the other Santa, something about him.

The little girl giggled. "I've been a good girl! Honest, Santa! Except that one time!"

Farnsy took his hand out of his pocket and kneeled down, so he was eye level with the little girl, and ho-hoed. "Now don't you look cunnin', dear. Santa knows you've been a good girl." Then he twirled his mustache and said, "Besides, everyone makes a mistake now and then, even Santa. Sometimes big mistakes." Farnsy stared right at the other Santa. Skinny fella, had a feeling he knew him from somewhere.

"But it doesn't mean you're bad. Just took a wrong turn. And you know, like in a car, you can always back up and turn around, take a different road."

Skinny Santa started backing away from the counter, leaving Farnsy standing there between him and Percy. The little girl was standing between the two Santas. The other Santa fished around in one of his pockets for something. Farnsy watched, then saw it wasn't a weapon. The skinny Santa spilled a handful of change into the little girl's hand like they were gold doubloons. "Now you take these over there to Fernald's when they open tomorrow," he said, pointing to the sandwich store across the street, "and get some penny candy, okay de-ah?"

And as the other Santa started for the door, he turned to the owner and said, "Sir, that's a sweet little angel you've got there. Merry Christmas to you all! And a Happy New Year! Ho, ho, ho. Oh, and thanks, Santa, you're a good cop. But get a shave."

FARNSY

Farnsy thought he recognized the other Santa's voice. In fact, he was sure he knew the other Santa. But something in Farnsy softened up. He'd just watched the man do a U-turn. Besides, no crime was committed, at least not carried out—the intent was there, but, after all, it was Christmas, or close enough to it. And like the Chief said, guns are always involved in everything a policeman does, even if it's just his own firearm. You want to use them sparingly. And if you figure another way out of a mess, that was a good thing. Farnsy never could remember who told him that. Maybe he'd just thought that up himself.

Percy thanked Farnsy, who told the little girl that, yes, there were a lot of Santas, but the best Santa was her father, standing right there next to her. Now he had to get on over to the Lincoln Home and visit the old folks.

Farnsy wouldn't let the owner give him any haddock for free. "Thanks, Percy," he added, "but I think that fish'd taste better if I paid for it, you know."

Percy scooped some crushed ice into a large plastic bag, then set the fish inside and tied it up with a twist tie.

"Should be okay, as long as you cook it tonight, Farnsy, after you're done at the home. Oh, here, take a lemon."

Farnsy put a dollar for the lemon on the countertop then ho-hoed a couple of times—"Merry Christmas! Merrrry Christmas!"—on the way out, warming up for his grand entrance at the Lincoln Home a few minutes away.

The gal from the home met him outside with a large red bag full of soft-chew, non-stick, low-sugar goodies all wrapped up and ready for him to hand out. "Perfect, Farnsy. The Professor was right. You look just like the jolly old soul himself. Everyone's been talking all week about Santa coming. It's like they're kids again, you know?"

Farnsy sprinkled some new snow all over himself for that authentic look. Then there they were, all those old folks waiting for him, gathered around inside the entrance. Some standing on their own, some with walkers or canes, a few in wheelchairs. A nurse stood nearby, just in case. Farnsy ho-hoed, "MERRY Christmas everyone, Merry Christmas! Ho ho ho!"

Farnsy thought they looked young again, like that little girl he'd just seen—looking up at him as though he were the real thing. Truth was, he sort of felt like he was the real Santa. So he reached into his red sack, pulled out the first gift, and walked over to an old woman in a wheelchair. "Have you been a good girl this year, young lady?"

She giggled and said, "mostly."

"Merry Christmas, dear!" He handed her the little gift then started to make the rounds of everyone at the party and a few folks too fragile to leave their rooms. He stayed there until he put the last of the gifts in the frail hands of the oldest resident of the Lincoln Home, who waved him closer to her face and whispered, "Merry Christmas, Farnsy. Next year you bring Mrs. Claus. Lucy's the one!"

Farnsy took another look at the old woman and saw it was Ernestina, the woman who'd handled the front desk at the station up to around the time Farnsy started work there. "Can't make any promises, Ernestina."

"Lucy's the gal, Farnsy, trust me. Heart of gold. Forgive and forget, bygones be bygones, the way I see things. Life is short, Farnsy. Take my word for it. You know, like that old kids' song, how's it go? Life is but a dream. Something like that."

How Ernestina knew about Lucy was a mystery. Sometimes it seemed like everyone in town knew more about his life than he did. Made him wonder if he shouldn't just call a town meeting and get everyone's advice.

Back home, Farnsy popped open a Pabst and sat down on the sofa with a small bowl of honey-roasted almonds, too tired to get up and

FARNSY

start a fire in the fireplace. Henry was sitting across from him on an old ladder-back chair. The cushion on the chair was stuffed with balsam needles and Henry loved it. That cat stared right at him, unflinching. Farnsy wanted to know what Henry was thinking.

"Henry, you're a good cat."

The cat stared.

"Okay, a great cat. Best ever."

The cat stared.

"Wish I knew what you're thinking, Henry."

Farnsy finished the honey-coated almonds and washed them down with a gulp of beer. He settled back into the sofa, and then his eyes met Henry's again.

"So tell me, Henry, is Lucy the one? You met Nedda last summer. Was it her dog? You didn't like Pearly. That it?" Farnsy paused.

"Jeez, what's a grown man doing, middle-aged, single, middle of his life, talking to a cat? No offense Henry, but my life's just a little more complicated than yours, old man. Even though I guess in cat years you're about my age."

Still no answer. Henry yawned, mouth wide open, his incisors showing as if he were the king of the jungle. Then he stretched out and curled up in a ball, facing Farnsy, eyes open, still listening.

"Okay, I get it, Henry. No more questions. You're telling me I've got all the answers. You're a real good listener, Henry. Okay, okay, I'll do it. I'll call Lucy. But after Christmas."

As Farnsy got the fish ready for the oven, he trimmed a couple of pieces for Henry, who ate them like he hadn't been fed in a week.

Moody's

Christmas arrived before Farnsy could think of anything special he could do to celebrate. He hadn't even been able to get a tree until Christmas Eve. Not that he hadn't looked forward to a little quiet at the end of a busy fall. After all, he really wasn't alone, not with Henry there, celebrating like a cat, knocking all the shiny ornaments off the lowest branches of the little balsam Farnsy'd picked out. He set the tree up across from the fireplace, so the needles wouldn't dry out. One Christmas his mother had made his father go out and find a new tree because there were more needles on the floor than on that tree, she'd said. Could hear them dropping.

It had been a good day, off duty and alone with his thoughts and the cat, but by the end of Christmas day, Farnsy had grown tired of looking back and wondering where Lucy was. Farnsy looked over to Henry and asked the cat what he thought about Lucy. The cat perked up and flicked his tail. Henry was good company, that cat. A little Christmas catnip, a new feathered toy on a string, and some of that canned cat food, warmed up with a little hot water, and Henry was happy as a clam, if clams are really happy.

All Farnsy had needed was a couple of days on the lake. Catch up on his sleep under the new comforter Lucy'd given him for his birthday. Bacon and eggs for breakfast. Let his beard get scratchy. Bundle up and bring in more kindling and firewood for the fireplace. Then sit in front of the fire with a cup of black coffee and listen to the news on the radio. Farnsy'd never seen the point in getting a TV. The news wasn't any better if you could see the people reading it. And with his schedule, the last thing he wanted was to get all wrapped up in some TV series. He had enough interrupted stories in his own life.

Farnsy liked Christmas. Not the long commercial build-up, which seemed to start earlier and earlier. He liked Christmas Eve and Christmas Day. When he was a kid, it was like all time came to a stop. Just Farnsy, his sister, and their parents. He loved the rituals and had done his best to keep them, even after his mother died and his father left.

Before Farnsy started wondering again how Lucy was, or where she was, or if she'd gotten the mittens, his phone rang. His sister out west. They caught up. "Merry Christmas, Farnsy!" she said. He told her about the bait he'd set for the Necco man. Then Grace told Farnsy she was planning to come back to the lake next summer. "The kids want more turtle-hunting time, Farnsy. We missed you last summer. Promise?"

Farnsy promised he'd take Grace's kids out turtle hunting. "And they're bigger now, so they could paddle with me out to Blueberry Island, too. Blueberries should be in season when you come."

Grace asked how Lucy was doing. Farnsy told her about Thanksgiving over at Lucy's mother's. Grace said, "Well, that's nice. Good. I'm glad." Then she said, "Okay, kids are getting restless. I'd better go. Hey, almost forgot. The kids loved that book about turtles. Sheesh, now they're all over me to get a pet turtle."

"Just tell them we'll get a pet turtle when they're out next summer. Catch and release, though." Farnsy told Grace that he loved her.

She said, "You too, Farnsy. Say hi to Lucy for me, if you see her, okay?"

Farnsy promised he would. After he put his phone down, his thoughts gravitated back to Lucy. Try as he might, he couldn't get his mind off her. And he wasn't sure he really wanted to.

What had Doc told him? "Sometimes the things we want most are the things we can't have. And sometimes the things we most need are right there in front of us, staring at us."

Farnsy passed Christmas in pleasant solitude, trying to sort out his tangle of thoughts about the woman in his life and his police work, which seemed to be stalled, same-old-same-old, and no leads or action on the case. He couldn't even solve the donut mystery.

He sat in front of the fire, trying to figure out the right thing to do so he wouldn't have any regrets when he hit 70, if he did, but no voices told him the right next steps. He had everything he needed. Except someone to share it with. Not that Henry wasn't great. He was even a fair snuggler, but still.

By the end of Christmas day, Farnsy had decided he needed someone who could talk back. Someone to swap stories with. Someone even to argue with and then afterward get all tangled up with. Lucy just kept popping up at the oddest times and it drove him crazy. The Professor had told him that was the surest sign you were in love. The kind that lasted. If they drove you crazy.

During his weekend off after Christmas, Farnsy slept in, wrapped up in Lucy's comforter like a mummy. From time to time, he'd take a look at the Christmas cards friends had sent him: photos from everywhere, and a couple of long family letters about people he didn't know and wouldn't ever meet, and places he'd never see, but it made him aware of the network surrounding him and that felt good. Farnsy felt almost as comfy and cozy as Henry looked, all balled up there on the couch. That night he had the dream again.

Farnsy was strolling along a wide, sun-dappled path, which he could tell was Boston Common. The Swan Boats meandering slowly around the little duck pond were full of happy people.

FARNSY

Children's happy laughter. Fat gold carp floated among the lily pads, surfacing to nibble bread crumbs the children threw into the pond. The warm air smelled of popcorn and cotton candy. At the intersection of two paths that crisscrossed the Common, Farnsy was startled to see Lucy walking toward him. They both slowed down and Farnsy, sensing an opportunity or some unseen urgency, asked Lucy if she would marry him. She looked surprised. "I'm really sorry, Farnsy, but someone else just asked me to marry him." She didn't say who, and Farnsy forgot to ask. But he was too late. Waited too long. Hesitated.

He woke up with a start and a sad sense of regret that didn't fade even when he realized it was a just a dream. But the fear that he might really be too late, might have missed his only opportunity, stayed with him. Like the universe was trying to tell him something. To just do something. Maybe Doc was right. He had to act. To be or not to be. Or maybe the universe was trying to tell him that Lucy was out of his orbit. He tried to call Lucy, at least to see if there was any truth to the dream. Each call went straight to voicemail. Finally, the day before New Year's, she picked up.

"Good to hear from you, Farnsy. I was wondering what you've been up to. Oh, by the way, thanks for the mittens. They're really pretty. Where'd you find them?"

He asked her where she was, and she said she was down in Boston. Her friend from the cosmetology program had an apartment in Cambridge. "When I told her I'd never been to Boston, well..."

Thinking of his dream, Farnsy asked if she'd been to Boston Common. "Not that the Swan Boats would be out in mid-winter."

She laughed. "Farnsy, that has got to be the strangest question you've ever asked. Where do you come up with this? Anyway, yes, we were over there yesterday. You know, to see the lights."

Farnsy told her about the dream, the running into her part, not the part where he asked her to marry him. She laughed and said, well, that's sort of how it seemed to her, too, them always crossing paths every now and then. Then they talked about when they might cross paths again. January, after New Year's, she said.

She was going to watch the big ball drop in Times Square. "With an old friend," she said. Farnsy was afraid to ask. It wasn't like he had any hold on her. She was as free a spirit as Nedda.

"Maybe February," she said.

"Valentine's Day?" he asked.

She paused. "Sure, okay, I'd like that. Meet you at Eider's? Corner booth, same's always?"

"I'll do my best, Luce. Listen, you take care, okay? Can I call you on New Year's, maybe?" Farnsy asked, then remembered she was going to watch the ball drop at Times Square.

"Shoot, forgot, Luce, those crowds in Times Square and all, it's pretty crazy."

"Don't be an old poop, Farnsy. Sometimes crazy is good! Gosh, sometimes I wonder about us, you know?"

All Farnsy heard was "us."

New Year's Eve that year was three temperatures all day: cold, colder, then coldest. And the snow started early, with small flakes that Mainers knew meant a long storm and big drifts. Farnsy's shift was over by late evening, and he was still on call, but Chief told him it'd been a long day and he should get some supper. He'd page Farnsy if he needed help. Farnsy sat in his cruiser thinking, still in uniform. Henry was okay at home with plenty of water and some holiday mix dry food in a dish. So Farnsy drove up Route 1 to Moody's for the New Year's special, New England boiled dinner, hoping they were still open and hadn't run out.

FARNSY

Farnsy stayed at the counter until Philomena Pelletier, who always worked the New Year's Eve shift because, as she told Farnsy, she was alone in life, locked the front door at 10. The last customers said they would've stayed but the snow was starting to drift up, so they had to get home. After a chorus of "Happy New Years!," it was just Farnsy and Philomena, and she hadn't been sweeping for more than a few minutes when there was a loud knock at the front door.

The last night of the year was always the worst. You just never knew who would see Moody's orange sign at the top of the hill and roll in off Route 1, park their rig at some crazy angle, crunch up the wooden ramp dusted by one more howling gust, pull open the second door and walk into that neon oasis, looking around the diner like a newborn, then stomp their boots, trail clots of old snow across the welcome mat, take a green seat at the counter and say to no one in particular, "Sweet Jesus, it's cold." But that's just what the man from the 16-wheeler did after Philomena unlocked the door to let the man in and Farnsy heard him say he just wanted to fill his thermos with some hot coffee and get back on the road. Philomena told Farnsy later that the man had a kind face, so she let him in. Besides, she said, pointing to Farnsy, "I got my own police backup."

Farnsy was sitting near the end of the counter where it curved around toward the restrooms. Ever since he'd seen that spy movie with Lucy at the Skowhegan drive-in, Farnsy always sat with his back to the wall so he could see what was going on. Only this time, he was just sitting there, alone, his after-dinner coffee staring back at him as he started to wade into a pool of memories, wondering what Lucy was doing down there in Times Square, when he heard the man from the big rig knock on the door. He watched Philomena go over and open up, and he heard voices. Then he watched the trucker come in, stomp the snow off his boots, and sit down at the counter next to the register. Philomena locked the door behind the man.

Instinctively, Farnsy slipped his hand down near his pistol like he'd seen Dirty Harry do once. Farnsy thought the man seemed lost, and it was probably kind of Philomena to let him in to get a cup of coffee, but Farnsy was on the alert. Philomena was supposed to close up, and maybe she would have if Farnsy hadn't been there, but like she told Farnsy later, you never knew who needed a cup of coffee and a warm place on New Year's. But Farnsy wondered why the man sat so close to the register.

"Coffee?" Philomena asked the man.

The man, whose Red Sox balaclava started to drip snow, just nodded, as if to let his brain thaw a bit, then said, "Yup. Black."

Philomena was ready with the BUNN coffeepot and had the man's cup brim-full by the time he'd taken off his jacket and draped it over the stool next to him. But the man wasn't a talker. Philomena gave Farnsy the nod. He'd trained the waitresses how to signal trouble, so she gave him that "check this out" glance with her eyes. Which was even more dramatic because on New Year's, Philomena always smeared on a dollop too much blue eyeliner. Anyone didn't know her might've thought she'd gotten two shiners in a bar fight. When Philomena asked him earlier that evening if he liked her new look, meaning her new Moody's apron, Farnsy said was it was fine by him if she wanted to look nice every now and then. "What do you mean, 'every now and then'?" she asked, like she was just about to dope slap him.

Philomena walked over to fill up Farnsy's mug, and said in a voice a little louder than normal, "Top that off for you, Officer?" and gave Farnsy a little tip of her head that said, "something fishy." To which Farnsy responded with his signal, a one-finger tap to his right eyebrow, which meant, "I'm on the case." Then he took a sip of his coffee real slow, thinking, What would Jack Reacher do now? But the first thing that came to his mind was that he might've had too much coffee.

After Farnsy emerged from the men's room, the door flapping behind him like he was Clint Eastwood walking into a bar in Deadwood, he strolled down along the counter and picked up the trucker's jacket to move it one seat away. It felt light, like something you'd wear in warm weather, and he could tell there wasn't a pistol weighing down one of its pockets. He took the seat next to the man and turned toward him so that his police badge showed brass. "My friend, where you headed this fine night, in a blizzard on New Year's Eve here on Route 1?" then added, "if you don't mind my asking."

The man in the balaclava said nothing. Just kept his hands wrapped around the coffee mug, staring at it like he was going to rub it and make a wish. Farnsy waited. He was about to say something like, "Hey, bud, you okay?" when the man in the balaclava turned to Farnsy and with an odd quivery look on his face, which in that bright light looked like a stubbly old battleground, fighting back tears. Then the man got all blubbery and blurted out, "Home." Then he lost the fight and started weeping, his face in his hands. "Sorry," he stammered. "Not doing too good."

Philomena, who could see trouble coming a mile away and around a corner, put her coffeepot down and got out the box of Kleenex she kept under the counter because it was that time of night, between trouble and dawn, she called her shift, and she motioned Farnsy and the driver over to a booth. She checked the two front doors again to make sure they were locked, then turned out the big neon light over the diner and slid onto the seat in the booth opposite the man, and they started talking, slow at first.

The man explained that he'd just done a run down South, to Tennessee, where he'd stopped in a roadside place "a little like this," he said, looking around, "'cept they had grits." Farnsy and

Philomena waited, let the man draw a breath. "And I was weak. You see, been away from home so long I forgot what my wife's voice sounded like. And that southern gal's accent, well, it was too much." Then he told them how he'd driven all that way back home, heading to New Year's up in Bangor, trying to get back to his sweetie before the ball dropped in Times Square, and the closer he got, the slower he drove, on account of the snow and all, and then he goes and takes the wrong exit and ends up here and it's past midnight and all he could think of was his sweet little wife in her flannel nightie up there, waiting for him. And here he was, a strayer, he says, just like his father.

The man commenced weeping, and after a few minutes he stopped and blew his nose into one of Julie's tissues. Farnsy thought the trucker seemed like a hooked fish that'd just spun itself out and then gave up. They talked and talked, and after some time Philomena got up and left them to talk man to man while she made them a stack of blueberry pancakes with real maple syrup and whipped up a side of fresh corned beef hash and a handful of bacon. About the time the sun started to come up, the truck driver looked over at teary old Philomena sitting there with her blue eyeliner running down her cheeks and Farnsy sitting there, the other side of the trucker, twirling his badge on the tabletop, and the man turned to Philomena and asked, "What do I do now?"

Farnsy and Philomena looked at each other. Then Philomena said, "I'm a woman. So I'll tell you what you do."

"Okay," the man said with a sniffle.

Like a mom telling her boy not to shoot birds with his BB gun anymore, Philomena says to the man in the balaclava, "You let me pour you a large coffee, cream and sugar, for the road. Then you go scrape the snow off your rig, and as you drive home, you think of all the good times you had with your Bangor gal. Remember that first kiss you had and just turn your dial over to her frequency, if you get what I mean. And as for that gal down South, never mention gettin' your prop fouled up in her lines. That's got nothin' to do with your gal in Bangor. Now I'm not saying it's right or wrong. Far's I'm concerned, you can have your grits every now and then, but Bangor's your home. And, what's more, you never even mention a word about Tennessee to that sweet Maine gal of yours." Then she paused for effect. "What's past is past. You can't go back. Got it?"

"Got it," he said.

The next time Farnsy went up to Moody's for a piece of blueberry pie and a black coffee just to see if his regular counter seat was still warm, he saw someone had put grits on the menu. Philomena said she figured if anyone wanted a little something on the side now and then, they might just as well stop right there on Route 1.

Fishing

Bruce was weighing a package for a customer when Farnsy walked into the post office next to Waltz's.

"Happy New Year there, Farnsy! Looks like you got some nibbles." Bruce nodded in the direction of the post office boxes. Farnsy had just about given up thinking someone else might take the bait. But he could tell Bruce was serious.

"Check your mailbox, Farns. I think you got something."

Fishermen check their lobster traps every day or so, and Farnsy realized he'd have to check his new post office box more often to see if his bait to lure the Necco burglar got any nibbles. The trail of Neccos he'd been chasing since the summer and through the fall had cooled off, so any new sign was welcome. And now here it was. As he worked the combination on the lock, he could see two envelopes through the little glass window on the door to his box.

One envelope had a Boston return address. The other was postmarked Greenville. Farnsy took one last peek into the box and found a piece of paper folded up, some writing scribbled on it, hastily, from the look of the handwriting. "Drop by the office, Farnsy. Got something. Margie, Slacktide."

Margie was an agent at Slacktide Realty. Maybe she'd heard something about the cottages. Another break-in maybe, more candy? Slacktide was on the same side of the street, about a block down, so Farnsy walked down there first, then he'd open the envelopes back at Waltz's.

FARNSY

"Margie's not in this early," the assistant said, "but she told me to give you this note if you came in."

Farnsy unfolded the paper and read.

"Farnsy—Bruce put my note in your mailbox. Got two voicemails yesterday. Someone asked did we know anyone named 'Oggie' on Damariscotta Lake. Second time he called, asked about the Gould cottage. You'd told us to be on the lookout, thought you should know." Margie had jotted down the caller's telephone number at the bottom. Good work.

Back at the station, Farnsy opened the envelopes. One was in longhand, from someone who said he was a Maine Guide, didn't know Oggie, but said he'd like to look at the Worthley collection, if he could. Business was slow, he wrote, and he could drive down any Saturday. The other letter, from Boston, was on embossed stationery, typed, and expressed "serious interest" in assessing Mr. Worthley's old lure and possibly making an offer for the entire collection. He'd want to see the whole collection, of course, and would like to know the address.

These were promising leads, at least one of them. Farnsy thought the Maine Guide sounded like a nice fellow and was likely a serious collector of fishing lures. Probably had a little collection of his own, since he wrote that he'd started collecting years ago. Still, you never knew, so Farnsy made a note to call the guide anyway. Maybe he'd have some information that could help. And since he'd mentioned not knowing Oggie, well, Farnsy didn't think the Necco man would add something like that. It's in the details like that where thieves get lost in the weeds.

The letter from Boston was more interesting. He and the Chief had speculated that a Mainer might've left the Necco wafers and taken the tackle boxes, but they'd pretty much figured that the person or persons behind the break-ins was probably from away, someone with a little spare change who knew the value of some of these lures down the food chain, at auction. Like Chief said, "money seeks money." And everything about the author of this letter, from his wording to the fancy embossed stationery and envelope, said money. Big money. Lexus money.

Farnsy called the other two real estate agencies in town and learned they'd gotten the same voicemail messages as Margie at Slacktide. Same phone number. Just hadn't gotten around to calling Farnsy yet.

"Heard you got some nibbles, Farns. Mind bringing me up to date?" Chief asked when Farnsy returned to the station.

Farnsy handed over the two letters. Chief looked up from the Maine Guide's letter and said, "Sounds innocent, but check it out. See if he's a registered guide. I'm with you. The guy sounds real." Chief paused, "But now this Boston letter. Could be our man. Might be. But it's still too early to get all giggly. I mean, there's that other big-time dealer you heard from, down in Connecticut. I wouldn't forget that one. For all we know, they could be in this together. What's your next step?"

"I'll check out the guide, but I think I need to get a letter back to the guy from Bean Town. See if maybe there's something behind his interest."

"You thinking what I'm thinking?"

"Like, maybe lunch?"

"Funny, Farnsy. Nope, I'm thinking when you write that letter, you might give him an address out near your place on the lake. Near where you think they're likely to hit this winter. And send it today." Chief paused. "I mean, you've baited the trap, now you got to set it."

"You mean like when a fish takes the bait and you yank the line and set the hook?"

"You got it, Farnsworth. There's hope for you yet."

FARNSY

That afternoon, Farnsy remembered what Lucy's Uncle Stubb had said about Ed, the man Farnsy'd bumped into on the bridge during Pumpkinfest. So he called Ed's number and let it ring a good long while. Ed loved to fish, and he had a nice spot on the lake a way down from Farnsy's cove. Ed finally picked up and said he was staying in the place over the winter and told Farnsy to drop by for a coffee. "Nothing hard, Farnsy, booze and I don't agree. Those meetings have helped and I'm back on the wagon, one day at a time. But I'll do anything for you, Farnsy. Not gonna forget you and me out there on that bridge, you know."

"Okay, Ed, all good. See you around 5:30."

Farnsy explained the whole Necco break-in story, start to finish, some of which Ed said he'd already heard, just not the part about the fake *Uncle Henry's* ad. The obit in the *LCN* he'd seen and wondered who that fellow Worthley was, never heard of him.

"Farnsy, I know most of the guys who fish Damariscotta."

"What about winter? Know any ice fishermen?"

"I'm one of them. Haven't been out yet this year. Soft ice. Especially around the narrows. Water almost never freezes up there nowadays. But other guys? There are a few who have some old ice houses, but they're a dying breed. Young guys now just drill a hole and set up a folding chair. Why?"

"Well, we think someone's been poking around, looking for old stuff, you know, old lures. During the summer. Then, if we're right, they'll come back this winter when no one's around, almost no one, and hit places where they think they'll get some lures, small stuff, things people won't even know is missing. Not until they start looking around for it, month or more later, and by then, the tackle's long gone. Off to New York, Philly, or Boston most likely. Chief and I agree: these guys on the receiving end probably haven't touched a fishing rod in years, if they ever did. But they got money to burn, and they know these lures are valuable, and easy to transport, easy to sell, and maybe even easy to make knockoffs and sell those."

"So, Ed," Farnsy continued, "I'd like to give your camp address to the fellow from Boston who wrote one of the letters. If you'd let me. Might be enough to get him up here, sniffing around."

"Sort of like putting apples in a porcupine trap, Farnsy. I like it. You want me to keep my eyes peeled?"

"That's right, Ed. And I might come out there myself if you don't mind. A little stakeout."

"So why don't you mention something about coming during the week because the owner is away weekends? You know, sweeten the pot. Then you and I sit here in the dark and bust him on the weekend?"

"Not sure about that, Ed. Police work isn't what you see on TV. Hit or miss and mostly miss."

"One thing I got, Farnsy, is time. Anything I can do to repay you, my friend, anything."

They shook hands.

"Thanks, Ed, appreciate your help. I'll let you know. Letter won't get to Boston in time for next weekend, but the weekend after. You here then?"

Ed said he wasn't going anywhere. Farnsy knew that feeling.

Back in the station, Farnsy used the portable typewriter they'd kept to fill in old government forms. The ink ribbon was worn, but he figured that just made his letter look all the more like it was typed by some old codger whose brother had just died and left him a couple dozen rusty old lures.

There were no more letters in his mailbox when Farnsy dropped by to mail his letter to the man in Boston.

Later that day, Farnsy called the Maine Guide and, just as he'd thought, the man was a nice guy, the real deal, who had a small collection of favorite lures that he liked to work on in the winter when he wasn't guiding. Turns out he knew Lucy's uncle. Sometimes it seemed like everyone in Maine was related, once or twice removed. Farnsy asked and the guide said sure, he'd heard of the Minnow, but he hadn't ever actually seen one, which was no surprise, he said, them being so rare and all. He wished Farnsy luck and said he'd keep an eye out when he was in Greenville up on Moosehead Lake. Maybe someone's seen something, he said.

"You never know," Farnsy said, then gave the man his phone number. Another set of eyes won't hurt.

The week before the Boston man said he'd come up and take a look, Farnsy made a few more calls. To snowmobile rental and repair places. They hadn't seen any suspicious behavior recently and couldn't remember any suspicious characters dropping in for repairs. Characters, some of them, the fellow joked, but not suspicious. Most of their business was local. Out of staters, he confirmed, trailered their own snowmobiles up to Maine. Most of them, one guy said, headed up to Moosehead, where they could let it all out. Another one offered that if Farnsy was looking for snowmobilers on Damariscotta Lake, it was a small number he was looking for.

"First off, the narrows is mostly open water even now. Winter's not like it was when we were kids. But the main thing is the pressure ridges," he said. "You hit one of those, full-throttle, on a wide-open snowmobile and you're either airborne or you're in a crumpled mess, spinning on the ice. Of course, late season, end of March, you got soft ice again. Ice looks good, but you get up close to tap it with a good stick and it's slushy and, well, last time I looked, snowmobiles don't float."

Farnsy figured that gave him about a month, maybe a tad longer, before it was ice-out on Damariscotta. But this coming

WINTER — *Fishing*

weekend looked good. Ed said he'd already dragged his ice fishing shack out on the lake middle of that week to about where it'd look like a serious ice fisherman was jigging bait for real fish: perch, pickerel, and large-mouths. It was about a hundred yards away from Ed's place and Ed had angled the shack so that the window gave them a good view of his camp in case anyone tried to break in there looking for lures.

Farnsy parked the Chief's snowmobile next to the ice shed and set up inside. Binoculars on a hook near the window. Lunch and thermos of hot black coffee on a small shelf. Ed had augured a nice hole in the ice, which looked a good foot thick. All Farnsy had to do, Ed told him, was to scoop out the slush every now and then, keep the ice from closing up the hole. Ed stayed back in his camp, ready to call Farnsy if the man from Boston showed up. Farnsy was scanning the lake for any suspicious activity, especially around the camps on the other side. Other than a few other fishermen out on the lake, one in an ice house and two others sitting on folding camp chairs out in the open, watching their jigs at nearby holes, there wasn't much going on.

Midafternoon, the wind picked up and the guys sitting outdoors packed up their gear. Farnsy heard their snowmobiles power down the lake to a pull-out he figured was somewhere over on the Bunker Hill side. Farnsy started packing up, too. Back at Ed's, Ed confirmed that he hadn't seen hide nor hair of the man from Boston. No calls, no turnarounds on the road into his cottage. Pretty much the way it is most weekends, Ed said.

When Farnsy got back to his place, he could see a light blinking on his wall phone. Voicemail. He heard a man's voice with a Boston accent explain that he was unable to drive up to Maine that day. An urgent matter. Sorry for the inconvenience. He'd reschedule at a later date. Left no number, but Farnsy could see from caller ID it was a Boston area code. When he called the number, it went straight to voicemail. And Farnsy left no message. A nibble on the hook, like when you see the bobber start to wiggle.

The next weekend, Farnsy waited in the ice shack from late morning until mid-afternoon. Ed came out for lunch. Brought two Reubens from Fernald's. With pickles and two Moxies and a bag of barbecue-flavored chips. There wasn't much action on the lake. A couple of kids on snowmobiles who looked like they were headed for the narrows and open water, but Farnsy watched them with the binoculars and they turned around well before the dark water. And no sign of any activity near any of the camps they could see from the shack. Ed said he'd seen some ice boats earlier farther down the lake. But these days, most folks liked to stay warm inside. Around three, one of the guys nearby who was watching a couple of ice jigs walked over to knock on the door and ask if they'd caught anything. When Ed told him they hadn't had a bite all day either, the guy said, "Well, that sucks. Least the Bruins won, you know. Guess we'll call it a day." Farnsy and Ed agreed that was probably a good idea. It was getting dark, anyway, so they called it a day too and closed up Ed's shack.

The next weekend, Farnsy was still hoping Lucy might come visit for Valentine's Day, so he asked Ed to keep his eyes peeled and call him right away if he saw anything.

Valentine's Day

Farnsy felt a cold coming on. Started in the morning and by day's end it was full throttle. All he wanted to do was to pick up some over-the-counter cold meds, head straight back to the cottage, and crawl under that down comforter Lucy'd given him.

Must be some kind of a homing instinct, he thought. Back to his mother or her mother, a long line of women, mothers, and grandmothers who practiced home medicine. Their remedy for winter bugs before pharmacy chains was simple: chicken soup if they had a chicken or, if they had potatoes, a potato poultice, which Farnsy's mom replaced with a hot water bottle. Mashed potatoes are for eating, Farnsy's father used to say. From his father, Farnsy learned the military way to clear your sinuses: run hot water from the tap in the bathroom sink until it's steaming, duck down close to the faucet with a towel over your head to create your own little steam room, then breathe deep, in and out, until you've had enough. Then repeat, as needed, several more times a day.

Five o'clock wasn't as dark in early February as it had been back in December when Farnsy's shift ended late afternoon, but it was still pretty gloomy. The road down to his camp was like a tunnel in some parts, trees and branches hunched over by the last ice storm and the weight of the snow, curving into an arch over the road lit up by his headlights. He flicked off his high beams now and then when he saw an approaching car. The road was clear of snow but iced over and Farnsy was real glad he'd put a couple 50-pound sand bags in the back of his pickup. The state didn't salt this road and the town didn't have a budget for salt. The old snow that plows had pushed onto the shoulder was hard-packed and peppered with kicked-up gravel. His pickup slipped in a couple of places where there was some black ice, so Farnsy slowed down even more.

Suddenly a vehicle came up from behind so fast it startled him. Farnsy hadn't even seen the car's lights coming, then there it was, right on his tail. Tailgating was a sport in New England, and some Mainers had perfected it to an art, but this car seemed to want to push Farnsy's vehicle right off the road. So Farnsy rolled his window down and held out his new arctic trooper hat with the shiny gold police badge on it, wiggled it a little, and the car behind him slowed down to an apologetic crawl and dropped back a couple lengths. Not half a mile later, the car pulled off down one of the side roads, an old fire lane, toward a new house perched overlooking the lake.

He nosed the pickup off onto his fire road a mile or so later. It was gravel, but hard-packed from generations. The twin tire ruts were getting deeper, and he could feel the car's undercarriage scrape the ridge in the middle of the road now and then. The road would need work next summer.

When folks talked about feeling like they were in a rut, this road was what Farnsy always pictured to himself. Looked like Tib had plowed it earlier that day, and although the snow had been falling lightly all day, the pines lining the road had prevented the snow from drifting up. There were a couple of deep new gouges where it looked like someone had spun out earlier that day. Even seasoned back road delivery drivers in Maine got hung up now and then, but he hadn't met one yet who wasn't proud they could get their rigs down those gravel roads off grid and back out again. One FedEx guy last winter skidded and got his bumper hung

WINTER — *Valentine's Day*

up on a small tree just up from Farnsy's place. Knocked on the cottage door, pitch-black out, to ask Farnsy if he had a chainsaw. The man took that tree down and drove out just as if nothing had happened. Left some good firewood behind too.

As Farnsy took the last curve, eyes on the edge of the road either side, he looked up and saw a light on in his place. Car parked next to it. He tapped the brakes until the pickup slid to a stop. Make that two lights on inside his place, one in the living room and a second in the back bedroom. He sometimes left the outside light on, but he must've forgotten because it wasn't on. The light in the bedroom went out.

Someone was inside and it wasn't Henry working the lights. If Henry could, he would. But it wasn't the cat. Farnsy inched the pickup forward. He stopped again. Opened his window. Smoke from a wood fire. Couldn't be the Necco burglar. Necco man didn't light fires. So, who was this? Or who were they? Farnsy felt around in the dark to find his firearm. Bear spray was in the glove compartment. No bears this time of year. But Farnsy was ready and, for the moment, he forgot about his sinuses and eased the pickup to a stop. He'd be visible if someone inside looked out the window, but Farnsy was certain he hadn't drawn their attention. He didn't recognize the car. Maine plates. Still no idea who this might be. This was all he needed now, his head feeling like a sack of potatoes full of whatever. Farnsy reached for his mag light, figuring he'd beam it at the person and gain an edge if there was a confrontation. As soon as he stepped out of the pickup, Farnsy saw movement inside the house. The curtain shimmied as Henry jumped up onto the windowsill next to the front door and watched Farnsy taking slow steps up the walkway he'd shoveled out what felt like a week ago but was just that morning. That cat didn't miss a trick. When Farnsy reached the door, he stepped to one side, grasped the door handle and yanked the door open.

FARNSY

He was met by a shaft of light, a gust of warmth from the fireplace, and there she was.

"Lucy! What the…?"

"What am I doing here? Farnsy, don't you know what day it is?"

"Saturday?"

"Oh, Farnsy. You've forgotten, you've really forgotten, haven't you? Tomorrow's Valentine's Day!"

"Mind if I shut the door here, Luce?"

"Farnsy, you sound awful. Sorry."

Farnsy sneezed. Lucy took a step back.

He hung up his coat and set his hat on the table near the door.

"Don't get me wrong—it's good to see you, Luce. Real good. Henry's good company, but it's not the same." He sneezed again.

"Let me get you some tea, Farns, and I'll put the wine back in the fridge. I'm into tea now. Good for you too. Chamomile's supposed to be good for colds," she said.

"Luce, hate to say it, and I know you're all gaga about teas, but right now what I'd love is a couple shots of Jameson's. One ice cube and a splash of water."

Farnsy plopped into a corner of the sofa across from the fireplace.

"Nice fire, Lucy. Earl teach you that?"

She was out in the kitchen. "No, you did. Remember that night? 'Come on baby, light my fire?' You forgotten that night?"

"How could I, Luce? You were still married to old Earl back then."

"Separated, Farnsy, for a long time then. Big difference."

"Maybe. But a ring's a ring."

She held up her left hand. "Ring's long gone, Officer."

Lucy always called Farnsy "Officer" if she wanted to start something. But this time Farnsy just cast her a look, his head feeling more and more like a bowling ball.

"Let me get that whiskey, Farns."

WINTER — *Valentine's Day*

In short order, Farnsy had a tumbler of whiskey in his left hand, a blanket wrapped around him tight, and Lucy there on his right side, lying down, cuddling up as if she were a big house cat. Henry was off somewhere. Smart cat. The fire popped now and then, and after Lucy put another log on the fire, the new wood sizzled, then smoked.

"You need dry wood, Farnsy. At least tarp it. All your stuff is wet," Lucy observed. Mainer through and through, Farnsy thought.

"I know. Keep meaning to do it, cover them up so they stay dry, but never get around to it, you know. Busy as heck this month, hasn't really let up since Thanksgiving at your mom's place. You heard about the Professor, right?"

"Mom told me. She was a real hoot. Isn't she the person who found your dad's Jitterbug?"

As they sat there together, bathed in warm silence, they watched the flames lick the air, flickering white-hot yellow. A log burned through and fell off the andirons with a sudden thunk, and the two halves rolled to either side of the fireplace. Neither one of them wanted to get up to find the tongs to put another log on. They were nestled together on the couch like chipmunks in a winter burrow. Henry curled up next to Lucy.

Farnsy finished his whiskey and set the glass down. Lucy had fallen asleep and he could tell that the cold pills were starting to take effect. He was hungry, but not much. A soup would be good. He tried to put a pillow under Lucy's head so that she could keep on sleeping, but she stirred and woke up.

"Nice, eh?" she asked.

"Yup, sure is."

"You thinking what I'm thinking, Officer?"

"Soup?"

She punched him in the shoulder.

FARNSY

"That's assault and battery on a uniformed officer."

"Well, then, take your uniform off, Officer Farnsworth."

"That an order, ma'am?"

"Citizen's arrest sort of order, yes it is."

She kissed him and held the kiss.

He pushed her away, gently.

"Lucy! You're gonna catch this crud. Trust me, you don't want this. It's been going around all winter and everyone says this bug's harder to shake off than a tick in spring."

"One soup, then, Farnsy, coming right up."

Hmmmmmmmm. Hmmmmmmmm. Hmmmmmmmm.

Farnsy's hand groped around in the dark like a spider with a mind of its own, looking for that humming phone. His dream made it sound like an old lobster boat, but by the time he heard the phone vibrate and drop onto the floor, he was awake and so was Lucy. Henry scurried off into the kitchen.

"Get that, will ya, Farnsy? Jeez," Lucy groaned.

Farnsy's fingers found the phone just under the bed, along with a dust bunny. Almost time for spring cleaning, he thought, as Lucy cuddled up there next to him, their old spoon position, and Farnsy put the little phone up to one ear.

"Farnsworth."

Farnsy listened. "That so?" he asked.

Farnsy sat upright and Lucy let go.

"Where'd they spot them?"

"Over around the narrows there? One of the old cottages?"

"Nope, that's not good."

"Ayuh. Be there just as soon's I can."

Farnsy set the phone down and started going through his mental checklist. He heard Lucy knocking around in the kitchen.

WINTER — *Valentine's Day*

The smell of coffee brewing began to fill the air. What the heck would he tell Luce?

She came into the bedroom, tying up her bathrobe. Any other day, Farnsy would've untied it and put the moves on, morning breath or not. But he was waking up to a case that might be breaking wide open.

"What was that all about? Sounded serious."

"It is, Luce."

"Who was it you were talkin' to?"

"The Chief, Lucy."

"So I guess you gotta go then, right?"

Farnsy thought a moment. "If I want to catch the Necco man I do."

"Man? Ever thought your man might be a woman?"

"Might be, Lucy. Might even be you. You know, trying to get my attention."

"Oh, I know how to get your attention all right." She opened up her bathrobe a notch and he came this close to jumping at the bait. "So what's going on? You gonna tell me now, Officer? Or later? Cause I can get it out of you, you know."

"Look, Luce, jeez. Not now. I gotta go. Someone saw something out on the lake this morning. Footprints around a cabin. Could be our man with the Neccos."

Lucy put down the coffee mug she'd brought back to the bedroom for Farnsy and shook her head and smiled. "Once a cop, always a cop, Farnsy. This how it's gonna be?"

"Not always, Luce," Farnsy lied.

"Oh, Farnsy, come on, you don't believe that and neither do I."

Farnsy nodded. Never could tell her a lie. With some men little lies might come easy. Not Farnsy and not with Lucy.

"Call me, will ya?"

"I will, Luce. You still be here when I get back?"
"Call me, okay?"

Farnsy drove around the lake as fast as he could, hoping Lucy would still be there when he got back. The boot prints, which the caller had said looked like a bear had been poking around, were just the next-door neighbor, who was checking his place for signs of a break-in. Seemed like word had spread and folks were getting a little edgy. When Farnsy got back to his cottage, Lucy's car was gone. She'd just left a can of chicken soup out on the kitchen counter and a slip of paper with a smiley face. The place felt empty. All he had was Henry and a head cold.

After Valentine's Day, the Necco case seemed to shut down tight. The ad ran again in *Uncle Henry's* and Farnsy had the *Lincoln County News* run a blurb about Mr. Worthley's fishing lure collection. This time, thinking he should sweeten the pot a little, freshen the bait, he inserted a reference to the cottage where the lures were temporarily stored. Anyone from away with a good map would've been able to find the right cottage. But there were no calls, no letters, no visitors from Boston. Though ice-out was only a few weeks away, the weather turned colder, cement-gray skies every day, which pretty much mirrored Farnsy's sense of gloom that he might never get this Necco guy. Farnsy still had the sense that the case might break open. Just because the man from Boston hadn't shown up didn't mean he wouldn't make an appearance before ice-out in March.

All the evidence they'd gathered so far indicated that the Necco man poked around in the summer and broke in during the winter. There was no other way. He or someone had been sniffing around that past summer, so there had to be something brewing this winter. And these were professionals he was up against, not smash-and-grab, hit-and-run thieves, because real pros take their time, plan, then pounce. That meant there were only a few more weeks of iced-up winter and only a couple of weekends when Farnsy could do an ice fishing stakeout and catch them in action. When Eddie told Farnsy he was going to take his shack off the lake in early March before the ice got mushy, Farnsy asked him if he could try one last stakeout before he pulled the shack on shore, maybe take Doc out there with him this time.

"Fine by me, Farnsy. Three strikes and all, you know?" Eddie said, "Maybe Doc'll bring you better luck. Really hope you can catch these guys."

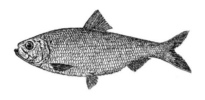

SPRING

The Alewife (*Alosa pseudoharengus*)

Alewives, so-named because their rounded silver bellies reminded folks of corpulent female tavern keepers, are herring that spend most of their lives in the Gulf of Maine. Every spring, from the middle of May to the middle of June, adult alewives return to freshwater to spawn, as they have for thousands of years. About 10-inches long and fork-tailed, alewives by the millions swarm up the Damariscotta River, through Great Salt Bay, then wiggle up the fish ladder at Damariscotta Mills into the fresh waters of Damariscotta Lake. Some folks like smoked alewives. To a lobsterman, alewives are just baitfish. After spawning, the adults return to the sea.

The Catch

"You smell anything, Farns?" Doc sniffed the air in the ice shack as he put down his playing cards and regarded his considerable lead on the cribbage board.

"You mean other than the smell of Ed's cigars and baitfish?"

"I smell a skunk, Farnsy. Get your money ready, son."

Ice-out was still a few weeks away. But the surface of the ice had already started to soften up during the day, Ed told Farnsy, leaving thin puddles here and there that froze up overnight. Farnsy wanted another set of eyes and ears while he waited for Necco man to make a move, so he invited Doc to join him. Plus, playing cribbage with Doc would help pass the time. Maybe bring a little luck.

There was always a chance the perp had moved on to cottages on other lakes. Maybe word had gotten out. But Farnsy wasn't going to give up as long as there was even a slim chance that the Necco man might make a move. Farnsy figured it was the last opportunity this season. The Necco man probably thought he'd been successful so far, so why not hit a few more cottages? From the perp's perspective, the odds probably looked pretty good. Farnsy was betting on that so he had a good feeling about this stakeout. Only a matter of time before Necco man slipped up.

"Not so fast, Doc, never say never. Fifteen two, four, and a double run is 12, right jack makes it 13. And I'm around the corner." Farnsy leapfrogged his back peg onto the last leg of the game board, Fourth Street.

"Okay, okay, no skunking, but the money's as good as mine, kid. Two bucks. Crisp."

Farnsy knew Doc's cribbage chatter was just an old-timer's attempt to irritate and confuse his younger opponent. Like a skunk would, if it could spray words.

Farnsy watched Doc shuffle up the cards then deal out six cards each, face down.

"Read 'em and weep, Farnsy, read 'em and weep. Even if you got a 20-hand you'd still lose. This were a tournament, you'd fold 'em up and start a new game, as far behind as you are now. You know I'll peg out, son, before you even have a chance to count."

"Well, Doc, guess I'm not one to give up."

"No, you're not. Anyway, Farnsworth, you gonna put some cards in my crib? Any time today would be good, I'm not getting any younger, you know. You either, by the way."

Farnsy wasn't rising to Doc's bait. He lay two cards on top of Doc's cards.

"Okay, now cut 'em Farnsy. Cut me a good one."

Farnsy cut the cards and flipped over a queen.

"Hello! Queen of hearts!" Doc exclaimed, "Luck be a lady! That card as good for you as it is for me? Say, you know, in this light you don't look so good, Farnsworth."

The cards had been running good for Doc, so he was in great form. Farnsy pegged six points and was halfway down Fourth Street, but Doc pegged two pairs and was out. Game over.

"Show me the money, son!"

Farnsy handed over a crisp $2 bill, then got up and stuck another log in the woodstove to take the edge off the chill that was returning to the ice shack.

"Want another one, Farns, rubber match? Old time's sake? Winner take all?" Doc wiggled the $2 bill like it was a worm on a fishhook.

SPRING — *The Catch*

Farnsy shook his head, then held up one hand for quiet. Something was up. Farnsy pointed to his ear and Doc listened. After what might've been a minute, the whining chain saw sound of a snowmobile grew louder, then throttled down. Farnsy was concerned that the smoke from the woodstove in the ice house might spook whoever was on that snowmobile, but the wind probably dispersed it pretty well and, besides, in Maine it was normal to smell a wood fire pretty much anywhere in winter. Doc and Farnsy leaned back in their folding lawn chairs and listened. The snowmobile went quiet, too. Dead silence. Only the crackle and pop now and then of the fire as the firewood hissed, still wet from the snow.

Farnsy reached for the field binoculars he'd borrowed from the Chief, pulled the strap over his head, then uncapped both ends of the binoculars and let his eyes adjust to the bright light and the snow. The sun was trying to peek through the overcast sky, which he took as a good omen.

Behind him, Doc unwrapped the wax paper from one of the bologna sandwiches he'd brought. You want a friend in a storm, Doc was your man. Farnsy kept his eyes riveted on the snowmobile that had just pulled up next to one of the old seasonal cottages about 100 yards away, one of a dozen or so in the section of the lake that hadn't been broken into last season.

After he'd read Doc's journal from last summer, the pieces had started to come together, and they all led to the conclusion that Necco man might be headed across the lake, over to where some of the oldest camps, fishing camps, were located. Farnsy had pretty much ruled out any other scenarios, and his first stakeouts in February had been a cold waste of time. Like Farnsy had told the Chief, if the perp was going to hit a few more cottages that season, then they'd at least narrowed down the window and that gave them a slight advantage. This was his last option that season if they were coming by snowmobile over the lake.

FARNSY

Farnsy concentrated his gaze on the camp where the snowmobile had stopped, now and then lifting the binoculars to his eyes. If he looked away, he'd miss something. He felt Doc put half a sandwich in his right hand and he started eating it, still watching the cottage for any sign of movement. The shack's window started to frost up from Farnsy's breath.

"Jeez, Doc, ketchup? On bologna?" Farnsy said over his shoulder with a mouthful of sandwich.

"All I had, Farnsy. Thought you liked vegetables. Didn't Reagan declare ketchup a vegetable back then?"

"I do, but ketchup's not a vegetable. Mustard with bologna. Maybe mayo."

"I stopped using mayo, Farnsy. Cholesterol. You ask me, I think ketchup spices up bologna. Might even catch on. You know, start a new trend."

Farnsy pushed the rest of the half sandwich into his mouth and waved Doc to shut up. He watched a person emerge from the cottage, get on a snowmobile, throttle it up, and buzz like a big bee to the next flower, over the ice toward a cottage a couple of places away. Farnsy shifted to the other window. The ice house was perfect. It was his little Trojan horse. Just another little house for ice fishing. Except the ice hole that Eddie had drilled was iced over now, and there was no fish line dangling into the lake. The air inside was permeated by the stale smell of cigars, fish, sweat, and a couple of hospital bed bottles that Farnsy and Doc had used every now and then because they'd been drinking black coffee all day.

Farnsy glanced at his watch. The snowmobiler was spending a lot of time in the second cottage. And finally, when the figure emerged, he was carrying what looked like a tackle box. Farnsy watched the person place it in a big black pack box that was strapped to the snowmobile where a passenger would sit. This guy, whoever he was, was working solo. Which made good sense, Farnsy thought. No one to squeal on you. Except maybe the snowmobile was a loaner from a friend or a rental. Chances were high, Farnsy thought, that it was simply "borrowed" briefly and might show up later on the police blotter as stolen property.

Now the question was: nab him now or follow the snowmobile trail across the lake? Farnsy did the math. By the time he could get his snowmobile outfit on and start up the machine outside that had been sitting there since early morning, the other snowmobiler would be at the other end of the lake and long gone. All he'd find would be a ditched snowmobile with an empty pack box. Someone might see the getaway car. Maybe not. Probably not, Farnsy thought.

By then, Farnsy had zipped up his suit and put his boots on. Doc took a quick look out the window. "Snowmobile's still there, Farnsy." A closer look with the binocs told the story. "Farns, looks like the guy can't get his snowmobile started."

"Must be an amateur, Doc. That's a beginner's mistake. Got to pull the choke on an old snowmobile. Pull it too far out, you flood the engine."

But there the man was, 100 yards away. Sitting on a dead snowmobile, still hoping it would start up. Farnsy knew he had only a few minutes before the man's engine would start, so he told Doc to wait and exited the ice shack through the back door, opposite side from the snowmobiler. Farnsy pulled his face mask and goggles down, pushed the starter, and knew that even at top speed he'd need at least a couple minutes to get across the lake, which was covered by a foot of new snow, over to the snowmobiler, who, for all he knew, might be armed and just waiting there for him. Could be a trap.

As soon as Farnsy throttled up and shot out from behind the ice house, he saw the snowmobiler look up, startled, then try to start his engine again. Halfway across the lake, one eye on the ice, looking out for pressure ridges and glazed-over ice puddles, Farnsy saw a puff of gray smoke from the other snowmobile as it started up, and he knew it wasn't going to be easy. Farnsy leaned forward to accelerate and made a beeline in the direction of the other machine, which was now making a huge arc across the lake as though looking for someplace to ditch.

This is good, Farnsy thought. I know this lake. This lake is mine. You're on my territory, buddy. And I want to know who stole my father's lure. Who is this candy loving burglar? Just then, the other machine straightened out and headed due south toward the end of the lake where folks stop to watch the eagles' nest in the summer.

Farnsy gunned his sled and tried to close the distance, but the other machine had a hundred-yard lead and seemed to be pulling away. The cloud of snow kicked up by the other snowmobiler was crusting up on his visor, and his face stung from the flecks of ice and wind. The two machines curved around the bend in the lake past the kids' summer camp, past Bunker Hill up on the right, and continued full throttle south, down the lake. Past the cove where Farnsy caught sun turtles for his sister's kids, then past Blueberry Island. Another five minutes at this speed and they'd hit the south end of Damariscotta Lake. If the other sled stopped there.

Farnsy felt for his handgun. It was back in the ice house, on the shelf next to his Yeti coffee mug. Must've taken it off when he sat down to play cribbage with Doc. That's great, he thought, just great. Well, what would a London bobby do? Most of them don't carry side arms, do they? Farnsy hunched down to lower his wind resistance and squeeze another mile an hour out of his sled, which still had plenty of fuel. The closer they got to the southern shoreline, the faster Farnsy's thoughts flew. When the end of the lake was about half a mile away, Farnsy spotted the Chief's SUV pulling off the lake road at the beach. He saw the Chief step out and hold his 30-30 across his chest, just standing there, ready for action. The snowmobiler slowed down, appeared to look around, saw he was cornered, then aimed his snowmobile at the Chief and came to a full stop not 20 yards away. He stepped off, hands in the air.

"Doc called it in, Farnsworth," Chief said, "so I figured I'd drive out to see if I could help, which is when I saw you in hot, or should I say, cold pursuit, coming like a bat outta hell down the lake. Look, Farns, this one's all yours. Use my cuffs."

"Guess you got me good. Speeding, right? Endangerment, something like that?"

Farnsy was as surprised as the Chief was when they heard a woman's voice. Young. Looked familiar to Farnsy, but he couldn't place her. She said her name was Nicky, Nicky Putnam.

Farnsy read Nicky her Miranda rights, anything you say could be used against you, and all that. She knew the words by heart and repeated them along with Farnsy.

"First time for everything," Chief said later in a staff meeting.

But the big surprise came when Farnsy asked the woman if he could check the contents of the box and the woman said, "Sure, why not, it's just my gear and some lunch."

Farnsy thanked her, wondering why she was so accommodating. Inside the box he found a pair of dry mittens, woolen socks, a heat pack, a survival blanket, three rolls of Necco wafers, half a Reuben sandwich that looked like it was from Fernald's, and a large round thermos.

Farnsy picked up the thermos by the handle. "Coffee?" he asked Nicky. If it was the hard stuff, he might get her on an OUI, too. He shook the thermos and heard a rattle. He looked over at the Chief, who was looking at Farnsy. Coffee didn't rattle like that. Something was knocking around inside there for sure.

"Mind if I open her up?"

"Might's well."

FARNSY

Farnsy tipped the thermos upside down and out dropped what looked like about half a dozen fishing lures, in a clump, hooks jumbled up, all sizes and shapes and colors.

"I'm arresting you for suspicion of theft of private property and fleeing the police," Farnsy said as he slapped the Chief's cuffs on her. Nicky sighed.

On the way to the station, Nicky sat in the back of the Chief's cruiser. She started to talk and didn't stop. By the time they pulled up at the station it was getting dark fast and they'd heard her whole story. Except for one detail.

"What's with the Necco wafers, Nicky?" Farnsy asked.

"My calling card," Nicky shrugged. "You know. Nicky? Necco? Get it? Like, I mean, who doesn't love Neccos? I thought it was nice, you know, leaving something sweet behind. Besides, I figured, like, the candy might throw you guys off my trail. Keep you guessing, and all." Then she looked out the station window and asked what time it was, and Farnsy asked her why she seemed worried. Nicky said she was supposed to meet her buyer up at Moody's around 5:30.

Chief and Farnsy conferred with the Sheriff outside the interrogation room, and they agreed they'd try to flip her. Which was easy, because they convinced her that if she helped them nab her buyer, they were sure the DA would look favorably on her case, maybe get her a reduced sentence. Her only priors were underage drinking and speeding, both more than five years earlier. She said she didn't think her buyer was the big fish, but she agreed to help them catch the guy if it got her some sympathy from the judge.

Farnsy looked over at the Chief, who nodded. Farnsy gave Nicky her phone and instructed her to call the man and tell him she was running a little late, just had some mechanical trouble with the snowmobile and all, which was partly true.

Farnsy and Chief drove Nicky up to Moody's in the Chief's personal SUV so as not to spook the man. As they drove, they instructed her to walk in like everything was normal. Then they told her to hand the man the thermos and wait until he gave her the money, then she was to excuse herself and walk calmly over to the ladies' room. They'd handle the rest. Of course, she was still under arrest, but they told her they'd do everything they could to get her off with a lesser sentence. Maybe even community service. No promises, though.

As they pulled into the big parking lot next to Moody's, Nicky said she didn't think the buyer had a firearm, but wasn't sure. So Farnsy said he'd walk in first just to scout things out. It being a little before supper time, there were a half dozen booths open and only a couple of old men sitting at the counter, two stools between them, and a woman sitting at the far end, where Farnsy liked to sit. He scanned the diner as if he were considering where he wanted to sit, solo, when he spotted a man sitting in a booth at the other end of the diner, in a corner, staring back. That was the man. Ben was his name, she had said.

Farnsy waited to be seated, then let a waitress guide him to a booth near the entrance. When Philomena bumped her way out of the kitchen with a plate of meatloaf in hand and spotted Farnsy sitting there, he gave her his secret, "I'm on a case," nose tap and she clammed up tight.

"Be right with you, sir," she said, playing along like the pro she was. The whole first act took about three minutes, which was precisely when Farnsy watched Nicky walk up the ramp from the big parking lot and push open the door, her thermos in one hand. The good thing about Moody's was that there was only one front entrance, which meant there was only one way out. No escape.

If anyone tried to run, Farnsy was in perfect position to stop them. Nicky walked right past Farnsy toward the man in the back booth and sat down across from him. She was a born actress. A minute or so later, the Chief came in wearing his old black leather biker's jacket and a red cap his wife had knitted for him. He stomped the snow off his boots on the rug at the entrance near the sign that said "PLEASE WAIT TO BE SEATED" and took a stool at the counter right near the register. Everyone was in their place, just as Farnsy had planned it.

Philomena brought Farnsy a coffee, handed him a menu, then left. She was tight-lipped. Farnsy could tell she knew something was brewing. Then, just as they'd instructed her, Nicky got up from the back booth and headed all the way up the aisle past Farnsy, past the Chief, and disappeared into the ladies' room behind them. Farnsy counted to 30 as slowly as he could, then stood up and walked down the aisle to where the man was sitting. The man looked up from his meatloaf, on which he was just about to slather more ketchup, and growled, "You got a problem, bud?"

Farnsy shook his head and sat down across from the man, who had a side order of grits with a perfect square pat of butter starting to melt on top.

"Not me who's got a problem." He pulled his coat back to reveal his badge.

"Shoot," the man said, "I thought you looked familiar."

That face, the hat. The guy with the Lexus. It all came back to Farnsy.

"Yup, me again. Remember? Thought so. So, here's my question for you now: You want to go peacefully and let all these good folks have a nice quiet supper, or do you want to go the hard way?"

Farnsy stopped talking to let a young mom go around him. Her son had a brightly speckled superhero backpack that was unzipped and toy dinosaurs of all sizes and colors were spilling onto the floor as he struggled along behind her. The mom stopped to pick a Tyrannosaurus Rex off the floor and the man said in a loud whisper, "The 'hard way?' You threatening me, Officer?"

"No threats. Just options."

SPRING ~ *The Catch*

"You got no proof. Besides, you're alone."

"Not really." Farnsy looked around and pointed to the Chief, who had tugged on his knit police cap and was making his way down the row of booths. When he got to their booth, the Chief slid onto the seat next to the man, who was still working on his meatloaf as though he hadn't a care in the world. A moment later, the Lincoln County Sheriff's cruiser nosed into a parking spot out front, its lights flashing. If they'd come a few minutes earlier, it would've blown their cover.

"Looks like the cavalry just arrived," the man said, straining to look out the window. "All this? Besides, you got nothing on me." He reached for the ketchup bottle.

"Oh, I think you're hooked. We're just reeling you in now, my friend. Jig's up."

Folks in nearby booths turned around to watch Farnsy slap a pair of cuffs on the man, read him his rights, search him for sharp objects, get his car keys, and then walk him down the aisle and out the door.

Outside, the Lincoln County Sheriff stood in front of his cruiser and grinned as Farnsy led the man outside.

"Nice catch, Farnsy, real nice."

Farnsy nodded and tried to suppress a smile, but then he was all business as he got the man into the back of the Chief's SUV and closed the door. This fish wasn't getting away.

Farnsy and the Chief agreed they should get the man's car over to the station for a thorough evidence check. It would take a couple of hours for the state fingerprint expert and evidence technician to get there from Augusta. By that evening, after the man posted bail, they'd have enough evidence to make charges stick.

It was the same car Farnsy stopped last summer. No doubt about it. And after the technician dusted the car for fingerprints and removed all of the other evidence from the trunk, it looked like the case was a lock: two old fishing tackle boxes, chock full of lures, and a small cardboard box stuffed with old fishing reels. The glove compartment produced a list of all the lures they were looking for, with pictures of some. A shopping list for their customers. They even found a couple of old obits, real ones, where there was some mention that the fellow who passed had liked to fish.

But the kicker, Chief told Farnsy, was what the Lincoln County boys had found in his briefcase: a list of all the cottages and a real estate map where they'd crossed off the cottages hit the winter before, one of which was Farnsy's, and even one or two they'd hit the winter before that.

"Must've been a warmup trial run last year. Well, practice makes perfect, I guess," the Chief said.

But the "piece of resistance," the Chief said, was finding that *Uncle Henry's* ad, stapled to the *LCN* obit. So Farnsy's lures had actually worked. That evening, the man did the math and started to talk. Said he'd work with Farnsy. Spilled everything, start to finish.

He was Benjamin Bradford Bennett III, an antiques dealer from Kennebunkport. All started with one lure, he told them. Then, he confessed, he happened to procure, was the word he used, a tackle box with old lures once owned by an old Maine Guide out in western Maine's lake region, in Oquossoc, out near Rangeley. Just stumbled on it at an estate sale and at a time when his antiques place had drifted onto some hard times in the downturn. "Didn't have the foggiest but put down $100 for the whole lot." He explained. "Folks laughed when I bid it up, but what I found in that box when I got back home was an old lure that anyone might think would scare a fish away. It was the Minnow. Looked it up and there it was. One of maybe a dozen."

B. B. Bennett drew a deep breath. "And then, I don't know where I got the idea, just got greedy, I guess. Anyway, I figured if

I could find a way to make a mold of the Minnow, maybe I could cast a few more of my own. Just a few, mind you, wouldn't want to attract too much attention. Only a few Minnows out there, known. So, I thought if I put them out on the market, one at a time, couple years apart, no one would take notice. I sold the first copy to a collector in Dallas last year. Retired oilman, all hat and no cattle. But big money. I don't think he ever caught a fish in his life."

The Lincoln County detective squeezed Bennett for more and found out that he'd set up a meeting with another dealer, a big wheeler-dealer, who was going to do a 50-50 split of the sales of the second Minnow Ben had cast and buy up all the other old lures to sweeten the pot. He had planned to meet the man in Boston. A few days before Maine's fishing season opened, because they thought it was appropriate. Bennett said he'd wanted to unload the fake Minnow as soon as he could. The Boston antiques dealer was Jonas Pepperell, Esq., of Back Bay, who, Bennett said, had a whispered reputation among New England dealers as a reliable source of antique fishing lures. As Bennett explained, Pepperell knew a used book dealer in Cambridge who handled old documents and had a good supply of old paper. That paper provided what looked like legitimate provenance for each of the three Minnows that Bennett had an associate cast, convincing proof of an ownership trail.

The man from Kennebunkport was desperate to claw his way out any way he could. But when the Lincoln County Sheriff staff contacted Boston to set up the arrest, they told the Chief that Bennett's story held up. Boston police already had their eye on Pepperell, whose uncanny ability to find old maps had started to raise eyebrows—and spark some jealousy—among some prominent New England antiquarians. And a warrant was pending for Pepperell for forgery and grand larceny. It seems he had made his own mold of Bennett's forged Minnow then started selling his fakes up and down the Northeast at some of the premier auction houses. Even fooled two of the top Northeast collectors, until they got a little suspicious that they'd each scored a Minnow. That's when the dam broke. Now the feds were on the case.

Outside the jail, Farnsy stopped to take it all in. The snow was starting up again and the sky was darkening. The Chief stood next to him for a moment.

"That was some damned fine police work, Farnsworth." Chief shook Farnsy's hand. He looked like he was tearing up some. "Real proud of you, Officer."

"Thanks, Chief, but it's not over yet. Still gotta get the man at the top," Farnsy said, then started to walk back to his vehicle.

"I suppose now you'll be looking at that Portland detective job."

Farnsy spun around.

"Oh, I have my ways, Farnsy. Got my own research assistants, you know? Big world, small town. Gotta have some vitamin C, you know. Connections, if you get my drift."

"Doc!" Farnsy said.

"Maybe. Now you get some sleep, Farnsy. You been up since the wee hours. And I'm gonna need you back tomorrow, 8 a.m. sharp, and wear your blues, 'cause you and I know the Portland Press will be all over this story. Boothbay Register. Maybe even the Bangor paper. As far's I'm concerned, the *LCN* has first dibs on the story. But we need to keep this quiet, Farns."

"You mean, no interviews? How're we going to do that?"

"We zip it. I'll talk with *LCN*. Dottie will hunker down and stall inquiries that come in at the front desk. Otherwise, Mr. Big in Boston gets off scot-free. It's like weeding your garden, Farnsworth. You want to get rid of dandelions, you gotta get their roots, too." The Chief started for his cruiser, then turned around. "By the way, Farnsworth, almost forgot, Doc tells me you're on a cribbage losing streak. Maybe Lucy can teach you how to play."

The Press

On the day before fishing season opened in Maine, Police Officer William Phineas Farnsworth sat in a beat-up stakeout van outside Boston's Union Oyster House, watching with nervous pride as his brothers in blue waited inside, wearing dark business suits to blend in, slurping Glidden Point, Pemaquid, and Mook Moondancers in honor of the occasion, as Benjamin B. Bennett III slid into a booth opposite Jonas Pepperell, Esq., and shook Pepperell's hand, then slid a small black bag across the tabletop toward Pepperell, who slid a white envelope over to B. B. Bennett III in a synchronized motion that looked practiced.

Their waitress, a Boston police detective who'd once waited tables, walked over to their booth, pencil behind one ear, and asked, "Having a nice day, boys?" She showed them her badge and then made the arrest as two Boston police detectives, a Massachusetts state trooper, and an FBI officer surrounded the booth.

Standing behind them, as a professional courtesy, were the Lincoln County Sheriff, Damariscotta Chief of Police Elwood Grenier, and Officer William Phineas Farnsworth. As the Chief had told Farnsy on the drive down to Boston, "We hooked them, but we'll let the Boston boys clean and cook 'em."

Bennett was led off separately as they'd agreed, while Pepperell was cuffed, Mirandized, and whisked off to the station in Boston, to be booked, charged with possession of stolen goods, interstate transport of same, and forgery. The *Boston Globe* had the exclusive. A reporter on the scene had gotten an inside tip from one of the oyster shuckers that he might want to get some oysters that noon and to bring a photographer. The *Globe* reported the next day, front page, above the fold, that a trial date would be set later that fall.

At Waltz's the next morning, Doc sat down next to Farnsy, who'd seen the headlines on top of the stack of the Boston papers as he took a seat but didn't want to make anything of it. Lucy'd already called him early that morning and embarrassed him, so he knew word was out. Doc nudged Farnsy, who had hardly slept the night before, and tapped the edge of the color photo that filled the top half of the *Globe* that Doc spread out on the counter between the two friends.

"Says here, 'Unidentified Maine police officer' in the caption, Farnsy."

Farnsy glanced at the photo and could just about make out his face, as the men behind the great Necco and fish lure caper emerged from the Union Oyster House, doing the perp walk, squinting in the bright spring sunlight.

"You any idea how proud I am to see this, son?"

A day after the *Globe* ran the story, the *Lincoln County News* sent a reporter and a photographer over to the station and spent what felt like at least an hour interviewing Farnsy, asking him to please stand over here next to his cruiser, then over there, please, and, oh, maybe just one more of you sitting there with that tackle box open and holding up a copy of the Minnow. Farnsy wished he could disappear like Henry did whenever he got out the nail trimmer.

The next Thursday, mid-April, the *Lincoln County News* came out with a half-page spread and a big photo of Farnsy sitting with Henry perched on the back of his old armchair. The headline read, "Damariscotta Police Officer Nabs Necco Burglar After 5-Mile Snowmobile Chase." The article started, "Damariscotta Police

SPRING — *The Press*

Officer William Farnsworth, known to his friends as 'Farnsy' and pictured here in a file photo with his Maine coon cat, Henry, captured the first suspect in a string of cottage break-ins that started a year ago after a six-hour stakeout and a five-mile snowmobile chase at top speed down Damariscotta Lake. Chief Elwood Grenier told the *LCN* that Officer Farnsworth's dogged detective work led to the arrest of a team of perpetrators after almost a year of detective work, gathering evidence and piecing all the clues together."

The Chief was quoted saying, "All of us on the Damariscotta Police team are really proud of Officer Farnsworth. He'll make a great police chief some day."

The journalist had clearly interviewed Doc, too, because her article described the early morning ice house stakeout and the suspended outcome of the cribbage game, and Doc mentioning that he was just about to skunk Farnsy. "Darned fine detective, Farnsy is, but a lousy cribbage pegger."

The article described how Doc figured they were headed down the lake and called the station, so the Chief drove over to the lake to provide backup for Farnsy when he made the arrest. Chief told the writer that this first arrest was just the start, that what Farnsy did next, convincing the young woman to assist them with the arrest of her Boston connection over in Moody's diner later that day, was nothing short of brilliant police work. Like hitting two flies with one swat, Chief told the *LCN* reporter. And it turned out that Bennett's connection to Pepperell was just the first link of a national ring dealing in antique fishing lures. The Minnow had evidently spawned, Doc joked, because it sounded like there were fakes starting to pop up at sporting conventions all over the country.

A day after the *LCN* covered the story, it was picked up by the *Bangor Daily News* and the *Portland Press Herald*. The Colby

FARNSY

Alumni magazine wanted to interview Farnsy and *Down East* asked a stringer to write a piece about The Minnow for their June edition. Then the story went national: the *New York Times*, *Chicago Tribune*, *Washington Post*. The *Wall Street Journal* ran a piece on the market for old fishing lures. Then it hit *USA Today* and papers that Maine snowbirds read in Florida and out in the Southwest. On the Internet, it was getting thousands of hits. In town, Round Top Ice Cream Shop announced a new sundae: the "Farnsy," topped with bits of Necco wafers. Not to be outdone, King Eider's Pub started giving customers a little cup of Necco wafers instead of M&Ms with their bills. The station phone never stopped ringing.

By the time CNN and the Sunday morning TV programs sent their crews to Damariscotta to prepare some atmospheric fluff pieces, folks in town were divided. The pessimists thought it would mean more tourists, more traffic in town, and longer backups on Route 1, if that was possible. The optimists said it would be good for business. Meanwhile, everyone wondered when they could say it was finally spring.

Fiddleheads

Farnsy couldn't recall when he first went out fiddleheadin'. All he could remember was that his mother woke him up on a sunny Saturday morning one spring and told him his grandfather was coming by to take him out to pick fiddleheads. She said when her father was growing up, times were tight, and they had to stretch a dollar. Now, Farnsy was old enough to go fiddleheading, and besides, his grandfather was getting on and could use the help. His father explained to Farnsy there was a time way back when most of the fiddleheads sold in the Yellowfront had been picked by his grandfather in the same secret spot where they were headed.

Fiddleheadin' was what Mainers did, if they didn't mind getting up early, every spring, or what passed for spring in Maine after the snow'd melted, the lake'd turned over, the sun'd had time to warm up the ground enough for plants to take notice, and everything started greening up.

Farnsy and his grandfather went out fiddleheading a few more springs before he passed. It wasn't just knowing where to find the fiddleheads, he told Farnsy, which were the little buds of ostrich ferns that poked up out of the early spring ground, through thatched layers of leaves and grass and twigs and things left over from the fall. Always near water, not too much sun, not too much shade. It was knowing how to snap them off with your fingers, he'd explained, so you didn't kill the fern. And how to cook them. And when they got back home, his mother showed

Farnsy how to clean them, steam them, and sauté them in butter with a sprinkle of salt. Nothing fancy, she said.

So when Doc called him up middle of April and said it was time to go out, Farnsy knew he meant fiddleheadin' and he didn't hesitate. "Same time, same place?" to which Doc said, "Ayuh. And bring your muck boots, son, season's starting early," then hung up.

Farnsy parked his pickup just off the side of the road, well-hidden from anyone who might see a parked car and try to poach Doc's secret spot. It wasn't so much that someone might pick all the emerging fiddleheads, but that they might pick off too much of the plants and the next year there'd be half as many fiddleheads.

Farnsy tugged on an old wool skullcap because there was still a chill in the air. And his muck boots. The only equipment a good fiddleheader needs is a five-gallon plastic bucket and an unscented trash bag to collect the bounty.

Farnsy leaned against his pickup, crossed his arms, and waited for Doc to drive up. Doc would have a thermos of black coffee with him. Farnsy knew that when Doc went fiddleheadin' years ago, he used to pour just a dite of Allen's coffee brandy into his thermos—give the coffee a little kick was the way he put it.

Doc finally pulled up, rolled down his window, and greeted Farnsy.

"Fine morning for fiddleheadin'." Which was a lot for Doc to say that early in the morning. Then he stepped out of his car and proceeded to unscrew the top of an old dinged-up thermos and pour some coffee into its top and another small coffee cup he'd brought along, turning the hood of his old Ford into a coffee table. Doc claimed the heat of the engine kept the coffee warm, which Farnsy didn't believe for one minute, but he still liked the way Doc thought, all economy of speech and motion.

Farnsy took the little cup in his hands and sipped. "Thanks, Doc."

SPRING — *Fiddleheads*

"Thank me when we get to the spot," Doc said, taking a sip and looking around. "I don't think anyone's been here yet this year. Not that I can tell, anyway."

They sipped their coffees, lost in separate thoughts but probably not too far off from one another. Farnsy thought he could feel the ground warming up and even hear the leaves budding.

"Guess we better get started."

The trick, Farnsy'd learned as a boy, was to pick fiddleheads at just the right time, when they were a few inches out of the ground. Catch them when they're still shaped like the head of a fiddle, a tightly wound curl of coiled green just about ready to explode into full-fledged fern, and you've got something real Mainers rave about, a local delicacy.

Someone from away might just buy some later in the Hannaford produce department, but Doc said store-bought fiddleheads are about as much like fresh picked fiddleheads as a Michigan blueberry is to a wild Maine blueberry.

Since time was of the essence, Farnsy and Doc didn't dillydally too long over their coffee. Just set their cups down and started off down the old camp road, heavily rutted from spring rains and runoff. Farnsy heard a woodpecker hammering not far away. He figured Doc hadn't heard it, even with his hearing aids.

"Guess they don't call it mud season for nothing," Doc muttered.

After a spell, Doc said he'd seen some new patches of fiddleheads late last season sprouting up near a stream maybe half a mile down the road. They walked on in silence, past a "No Hunting" sign that was speckled with holes some knucklehead had made with a shotgun. Farnsy noticed Doc seemed slower than last year, a slight limp.

"Want me to cut you a walkin' stick, Doc?"

Doc stopped up short and took in Farnsy with that look of his. "You saying I'm getting old?" He paused for effect, then said,

"S'not like I need remindin,'" and started walking again, just a little brisker than before.

"Just trying to help, Doc."

"When I need help, son, I'll call you."

They kept walking.

After a while, the road split. Farnsy followed Doc down to the left, and soon after that the road flattened out and he could hear a small brook burbling like it was happy to be ice-free. The ground leading to it was swelling up, everything straining for the sun. The trees were starting to bud.

Farnsy scanned the ground. He'd learned as a kid that once you start seeing fiddleheads, you see more. It was like your eyes adjusted so that when you know what to look for and after you see the first few, you start to see them everywhere. That's why someone going out alone for the first time fiddleheadin' usually came back with an empty bucket and stopped at Yellowfront for the store-bought kind.

Farnsy took another look and saw a clump of fiddleheads right at his feet, staring up at him. By then, Doc was already bent over as best he could, pinching off two or three fiddleheads from each clump, taking care to leave a few for next year. Good fiddlehead hunters of any kind always leave something to grow.

"Not that one, Farnsy. See that little donut hole there? It's gone by. This is the one you want."

Fiddleheads seemed to like their distance, like some Mainers. Doc pointed Farnsy to a spot not far away. "Some more over there."

A good fiddleheader keeps his favorite spots a tight secret. Last thing you wanted was to get there to find some yum-yum'd dug up all the fiddleheads with a damned shovel or picked all the heads off each clump. Either way, there'd be nothing left for anyone the next year.

They stepped through the bushes over to another spot, where there were a few more fiddleheads and then a few more after that.

Then they both stood up at about the same time and stretched out, this work being pretty hard on the back, which Farnsy figured was why old-timers took their grandkids out to help picking—and teach them something about hard work while they were at it.

On the way back up to their cars, Farnsy was glad they were taking their time. Doc was stopping every now and then. Seemed like Doc was trying to stretch time out, too. Or maybe it was his hip bothering him. Then Doc stopped and turned around to face Farnsy.

"What about Lucy?"

"What about her, Doc?"

"You didn't know she's coming back to town?"

"You kidding, Doc?"

"Some detective you are Farnsworth! You ought to spend more time at Waltz's counter. Maybe all this publicity has got you thinking too much."

Doc stopped to take another breather and leaned against a tree.

"What I hear, she's about finished up with that course she was taking over in Augusta. Thinking about setting up here in town. You know, get some of the summer tourist trade before fall."

Farnsy stared off. Last time he'd seen her was out at his place on Valentine's Day. Just a couple of "how you doing" phone calls since then, and of course when she called him after the big arrest in Boston. But everything seemed to have speeded up after the case broke wide open, and he'd lost touch again. Maybe Lucy was right about him being a cop day and night.

"She's a good woman, Lucy is, Farnsy."

Farnsy nodded. "Right, Doc. But she's a free spirit. And by God, she's hard-headed."

"Farnsy, she's a Mainer. Through and through. Like you. Good teeth, too, you don't mind me saying."

Farnsy nodded.

FARNSY

"Farnsy, it took me a long time to understand this, but here you go: There's a universe of women in every woman. A universe. To explore and get to know and to share life with. And take it from me, 'cause I lost my dearie some years ago, you've got damned little time with your gal before things start to speed up, then go downhill, and before you know it, it's all past tense and all you have are regrets for things you said, or left unsaid, or did, or wish you hadn't, and a bucketful of the happiest memories and laughs of your life." Doc adjusted himself. "And that's what keeps you going, those sweet memories, Farnsy, when things get tough. And they will, trust me, they will. So, you and Lucy had better start making some memories together or you'll have nothing to remember, Farnsy, except all this police stuff. Call her, Farnsy. You feel the way you do, you better do something fast before someone else does. Like that dream of yours, the one where you lose her there in the crowd on Boston Common. Someone's trying to tell you something. Let me tell you, Farnsworth, you can go back to get a hat you left someplace and you can go back to your favorite fiddlehead patch, but you can't go back when it comes to women. If you miss that moment, it's gone. You can be friends and you can be friendly, but you'll never be partners and lovers. Like with that gal in Portland. Same might be true with Lucy if you let her go. You already lost her once, to Earl. Don't want to make that mistake again, you know." Doc swatted away some blackflies.

"What's more, this on-again, off-again stuff is just plain tiring, Farnsy. For you, for Lucy, and it sure as blazes is for all the rest of us. Seems like you and Lucy are the only ones who can't see you're made for each other. Cripes, Farnsy, love isn't all they make it out to be, all roses and perfume. It's messy, my friend. Always has been and always will be. But you two are as tangled up in each other as any couple ever. Time to fish or cut bait, Farnsy. You're gonna lose that girl if you don't do something, and I mean soon."

Doc paused to take a breath. "And what do I know? Maybe you've screwed this up already. Besides, Lucy's right. You're a good cop and that's what this town needs. But you've got to take stock. Good as that cat is, Henry's no substitute for your Lucy. So there now, I've said my piece and I'll shut up."

Farnsy could hear a car coming and start to slow down, as if to see if they'd got any fiddleheads, but when the driver and passenger saw Farnsy and Doc standing there, they kept right on going. Probably come back when they'd left.

"You hear what I'm saying, Farnsy?" Doc paused. "Take it from an old man. You only get one or two second chances."

"Thanks, Doc, I hear you. Loud 'n clear."

Doc patted Farnsy on the back. "Okay, now you get those fiddleheads in your fridge. Lucy knows how to cook 'em. If you get my drift."

Farnsy shook his head and laughed. "Thanks, Doc."

Aunt Josie

One Sunday in late April, after Lucy had finished her cosmetology course in Augusta, she called Farnsy and said if he had time she could sure use some help with her great aunt Josie, who had a little summer place out near China Lake.

"She's close to 85 and has taken a turn for the worse. Literally," Lucy said. "She told me she thought she saw an animal on the road, so she swerved to avoid it. Only thing is, she turned right into a big pine."

"She okay?" Farnsy asked, trying to picture the sweet old Lithuanian woman, who'd called him "Mr. English" years ago when he went out there with Lucy to help pick raspberries and weed out the dead stalks. Her garden had been a chaos of flowers, berries, beans, and potatoes. After he finished in the raspberry patch, she'd asked Farnsy if he could putty a couple of windows on her shed. For lunch, Josie had brought out baked kugelis with sour cream, an old family recipe. Farnsy remembered feeling like he was being enveloped, embraced, in a strange new world, Lucy's world.

She's fine, but thanks for asking, Farnsy. You know Josie, she never drives faster than 25, and that old Buick of hers is built like a tank. They took her to the hospital for observation right after the accident, but when I talked with her on the phone today, she said she told them she'd walk out of there in her nightie if they didn't let her go home."

"Wow, she's one tough cookie, your auntie. So how can I help?"

SPRING — *Aunt Josie*

Lucy took a deep breath, then said, "Well, Farnsy, for starters, I think someone needs to have a talk with Auntie about her driving. If she keeps up, well, it's only a matter of time before something awful happens, you know."

"So, you want me to have 'The Talk.' With your auntie. Out near China Lake. Today?"

"That's right. You know, put on your uniform, pick me up, and we'll drive over there and have a talk."

"Can't Lucy. Not exactly police business, you know."

"Come on, Farnsy, she's a sweet old woman. You know her. Old country. Chief won't mind. I think she likes you. Can't figure out why."

"Okay, okay. Pick you up in an hour? That work for you? Your mom's place, right? I'll bring my police cap."

Farnsy put on his best khakis and a clean T-shirt, grabbed his police cap, and drove his pickup over to get Lucy. He wondered what it would be like for someone to have The Talk with him when he got as old as Auntie. If he got that old.

Farnsy and Lucy had a good Sunday-afternoon-drive-in-the-country sort of conversation. After they'd figured out something like a strategy for getting the car keys from Josie, Farnsy asked Lucy how things were going. She'd loved her courses in Augusta, she said. Learned a lot about coloring and some new cutting techniques.

"The scissors they have, Farnsy, you wouldn't believe."

"Really? I thought scissors were scissors," he teased.

"Farnsy, they had the best. Japanese. Ask me how much they cost."

"Okay, how much?"

"Start at 700 dollars."

Farnsy shook his head. "Be lucky to get that much for your auntie's car."

"Well, my instructor said I should look into working on a cruise ship. You know, the kind that sail into Portland or Bar Harbor."

"Don't they sail down to the Caribbean?"

"That too."

Farnsy slowed down to let a driver pass.

"I mean, I'd like that. A lot. But Winnie just told me that one of her stylists took off for the other Portland, so now there's a chair free."

"So," Farnsy said, "you..."

"Which means I'd get all of her clients. And she says I can do some color work, too."

"Sounds pretty good."

"And I've done some thinking. That friend I went down to Florida with, you remember him?"

Farnsy nodded.

"Well, he and I got to talking. And there are some places down in Boston where I could get a chair next fall. He's going to get a chair in a shop called The Cutting Edge. Says it's really hip. Lot of students and well, you know, big city and all."

Farnsy was trying to picture Lucy cutting the hair of some young professor.

"But I'm not sure. Been thinking maybe I should open my own place, you know. Mom says there might be a space opening up in Newcastle near the bridge. I've looked at it and it might work. Could have another chair in there. Maybe add a nail station after I get established. Winter comes, I could offer home styling service. No one's doing that, and with all the retirees around here now, well, I think it could be good business. You know?"

Farnsy agreed. There were so many thoughts and memories swirling around Farnsy's head, and the conversation with Lucy flowed so easily that he lost track of time, and suddenly he could see China Lake through the pines. His pickup found the road down to Josie's place.

Her camp had to be the smallest one he'd ever seen. Tiny front porch, big enough for a small table and four chairs and not much else. It was where he'd had lunch with Lucy and Auntie and Auntie's brother Tony some years ago. Dill soup and meat buns. What would have been the front yard was her garden, an abundant chaos of flowers and rows of sprouting vegetables, and a huge raspberry patch spreading off to one side.

Farnsy had never seen the second floor of Auntie's summer camp but couldn't imagine there being more than two tiny bedrooms upstairs. Downstairs, he remembered seeing a tiny sitting room, in front, a parlor where one of Auntie's braided rugs spread across the floor. Lucy told Farnsy a couple of skirts she'd outgrown were braided into that rug. The kitchen was in the back and had a woodstove and a tin sink with a hand pump. Standing outside on the porch, Farnsy smelled a soup of some kind, for sure. And pork. Auntie always had a pig until a few years ago, Lucy'd told Farnsy in the car on the way out, and she even named them. Every year, Lucy explained, when she was little, she'd eaten Auntie's meat buns, wondering where that pig had gone. When she found out, Lucy went vegetarian for a while.

He knocked on the screened door. They peeked in and could see Josie in her kitchen, in a flowery apron, standing at the stove. The unmistakable smell of her dill soup infused the air on the porch where Farnsy stood, salivating.

"Lucy, dear! You like meat buns, Mr.?" Auntie swept a lock of her gray hair behind one ear and smiled.

"Yes, he does, Auntie. You remember Farnsy, don't you? Can we come in?"

"Of course, dear. You want my car keys now?" Auntie smiled.

Josie never minced words. Straight to the point.

Lucy informed her that they were coming to help her sell her car to Mr. Bauer, who owned the barn where Auntie kept her car in the winter. He'd been interested in Auntie's car for years. And

FARNSY

he promised to drive Auntie into town once a week if she sold it to him.

Farnsy had two bowls of Auntie's dill soup and four meat buns to Lucy's one bowl and one bun. Auntie, who'd never had any kids of her own, watched Farnsy with a bemused smile, as if she were a mother proudly watching her son.

The car key was in the middle of the table when Farnsy dabbed his mouth with the cloth napkin. There wasn't any song and dance, no negotiations or reasoning or argument. Josie simply handed her key to Farnsy, then hung her apron on a hook in the kitchen, tied her hair back in the mirror, and walked with him and Lucy out to his pickup for the drive over to Mr. Bauer's place. They drove there in silence like actors, practicing their lines. As Farnsy pulled in at the Bauer farm, he could see Josie tearing up.

They sat there for a few minutes, windows up, the hush of the air conditioning, both looking straight ahead at Josie's car, all polished up now, the front bumper back where it belonged. Mr. Bauer had gotten the car out of the space under his barn and dusted the winter off her. Josie pulled a hankie out of her blouse, tapped away the tears and said to Farnsy, "Thank you, mister." Then, "I'll be okay."

And before Farnsy could say what he was thinking, Lucy said, "Okay, now let's go up there, knock on his door, and squeeze old man Bauer tighter than a turnip. I'm not coming out of there with anything less than 500 dollars. Why, if anything," she said, gathering steam, "If anything, it's worth at least a good 600. I don't much care what that blue book says. Mr. Bauer knows that Auntie changed the oil like clockwork. And she hardly drove it anywhere."

Bauer looked somber as they sat down at his kitchen table, like he was getting ready to do some hard bargaining, but Aunt Josie surprised them all and jumped right in. "Mr. Bauer, you know why we are here. I want 1,000 dollars for the car. You know it's worth every penny."

Farnsy looked to Lucy in astonishment. Where'd this come from?

Mr. Bauer took a moment, then came to his senses. "Well, now, that's interesting, because that car's so old, Henry Ford himself might've driven it. I'll give you 200, 250 tops, but that's only because I think I can sell your car to collectors for parts, and that'll take me two years. At least. And that doesn't include the repairs I just made to your fender."

Mr. Bauer reached for the soda bottle in front of him and pulled the cap off with an opener on the wall near the door.

Josie said he could get twice that for the engine, because the car only had about 5,000 miles on it, seeing as she'd only driven it around town and once a year over to the Skowhegan summer theater back when her husband, rest his soul, was alive. "That car's not an antique," Josie said softly, "it's classic."

By the time they finished, old Mr. Bauer was out $600, and he and Josie shook hands. Josie tucked the six bills into her purse, thanked Mr. Bauer, and wished him well. Then she asked Lucy if she and her boyfriend wanted to go out for an ice cream sundae.

"Next time, Auntie, thanks," Lucy said, winking at Farnsy. "Officer Farnsworth and I have a date back at his place."

The Accident

Dottie's voice from dispatch said it all. The intersection of Belvedere and Route 1. Most dangerous intersection in town. Farnsy felt like he was driving through molasses but arrived on the scene a few minutes later and saw everything lying at crazy angles with papers and bits of things all over the place. The car was upended like a turtle and the smell of gasoline hung in the unforgiving cool night air. One headlight was still on, and a directional blinker seemed to keep time with the rock music still blasting away on the radio.

Godawful it was. An upended puzzle box, pieces all scattered in fury. Farnsy called Dottie to tell her it was a fatal for sure, and the protocol kicked in. She called EMS, the fire department, the wrecking crew, and the funeral home. Then the district attorney. The DA was a formality, but Farnsy knew the others would arrive soon. Lincoln County would send out an accident reconstruction specialist who would arrive a bit later. Farnsy's job now was to maintain safety at the site, so he set out four traffic flares to slow down any traffic and move them around the scene. The flares fizzed orange in the night mist. It was near midnight, so there was only the occasional passing car, which would slow down long enough so the occupants could take a look, then pick up speed as if to shake off what they'd just seen: something so private that it seemed ripped out and on naked display.

But the worst of it was seeing Skip Tucker's boy lying there on the cold asphalt, all messed up, groaning and bleeding, twisted out of shape, shards of glass strewn across the asphalt and then the white bones sticking out of him, the rain starting to drizzle again. It looked to Farnsy like Skip's car must've been airborne when it crossed the median and slammed head-on into a tree.

Farnsy found the boy's date on the other side of the road, off on the shoulder. Like a rag doll flung there, landing awkwardly like she was sleeping in the weeds. Dressed all nice for the prom. She must've been from somewhere else because none of the EMS guys knew her. One of them thought he recognized her, but it was all the same because they could see that she was dead, just lying there, quiet and peaceful. Farnsy remembered thinking that she was pretty. It hit him, how young they were. Just starting to figure things out.

Skip's kid's groans swelled to screams, now and then some kind of a prayer. "Please Jesus, oh God, someone help me." Farnsy couldn't shake the boy's voice out of his mind. They figured out the girl's name because Skip's boy kept asking for her. "Betty, Betty." A nice name you didn't hear much anymore. The kind of name you'd give a girl who had moxie, a strong name. But she was gone, so Farnsy stayed next to Skip's kid until they got him on a stretcher and the ambulance raced off, its red taillights swallowed up by the darkness as it turned toward the hospital in Damariscotta and the siren's sounds dissolved. And they found the girl's address in her pocketbook.

While one officer swept the road, another measured the skid marks and took photos of the skid marks and the empties strewn about the road. For his report, Farnsy sketched the scene in his notebook, where they'd found the kids and the empties. After the rain stopped again and they had cleaned up the site as best they could, he told the fellas and the one gal that they should go home. There wasn't anything else they could do. Farnsy stayed until they'd left, then said a little prayer, not that he was a church sort of guy, but because he thought, well, you never know. And he wept. Then he drove over to Skip's place to give him the news and then to the girl's parents up in Jefferson, just past his place on the lake.

Farnsy woke up groggy the morning after the accident. Still in that world of heartache and sadness. Everything had happened so suddenly the night before that it all seemed like a dream. Nightmare was more like it, all that splintered glass and tangled mess scattered across the rain-slicked highway.

He showered and shaved and drove back to the scene to see if there was anything else he could do or if there was something he might've missed. All the big bits and pieces were cleaned up. The blood splatters, now brownish, were still visible. They'd said it would rain again later that day. But a memory like that wouldn't wash away fast. They were just a couple of good Maine kids out having fun and headed home after a spring dance. Farnsy put that in his report.

When Skip came to the station a few days later to thank Farnsy, they hugged and bawled tears they didn't think they'd ever have to shed. Skip told Farnsy his boy was the best sternman any father could want.

"You did everything you could to help my boy," Skip said. "Thanks, man."

Farnsy couldn't find any words. What do you tell someone you know who's just lost his youngest son on some lousy highway before the kid'd even started living? All Farnsy could tell Skip was just to put one boot on at a time, one day at a time. It was the best he could think of, and the words felt empty even as he spoke them, but he hoped Skip might find something in them.

Farnsy caught himself looking up from whatever he was doing a day or so after the accident and staring off at something he couldn't see. He hoped the predictability of his routine might distract him or that something else, something new and good, might displace the memories.

SPRING — *The Accident*

"Farnsworth," Chief said, catching Farnsy staring out the window of the station's kitchen, "take the afternoon off. For that matter, no, take the day off. We need you, but you need time out. Trust me, Farnsy, we're all behind you. This is lousy stuff. And we're not as tough as we think we are. Anyway, consider this an order. No debate."

Farnsy sat in his pickup outside the station for a moment, thinking maybe he should drive out to Pemaquid to think. Maybe that would shake it off. But Henry needed him. And maybe he needed the cat. So he drove back to the lake.

Farnsy fell asleep on the couch. When he woke up, the cottage was dark, it was dark outside, and there was a slight chill in the air. It felt like rain again. Henry was kneading Farnsy's chest because he was hungry, and the phone was ringing.

"Sorry, Henry," Farnsy said as he set the cat down and stumbled over to the phone.

"Farnsy, that you?" He heard Lucy's voice.

"Guilty as charged, Luce. Time is it?"

"Late, Farnsy. Almost 10."

"What's up?"

"Well, I was just going to ask you the same question. I heard about the accident."

"Yeah, it was bad, Lucy. Real bad."

"Want to tell me about it?"

"No, but how'd you hear about it?"

"Farnsy. Really?"

"Yeah, I mean, I just finished my report." He paused, "What day is it?"

"Farnsy, you know what they say about bad news."

"Not really, what?'

"Travels fast."

"Guess so. Give me a second, Luce, gotta feed Henry, okay?"

"Okay, Farnsy. Guess I know where I stand. Police work, Henry, Doc, more police work, then me."

"Luce, come on. You know that's not the way I see it."

"So then, how do you see it, William Phineas Farnsworth?"

"Not like that. Change of topic?"

"Okay. You remember that styling job I mentioned down in Boston?"

"Luce, it's Henry. He's driving me crazy here. Hold on a sec."

After he'd scooped some cat food out of a new can, Farnsy went back to the phone, expecting to hear a dial tone. Instead he heard the late news in the background on Lucy's phone.

"You still there?" he asked.

"Been holding my breath the whole time, Farnsy. I'm getting pretty good at that. Henry's a lucky fellow."

"Well, Luce, all you need to do is rub up against my leg now and then, you know?"

"Good thing this isn't a party line, Farnsworth."

"So this Boston job."

"Right. I've been thinking a lot recently. My mother's place is starting to feel a little cramped, so it's tempting, that job. Good tippers, too, down there, they say."

"But?"

"But I've decided to take the chair in that salon near the bridge. For now, anyway."

"Thought you wanted someplace exciting."

"You okay with that?"

"Of course. Luce, to tell the truth..."

"Whole truth and nothing but?"

"Like I was starting to say, to tell the truth, I think it's good. Be nice to have you back."

They paused.

"You still there, Farnsy?"

SPRING — *The Accident*

"What I'm trying to say is that I wouldn't have to arrest you if you came over tonight. Henry misses you. And so do I."

They paused.

"Been doing a lot of thinking since the accident."

"And?"

"And it just makes you wonder how short life is. How fragile everything is. How you can lose it all in a second."

"Yeah," Lucy whispered, "I know what you mean. When we went out to Josie's place, it got me thinking about how old she is and how long ago it was I used to feed her pigs when I was a kid."

"Yeah, that was a good visit, Luce. Sweet old gal. Glad we could help her. Look, why don't you come over? I'll pop a frozen pizza in the oven. Should be done by the time you get here."

"I'll bring a bottle of mom's favorite red wine."

"And a toothbrush."

"Okay. And a toothbrush. Oh, and by the way, I'm going to need some help putting up some shelves in my corner of that salon. That a fair deal?"

"Sure, Lucy. It's getting late."

A few days later, Farnsy saw someone had set up a little white cross and a wreath on the side of the road where it all happened. Flowers and teddy bears huddled around the cross. Maybe a week or so after that, Farnsy spotted Skip headed downriver in his fishing boat, alone.

Crazy Moon

"Must be something in the air," Chief muttered under his breath when Farnsy arrived at the station late that Saturday morning. "Never seen anything like it. Nuts."

"Full moon tonight, Chief, and it's Saturday to boot. You know what they say," Dottie smiled in Farnsy's direction.

"Mind filling me in, Chief?" Farnsy asked.

"Well, we got a triple whammy over at Hannaford, Farnsworth: a blue lobster. Report of a skunk wandering around the McDonald's next to Hannaford. Seems he's got a McFlurry cup on his head. And then some snowbird complaining about the asparagus."

"Hannaford?"

"Yup, a Hannaford trifecta. And that's just for starters. Now Dottie tells me someone called in a complaint. Seems that old Hamlin's doing his business again, right out there next to the Bristol Road."

The phone at dispatch rang again. Julie held her hand over the mouthpiece, "Chief, caller says a Portland news crew is headed up to Hannaford. They want to do some interviews around the lobster tank. Want to know if you'll do an interview?"

"Jeez Louise. That all?"

"Well, now that you ask, the manager over at Sherman's Book Shop called earlier. Forgot to mention this. Said someone's dressed up in a giant tick outfit handing out tick safety brochures in front of their main window, scaring people away."

Farnsy chimed in. "Chief, let me take the Hannaford action. I've had a little experience with TV interviews recently. And I can handle the skunk. You okay taking the tick imposter, Chief?"

"What about old Hamlin out there?" Chief asked.

Farnsy thought about it a moment. "Why doesn't Julie call our informant out there and ask her. Look, I mean, we all know who it is. Just call Millie and ask her to call us as soon's Hamlin's back at it. So we can catch him in the act, if you get my drift."

"Good thinking, Farnsworth. There's hope for you yet, you know. That's the plan. Everyone on it?" They all nodded. "Okay, good. Now what are you waiting for?"

Farnsy pulled into the parking lot next to the golden arches and saw a handful of folks standing in a loose circle around what had to be the skunk with a giant McFlurry cup around his head. Must've been doing some dumpster diving, Farnsy guessed. Every now and then the critter stopped, as if to get a breath, arched its tail like it was getting ready to spray, someone screeched, the circle widened, and the whole dance started again.

Farnsy recognized most of the folks gathered there. A couple of them, he figured, must be from away. Looked like they'd walked out of an L. L. Bean catalog. They were standing behind the locals, all of whom had probably had their fair share of tangles with skunks. Or at least their dogs had.

Like a bullfighter with his cape, Farnsy stepped gingerly into the ring, the blanket from his trunk draped over his left arm. "Okay, now, folks, please step back, and let's all be quiet. You wouldn't be happy either if you had one of those things on your head."

"Not the end stuck in the cup we're worried about, Farnsy," one of the locals joked. "Looks to me like that little fella's working end is locked and loaded."

FARNSY

Farnsy'd never gotten quite this close to a skunk and certainly not a skunk in distress. But he held out the blanket, which he'd folded in half just in case the skunk let loose, figuring the blanket offered a little protection from any aromatic discharge. Farnsy motioned for silence and stepped closer and then still closer. Until the skunk tired out and stopped wiggling.

Farnsy tossed the blanket over the skunk and the McFlurry cup, and if there was any spray, he couldn't smell it. He waved one of the locals over and they got the blanket around the creature real tight, with just the McFlurry cup sticking out.

"Okay, now, folks, this is what I'm going to do. I'm going to yank this cup off the skunk then run like hell. I suggest you do the same. Because if this little guy tags you, you'll have a fragrant souvenir for a week or so."

Farnsy looked around to make sure everyone was out of range, then he gave the nod and off came the cup, off came the blanket, and everyone scattered back as far and as fast as they could. The skunk looked around, sniffed the air, wobbled his tail, hesitated, then bolted in little wobbly leaps off into the bushes. The crowd erupted in applause. But Farnsy didn't have time to spare because he saw Portland TV crew's van pulling up over in front of Hannaford a hundred yards away. They were parked in a No Parking zone, but Farnsy figured that was the least of his worries for the moment.

Jim, the new manager from away, was standing at the entrance as Farnsy pulled up behind the TV van.

"Big Day, Jim! This blue lobster part of Hannaford's new publicity campaign?"

"Hi Farnsy, thanks for coming. I let the TV crew in already. They seemed nice enough and besides, I don't think corporate will complain about a little free advertising."

"Hope you're right, Jim. Where are they now?"

"Back of the store, between the cheese display and the shrimp. And you heard about the guy in the veggie department, right? Comes up from Rhode Island and says our asparagus isn't really local if it's from Massachusetts."

"That's next," Farnsy said. "I'd like to see this blue lobster first if you don't mind."

The news producer caught Farnsy as he approached the lobster tank, where a few shoppers had gathered, witness to a lesser miracle. Farnsy agreed to do the interview next to the tank where the blue lobster was sulking. Someone on the TV crew poked the lobster so that he'd move to the front of the tank, where he was now, under the glare of TV lights, his claws up as if ready for a fight. Farnsy thought he looked like a good two- or three-pounder and wondered if it would taste as tough as it looked, steamed.

The fellow from the Portland TV station asked a few softball questions, and Farnsy played right along, said yes, he'd heard of fishermen pulling up orange lobsters and even one that was half blue and half orange, right down the middle. "But a lobster this blue is rare," Farnsy said with a serious voice. "I'm guessing he must've eaten a lot of Maine blueberries."

The cameraman smiled, gave a thumbs up, and turned the camera toward Jim, who told the crew someone had already bid $100 for the blue lobster. But he was going to wait for the best offer, then donate the profit to a food bank in town.

Smart fella, Farnsy thought as he left the circle of TV lights and headed around the corner over to the produce department, where the rhubarb about the asparagus was calming down. The man from Rhode Island, who claimed to be something of an expert, said the "Local Produce" sign was false advertising. He knew this asparagus couldn't be Maine produce. If he wanted Massachusetts asparagus, he'd have bought some there on his way up to Maine. Farnsy listened politely, then said that some 200 years ago, Maine had been part of Massachusetts, so technically speaking, Massachusetts was "local," historically speaking, at least.

The man shrugged and tried to smile. "Good one, Officer. Thanks for the history lesson. Maybe I got a little carried away here." He apologized to the young man in charge of produce, who put a rubber band around a few asparagus stalks and handed the bunch to the man from Rhode Island. He wouldn't be the first person from away who thought locals were having a good one on him.

Farnsy excused himself. "Got a call coming in, sorry, but glad everything's okay now."

It was Dottie from dispatch. "Farnsy, old Hamlin's on his hopper as we speak. Millie says he took the Sunday paper with him, so you've probably got a few minutes to get there. Chief's tied up in town. Had to handcuff the tick man."

Farnsy made a beeline over to the Bristol Road. Hamlin King was something of an institution in town. Everyone said Ham was the laziest man in Lincoln County. And probably one of the last people in Damariscotta with a real privy. Soon's the first good snow hit the ground, old Hamlin would start pissin' and moaning about how far his privy was from his back door. Truth was, that privy wasn't but 20 steps at most from his house, but the trouble was, the Bristol Road wasn't but 20 yards off in the other direction.

If Hamlin propped open the privy door with his good foot he had a wicked good view of the Damariscotta River. In summer, that privy didn't seem all that far away to Hamlin, but come winter he was disinclined to spend any extra time out on the hopper reading *Uncle Henry's Weekly Swap or Sell It Guide*. Well, Hamlin was the one who'd built it so he had only himself to blame.

Late one winter, a few years ago, when Hamlin was down to his last half cord of firewood, he calculated he could make it to spring if he used the pine panels off that privy to heat his house. Board by board, Hamlin King stripped his privy down to its bare essentials, until sometime later that spring, anyone driving along the Bristol Road could look up and see old Hamlin sitting out there on his throne, King of the Bristol Road, studying *Uncle Henry's* like a New York stockbroker reading the ticker. Hamlin'd look up and wave to the cars just as though it were the most normal thing in the world for a man to be doing his business out there right next to that road. Then, every summer, he'd get some old planks and rebuild that privy just like new. Real proud of himself he was.

Farnsy pulled up on the shoulder of the Bristol Road and walked through the brambles at the road's edge and across the field up close to where Hamlin still sat, reading *Uncle Henry's*.

"Can't a man get any peace and quiet around here, Farnsworth?"

"Well, now, Hamlin, that depends on where a man's sitting."

"Didn't I hear the governor say something about Maine being open for business?"

"Well, I'm not sure he meant this kind of business here, Hamlin."

Hamlin put down his *Uncle Henry's*. "Suppose you want me to buy some wood and put up some walls?"

"That'd do it for me. And I think your neighbors would appreciate it, too, Mr. King."

Hamlin muttered something about his rights.

Back in the station, the Chief chuckled and said it sounded like Farnsy had gotten to the bottom of things with Hamlin. Said the Hannaford manager and the owner of the McDonald's had both called to thank the Chief for his quick response. The asparagus sold out and the top bid for the blue lobster hit $500, so he was en route to some la-de-da restaurant in Portland. That evening, the Portland news carried a short piece about a lobster eating blueberries, followed by an interview with a UMaine professor who was an international blueberry expert and dismissed Farnsy's theory that the lobster had eaten a pint of Maine blueberries.

A week later, the *Lincoln County News* noted the skunk incident in the Damariscotta Police report and, possibly coincidentally, the *LCN* launched a new weekly advice column for out-of-staters. The first column instructed folks from away how to approach a skunk and made clear that Maine lobsters don't eat wild Maine blueberries, and if they did, they wouldn't eat their bloated Michigan or New Jersey cousins, which the columnist described as being the size of softballs and having about as much flavor.

The paper wrapped up the series in the issue just before Memorial Day with a final advice column listing some of the dumb questions that people from away ask—and shouldn't: Never ask a local how they get all the boats in the harbor pointing in the same direction. Or where all the water goes at low tide. Or where they can see a flock of moose. Or who paints all those pretty little lobster buoys. Or which way to East Vassalboro. The article promised to publish the answers to those and a few other questions in the following week's *Lincoln County News*.

Rainy Day

Something moved Farnsy to stop at the old cemetery next to St. Patrick's Church. It was where his mother was buried, near her parents, and where his father, wherever he was then, would be buried too. It was a warm spring morning, and the Portland radio said the temperatures were going up. A light rain, more of a mist, had started to fall by the time he found her grave. He tugged up a couple handfuls of dandelions that had settled in near her stone. The ground was soft, so he got most of the roots. He stood there, lost in his thoughts, trying to find one that would stay put, still not knowing what forces had coaxed him there. He remembered his mother telling him and Gracie about the time their grandfather made his baked beans for a church supper one Saturday, and the chorus of farts that had percolated up and down the pews during mass the next day. The ripples of giggles. And how Father McKetchie turned to the altar boy and asked him to please, God, light more incense.

"Ma," Farnsy said in a whisper, thinking maybe that's how you might best be heard if you were talking to someone who was dead. "Ma, Farnsy here." He stopped. "I think I'm going to ask Lucy to marry me. She's a good girl. I think you kind of always liked her." He stopped again. "I know she's been married before, but some things just don't work out, you know. Not like you and Dad." He stopped. "I can't live without her. She drives me crazy sometimes. But it's a good crazy, you know. Anyway, I thought you should know. Just wish you could be here." It was time to go. "Love you,

Ma, miss you. All of us do. Anyway, don't worry about me, everything's gonna be all right. Hey, didn't I get pop's Jitterbug back? The one you framed?" He paused. "Okay, yeah, you're right, the Professor found it. But things worked out, didn't they? Just like you always said they would." The rain slowed down. "Love you, Ma." He listened. "No, I love you more."

Main Feature

Farnsy looked out at the lake and chuckled about something Doc had said the other day about how it looked like someone had put a couple of quarters in the sun machine. Dawn was blooming bright after the big storm had scraped along the coast the night before. Farnsy took it as a sign that this Memorial Day would be a good day and a good start to a new season on the coast.

Summer people had started to trickle in, some of them as early as mid-May. But most didn't leave their winter homes for Maine until summer was already there, ready and waiting for them.

Farnsy was on duty. Heavy traffic was predicted and that meant more stops than usual. Some warnings and some tickets and a lot of questions about how to get somewhere. Lots of smiling folks strolled the sun-warmed sidewalks in town, peeking in shop windows set up to lure in the summer visitors. Things were humming and it was promising to be one of the best Memorial Days in some years.

By day's end, Farnsy had nailed the Chief's prize for the first speeding ticket of the new season: New York plates, 25 miles an hour over. The driver even thanked Farnsy for his service and said it was just nice to be there in Maine. The rest of the day was a normal Memorial Day. Must be the sun, he thought. People's moods always seemed to follow the weather. Some people's, anyway.

After his shift, Farnsy checked in at the station to see if the Chief needed him, but Chief knew Farnsy had a big date planned that evening. Even though he could've used an extra hand, he waved Farnsy off and said, "You're off duty, Officer Farnsworth. Off means off. Skedaddle. Go home and get cleaned up. Lucy's not gonna like it if I send you to her smelling like that."

Farnsy was out the station door before anyone could say anything else, his mind leap-skipping ahead, thinking of all the things that might go wrong. Doc had tried to help. "One step at a time, one day at a time," he'd said when Farnsy told him his plans. By the time Farnsy's pickup crested the hill at the Bunker Hill Church, he'd put work behind him and all he could think about was feeding Henry, then showering, shaving, slapping on some Old Spice, and getting back to the Lincoln Theater by quarter to seven for his movie date with Lucy.

Titanic was playing. It was the same movie he and Lucy had seen on their first date back when they were kids.

"You sure?" Lucy'd asked Farnsy when he'd called her. "Well, okay, Farnsworth. I just hope we get to see the ending this time."

Farnsy got to the theater early, but Lucy was already there. He spotted her as soon as he came up the wooden stairs to the lobby and was enveloped by the smell of fresh popcorn and the sound of happy voices. She was standing next to the little ticket booth, chatting with Buck, who sold Farnsy two tickets, which he tore in half, keeping the stubs. Buck gave Farnsy a wink.

"You look beautiful, Lucy" Farnsy said. "Like that scene in *Moonstruck*, you know?"

Farnsy was wearing his cleanest pair of no-iron khakis and a new purple polo shirt he'd bought for the occasion at Renys, thinking Lucy would like that color.

"Nice, Farnsy. I didn't think you were a purple guy."

"I'm in blue all day long, Luce. Time for a change." He was starting to think things might work out. "Popcorn?"

"Sure!"

SPRING — *Main Feature*

They decided on a medium root beer, two straws, and a large bag of popcorn, because if there was ever a popcorn movie, they agreed this was it. Standing in the lobby, Farnsy and Lucy could hear the previews: ear-busting music and sounds of car chases, gunshots, and explosions.

"What are we waiting for, Farnsy?" Lucy asked, looking around the lobby, seeing they were the last ones.

"Luce, you'll see. This way—follow me."

Farnsy took Lucy's hand and led her to a small white door on the other side of the lobby. He turned to her and said, "Just like that last time, Luce, the balcony. You coming?"

She giggled, brushed her hair back behind her ears, and he led the way up the narrow stairs to the balcony, which was now stuffed with fancy movie and sound equipment, all digital, no old-fashioned movie reels spinning. And not much room to sit, except Farnsy had arranged with Buck for a comfy old loveseat, courtesy of Sproul's furniture store.

"Farnsy, you're amazing!" she whispered. "Our own private showing." Then she sat down, settling into the sofa with a swish.

"Other side, Lucy. I'm right-handed." Lucy smiled and scooched over. Farnsy balanced the bag of popcorn and the drink on the ledge in front of them as they settled in, the last trailer blasted their ears, and a list of every local donor to the theater scrolled by alphabetically, a blur of letters and names. Farnsy recognized most every one of them.

After the main feature started and the *Titanic* commenced its doomed voyage, Farnsy and Lucy shared sips of soda and their fingers found kernels of hot, buttered popcorn in the dark, just like years ago when they were kids. Farnsy put the soda down at his feet and took the bag of popcorn from Lucy, setting it gently on the floor off to one side so they could watch the movie. He could feel the warmth of her thigh resting against his, and all the memories came back, as if nothing had changed, even though so much had. It felt good. They held hands, interlocking fingers until it hurt and they had to let loose a bit, squeezing only when the scene was good. Lucy leaned her head on Farnsy's shoulder whenever there was a scary scene or a sad one. He reached his arm up around her and pulled her closer still. He remembered doing this as a kid and feeling his arm fall asleep, but being too scared to move it because it'd taken him most of the film to inch his hand around her. This time it felt as though she blended right in with him on that little sofa, and he felt like they could stay there forever.

The iceberg scraped the hull of the ship and huge chunks of ice scattered across the great ship's deck. Lucy squeezed Farnsy's arm and said, "I can't watch."

"Lucy, I've been thinking."

"Farnsy, shh, can't this wait?"

"You know how it ends, Luce."

"Sure, but..."

"Luce, I've been thinking." Farnsy realized he'd forgotten the script he'd rehearsed. "I've been thinking..."

"Shh," she whispered, clasping his arm.

"Lucy, have you ever thought about us..."

"Us? Us, what?"

"I mean us, as in maybe, well, have you ever thought of getting...?"

The great ship listed again and more clinging passengers fell into the icy water.

"What?!" Lucy turned to Farnsy.

"Well, you know what I mean."

"No, Farnsy, I don't."

"Jeez, Luce, whisper, you're not making this easy."

"Can't this wait? My gosh, Farnsy, can't we just watch the ending?"

"Lucy, have you ever thought, would you...?"

"Would I what, Farnsy, gosh sakes, what's gotten into you?"

SPRING ~ *Main Feature*

Farnsy knelt down on one knee, holding open a small red box in both hands. It held a gold ring with Maine tourmaline set in the middle. "Would you marry me, Lucy? What I mean is, would you be my husband? Shoot, you know what I mean."

"Farnsy, oh my God, it's beautiful. Is that tourmaline?" she said, smiling through her tears. More passengers tumbled off the ship's decks as the great vessel lurched once more.

"But I'll have to think about it, you know."

Farnsy watched her lean back in her seat. What now? he wondered. All the what-ifs he'd prepared for, just not this one. What now? His script was out the window because life isn't like a movie.

He stared at the screen and watched as the arctic sea was about to swallow up the *Titanic*. He heard a whisper next to him. "Guess that's long enough."

"What's long enough?"

"Okay, I've thought about it, and yes, I'll be your husband. If you'll be my wife..."

While the great ship sank, Farnsy and Lucy tangled up, all arms and kisses, and didn't stop until one of them kicked the popcorn bag and it landed on a couple of old-timers in the back row of the seats below them.

"Hey, who's up there? Cut that out," one codger yelled, looking up at the balcony overhead to see if he could find the culprit. But the credits were rolling and Farnsy and Lucy stayed up in the balcony until the theater had emptied out and Buck had turned the lights back on and started sweeping up.

"You two ever coming down?"

"Never!" they yelled.

Around noon the next day, Lucy told Farnsy she'd thought things over and wanted a real ceremony. "On the Fourth," she said, "which is appropriate because every marriage has some fireworks." She'd made some calls, she told Farnsy, and there was a cancellation at Lakehurst Lodge, so that's where they'd have the reception. And she'd reserved the lawn next to the Pemaquid Lighthouse for the ceremony because she knew how much Farnsy liked to go out there, and besides, they'd gone out there a couple times to talk. "Something special about that place," she said. She explained that she knew someone who knew someone down in Bristol who had a friend and got last-minute permission to reserve the rock-stubbled lawn next to the lighthouse for their ceremony. Plus, she said, it would be high tide during the ceremony, and she wanted nice photos out there on the rocks with the waves. She had a photographer lined up.

Farnsy listened and agreed, mostly because he had no alternate plans and because it all made sense and everything seemed to be falling into place, was as though it were preordained. The speed with which Lucy made arrangements for their wedding and the reception made him wonder if she'd had this up her sleeve all along. Maybe she even knew he was going to propose.

But for the life of him, Farnsy couldn't figure out how Lucy'd managed to reserve the Lakehurst Lodge on Pemaquid Pond. And rent four Lakehurst cottages for two nights on the Fourth of July weekend. He knew enough not to ask. Lucy had as many friends in town as he did. So if she were calling in favors, Farnsy was certain she'd run out of them.

Like Doc said, "Small secrets and a little mystery are the mortar of a good marriage." Farnsy wasn't complaining, but based on all the evidence, he was convinced that Lucy had known he was going to pop the question in the balcony long before he'd ever thought about doing it.

Then, one Saturday, precisely three weeks to the day before their wedding, Lucy called Farnsy from her mother's place to ask him what color socks he was going to wear. Farnsy stared out at the lake, his second mug of coffee in hand, and searched the shimmering water for the right thing to say, trying not to say what he felt like saying. Ever since he'd proposed to Lucy in the Lincoln Theater, things seemed to be picking up speed. He felt deer-in-the-headlights dazed. In the background, he heard Corrie's voice.

"Farns, I know what you're thinking. Just not white socks, okay?" Lucy whispered.

"Yes, dear," Farnsy said, thinking it wouldn't be the last time he ever said that.

When Farnsy called his sister, Grace, to tell her he and Lucy were getting married, Grace said Lucy had already called her that morning with the date and asked if she'd fly out with the kids and be her bridesmaid.

"You know I wouldn't miss this, Farnsy, not for anything," Grace said. "We were planning on coming out East this summer anyway, and the kids made me cross my heart and promise you'd take them turtle hunting again. Lulu says she wants to hold the net this time. You good with that?"

Grace said she'd get their mother's gold wedding ring expressed to Lucy so she could get it resized before the ceremony. Everything was happening so fast, Farnsy'd forgotten about a wedding ring.

"Just seemed right, Farnsy. I know Mom loved Lucy as much as the kids and I do. And besides," she added, "it's an antique and you know, every bride needs something old, something new, something borrowed, something blue."

Farnsy said he was real glad Grace and the kids were coming and offered that if Lucy needed something old, maybe Doc would do.

"Lucy's going to ask him to officiate, you know," Farnsy added.

FARNSY

"Yeah, Lucy told me. She said he's already agreed to get certified as a justice of the peace. But don't worry, she's told him to keep it short. Love you, Farns. Gotta go."

"Love you too, Gracie. But when did Lucy tell you about Doc? I mean, I only just now..."

"Have to run, Farnsy, sorry. Doesn't matter when Lucy told me. Anyway, the kids are just getting up. But everything's gonna be all right, okay? Oh, I'm bringing a little surprise for you, too."

"Okay," Farnsy said, "sure hope so. But what's this about a surprise?"

"That's why they call it a surprise. You just have to wait, Farnsy." She hung up.

The Beginning

The morning of the wedding broke hot and sunny. Not a cloud in the sky. Lucy had told Farnsy his job was simple: shower, shave, and show up on time. Lucy and her mom had handled all the plans with military precision. The dressing rooms she reserved at the Pemaquid Hotel were just a short stroll from the Pemaquid Lighthouse. Then there were the preparations for the reception back in town at Lakehurst Lodge: the flowers, the food, the drinks, the music, the tables and chairs. The invitations were easy: family and friends. And friends of friends. Henry would stay home and watch the cottage. He'd be fine for one night. Lucy seemed pretty happy checking things off her gotta-do list, as long as her mom was there to help. Farnsy figured there were plenty of times someone might need a third opinion, but this didn't seem to be one of them.

Farnsy buttoned up his police tunic, which Lucy had asked him to wear, gave it a little tug, smoothed it out, took one last look in the mirror at himself as a single man and left the Pemaquid Hotel to join the family and friends who were straggling over to the rocky lawn next to the lighthouse.

A few puffy clouds glided overhead, and a fresh sea breeze scurried the clouds along. The tide was high and the surf surged and foamed over the rocky ledge into the tide pools below the lighthouse. The salt air smelled of seaweed sunning in tide pools. Seagulls swooped overhead, on the lookout for picnic sandwiches. The white lighthouse was freshly painted and picture-perfect.

FARNSY

Farnsy smiled, thinking about the red socks Lucy'd given him last Christmas that he'd tugged on earlier that morning. Well, they're not white, he thought. When he caught up with Doc, who was making his way slowly across the parking lot over to the lawn next to the lighthouse, Doc turned to Farnsy, "It's a real Irish blackthorn walking stick, Farnsy," Doc said, holding it up for Farnsy to see, "Not a cane. Canes are for old farts."

Then he added, "You know, son, if you want to back out, there's still time to grab a seat on the next bus to Boston." Doc pretended to look at his pocket watch, "Yup, the afternoon bus'll be pulling up in front of the library about an hour from now..."

Farnsy grinned, "Doc, you and I know, the river only flows one way, Doc."

"Not the Damariscotta River."

"You got the license, Doc?"

Doc tapped a pocket of his blazer. "Right here. And this other certificate I got here says I have the power to marry anyone, long as they're not wearing white socks."

Tourists waiting in line outside the lighthouse watched the wedding party gather on the lawn nearby. Spotting Farnsy dressed to the nines and figuring he must be the groom, a guy in line cupped his hands and shouted, "Don't do it!" It was the kind of sun-dappled day when happy laughter and grins came easily. Another voice shouted, "Good luck!"

Doc and Farnsy took their places on a slight rise in the middle of the lawn as family and friends gathered before them, facing the sea stretching out to Monhegan and past. Now and then the surf could be heard breaking over the rocks below. Doc looked solemn but had a pleasant smile as he watched the CLYNK kid help some older folks take their seats on the folding chairs that Lucy's mom, Corrie, had remembered to bring last minute. Farnsy spotted the Chief's cruiser rolling past the little ticket booth for the light-

SPRING — *The Beginning*

house parking lot. As Farnsy's best man, the Chief had the honor of bringing the bride to the edge of the lawn. He hit the siren and lights, and all heads turned around to watch the Chief help Lucy step out of his cruiser. Her dress was sky blue, and she had a small bouquet of blue and white hydrangeas in one hand. The Chief, bulging in his ceremonial tunic, his badge glinting in the sun, left Lucy standing between her mother and her uncle, then strode down the narrow aisle to take his place next to Farnsy. "Picked a good one, Farnsy, a real keeper," he said, still smiling.

Farnsy spotted Lucy and her mom standing over near a blooming rosa rugosa bush, waiting until latecomers found a seat. Uncle Stubb stood near them, hardly recognizable in a light blue seersucker suit and tie. It looked like everyone he knew was there, folks from all around town, even Philomena from Moody's, her mascara blurred with happy tears. Folks were chatting and nodding and smiling as their eyes met Farnsy's. He'd ticketed and warned more than a few of them.

As Farnsy tried to get a headcount, he spotted Grace helping her kids find a place to sit on the grass up front. As soon as she got them squared away, Grace swished over to her place as bridesmaid on the other side of Doc. Farnsy glimpsed Grace's kids, Maggie and Lulu, waving to him and pointing to the row behind them, where he saw a man in Ray-Bans and a beat-up Red Sox cap. It was Jack, his father, sitting there suntanned and smiling. They locked eyes and his father broke into that grin of his. So this was Gracie's surprise. Farnsy grinned back and Jack lifted his hand as if to salute.

In spite of the sea breeze, the sun was hot. A few ladies began to fan themselves, and some of the men dabbed at the sweat on their faces. As soon as everyone had settled in and quieted, Doc nodded to Lucy and Corrie, who were waiting at the back of the gathering in the middle of a little conversation. They missed his signal, so Doc tried again. No response.

FARNSY

Finally, Doc cleared his throat and bellowed, "Someone want to remind the bride and her mother there's supposed to be a wedding up here? You ready, Stubb?" A titter of laughs rustled through the folks assembled.

Farnsy watched Lucy take her Uncle Stubb's arm. Her mother on the other arm. Corrie had told Lucy she couldn't give her daughter away. "Lord knows, you're your own woman, Lucy." But Stubb said he'd be proud. So they agreed to share the honors.

The audience turned to watch the beaming bride stroll slowly down the aisle through a smiling chorus of oohs and ahhs. As she neared Doc and Farnsy, Stubb stepped aside and Corrie walked Lucy the last few steps over to Farnsy, whispered something to him that made him smile, then took the seat between Stubb and Farnsy's father, Jack. Farnsy thought Lucy looked more beautiful than ever, that wildflower tucked in the curls of her hair, her blue dress. Something old, something blue, he remembered.

Doc explained that he took his role seriously, so he wanted to take the opportunity to say a few words. Folks groaned. First, he said, "Like many of you, I was concerned about this marriage starting out on the rocks." The assembled friends and family groaned louder. Doc continued, "But we all know every marriage has some high tides and some low tides." The audience groaned again. "Well, folks, it's getting hot and we're all hungry. I think it's high time we got these lovebirds together." The audience applauded. "So, let me ask the assembled here today if anyone among you can give me three good reasons why these two, Lucy and Farnsy, shouldn't be joined at the hip for as long as they can stand it?"

"Just three?" someone in the back called out. The audience tittered. Doc could've said anything and they would have laughed. It was that kind of a day.

"Settle down now, folks. I know three's as high as some of you can count." He paused. "We, the friends and family of Lucille

SPRING ~ *The Beginning*

Granger and William Farnsworth, are gathered together here on the foundation of this great granite rock to witness and to celebrate their union in marriage.

"Lucy, Farnsy, we're all delighted that you two've finally decided to tie the knot. We know this is a decision you've not entered lightly. And that's a good thing, because love and marriage is a delicate balance. Not 50-50. Sorry, nope. Some days it's 70-30. Other days it's 10-90. Based on my experience, if it averages out to around 50-50, you're pretty lucky. My point is, marriage isn't a steady state. It's always changing, like the ocean around us. So, if you're ready to take the plunge into an ocean of love, Farnsy, if you're willing to bring home the bacon and do everything on Lucy's 'honey-do' list. And Lucy, if you're willing to fry up some of that bacon for Farnsy every now and then, you may repeat your vows before these witnesses, but remember, some of us are hard of hearing."

"Lucy," Farnsy started, "in front of these gathered friends and family, I take you as my wife and promise to love and protect and cherish you, in sickness and in health, for richer or poorer, as long as we both shall live."

"Farnsy, in front of these gathered friends and family, I take you as my husband and promise to love and cherish you, in sickness and in health, for richer or poorer, as long as we both shall live."

Doc handed Farnsy his mother's ring.

Farnsy held the ring up for everyone to see. "With this ring, I marry you, Lucy Granger, and take you to be my wife and my hairstylist as long as we both shall live."

Doc reached into his pocket and pulled out the other ring, handing it to Lucy with great ceremony.

"With this ring, I marry you, William Farnsworth, and take you to be my husband and promise to put up with your crazy schedule as long as we both shall live."

"I now, at long last, and to everyone's great relief, pronounce you man and wife! You may kiss your bride, Farnsy!"

The audience and tourists nearby burst into applause.

"Okay, folks," Doc said as he scanned the happy faces assembled, "See you at Lakehurst!"

Older folks got a head start across the lawn so they could get a good parking spot at Lakehurst, while family and friends milled around and took pictures. Farnsy had just finished shaking hands with Doc and the Chief when his father approached. Jack tucked his sunglasses in a pocket and had his ball cap in his left hand and his right hand outstretched. Farnsy took it. Neither man spoke at first, then Jack grabbed Farnsy and hugged him tight.

"Son, I'm so proud of you. When Grace told me..."

"That's okay, Dad. We were just worried about you. I mean, your notes were great, but we just hoped you'd find the road back to Maine, you know?"

"I know, Willie. Looking back I don't know what got into me. Cripes, after your mom passed, well.... I feel different now, though."

"Pop, you sticking around for a while?"

"Today?"

"No, here, in town, for a while. Couple days, maybe? You know, I could use some help catching turtles with Grace's kids."

His father looked around and found Corrie standing off to one side. "Corrie's putting me up this week. Says I can stay longer, if I want. She's real nice. And you and I've got a lot to catch up on, Willie. Grace, too. But I want you to know I'm real proud of you. Chief tells me you're doing a great job. And Grace showed me all the articles on the Necco wafer case. Say, thanks for getting the old Jitterbug back. May have to try her out, just for old time's sake, see if the fish are biting." His father stopped. "You know

SPRING — *The Beginning*

your mom and I always liked Lucy, since way back. You're a lucky man, Willie. Just like I was lucky in love. If I learned anything driving around, it's that family is everything. Thick and thin. Life was meant to be shared."

They hugged. "See you over at Lakehurst, son. I want the second dance..."

Folks said the reception at Lakehurst was the best ever. Lucy and Corrie had found a three-man blues band in *Uncle Henry's* and traded the band members free haircuts for a year in return for their gig. They plugged in their guitars late that afternoon and played until midnight, fueled by Oxbow's summer ale.

The buffet table was three picnic tables long, end to end, and it was all potluck: tuna casserole, baked beans, lobster mac 'n cheese, spiral ham, creamy clam chowder, bowls of salads—tossed salad, potato salad, Jello salad, coleslaw—burgers on the grill and fresh buttered corn. Lucy lost track but everyone brought their best recipes in Tupperware and Crock-Pots.

The big surprise was the huge chocolate donut–shaped wedding cake that Julie from Waltz's Soda Fountain rolled out to the center of the dance floor at the end of the evening. Microphone in hand, with Farnsy and Lucy waiting to cut into the donut, which was the size of an automobile tire, Julie told everyone that Farnsy may be a good detective, one who'd nabbed the Necco burglar, but after a year of trying, he still hadn't cracked the mystery of who baked the donuts at Waltz's.

"Some detective, Farnsworth. You crack the Necco case wide open, but you couldn't figure out the identity of your donut baker?" she paused for effect. "Well, you're looking at her. I make the donuts."

Doc shook his head. "That beats all."

FARNSY

Toasts punctuated the evening whenever the band took a break. Near the end of the celebration, someone offered Lucy the microphone. She told folks the story about Farnsy and his socks.

"Not those old white ones," she said, describing her call to Farnsy the day after he proposed. "I thought the phone line'd gone dead, then I hear Farnsy say, 'Luce, I'll tell you what. On the day of the wedding, I'm going to close my eyes, reach into my top drawer, and pull out the first pair of socks I find.'"

Everyone laughed.

Doc took the mike and said he was just happy that Lucy and Farnsy had finally tied the knot. Someone asked what knot Doc used to hitch them up. "Slip knot?"

Farnsy watched Lucy work the crowd, like a hummingbird, buzzing from table to table, leaving a rippling pool of smiles and laughter every time she moved on. He thought she was the most beautiful woman he'd ever seen.

They slow danced the first dance of the evening to the music of "You Are So Beautiful," under the steady gaze of the huge moose head hanging over the grand fireplace. As the last words echoed in the now quiet hall, and the band kicked up the beat and started the opening to "Sweet Home Chicago," Farnsy felt a tap on his shoulder and heard his father say, "Next dance's mine, young man..."

Every once in a while, someone would pick up the microphone and tap a glass and tell a story about Lucy or Farnsy or both of them. The old memories flowed.

It was good to see his old man again. You don't know a puzzle piece is missing until all the other pieces are in place. So he was staying at Corrie's place. And he agreed to stop by the cottage in a couple of days to help Farnsy take Maggie and Lulu out turtle hunting, just like the old times. Farnsy was still trying to absorb it all when he waved off a refill of his champagne. He noticed Lucy was still nursing a glass of water.

SPRING — *The Beginning*

"Luce, can I get you some bubbly?"

"Thanks, sweetie, I shouldn't. Maybe just a little sip of yours." She glanced at Gracie's kids out on the dance floor. "Aren't Gracie's kids cute? I can't wait..."

Just as Farnsy was going to ask her what she couldn't wait for, the band cranked up Johnny Cash's "Ring of Fire": "Love is a burning thing..."

"That's our song, Farns. One last dance?"

Just before midnight, the Chief, who was their designated driver, pulled up near the entrance to the Lakehurst pavilion, lights flashing, and Lucy and Farnsy scurried down the gauntlet of friends and family and folks from around town as they tossed rice and hooted and cheered. After the Chief dropped them off at Farnsy's cottage, Farnsy scooped Lucy up and carried her over the threshold.

Epilogue

Farnsy opened one eye, then the other, his head nested in one of the new feather pillows Lucy's mom had gotten them for her bridal shower. He could tell by the angle of the dappled reflections from the lake on the ceiling of his bedroom that it was still morning. He was waking up into a blur of memories, blinking like a newborn. He propped himself up to see what Henry was doing and looked around. No Henry. Smart cat, out in the kitchen with Lucy. She was frying up some bacon. And they were married.

He flopped back onto the pillow, spent. For no reason, he remembered saying something about how you only get married once as they cut the donut cake and Lucy laughing as she fed him a piece of the huge donut cake, saying, "Or twice!" Then Doc said, "Jeez, look folks! He's eating out of her hand already!"

Farnsy heard a soft knock on the bedroom door. He heard it again.

"Farnsy, you up, honey?"

"That you, Luce?"

The door nudged open a crack and Henry scurried in, as if reminding Farnsy not to forget his morning wakeup cat massage routine.

"Now, William Phineas Farnsworth, who else'd be whispering sweet nothings to you today?"

"That's Police Officer William Farnsworth to you, Luce. A little respect..."

"Well, I'm Mrs. William Phineas Farnsworth," Lucy said proudly. "But if you think I'm gonna bring you breakfast in bed, guess again, Officer. So get some clothes on and splash some water on your face and come out to the porch because I'm making eggs Benedict, real bacon, the way you like it, and they're no good cold."

"That coffee I smell?"

She tossed him his bathrobe. "Oh, and don't get used to this, Officer, 'cause next anniversary it's your turn." She blew him a kiss.

Henry stretched out on the windowsill, watching the hummingbirds at the feeder, his tail flicking. Good thing he's an indoor cat, Farnsy thought.

Next anniversary? Sounded like Lucy could see into the future, their future, all unfolded before her like a road map. Farnsy was just waking up to the here and now when he recalled someone, he couldn't remember who, saying something about the joy of kids, how they couldn't wait to see some "productivity" next spring. No, wait, it was his sister, Grace, who asked Farnsy when Maggie and Lulu were going to have some cousins so they could all go turtle hunting together.

Farnsy spotted Henry on top of the bureau, where Lucy had already filled the top three drawers with her things, and watched the cat get ready to knock stuff off onto the floor. Farnsy jumped up, picked the cat up and headed out to the kitchen for his first breakfast with Lucy, his wife. The cottage felt infused with new life. Something he couldn't quite put his finger on. And it wasn't the bacon sizzling on the griddle. He was in a new time zone now: there was before Lucy and now. It felt strange talking about things he was going to do in this new time, saying "we" or "we're."

Farnsy poured more coffee into Lucy's cup and, bathrobes still on, they walked barefoot out to the end of their wooden

SPRING ~ *Epilogue*

dock where something caught Farnsy's eye. Tied to a cleat at the end of the dock was a dark green canoe, two paddles lying inside, and a note attached.

> *To Lucy and Farnsy!*
> *with love,*
> *from Corrie and Jack*
> *May you never be up a creek without a paddle!*

"You up for a paddle?" Farnsy asked.
"Depends on where I'm sitting."
"You know the J-stroke?"
"I'm a Mainer, Farnsy. But there's something I think we need to talk about."

Staring at the little baby seat in the middle of the canoe, Farnsy wondered if that was the way it would be from now on—that he'd be the last one to know.

Perley standing proudly at the Waltz Soda Fountain, taken in 1948 when the Waltz Pharmacy opened.

Perley and Gerry sitting at the counter of the Waltz Soda Fountain, taken in 1952.

About Waltz Soda Fountain

These vintage family photos (left) were generously provided by Christie and Dean Jacobs, the grandchildren of Perley Waltz, a pharmacist, and his wife Geraldine "Gerry" Waltz, who opened the Waltz Pharmacy in August 1948.

Jo-Ann, their daughter, started working at the soda fountain when she was 16. Eventually she and her husband, pharmacist Winton "Winty" Jacobs took over. They ran the pharmacy until it closed in 2011. Winty died in 2012, and Jo-Ann in 2013. When the family decided to close the pharmacy, they opted to keep the soda fountain open. Jo-Ann and Winty's children, Christie and Dean Jacobs, run the soda fountain today and own the business and the building with the Reny family, their neighbors at Renys Underground. Christie said their mother was the driving force behind keeping the soda fountain open. "She felt it had been an important place for community gathering since 1948 and hoped that would continue," Christie said. The soda fountain closed in December 2012 for renovations. Renys Underground expanded into the space the pharmacy had occupied. The soda fountain reopened in May 2013. Source: "Waltz Soda Fountain: A Tradition for 70 Years," by Suzi Thayer in the *Lincoln County News*, December 22, 2018.

The soda fountain was closed during the pandemic but will reopen in the spring of 2022. The Jacobs and Reny families continue to preserve one of the last traditional soda fountains still operating in Maine.

Acknowledgments

From time to time, some errant impulse moves a writer to start scribbling. So it was, more than a decade ago, when two writers, Sharon and Steve Fiffer, cofounders of the Wesley Writers Workshop in Evanston, Illinois, gave participants a writing prompt one week:

"Farnsworth forgot his toothpaste."

From those four words sprang this story about Farnsy. (The toothpaste scene didn't make the cut.) Since then, whenever I thought I'd lost my narrative thread, Steve and Sharon's encouragement and sage advice sustained me. Were it not for the Fiffers and my fellow Wesley Writers, this novel would not exist.

Writing only seems a solitary enterprise to a non-writer. But the truth is no novel would ever see the light of day were it not for the support, candid feedback, and encouragement of many people. The first among them is my wife, Carolyn. Without her belief in my writing, her critical review of countless drafts, her patience, and her encouragement, Farnsy's story would have languished in an early draft.

Special thanks are due to several people:

My dear sisters, Susan Holland and Betsy Binder, two voracious readers, who read several drafts and gave me invaluable critical feedback.

FARNSY

My good friend Lorna Stern, who has an eagle eye for details, an ear for language, and an uncanny ability to untangle phrases. (There's one sentence somewhere in *Farnsy* that's all hers.) Lorna also gets credit for that corker of a cover photo of the Waltz Soda Fountain, emptied by the pandemic, but waiting for conversations to resume.

My brother-in-law Dr. Kent "Kink" Farris, who, early on, saw something in Farnsy and organized my first public reading one summer for family and friends at Sandy Point. Kent may be a proud Tennessean, but he's almost a Mainer.

In Damariscotta, I'd like to recognize the staff and volunteers in the award-winning Skidompha Public Library, who preserve a place where a writer can find quiet refuge.

In particular, I want to thank two librarians:

Terry Hapach, the tireless head librarian, for her help researching antique fishing lures and Native American place names, and

Pam Gormley, the retired director, who kindly read a late draft of the story.

And I want to thank my neighbor, Carole Fraser Fowler, also a retired library director, for her perceptive editorial eye.

My thanks and appreciation go out to Damariscotta Police Chief Jason Warlick for his patience answering endless questions and for providing expert advice on police equipment and procedures. (Nota bene: Chief Warlick does not make his own jerky and reports that he used to have Necco wafers in his duty bag but hasn't replenished them in a couple of years.) I commend Chief Warlick and his team for their commitment to community service. Police work is challenging and, at times, dangerous. Sadly, it is often thankless. This story is my way of thanking them.

Thanks to the Reny and Jacobs families, in particular, Mary Kate Reny, Bob Reny, John Reny, Christie Jacobs, and Dean Jacobs for their help with details related to the history of the Waltz Soda

Acknowledgments

Fountain. Special thanks to Christie and Dean Jacobs for their permission to use the photograph of the Waltz Soda Fountain by Lorna Stern on the front cover and for providing two vintage family photos of the soda fountain. My thanks to both families for their roles in preserving this gem, this simple gathering spot for folks of all ages, now in its 73rd year.

My thanks to Kirk Vashaw, Chairman and Chief Executive Officer of the Spangler Candy Company in Bryan, Ohio, for kindly giving me permission to feature Necco wafers in this novel. I have loved Necco wafers ever since I was a kid and am delighted that Kirk and his team were able to rejuvenate the iconic New England Confectionary Company (NECCO) wafers. Necco is a registered trademark of the Spangler Candy Company.

Thanks to Maine mystery writers Bruce Robert Coffin and Matt Cost, who generously took time to read and comment on the work of an (older) new author.

For their expert help with details about the origins of Native American place names in Maine, my thanks to Professor Joseph Hall at Bates College in Lewiston, Maine, and Professor Darren Ranco at the University of Maine in Orono.

Finally, I want to thank my daughters, Margaret Anthony and Lauren Farris, who never tired of hearing the same stories over and over as they were growing up (until my lectures started when they were teenagers). *Farnsy* is for their kids, my grandkids, Charlotte, Benjamin, Evelyn, and Dillan, because if their Gramps can write a novel, then they can do anything they can imagine.

Honoring Native Americans, the First People

I want to acknowledge and honor the Wabanakis, or the "People of the Dawn," who first inhabited this place we call Maine over 12,000 years ago and still live here. You can hear their voices in place names like Damariscotta (derived from *Madamescontee*, or "place with many alewives") and Pemaquid (derived from *Pomaqot*, or "point of land extending out away from you"). Wabanaki speakers refer to their land as the Dawnland. For instance, the Passamaquoddy word for the region that includes Maine, *Ckuwaponahkik*, means "place where the sun first looks our way."

About the Author

William Anthony lives part of the year in Maine with his wife and an English Lab and a Maine coon cat. When he's not writing or painting, Bill's out on the Damariscotta River in the *Susan B.*, a Maine-built Pulsifer Hampton. Though Mainers would say he's "from away," Anthony considers himself a Mainer. So far, most Mainers have been too polite to correct him. Bill has spent his life listening to stories, reading stories, and studying, recording, and telling stories. Bill believes that storytelling is essential to being human.